By the
LIGHT
of a
THOUSAND
STARS

Books by
Jamie Langston Turner

Suncatchers

Some Wildflower in My Heart

By the Light of a Thousand Stars

A Garden to Keep

No Dark Valley

Winter Birds

JAMIE LANGSTON TURNER

By the
LIGHT
of a
THOUSAND
STARS

BETHANYHOUSE
MINNEAPOLIS, MINNESOTA

By the Light of a Thousand Stars
Copyright © 1999
Jamie Langston Turner

Cover design by Lookout Design, Inc.

Unless otherwise identified, Scripture quotations are from the King James Version of the Bible.

Published by Bethany House Publishers
11400 Hampshire Avenue South
Bloomington, Minnesota 55438

Bethany House Publishers is a division of
Baker Publishing Group, Grand Rapids, Michigan.

Printed in the United States of America

ISBN-13:   978-0-7642-0298-8
ISBN-10:   0-7642-0298-7

The Library of Congress has cataloged the original edition as follows:

Turner, Jamie L.
   By the light of a thousand stars / by Jamie Langston Turner.
      p.   cm.
   ISBN 0-7642-2153-1
   I. Title.
PS3570.U717   B9   1999
813'.54—dc21

99-6527
CIP

FOR JESS

who is going with me

"The father of the righteous shall greatly rejoice:
and he that begetteth a wise child shall have joy of him.
Thy father and thy mother shall be glad,
and she that bore thee shall rejoice."

PROVERBS 23:24, 25

JAMIE LANGSTON TURNER has been a teacher for thirty-five years at both the elementary and college levels and has written extensively for a variety of periodicals, including *Faith for the Family*, *Moody*, and *Christian Reader*. Her first novel, *Suncatchers*, was published in 1995. Born in Mississippi, Jamie has lived in the South all her life and currently resides with her husband and son in South Carolina, where she teaches creative writing and literature at Bob Jones University.

February 17 — March 18
Della Boyd

May 26
Dottie

July 29

DOTTIE

A Few Short Years

1

Lying on her daughter's bed, Dottie Puckett heard sounds as if they were magnified a hundred times that day. She heard the usual things you'd expect to hear—an airplane, distant traffic, the air conditioning turning on and off. And she heard other things, too—a high-pitched motorized whine from somewhere nearby, the chatter of a squirrel outside the window, a tree branch brushing against the gutter, the coursing sound of water through a pipe, her own breathing.

Sounds told you a lot. Today they told her that people and things were going about their normal business in spite of what had happened here at this house only three weeks ago. Though everybody thought she was mild-mannered and good-natured, Dottie knew that what she felt right now was closer to anger than anything else. Not that she was angry at the planes and cars and water pipes, for goodness' sake, but why is it, she thought, that I have to go on breathing in and out when Bonita is lying in a box a mile down the road?

A mile down the road. They had made a short day's walk out of it one time, she and Bonita. It couldn't have been more than three or four years ago. Bonita would have been twelve or thirteen at the time. Dottie had packed a lunch for them of cold chicken left over from supper the night before and pimento cheese sandwiches, and the two of them had walked down one Saturday in early spring to pay a surprise visit to Birdie Freeman, whose house stood right next to Shepherd's Valley Cemetery along Highway 11. They could have driven, of course, but the whole point of it was to take a springtime walk. They meandered a bit on the way, detouring into a wooded area to look for birds building their nests, a subject that had fascinated Bonita at the time, and stopping to peer into the windows of an old abandoned farmhouse next to an empty field, trying to imagine things about the people who had lived there. Bonita had picked a bouquet of wild hawthorn and forsythia growing at the side of the house to take to Birdie.

If Birdie hadn't been home, they already had it planned that they would take a turn through the cemetery, eat their lunch by the willow trees, and start back home. But she was home, hanging out towels and sheets on her clothesline. They heard her humming as they approached. Her small hands were brisk and efficient with the large white sheets. Dottie had motioned to Bonita, putting her finger to her lips, and they had stood watching Birdie a full minute or two before she knew they were there.

Even though she didn't want to think about it now, Dottie remembered how joyfully Birdie had greeted them, scolding them for bringing their own lunch, then pulling them into her house to see the new braided rug she and her husband, Mickey, had made by hand from old fabric scraps. Birdie had fixed herself a sandwich and had eaten lunch with Dottie and Bonita by the willow trees behind the cemetery. And though Dottie especially didn't want to think about this part, the three of them had walked through the cemetery before it was all over. Bonita had read the names and epitaphs aloud, and Birdie had loved the one that read *A Saint on Earth as He Is in Heaven.*

If someone had told the three of them that spring Saturday that within a few short years two of them would be buried right there in that very cemetery, they wouldn't have believed it. It was far too unlikely. But the unlikelihood of that paled in comparison to the way Birdie and Bonita had both died.

Dottie took hold of the bedspread beneath her and crumpled a handful of chenille in each fist. She breathed in deeply and held it while she slowly counted to ten. *Don't say the word* died, she told herself. *Don't even think. Just listen. Stop remembering things.* She decided to close her eyes so she wouldn't be distracted by the things she saw in Bonita's bedroom, not that there was much left of Bonita in the room. Only her furniture, really, and the curtains they had made together last summer when they were redecorating her bedroom for her sixteenth birthday. Right before she squeezed her eyes shut, Dottie saw in a blinding flash the pink ruffled valance on the window facing the front of the house. *Don't think about it,* she thought. *Don't think about how Bonita tore that ruffle out and resewed it three times to get it even. Just listen.*

She couldn't have said how long she lay there with her eyes closed. She might have fallen asleep, for when she opened her eyes again sometime later, the angle of sunlight coming in through the windows seemed different. She glanced around for a clock but knew there wasn't one in here. But as she had no idea what time it had been when she had slipped off her shoes to lie down on Bonita's bed, a clock wouldn't have told her how much time had passed. The words echoed inside her head. *Time passing time passing time passing time . . .* The passing of time, which had once seemed so important in marking off small accomplishments and segments of life, now seemed utterly meaningless. Time passed, and what it took with it couldn't be retrieved.

Think of Bible verses, Dottie told herself. Though she knew reams of Scripture by heart, the one that sprang first to her mind was the old standby. *"The Lord is my shepherd; I shall not want. He maketh me to lie down in green pastures: he leadeth me beside the still waters."* A picture of the three of them eating lunch under willow trees behind the cemetery came into her mind. *"He restoreth my soul: he leadeth me in the paths of righteousness for his name's sake."* Again she clutched at the bedspread. She felt no restoration of soul, couldn't see any righteousness for all the brambles that had overgrown her path. *"Yea, though I walk through the valley of the shadow of death, I will fear no evil: for thou art with me; thy rod and thy staff they comfort me."* She heard herself cry out and immediately clapped her hand over her mouth. All her life she had recited these verses, yet now, when it counted most, the truth seemed to elude her. She felt the cold, hard presence of evil in the shadow of Bonita's death, and instead of comfort, she felt that her soul had been beaten with a rod and staff. *"Thou preparest a table before me in the presence of mine enemies. . . ."*

She couldn't continue. She had to stop this. A sudden, desperate dread of what was to come seized her. Where was her faith? Was this how it was going to be for the rest of her life? Lay hold of Scripture, she told herself, and as she cast about frantically for another passage, the words of Job's wife suddenly shouted in her mind: *"Curse God, and die."* But just as swiftly Job's reply offered itself: *"What? Shall we receive good at the hand of God, and shall we not receive evil?"* He had told his wife she was speaking as a foolish woman. And that's just what you're doing, Dottie told herself. You're speaking as a foolish woman. Again she thought of Job's answer: *"Shall we receive good at the hand of God, and shall we not receive evil?"*

Oh, but I would gladly give up a thousand good things I've received from God's hand, thought Dottie, if only I could have Bonita back. Again the smothering thought came to her that had first come to her at Bonita's funeral: *For the rest of my days on earth, I won't see Bonita. I won't hear her voice or touch her ever again for as long as I live.* She bit her lower lip until she felt pain. They had told her that Bonita hadn't felt any pain, that in all probability she had died instantly.

Things had seemed so simple before. Had anybody asked her how to suffer great loss, she would have quoted verse after verse, stringing them together like shiny beads. "God is good," she would have assured the person, "his merciful goodness endures to all generations," "all things work together for good," and "the steps of a good man are ordered by the Lord." Good, good, good, good—a pretty little bracelet to wear. Here. Put it on and finger the beads whenever you feel a little uneasy, like good luck charms, and soon all the bad feelings will go away for good.

She felt ashamed of herself, a deep, searing sense of guilty failure and betrayal. How could she live her whole life believing the Bible as the bedrock of truth and then turn so suddenly, disgracefully doubtful? She remembered something her pastor had once said. "Untested faith is easy." So this is the hard kind, she thought. Tested faith. She knew she wasn't scoring very high on the test so far.

She thought again of Job's reprimand to his wife and remembered the end of the verse: *"In all this did not Job sin with his lips."* The words repeated themselves, and even though it wasn't much, she saw the dimmest, slimmest shape of something to grasp. She felt the faintest stirring, as of a rope cast into the floodwaters, and she reached for it, though she couldn't see its source. She knew, of course, that strictly speaking her thoughts had already disqualified her from living up to Job's example. But couldn't she with God's help remain true and faithful in her spoken words? She wanted it to be said, "In all this did not Dottie Puckett sin with her lips." That wasn't being irreverent, was it?

She thought of the psalm that kept repeating the same phrase over and over. She couldn't remember which psalm it was nor the exact phrase, but she was forming a plan. She would make her days like that psalm, affirming God's goodness over and over. She would do or say something as part of everyday life, then repeat the phrase, do something else, say something else, then repeat the phrase. Even *while* she was doing things, she would repeat the phrase. Maybe it would keep away those other thoughts. *His mercy endureth forever*—that was the phrase she would use. All day long she would say the words and keep the thought before her. Hang on to it, she told herself now. Don't let go. Hold it fast.

Suddenly she heard a door open and her husband's voice. "Dottie?" There was a pause and then footsteps coming through the kitchen. "Dottie, sugar?" Dottie didn't answer but lay very still. She hadn't meant for Sid to find her lying on Bonita's bed. He had taken great care to keep her out of Bonita's bedroom, locking the door and putting the pathetic little stick of a key in the back of his top drawer in a black velvet box with the cuff links he never wore. It hadn't taken Dottie long to find it once she had set her mind to it. She knew Sid only wanted to protect her, and she didn't want him to know she'd gone looking through his things and sneaked in here. She should have talked with him about it first. He would have listened to her. He always did. Unlike what she heard about many husbands, Sid was a good listener. He would have unlocked the door for her if she had only asked.

He went through the whole house calling for her. She heard him pick up the phone in the kitchen and call down to the Texaco station. It was only a few hundred yards from the house. He could have opened the side door and yelled just as quick. "Hey, Max," she heard him say over the telephone, "did you hear your mama mention going somewhere today? I can't find her here in the house anywhere." A few moments of silence, then, "Well, no, I don't expect she's out there, but I'll take a look. I'll be back over directly. You okay for a couple more minutes?" It never had worried Dottie before when Sid left Max at the station by himself, but now she found herself imagining all kinds of things that could happen. Max was a big boy for his age, but he was still only eleven.

She waited tensely for the sound of the back door. As soon as Sid went outside, she was going to get up and go into the bathroom. She'd just have to make Sid think he had overlooked her earlier. Or better yet, she could go out on the front porch. Of course, he would wonder why he hadn't seen her there when he had walked over from the station, but she could think of something without telling an outright fib.

But instead of hearing the back door open, she heard Sid's steps return to the hall. "Dottie?" he said again. He paused as if ready to turn back, but then with a sinking heart Dottie heard him coming down the hall toward Bonita's bedroom. She looked at the doorknob and begged silently, Don't turn, please don't turn. If she had only thought to lock the bedroom door again from the inside—that was a careless oversight. Of course, she hadn't expected to stay in here so long. She had thought she'd come in for just ten minutes or so and be out well before Sid came home for his afternoon Coca-Cola, which she knew was actually just an excuse for him to check on her.

Sid's footsteps stopped outside Bonita's bedroom, and Dottie saw the knob turn slowly. She knew exactly what expression would be on Sid's face as he swung the door open and saw her lying on the bed. She turned her head to the window so she wouldn't have to see his face. *His mercy endureth forever*, she said to herself. After all, she wasn't doing anything wrong, really. Why should her heart be beating so hard? She heard him make a noise deep back in his throat.

"Oh, Dottie, sugar," he said in a wounded voice. He entered the room slowly, his rubber-soled work boots making little squeaks against the hardwood floor with each step. He reached the edge of the bed. "What are you doing in here, sugar?"

He sat down on the bed and laid his hand over hers. She knew if she pulled his hand to her face, she'd smell axle grease, motor oil, gasoline.

Neither of them spoke for a long moment as he patted the back of her hand gently. Then he repeated the question. "How come you're in here?"

"I'm thinking," Dottie said. *His mercy endureth forever.* "I had to face coming in here sometime, Sid. We couldn't keep the door locked forever." She still wasn't looking at him. She knew it would make him feel bad, but she couldn't resist adding, "I don't know why you had to go and strip her room of everything that was *her*."

Through the window she saw a bird, something large and hawklike, soaring across the summer sky. Summer—what a horrible time to suffer, when the sky was so blue and grass so green and the sun so close to the earth. She wondered for a moment whether it was still July. The accident had happened on July 6. That was the last date on the calendar she had been aware of. She tried to figure it out. Yes, it would still be July—sometime near the end, probably. It must have been close to three weeks ago, but it could as easily have been four or only two. She could imagine herself a year from now thinking, Was it fifty weeks ago or only five? *His mercy endureth forever.*

Sid stopped patting and pressed his hand against hers. Dottie turned her hand over so that their palms were touching. She swallowed hard, still looking toward the window, and said, "Oh, Sid, it's just so hard to—"

He didn't let her finish. "I know, sugar, I know," he said. "You're doing so well, and I'm so proud of you. We're going to get through it. We will, sugar, I promise. God's not going to let us down." He touched her chin with his other hand, and she turned her face toward him. "You're doing good, Dottie," he said tenderly.

Though she shouldn't have, she felt a sudden hot flare of irritation. Those were the exact words he had kept saying a year ago when he had taught her to drive a car with a standard transmission. "You're doing good, sugar. I'm so proud of you," he had said over and over as the little Honda had lurched around the streets of Filbert and Berea.

"I'm not learning to drive a car, Sid," she said now and immediately wished she could take back her words. *His mercy endureth forever.* For one thing, she could tell from the look on Sid's face that he didn't even know what she was talking about. No doubt he was wondering what driving a car had to do with anything.

He let it drop, though, then smiled at her and said, "Guess what I did this morning before you woke up."

"What?"

"Planted those iris bulbs Dennis Abernathy gave me. Planted them out by your beauty shop sign." Then, as if she didn't know where her own sign was, he added, "Right at the end of the driveway where you'll see them as soon as you pull in."

Dottie thought of the damp, lumpy brown paper bag that had sat by the back door for weeks and weeks. One day in June, right after Dennis Abernathy had brought them by, she had looked inside it and felt a shiver go over her. It will be a miracle if those ugly, deformed-looking things ever bloom into irises, she had thought at the time and then rebuked herself at once for her flippant use of the word *miracle*. Of course they'll bloom, she had told herself. Millions of beautiful flowers come from dirty brown bulbs just like these. That's the way God planned it.

This was just the kind of thing she used to delight in drawing a lesson from before Bonita's accident. She could just hear herself saying something like "See, God always brings something lovely out of the worst circumstances!"

"You know, sugar," Sid said, then paused, as if struggling for the right words.

Dottie had a sudden wild fear that he was going to try to make such a parallel himself, and she felt a smoldering retort on the tip of her tongue before she remembered that Sid's mind didn't generally work that way. He saw things as what they were, not what they represented, and there was something reassuring in that now. *His mercy endureth forever.*

"I've been wondering if it might not be a good idea . . ." Sid stopped to nibble on the inside of his lip, then started over. "Have you given any thought to when you might start taking customers again?" The words came out in a rush. Sid looked away from her quickly, then back again. Every part of his thin face—his sad, earnest eyes, his pinched mouth, his furrowed brow—was pleading not to be taken wrong. "Ladies keep calling," he said. "They want to help you, sugar. They've been bringing things by for weeks now, you know, and nobody blames you a bit for wanting your privacy and keeping to yourself, but"—he appeared to be making a supreme effort now—"well, maybe it's time to let 'em come in, sugar. Maybe it's time to get your hands busy with something and . . ." He shrugged at her apologetically. "Oh, I just want what's best for you, Dottie," he said.

From somewhere deep inside her, she didn't know where, Dottie found the strength to say words she didn't want to say but knew she should. She sat up and swung her feet to the other side of the bed from where Sid was still sitting. "Well, I don't know," she said slowly. "Maybe you're right." She got up and pulled her knit top down over the waistband of her pants, then walked around the bed to put on her shoes. Sid had evidently pushed one of them up under the bed, and he fell to one knee, scrambling to find it for her.

"Here, sugar, raise your foot, and I'll put it on for you." He held her foot tenderly, then squeezed it and bent forward as if ready to kiss it.

Dottie felt a small pricking of pity for Sid. She hadn't exactly been very receptive to his attempts at affection lately. Holding her foot, it was as if he were saying, "I'll take any outpost I can get into."

She wiggled her foot impatiently. "Hurry up, Prince Charming, I need to make a phone call," she said, and he quickly slipped her shoe on. She had no idea who it was she meant to call. She hadn't even intended to say that. So who would it be? If she had to start again, which one of her customers would she want to take back first? And no sooner had she asked the question than Lily Beasley's face came to mind. She realized suddenly that she missed Lily. Her husband worked for Sid off and on at the gas station, and Lily had been a regular customer of hers for over ten years now. Yes, she'd call Lily Beasley and tell her she was opening her shop up again next week and wanted to see her first. Lily was one of the nicest women she knew.

She walked into the kitchen, Sid trailing along behind her.

"See your bonsai, sugar?" he said, and she saw that he had moved the little tree to the windowsill above the sink. "I've been watering it for you every day."

It looked healthy, which seemed unfair to Dottie. Just one more example of everything going about its normal business while her world fell apart. At least it wasn't blooming—that would have been too much.

She picked up the phone and dialed Lily's number, surprised that she could still remember it. As it rang, she lifted her eyes to Sid, who was still standing in the kitchen doorway smiling at her.

"I'm so proud of you," he whispered, and less than a second later she heard Lily's voice on the other end of the line.

She shut her eyes and took a deep breath. *His mercy endureth forever.* "Hey, Lily, this is Dottie," she said. "Can you talk a minute?"

August 23 – September 5

CATHERINE

Our Lowly Estate

2

One Wednesday morning in late August, Catherine Biddle was sitting at the only stoplight on Highway 11, just three miles away from Dottie's Be-Beautiful Style Shoppe, when she almost turned around and headed back home.

A question had just come into her mind: *Why am I doing this?* But in the few seconds that it took for her to note that the stoplight had changed to green and to move her foot to the accelerator, Catherine had thought of her answer—in fact, of three answers. First, because she needed a trim and set; second, because Nancy had been getting careless lately; and third, because—Catherine prided herself in the fact that she wasn't one to deny real motives the way some people did—because she was curious. Curious about how the likes of Dottie Puckett would handle death. Anyway, she couldn't have turned around and gone home if she'd wanted to. She'd have to get gas first. The little red needle was below empty.

Passing a strip of stores the people of Filbert called "the shopping center," she glanced into the rearview mirror and reached up a hand to try to fluff her bangs. If the truth were to be known, Catherine's auburn hair was probably her greatest source of pride. What Nancy had been thinking of when she had attempted this new style, Catherine couldn't begin to fathom. She hadn't even asked Catherine if she wanted to try it but had just up and done it, snipping away while Catherine had sat innocently with her back to the mirror describing her new dining room ensemble, totally unaware that Nancy was in the act of ruining her looks. She'd have to tell Dottie to do whatever she could with the botch-up.

Catherine clutched the steering wheel of her Buick Park Avenue with both hands as she drove past the stretch of woods where a car had wrecked last year—had left the highway and plowed right into the trees, the paper said. The driver had had a heart attack and had killed his wife while he was at it. In fact, Catherine had met the woman at Dottie's beauty shop one day three or four years ago, long before the wreck. Birdie Freeman was the woman's name. Catherine had recognized the name right away in the newspaper account of the wreck and had immediately called up a picture of the mousy-looking little woman. Actually, "mousy" was putting it mildly. Birdie Freeman had had absolutely one of the homeliest faces Catherine had ever seen. A terrible overbite and a hairstyle from the Dark Ages—just a single long braid coiled and pinned on top of her head.

Birdie Freeman had been leaving Dottie's house that day a few years ago when Catherine had been arriving, and Dottie had introduced the two of them. "Birdie just dropped by to leave me some of her famous apple dumplings and *this*," Dottie had said, holding up what looked like a tiny little tree in a pint-sized container. "She tells me pretty little white blossoms are going to burst out all over these twiggy branches one of these days." Dottie had turned the plant around, studying it from every angle.

"It's a bonsai," Birdie Freeman had said. "A Serissa, that's its real name, but I like its other name better—Tree of a Thousand Stars. Isn't that pretty?" She had reached over and patted the bonsai as if it were a well-behaved baby. "The blossoms look like tiny white stars, you see," she added.

Catherine had frowned at the little tree. There sure wasn't much to it. "Well, I wouldn't lay any bets on it," she had said. "It doesn't look like it has any intention of blooming." Catherine couldn't count the number of plants *she* had bought, hoping they'd bloom and finally throwing them in the trash when their leaves turned yellow and limp.

Birdie Freeman had clapped her hands and laughed. "Oh, you've got to have faith! Just wait and see!" Then as she made her way out the door, she had whirled around. "Say, how would you like one for yourself?" she asked Catherine. "I have plenty more where that one came from. It's as easy as pie to start a little slip from a cutting."

"No, thank you!" Catherine had said. "I like a plant that has some pep to it."

Birdie had laughed again. "Well, let me know if you change your mind. I wish I could stay, Dottie, but I've got to run." And she had left. Catherine had felt like calling after her and asking the poor little woman why she didn't stay and let Dottie do something with her hair.

Catherine was passing the Shepherd's Valley Cemetery now, and, as she always did, she glanced at the house just beside it. One of her neighbors had told her after the wreck that Birdie Freeman had lived right next to the cemetery on Highway 11, so Catherine knew it had to be that small white house with the black trim. She couldn't help wondering if that sorry-looking little tree had ever bloomed as Birdie had promised. Probably not.

Somebody else had moved into the house now—somebody with a lot of children from the looks of things. Two of those low-slung plastic tricycles cluttered the front sidewalk, one of them turned over on its side, and miscellaneous bright-colored toys were strewn all over the yard. A tire swing hung from an oak tree. Some days when Catherine passed this way she could see three or four little children zipping around the yard, and sometimes a woman was sitting on the front steps with a baby in her lap. She had often wondered if that woman had any idea what was ahead of her when her children got to be teenagers.

Farther on Catherine passed Sawyer's Plywood and a Dairy Queen on the right, then just past the Sunny Dale Feed and Seed and a ramshackle produce stand she passed the Texaco station that Dottie Puckett's husband ran. Immediately past that was a gravel driveway marked by a lopsided mailbox upon which was painted in white letters *SID PUCKETT*. Catherine couldn't believe that the Pucketts hadn't changed mailboxes after what had happened right beside it only six weeks ago, but she was positive this was the same old mailbox they'd always had.

Next to the mailbox was a small handmade wooden sign that read *Dottie's Be-Beautiful Style Shoppe*. Signaling to turn left, Catherine looked closely at the road and the grassy area alongside the mailbox for signs of the accident. She thought she might see skid marks or upturned earth, but she didn't. Evidently somebody had come along and fixed things up. Catherine turned into the driveway and slowed almost to a stop, surveying the house at the end of the long gravel drive. It never ceased to amaze her how tacky some people's tastes were.

What could have been an ordinary-looking house stood out against the open fields like a red flag—only, of course, it was blue. And not a nice, conventional pastel blue or even a slightly bolder Williamsburg blue, but the frivolous blue of a robin's egg. Why, the house was only a step away from turquoise! Catherine Biddle couldn't imagine the day when she'd sink so low as to live in a house that was the color of an Easter egg.

As she drove slowly down the driveway, the crunching of the gravel under her tires irked her. Why couldn't the Pucketts put in a regular paved driveway like civilized people? The gravel was just another sign of the low standards some people had. Even the sound of the word was ugly—*gravel*. Catherine opened her mouth and said the word out loud, making it as ugly as she could with a sharp, nasal twang.

It irked Catherine, too, to think that she would have to get gas at the Texaco before she drove back home. She wished she had noticed that the car was on empty before she had left Berea. Give Dottie ten dollars for doing my hair, she thought, then turn around and give her hick husband another three or four—there goes almost fifteen dollars just lining the pockets of people who couldn't tell the difference between sterling and silver plate if their lives depended on it.

But it couldn't be helped. She wouldn't let Nancy touch her hair again after the mess she had made, and the only other girl who did hair over in Berea was named Swee-yung Chan. Catherine wouldn't even shop at the drugstore in Berea because it was owned by a Taiwanese family, and she sure as sure wasn't going to let some Oriental give her a shampoo and set.

Catherine's husband, Blake, had told her about the foreigners years ago before they moved to this part of South Carolina, told her there were all kinds of them—Koreans, Germans, Poles, Japanese, French. And more of them poured in every year, it seemed, most of them drawn to the area because of some big industry, like Michelin or Hitachi or BMW or one of the textile mills. "Well, they won't bother me," Catherine had told Blake, "as long as they keep to themselves and leave me alone!" That was her motto in life: Leave Me Alone. And that was the very rule Dottie Puckett had so frequently violated when Catherine used to be her regular customer.

She pulled up next to the large fading sign beside the carport. Just like the smaller one by the mailbox, this sign read *Dottie's Be-Beautiful Style Shoppe*, but this one was in a ridiculously fancy black script with little curlicues springing up from the letters like overpermed hair. Catherine remembered Dottie saying that someone at her church had made the sign for her years ago when she first opened her shop.

Catherine parked next to a dark gray Chevrolet but sat for a minute while the dust settled, still peeved about the gravel driveway. Some people just didn't care about making things nice for their company. It sure couldn't be the money. Sid Puckett had to be doing a good business at the Texaco, seeing it was the only gas station along Highway 11 and only three miles off the new highway now. And everybody knew Dottie brought in a good bit off her beauty shop, even more now that she'd gone up from eight dollars to ten.

Before she got out of the car, Catherine took out her brush and tried to swoop up the sides of her hair. She sure didn't want Dottie feeling sorry for her having a hairdo that looked like somebody did it blindfolded. She opened the car door and waved both hands in front of her face as if driving away smoke. Maybe Dottie was looking out the window right now and would see her and then suggest to Sid that they put in a real driveway.

Hoisting her purse strap higher on her shoulder, Catherine slammed the car door and stood glaring at the sign. Why, it wasn't fading; it was just coated with dust, that was all. Catherine walked right up next to it, reached up, and traced the *B* with her index finger, then studied the thick smudge on the tip of her finger. Well, it looked like Dottie Puckett's standards had slipped during the two years since Catherine had been here last. She used to be real neat and particular.

Of course, Catherine had to admit as she followed the sidewalk up to the side door, it *had* been a dry summer, and Dottie and Sid *had* had other things on their minds lately besides a dusty sign. Walking up the steps, she felt a sudden thrill of expectation mingled with a peculiar reverence. To have the opportunity to see the effects of great sorrow on someone else—well, it wasn't *fun*, of course, but it was . . . interesting.

And it was even more interesting in this case because of all the things Catherine remembered from her years as a weekly customer of Dottie's. All those years of sitting in Dottie's black vinyl swivel chair and listening to her virtuous talk. All the years of eluding Dottie's invitations to visit the Willing Workers Sunday school class or come to a potluck supper at the Church of the Open Door, where she attended. All the years of deflecting Dottie's gentle but insulting questions about her *soul*, as if that were anybody's business.

Catherine stopped just a moment, her hand firmly grasping the doorknob, and reminded herself again of the final insolence that occurred over two years ago, the day she had vowed never again to come to Dottie's shop, to drive all the way to Greenville for a hair appointment if she had to.

Catherine had always wondered if Dottie even realized what she was saying at the time. She had looked so simple and *blank* after she had said it. Catherine could still feel the rush of blood to her face, the hot prickling on the back of her neck as she heard Dottie's words. When it happened, Catherine had been holding a cheap pink plastic hand mirror, still sitting in the swivel chair, studying the back of her hair—always the final act in the weekly hairstyling ritual—when Dottie had bent forward, her plump hands clasped under her chin. "Catherine," she said, smiling, "won't you please think about what I've been saying? I want you to be happy, and so does God. One of God's gifts to His children is *joy*. He loves us, and He regards us in our lowly estate."

As she recalled now, she had shot out of the chair, dropped her eight dollars on the little rolling table that held Dottie's perm rollers and tissue squares, and said, "I'll thank you not to include me in your lowly estate!"

All the way home she had fumed. Dottie Puckett could consider her own estate as common and low-down as she liked, but she'd better think twice before she lumped everybody else into the same class. Lowly estate indeed. Catherine's family, the Ashtons, had been just a step shy of aristocrats back home in Biloxi, Mississippi. They had owned a small yacht, employed two housemaids, and even boasted a coat of arms. Her father had been a trial lawyer, and her mother had never lifted a finger around the house.

Catherine herself had studied art and drama at Ole Miss and still remembered all her lines as Amanda Wingfield from *The Glass Menagerie*, a performance during her senior year that the newspaper review had described as "an admirable effort, especially in light of Miss Ashton's youth." Catherine had always wished they had left out that part about her youth—it somehow made it seem less complimentary. And she also wished they had substituted the word *success* for *effort*. Nevertheless, it had been the high point of Catherine's whole life, and even though she still played the role of Amanda Wingfield every few years over at the Abbeville Opera House here in South Carolina, nothing could compare to her glory days in college. Dottie Puckett might come from poor white sharecropper stock, but Catherine Ashton Biddle surely didn't!

Catherine opened the door now and heard the jingle of the bell hanging from the doorknob on the other side. She stepped into the air-conditioned coolness of the beauty shop, thankful that if Dottie had to have a gravel driveway, at least she had had sense enough to have a small window unit installed to keep her customers comfortable in the hot months. The beauty shop was empty, but Catherine heard voices through the open door leading into the kitchen. "Be right there!" called one of them, and Catherine recognized it instantly as Dottie's. She hadn't heard Dottie's voice in more than two whole years—not counting all the times Dottie's words had played in her mind—yet it was a voice she knew she would recognize instantly anytime, anyplace.

Looking around, Catherine saw that the Be-Beautiful hadn't changed a bit in the two years since she'd quit coming here. The shop was actually just an addition on to the side of Dottie and Sid's house, a single little room with only the bare necessities—one sink with a sprayer hose, one hair dryer, a small couch scattered with a few back issues of *Grit, Reader's Digest*, and *Guideposts*, a counter with a large mirror, and a black swivel chair.

She noted that the salmon pink walls were still decorated with the same foolishly outdated pictures and posters as before. Dottie had told her once that Sid had found the posters rolled up together in the corner of a junk store outside Clinton. "Soft 'n Lovely Shampoo—It Caresses Your Tresses," announced one, the words coming from a cartoon bubble above the head of a fresh-faced Donna Reed look-alike. Another one praised the "Luxurious Holding Power" of "Silken Strands Spray Mist" and pictured a teenaged girl of the sixties wearing a pastel peach mohair sweater. Catherine had always felt as though she were stepping back in time when she came here.

It struck her now that everything was the same—the same yellow gingham curtains at the windows, the same Coca-Cola clock on the wall above the hair dryer, the same Quaker State wire rack Sid had cleaned up and brought over from the Texaco for Dottie to store her shampoos and styling gels in. Catherine walked over to the counter where Dottie had all the implements of her trade laid out. Now here was something different. The picture of Bonita and Max that Dottie used to keep right here beside her appointment book and the telephone was gone now.

"Well, Catherine Biddle, it's good to see you, honey," Dottie said, hurrying in from the kitchen, her other customer trailing behind, blinking at Catherine stupidly. "I was just showing Muriel here the cake Lily Beasley made us. You and Muriel know each other, don't you?" Catherine lifted her chin and gave a short nod as Dottie continued. "I'll show you the cake after we finish. That Lily is just an artist when it comes to decorating cakes. You remember her, don't you? Her husband, Benny, is the mechanic who works with Sid."

Catherine nodded again. She remembered Lily Beasley all right. A Negro woman who used to have her hair appointment right after Catherine's, who would usually come while Catherine was sitting under the dryer, as a matter of fact. Catherine had disapproved of the familiar way she and Dottie cut up with each other, almost like sisters, and she had finally changed the time of her appointment so she wouldn't always be running into Lily Beasley.

"I swanee, you never *did* see the likes of that cake," Muriel said, her cheeks flushed with excitement. "I couldn't any more do a thing like that than the man in the moon! Shaped like an open Bible with gold all around the edges of the pages and Psalm 23:4 written out in *real writing* just as even and steady as can be—and a red ribbon down the middle, only of course it's not a real ribbon at all. It's all done with frosting!"

Muriel's hair was wound tightly on small wire rollers, and she spoke in a breathy voice, panting a little between every few words. With the white towel draped about her neck, she reminded Catherine of a boxer between rounds.

Dottie smiled at Catherine. "Long time, no see," she said. "You still look like somebody that's stepped right out of a magazine."

It was the same smile as before, sweet and girlish for a woman Dottie's age and size, but her eyes looked darker and smaller than Catherine remembered, set deeper into her broad face, giving the effect of something slowly settling over time. Was this just a natural sign of aging, Catherine wondered, or had this happened over the past month and a half? Is this how death and sorrow had stamped its mark onto the face of Dottie Puckett? How well she recalled Dottie's green eyes, so unnaturally bright that day she had chirped, "One of God's gifts to His children is *joy*."

And how well she remembered the anger that had seethed within her as she sped down Highway 11 back toward Berea. It was easy for Dottie to talk about happiness and joy, to wish it on other people, to smile and nod and talk about things like love and God. She had an easy life. Catherine remembered passing a dilapidated cabin along the highway that day and catching sight of the stooped backs and wide straw hats of two old people hoeing, like a scene from another era. She had wondered briefly what *they* would say if informed by Dottie that God regarded them in their lowly estate. Catherine could have helped them think up a reply: "Oh, is that so? Then why doesn't He do something to show His regard? Why doesn't He send somebody from Publishers Clearing House out here with a check for a million dollars?"

Dottie just took happiness for granted, Catherine had thought as she had flown down the highway that day. Even though she knew for a fact that Sid Puckett hadn't even finished high school, it didn't seem to matter one iota to Dottie. And Catherine had to admit that even though he had about as much class as a scarecrow, at least Sid had manners. He looked at Dottie like he thought she was the homecoming queen and he had the good luck to be her freshman escort. He was always doing things for her, like taking her out for supper at C. C.'s Barbecue over in Filbert and bringing her bouquets of wild violets in April, which she used to put in a little Mason canning jar, of all things, and set on the counter among her combs and scissors. Of course, he wasn't much to look at—pale and slight. The two of them looked as mismatched as could be, but still, he did treat Dottie right.

Dottie didn't have any idea what it was like to be stuck with a cantankerous husband, one who accused her of nagging and picking and overreacting. One who kept telling her that a husband had a right to expect certain things out of a wife, things like loyalty and support, like cheerfulness and contentment. One who didn't have a shred of appreciation for her old family name and the fact that she still had her figure.

Here he was still harping after all these years about what he called her "snobby ways."

For being so book-smart, Blake certainly was a dunce about how to run a family. Surely it didn't take a genius to figure out that you couldn't take a woman like Catherine out of the grace and glamour of Old Biloxi and plunk her down in the sticks of South Carolina and then expect her to be happy! Or that you couldn't leave town for long stretches at a time and expect your kids to grow up perfect and everything to run like clockwork at home.

"Well, you aren't so contented yourself," she had shouted at Blake during one of their arguments, "or else you could accept me the way I am!" And he had left home again right after that on another one of his business trips to negotiate a production contract or attend some management seminar, trips Catherine was sure were not always necessary.

She remembered her lines from *The Glass Menagerie*: "Gone, gone, gone. All vestige of gracious living! Gone completely! I wasn't prepared for what the future brought me." Catherine had never dreamed when she was reciting those lines in college that twenty years down the road she'd be looking back on a life as disappointing as Amanda Wingfield's, that she, too, would have a husband who had begun to fall in love with long distances.

But Dottie Puckett thought happiness grew on trees. She used to mention some detail of her happy childhood almost every time Catherine had a hair appointment, talking about her parents as if they'd been canonized! She'd had no way of knowing, of course, that Catherine's own recollections of childhood were far from happy, that her most vivid memory was of the day after her sixth birthday when her mother had raised herself up in bed, pointed a shaky finger straight at Catherine, and said, "You're the reason I've been in bed for six years," and as Catherine had fled the room she added, "I wish you had never been born." If she had shouted it, it might not have been so devastating, but she had whispered it, and even at the age of six, Catherine had known that while the things you shouted usually came off the top of your head, the things you whispered most often came straight from the heart.

As clear as day she could remember running straight to her father's study after leaving her mother's bedroom. Normally when the door to his study was shut, as it was that day, Catherine and her sister knew not to disturb him, but her six-year-old mind had been in such upheaval that she hadn't even thought about the rules as she burst in. Her father had been working on a case and was hunched over his desk. From the banker's lamp with its green glass shade, a pool of yellow light fell on the papers and books cluttering the desktop. She had stopped a moment at the door, searching for hope in her father's face.

But she could hardly see his face as he scribbled on a legal pad. She couldn't have put it into words at the time, but all she needed, really, was a minute of love, or less. A few seconds would have done. She just needed to hear certain words from his mouth. She had stepped forward quietly, and when she was close enough to reach out and touch his arm, she had whispered, "Daddy, do you wish I had never been born?" Had he shoved his papers aside and taken her into his lap, things could have turned around. The open wound couldn't have been closed up and healed immediately, of course, but maybe it could have been stanched and bandaged so that the scar would have been small. She had often wondered about this.

As it was, he had sighed and lifted his eyes to the ceiling for what seemed like forever to Catherine. When he had finally looked at her, something in his eyes, before he even spoke, told her that hope was not to be found here. The white part of his eyes was shot through with tiny veins of red, and he appeared to be looking right through her to the wall on the other side of the room. "Catherine," he said, and her heart fell, for everything had depended on that one word. If he had said "Cathy," the room would have exploded with sunshine.

"I'm right in the middle of the most important case of my life," he said to her. She remembered it word for word. "Whatever it is you want to know, go ask your mother. Whatever she says is fine with me."

Well. So much for that. Catherine knew exactly what her mother would say, had already said, in fact. And her father just said he agreed with whatever her mother said. So all was lost. In the space of five minutes, she had stood on the edge of the world and then fallen off. She left her father's study, went to her bedroom, and closed her door. She then picked up a doll she had gotten as a birthday present the day before and twisted its head off.

"I want you to be happy, and so does God," Dottie Puckett had said to her that day two years ago. And just how did she know that? Catherine had wondered. Had God faxed her a personal message about her customers, a private revelation of His plan for each one? Would Dottie find cause for happiness if her own mother had hated the sight of her? If her father had looked right past her as if she didn't exist? If she had been yanked from a genteel environment on the Gulf Coast without even being asked if she wanted to move? If her husband had then gone off and left her every chance he got and the children she had vowed would be the happiest children on earth had turned on her?

"One of God's gifts to His children is *joy*," Dottie had said. Catherine couldn't help wondering, though, what Dottie's thoughts on happiness were these days, now that she had learned what it was to suffer. Did she feel that God was regarding her in her lowly estate as a grieving mother?

Catherine realized that Dottie had gotten Muriel settled under the hair dryer and was now standing over by the sink, holding a red plastic cape out to the side like a pudgy matador, looking at her expectantly, as if she had said something and was waiting for an answer. And does God want *you* to be happy, too? she felt like asking Dottie now. Does He want you to have joy? Is that why he snatched your daughter away? She stalked over to the sink.

"You've got a mean streak running clear through you, Catherine." Blake had said that to her one time. But she knew it wasn't true, not really. There were other adjectives that applied, such as curious, inquisitive, persistent, frank, opinionated—but not mean. But Blake had taken to calling her "Cat" for short and would do so right now if he knew she was here at Dottie's. She could just hear him: "Sniffing out another tragedy, huh? Prying and poking, trying to make somebody else hurt."

Oh, sure, sometimes she wished she could grab back things she said or undo certain actions, but who didn't? She remembered Tom's lines from the end of *The Glass Menagerie* about all the ways he had tried to forget his failures. But he couldn't do that. Nobody could. You couldn't blow out the candles of your past. That was part of life. You had to keep on going and make the best of your mistakes. You sure couldn't go around afraid to open your mouth just so you wouldn't have regrets later on.

Catherine sat down in front of the sink and allowed Dottie to tuck a towel around the neck of the plastic cape. She closed her eyes as Dottie turned on the water and tested it against her hand. She felt the fine mist on her forehead and then the warm flow of water, the cool squirt of shampoo. She felt Dottie's large, padded fingertips kneading her head, working up a thick lather.

Before, Dottie had always talked during this part, raising her voice a little above the rush of the water, telling Catherine about one thing or another—never anything serious or heavy at this point, just everyday things about the crowder peas in her garden or the geraniums Sid had planted out by the front sidewalk or something Bonita or Max had said. But this time she was quiet, moving her hands over Catherine's scalp slowly, randomly, as if she had lost track of what she was doing.

Catherine opened one eye. Above her, Dottie worked silently, her eyes half closed. Her wide face was heart shaped, like a big pink valentine. It struck Catherine that Dottie could have been pretty in her youth. Even now, in spite of her weight, she could spruce herself up with a few little makeup tricks and look as good as some of those women in the ads who modeled large-sized clothes. Personally, Catherine had always thought Dottie's hair looked unkempt with all that confusion of natural curl. She wondered how she even got a brush through it.

Her color wasn't as rosy as it used to be, Catherine thought, and she still didn't have any flair for fashion. Catherine frowned up at the gauzy lavender scarf around Dottie's throat—the kind women had worn back in the fifties. It was tied jauntily like a sailor's neckerchief. Catherine knew if she were to ask Dottie who Ralph Lauren, Liz Claiborne, Calvin Klein, and Ellen Tracy were, she wouldn't have the foggiest idea. She'd probably think they were politicians or movie stars.

Normally people who wore tacky clothes irritated Catherine, but somehow today Dottie's scarf struck a melancholy note. She tried to imagine Dottie waking up this morning, putting on her plain white blouse, then opening a drawer to find an accessory, pulling out the scarf, tying it with her large, capable fingers, then walking out to the beauty shop, raising the shade at the window, and flipping the sign to read *Yes, We're Open*. To think of a woman burying her girl one week, then tying a lavender scarf around her neck a few weeks later—well, Catherine wondered if Dottie had been tempted to cinch the scarf tighter and tighter until she choked herself.

It used to gall Catherine that Dottie reveled so in the joys of motherhood. *Bonita this* and *Max that*, as if she were the only woman who'd ever borne children. Early on she had asked Catherine about her own children and had looked briefly shocked when Catherine had answered tartly, "Yes, I have children, three of them, and they keep my life in a constant tumult. I never know which one's going to stir up some new hornets' nest of trouble. It's too bad a person can't have a trial run at motherhood before she commits the rest of her life to it!"

And how was Dottie to know she didn't really mean it? How could anyone know how violently Catherine loved her children in spite of all the distress they caused her? She had vowed to herself to be the kind of mother she had never had, but somewhere along the line she had made a mess of motherhood. Sometimes she heard herself blaming her children for things she knew were probably her own fault. But it was all so hard to figure out. Kids pushed you into a corner.

She remembered suddenly that Blake still didn't know about Hardy's latest escapade. She had withheld it out of spite for his having been gone from home for two weeks, and now she found that she didn't have the energy to drag it all out again and rehash it. She couldn't even remember all the details now. Besides, Blake might fly into a fury again like that time last month. He had almost killed Hardy then—or else Hardy had almost killed him. She wasn't sure which. She would never forget the awful sounds that had come up from the basement that night back in July. It seemed like those were the only times Blake and Hardy talked—when they were fighting about something Hardy had done.

Sometimes in the past Bonita or Max would come running into Dottie's beauty shop, always kicking up a ruckus about something they just *had* to show their mother. Catherine remembered Bonita well. Once she had spilled some Barq's root beer on the strap of Catherine's new Aigner purse that was sitting on the couch. She had apologized, going on and on about it, and even tried to dab off the root beer with a Kleenex, but Catherine had rubbed it again at home—hard—and treated it with a special oil.

Although she was a big-boned girl, Bonita Puckett had always been flighty and excitable, without a trace of the sophistication that girls her age usually started cultivating. She had had a high-pitched voice, a round pink-cheeked face like her mother's, and a headful of dark hair flying out in all directions. Catherine wondered now if Dottie had done something nicer with her hair when they buried her.

Even when she got to be a teenager, Bonita Puckett had acted childish in a lot of ways, never seeming to develop an interest in things like makeup and loud music and going out on dates. She had never made any effort whatsoever to act grown-up, which Catherine thought was the oddest thing about her. The girl didn't seem to know that teenagers weren't supposed to *care* about anything. She had never learned the haughty, sullen expressions that Catherine's own children had mastered at an early age. She was always smiling and carrying on far too eagerly over some little thing. Of course, the last time Catherine had seen her was two years ago, when Bonita was fifteen, but she couldn't imagine a girl like Bonita would have changed much.

A lady in Berea who had gone to the funeral said there was standing room only. She had told Catherine that the man who had struck and killed Bonita out by Highway 11 while she was walking back to the house after checking the mailbox had had a nervous breakdown and had put in for a job transfer to Winston-Salem, North Carolina. He had been fiddling with the dial on his radio while driving from Greenville to Derby and lost control of his car.

Some folks said this section of Highway 11 was jinxed, judging from all the wrecks on it. And the odd thing was that there was a pattern to it all. The last two wrecks had killed Birdie Freeman and Bonita Puckett, who both happened to go to the same church. Before that two men had been killed in two separate wrecks close together, and both of them were retired and in their late sixties. And Catherine had heard that years ago two women had had a head-on collision along Highway 11, and both of their children, who were riding on the passenger side in the two different cars, were killed.

The shampooing was done now. Catherine sat up and squeezed her eyes shut while Dottie blotted her hair with a towel. She wondered how many times a day Dottie thought of Bonita, turning around expecting to see her, then remembering she wouldn't ever be there again. She wondered which was harder, to have a daughter who was a constant worry day after day or to have a good girl and then lose her. But that was easy to figure out. Losing a child, any child, would tear a mother's heart out.

Dottie led the way to the black swivel chair, each step accompanied by the swishy rubbing sound of nylon stockings. Why Dottie would even bother with panty hose in the heat of the summer, just weeks after a family tragedy, was more than Catherine could comprehend. She sat down, and Dottie stood behind her, smiling faintly while she combed through her hair. Catherine wondered what was going through Dottie's mind. Was she thinking, "My word, Catherine's hair sure is getting thinner" or "She sure could use a color touch-up"? Did a person even notice things like that after losing a child?

"What are we doing for you today, honey?" Dottie asked. "You wanting me to cut it a little bit or just style it? You got you some perm left on the ends, I see."

"Well, I just want it *fixed*," Catherine snapped. "My regular girl went temporarily insane last time, and I can't do a thing with it. It's too short in some places and too long in others. I've been ashamed to go out in public."

Dottie smiled again, then picked up a large book from the bottom shelf of her rolling table and thumbed through the pages, pursing her lips and blowing out short, rhythmic patterns. She pointed to a picture and said, "How do you like that?"

Catherine frowned at the picture. "Well, I like it fine, I guess, although it's a little shorter than I usually wear mine, but . . . don't you think it's a little ambitious for my hair?"

"Well, let's just see," Dottie said. "We need to get some of this part up on top blended in with the sides first." She sectioned Catherine's hair off with neon blue plastic clamps. "I've always just loved your red hair," she said as she reached for the scissors. Catherine started to correct her about the color, which was auburn and not red, but she decided to let it go.

She had almost forgotten how much she had missed Dottie when she had quit coming here and switched to Nancy. Not all her holy talk, of course, but her hairstyling skill. She let herself relax in the black vinyl chair. This was nice—it was quiet and tidy here at the Be-Beautiful. Nancy's shop had been a hive of activity, with the radio always tuned in to the rock station in Spartanburg.

Catherine breathed deeply as she watched Dottie wedge her fingers into the handles of the small sharp scissors. She felt a decided sense of satisfaction as she saw the first tufts of hair fall against the plastic cape, and for several minutes Dottie clipped in silence, her brow furrowed in concentration. The thought was beginning to take root in Catherine's mind that she just might start coming back here on a regular basis. Especially since Dottie didn't seem to be talking about God with every other breath now.

That is, at least not until Catherine herself went and spoiled it all a few minutes later by making an innocent comment. If she had only kept her own mouth shut, she scolded herself a moment later, maybe Dottie would have remained quiet, too. But no, she had to go and say something that got Dottie started up.

And it was that ugly scarf that was the cause of it all. Catherine couldn't get the scenario out of her mind, kept seeing Dottie pull the scarf out of a drawer and hold it up to approve the color, then tie it around her ample neck. Over and over she imagined it, marveling at the simple dailiness of such an act by a mother bereft of her child. And finally, just to break the silence, Catherine said, "I had an aunt who had a scarf like that in practically every color of the rainbow."

Dottie stopped cutting, held the scissors in midair, and pressed the other hand against her neck as if to help herself swallow. The hair dryer was still humming steadily in the background, and a truck lumbered by out on Highway 11. Dottie's face softened as she touched the scarf, and she said, "Why, thank you, Catherine honey. My girl, Bonita, gave me this, must've been going on ten years ago now. She couldn't have been more than seven or eight." She patted the knot of the scarf lightly, then added, "I'm sure you know about the accident we had out here a little bit ago."

Catherine sat rigid, horrified. She certainly hadn't expected the subject of Bonita's death to actually come up in the conversation. She sat mutely, staring straight ahead. Dottie pumped the chair up a little higher and resumed cutting, but only a snip here and there now. She walked around on both sides, studying the symmetry, clipping a few hairs, nodding in an absentminded way.

"I think that's just about got it," she said. "This'll do a lot better for you. Now let's set it and then see how you like it." She put her scissors down, then touched her scarf again as if to remind herself of something unfinished. "People tried to be so thoughtful after it happened," she said, combing through Catherine's hair, "but what they did was clear out practically every single remembrance of her."

Don't say a word, Catherine told herself. *Sit still and don't open your mouth again.* But Dottie continued talking as she began to roll neat little swatches of Catherine's hair on small wire rollers. Catherine had forgotten how nimble her large fingers were with a comb, curlers, and picks.

"The church ladies came," Dottie continued, "and took away all her things, and Sid closed the door of her room up tight. And when I found the key and let myself in a few weeks later, it was like a spare room for company—not one sign of her at all. Not a single one of her personal things sitting around."

She paused a moment. Catherine saw Muriel Spears looking over at them longingly, as if wishing she could hear what was going on.

"Not a single clue that a little girl had grown up in that room," Dottie said, almost whispering now. "Sid felt so bad, said he never dreamed it would come across that way to me, like we were trying to erase her. He said *he* was the one to blame, for he'd told them to cart it all off. Then the next day I remembered this little scarf Bonita had given me, and all of a sudden I was better."

If Dottie's voice hadn't squeaked just the least bit at the end, Catherine would never have even looked up, but it did, and when she glanced up from staring at the plain beige linoleum, she was appalled.

Of course, it didn't really qualify as *crying*. It was more of a welling up in Dottie's eyes. It wasn't anything like the wild, wracking sobs and tears Catherine herself produced whenever she cried, but still she was appalled. She had wanted to see the effects of Bonita's death on Dottie, yes, but she sure hadn't counted on *this*. She knew what Blake would say if he heard she had made Dottie cry: "Well, I hope you're satisfied with yourself." And how could she ever explain that she hadn't done a single thing but make a simple remark about a scarf?

"Bonita had found it in a bunch of old things her grandma had boxed up to get rid of," Dottie said, "and she asked her for it, then went and wrapped it up and gave it to me—I think it was for my birthday, but it might have been Mother's Day. They come real close together. Anyway, she knew how much I liked this color." Dottie paused and lifted her head back, blinking rapidly as if to clear her eyes, then continued. "But I know now that it was more than just a gift from Bonita. It was—" She broke off with a short laugh.

Catherine looked up with alarm. Was Dottie having *hysterics*?

Muriel Spears lifted the hood of the hair dryer a little and called out, "I think I'm about done, Dottie. It's got mighty hot under here."

"All right, honey," Dottie said. "I guess I forgot how fast your hair dries. I'll be right with you."

Muriel got up from the dryer and went to sit on the couch. She didn't pick up a magazine, Catherine noticed, but riveted her eyes on Dottie and leaned forward as if ready to join the conversation.

"So anyway," Dottie said, turning back to Catherine, "I was just so thankful that I remembered this little scarf. It's been such a comfort. And I can't begin to tell you how kind everybody's been to us through all this, and they're *still* doing things—like that cake Lily Beasley brought over this morning. And a potted begonia somebody sent us from the florist yesterday. And meals galore. And well, just like you coming back here after all this time."

For a few seconds Dottie was silent as she concentrated on the smaller rollers at the bottom, and Catherine began to hope that she was going to drop the subject. But it wasn't to be.

"I've worn this scarf every day since I found it folded up in my drawer," Dottie said. "Oh, and I was starting to tell you—I know now that it wasn't just a gift from Bonita. It was a gift from God, and—"

"I sure hope I can make it back to Berea by noon!" Catherine said abruptly. "I've got to get to the dry cleaners before it closes. It's the silliest thing in the world for a business to close at noon on a weekday! It was the wishes of the original owners, they told me, and I said, 'Well, what about the wishes of your customers?' "

Dottie straightened up and smiled at Catherine through the mirror, leaning forward and cupping her hands around Catherine's ears. There was no trace of tears now, and Catherine wondered if perhaps she had only imagined them.

"There, I'm all done," Dottie said. "We'll get it dried, then see what we've got." As she followed Catherine over to the hair dryer, she said, "I know Bonita's in heaven, but I sure do . . ."

She trailed off, and Catherine thought she heard her sigh, though she couldn't be positive because Muriel Spears chose that exact moment to knock a magazine off the couch and onto the floor and then cry out, "Oh, my lands, if I'm not the clumsiest thing!"

Catherine suddenly recalled a phrase from *The Glass Menagerie*—

something about "the long delayed but always expected something that we live for." That's the way people like Dottie were about heaven. Living for something that everybody knew was just a desperate invention, a last-ditch effort at hope.

Why had she come back here to Dottie's anyway? She ought to have known better. People like Dottie Puckett never changed, not really—not in any long-term way. And the awful thing about it was, you couldn't snuff out her effect on you, like a candle. She stuck with you. You'd try to leave her behind, but you'd keep remembering things she said. Even when you were making fun of her, even when you were mad as all get-out at her, there she was planted in your mind, her expansive face smiling, her slow voice saying, "One of God's gifts to His children is *joy* . . . He regards us in our lowly estate . . . Bonita's in heaven." Dottie was easy to imitate. Catherine had mimicked her any number of times for Blake and the children.

Just then the telephone rang. Muriel had taken Catherine's place in the black swivel chair as Catherine had settled herself in the chair under the dryer hood.

"Just make yourself comfortable, honey," Dottie told Catherine. "Let me grab the phone, then I'll get you started."

Catherine watched Dottie retreat to answer the phone. She saw her open her appointment book. Catherine guessed she had seen what she came here to see, but what exactly would she say if giving a report titled *How Dottie Puckett Handles Death*? She stared hard at Dottie, who was nodding into the telephone and flipping the pages of her appointment book. "Dottie Puckett is sadder and quieter than she used to be," her report might begin.

"Well, now, yes, it looks like next Wednesday morning is free except for Muriel Spears," Dottie was saying, twirling the ends of the lavender scarf around her fingers. "Muriel's got a standing appointment every Wednesday at ten."

Catherine realized after she spoke her first word that she was talking much louder than she needed to. "I forgot to tell you I want this same time next Wednesday!" she shouted, frowning as she said it. Dottie looked up in surprise, her mouth falling open.

"Oh, wait a minute," Dottie said into the phone, "I do have some-body else at ten-thirty. Can you come at eleven?"

Catherine watched Dottie let loose of her scarf, click her ball-point pen, and lean down to write in her appointment book. "But she still keeps up with her schedule and talks about the goodness of God," her report might continue.

After Dottie hung up, she came back to the hair dryer and bent over in front of Catherine. "I'd be so honored to have you back as a regular, honey," she said.

And Catherine, her lips pressed tightly together, looked into Dottie's small, bright eyes and thought, I might come back as a customer, but don't go getting your hopes up about anything else, Dottie Puckett.

Then the hood of the hair dryer came down, and Catherine was enveloped in a warm flush of air. Dottie patted her hand and said something, but Catherine couldn't make out her words.

A Distant City

3

Thirty minutes later Catherine pulled out of Sid Puckett's Texaco and headed back down Highway 11 toward Berea. If she had known what awaited her at home, she thought later, she would not have spent the entire twelve miles feeling so proud of her new hairdo and sneaking glances at herself in the rearview mirror. She would have used her time to plot an escape.

As it was, though, she flew blithely down the highway, thinking about a hundred piddling things, like picking up her new pink suit from the woman in Derby who did all her alterations, buying fresh peaches if there were still any to be had, running by the bank and then by the public swimming pool to give Olivia money, stopping by the cleaners for Blake's shirts, checking the gift shop in Derby for potpourri to put in her new porcelain pomander, calling Elaine Berryhill to ask for the quiche recipe she had promised to bring to the last meeting of the Friends of the Library, but which she had forgotten, and so on.

If she had known an hour later when she turned onto Brookside Drive in Berea, after having completed her errands, that her life was about to be thrown completely off kilter, Catherine would have jammed her Buick into reverse and sped in the opposite direction as fast as her brand-new steel-belted radials would take her. But since she didn't know it, she drove haplessly down the street where she lived, taking note of the Burketts' new riding mower sitting ostentatiously in the middle of their front lawn—"Okay, okay, we all see it!" Catherine felt like yelling out the window—Trixie Thorndike's new border of monkey grass, and a truck from Hank's Appliances parked in the Chewnings' driveway. It seemed to Catherine that the Chewnings, who had moved onto Brookside just a week ago, were having something new delivered to their house every single day.

The first thing Catherine noticed when she pulled into her own driveway across the street from the Chewnings was that the front door was standing open so that her new eucalyptus wreath didn't show. And right on the heels of that she noticed a common brown grocery bag sitting on the front porch beside the wicker rocking chair. And no sooner had she seen that than she saw an unfamiliar tan umbrella, a large one such as men carry, neatly closed and hanging from the brass mailbox. She felt a vague warning flutter in the pit of her stomach, but even then she had no idea of the surprise she was in for.

She pushed the button to open the garage door and pulled slowly into her parking space on the right, closest to the kitchen door. She sat in the car for a moment before getting out. She had the distinct impression that a visitor was inside her house, and she was in no hurry to greet whoever it was. If she took her time, maybe the person would leave through the front door and never even know Catherine was home.

Who had let him in anyway? Blake was at work, or at least that's where he was supposed to be. She sometimes wondered if he really did go to his office every day when he was in town. She had even telephoned at random times to see if he was in, and then hung up. Olivia was at the swimming pool. Catherine had just seen her and given her a twenty-dollar bill, which Olivia had grabbed out of her hand without so much as a thank-you. Philip was probably around the neighborhood somewhere, most likely down the street at Andy Partridge's house playing Nintendo.

Hardy was probably home, even though he shouldn't be. He should be out looking for a job, as she had told him to do every single day since the first of June, a command that he either pretended not to hear or openly scorned. "Hey, yeah, that's a great idea for summertime fun," he had said to her just this morning. "I'd love to get up early every day and go take orders from some fat, middle-class authority figure." It had to be Hardy who had let the person in. Catherine certainly hoped it wasn't that deadbeat friend of his with the tattoo of a skull and a knife dripping blood right in plain sight on his arm, the one Blake had warned Hardy not to bring here ever again. But even as she considered the possibility, Catherine dismissed it. None of Hardy's friends would carry a tan umbrella.

She opened the car door, gathered her parcels, and got out. Glaring into the backseat at Blake's starched shirts, she slammed the door shut with her elbow. Blake could just come out and get the shirts himself when he got home. She couldn't carry everything in one trip. It was enough that she had picked them up from the laundry when he could just as easily have done it on his way home from work tomorrow.

As Catherine opened the kitchen door and stepped inside, the topmost peach from the bag she had bought at the roadside stand along the highway fell to the floor. Being plump and ripe, it didn't roll but just landed with a dull plop against the dark green ceramic tile. Catherine could see that the skin had split open partway and little droplets of peach juice had spurted out onto the tile. And somehow right at that same moment as she stood there glaring at the peach, her keys fell to the floor with a clatter.

"Well, of all things!" she declared, then stepped over the peach to the island counter, where she deposited her packages and purse with an enormous sigh. If Hardy would have come out to help her carry things in, she wouldn't have dropped anything. But the idea was ridiculous, and she knew it. When had Hardy ever exerted himself to help her carry anything? Well, now that she thought about it, she did remember his helping her carry his new television set downstairs to his room in the basement earlier this summer. When she had caught her heel on the stair carpet and almost lost her balance, he had shouted, "Hey! You make me drop this, and I'll . . ." She had regained her footing, and he hadn't finished the sentence. She still wasn't sure where he'd gotten the money to pay for the TV. When she asked him he said, "I saved up my allowance," but she doubted that.

She yanked a paper towel from the roller, then stooped to pick up the peach with one hand and swipe at the floor with the other. Sparkle Flynn, the cleaning woman she hired once a week, would be in on Friday to do the floors, so a quick wipe-up would do for now. She threw away the paper towel, set the damaged peach on the counter next to the sink, then retrieved her keys from the floor and tossed them on top of her purse.

She had half expected to hear voices coming from the living room or den, but the only thing she heard as she stood in the middle of the kitchen with her hands on her hips was the muffled racket of Hardy's music coming from downstairs. From the kitchen she could see into the dining room, and she moved so that she could admire the new floral table runner with its heavy blue tassels on the mahogany sideboard. She still wondered, though, if burgundy tassels would have looked better with the wallpaper.

She walked from the kitchen through the hallway and into the den. No one was there. She turned and looked across the hallway into the living room. It, too, was empty. She scowled at the open front door, then walked over and closed it firmly. That eucalyptus wreath had cost a small fortune to put together, and it was all for nothing if it couldn't be seen from the street. She had kept telling the floral designer to add another couple of silk roses here, then a few more sprigs of berries there, and then some curly willows, and when she heard the final cost, Catherine had said, "Well, my word, you'd think that stuff was made out of solid gold!"

She moved now toward the draperies and adjusted a tieback, then noticing that a sofa cushion was out of place, she straightened it. Catching sight of herself in the mirror above the fireplace, Catherine turned her head from side to side. Dottie Puckett really knew how to fix hair, she thought.

It suddenly dawned on her that it hadn't even entered her mind to be afraid. Here she was going from room to room, looking for a stranger! She was alone in the house for all practical purposes, since Hardy sure couldn't be counted on to be of any help, even when he was home. Well, she *wasn't* afraid. Nobody with ulterior motives was going to leave his umbrella in plain sight and forget to close the front door. Still, she paused and laid a hand across her chest. She briefly imagined herself on stage— the heroine in a suspense drama, unsuspecting of imminent danger.

"Is anybody here?" she called down the hallway. She thought she heard something bump in one of the bedrooms but decided it could have been Hardy downstairs. "What do you want?" she called, then immediately felt foolish. What would she have done, she wondered, if someone had replied, "Oh, I'm looking mostly for diamond jewelry, but I'll take cash, too, if you have it"?

"I've got the phone with me!" she said, though she didn't. "I'm dialing my husband right now." Slowly she stepped down the hallway, peering first into the bathroom, then into Olivia's room. No one was there. She pushed the door of Philip's room open and surveyed the disaster. It looked like the aftermath of mortal combat. It stank to high heaven, too. There was no telling when he had last cleaned the gerbil's cage. A half-eaten sandwich was sitting on the edge of the chest of drawers next to the door. Catherine reached over and touched the bread with a forefinger— hard as toast, just as she'd expected. No intruder in his right mind would want to step foot in here, she thought as she heaved a sigh and closed the door.

Nobody was in the laundry closet, nor in the master bedroom at the end of the hall. Tiptoeing across the mint green bedroom carpet toward the master bath, Catherine glanced at the king-sized bed. The large gold-framed Monet print looked just right above the headboard. That other thing, a geometric abstract, never had fit in with this room, especially in the black frame. It wasn't such a bad piece, really, but it was all wrong for the room. Though she had tried to tell Blake so when he had dragged it home from an art show in Columbia years ago, he had been stubborn and insisted on hanging it above their bed. She was glad she had finally moved it to the guest bedroom across the hall. For that matter, Blake was probably glad, too, since he slept in the guest room most nights now. He could lie awake all night and stare at it to his heart's content, Catherine thought angrily.

The guest bedroom was the only room left to check besides the basement, and though the door was closed, it didn't alarm her at first. Blake often closed it when he got up early in the morning and went to the hall bathroom to take a shower. Catherine suspected he did it so the children wouldn't see that the bed had been slept in. And though she vowed every morning to leave the guest bed unmade since she hadn't been the one to mess it up, she always slipped in at some point during the day and made it up. She had made it up this morning before she had driven out to Dottie Puckett's for her hair appointment, and she had also picked up Blake's trousers from the foot of the bed and hung them back in his closet in the master bedroom. The truth was that she didn't want the children asking questions any more than Blake did.

A sudden chill of knowledge gripped her as she laid hold of the doorknob now. Perhaps it was another soft sound—a rustling this time—that she thought she heard behind the door, or perhaps it was the sixth sense that she had always prided herself on having. At any rate, she knew as sure as anything right before she turned the knob and swung the door open that someone was in the room.

Her mind struggled to sort through things as she first took in the sight. A woman, her gray hair disheveled, sat on the edge of the bed, squinting at her as if disoriented. Her shoes—a pair of black crepe-soled lace-ups—were neatly stowed under the nightstand. A large canvas satchel with a strap buckled around it leaned against the dressing table, and a black handbag sat on the floor beside it. A navy raincoat was draped over the ladder-back chair next to the door. Another brown grocery bag like the one on the front porch sat at the foot of the bed, the head of a stuffed raccoon peering out the top.

Catherine's eyes darted back to the woman's face, a pale oval of confusion, and at the same moment that Catherine pieced it all together and said, "Della Boyd?" the woman spoke up, patting at her hair distractedly with one hand while pointing to the raincoat on the chair with the other.

"It was pouring down rain in Yazoo City when I left on the bus yesterday," she said.

Catherine didn't know what to think, and for a moment she couldn't speak. What in the world was Blake's sister doing sitting in their guest room? Why wasn't she back home in Mississippi? It didn't make a bit of sense. Though she knew it wasn't a very cordial greeting, Catherine took a step into the room and said quite loudly, "What are you doing here, Della Boyd?"

"I was just taking a little rest here on the bed," Della Boyd said. "The bus got held up between Birmingham and Atlanta." She was using both hands now to press her hair flat against her head, and her face still had a dazed look, as if somebody had hit her with a heavy object and she was trying to remember who had done it and why. "A van and a big truck had a wreck on the freeway," she said in a tone of wonder. "Both of them turned over on their sides and blocked all four lanes of traffic. There were ambulances and police cars everywhere flashing their lights. We had to sit in one spot for over a whole hour."

"But what are you doing here at our house?" Catherine repeated, raising her voice and taking another step toward Della Boyd on the bed.

"The man in the seat behind me on the bus had him a little miniature checkerboard," Della Boyd said, plucking at the hair around her ears now, "and he sat there playing checkers with a colored man across the aisle the whole time." She turned and looked toward the window, then added, "The colored man beat him almost every time."

"I don't care who won a stupid game of checkers on a bus in Birmingham—"

"It wasn't in Birmingham," Della Boyd interrupted, shaking her head briskly, though still patting at her hair with both hands. "It was between Birmingham and Atlanta. On the freeway. A truck and a van turned over—"

"I know, I know!" Catherine said. "They had a wreck and turned over, and there were lots of ambulances! But why are you here? You didn't write and ask about visiting. Are you on your way somewhere?"

Della Boyd gazed up at her with her mouth slightly open, both hands lifted from her head now, poised in midair. "Why, I was on my way here," she said.

"But *why?*" Catherine asked. "Why are you here, Della Boyd? We weren't expecting you. You never told us you were thinking about coming." When Della Boyd didn't answer, Catherine added, "This isn't a good time for us to have company."

For a few seconds Della Boyd appeared to be paralyzed. She just stared up at Catherine, unblinking, hardly even breathing. Then she made a gurgling noise almost like a giggle, though Catherine was sure she wasn't laughing.

"My house burned down," Della Boyd said. "I left Yazoo City because my house burned down. It burned to the ground. I can't live there any-more."

"What? Your *house* burned down?" Catherine said. She studied Della Boyd closely, looking for signs of deception. This was a suspicious-sound-ing story if she had ever heard one! "And why didn't we hear anything about that, Della Boyd?" she said. "When did it happen? Are you making this up?"

Della Boyd closed her lips and let her hands fall into her lap, then stared down at them, clasping them together tightly, as if afraid they might fly away. "It was some kind of electrical short, they think," she said after a moment of silence, during which Catherine was trying to decide what in the world she should do first—call Blake at work or call the bus station and find out about the next bus back to Yazoo City. She thought of those parcels that came in the mail, the ones you didn't want. You just marked *Refused* on them and sent them right back. She wished she could do that right now.

"Why did you take a bus, Della Boyd?" she asked. "Why didn't you drive your car?"

Della Boyd looked up at her and offered a small, sad smile. "I sold my car," she said. "Mr. D'Angelo bought it from me. He came to see it one day last week and took it for a drive, then wrote out a check for it right on the spot." She pointed to her purse on the floor. "I have the check in there. It's for six thousand dollars." She relaxed her hands and began slowly smoothing the folds of her navy skirt.

Catherine noticed that she was wearing the string of pearls Blake had sent her for Christmas one year.

"Mr. D'Angelo has the nicest handwriting for a man," Della Boyd said in a dreamlike voice. "He fixes clocks, you know, so I suppose that's why his hand is so steady. He has a little shop in his basement. He fixed my mantel clock for me last spring, and—"

"Look, Della Boyd, I don't care if Mr. D'Angelo fixes jackhammers!" Catherine cried. "This whole story of yours just sounds fishy! Some-thing's wrong with you! You're acting like you're making all this up. Now, let's get it straight. You say your house burned down? And you sold your car? And you took the bus from Yazoo City all the way here to Berea? And now you're . . ."

"Well, it didn't come right into Berea," Della Boyd said. "I had to take a taxi from the Greyhound station in Filbert."

"Well, of course, but that doesn't matter," Catherine said testily. "So now you're here in Berea, and you're planning to do *what*?"

"Well, I'm going to live here," Della Boyd said simply. "I've got the money from my insurance company, and I've got Mr. D'Angelo's money. I didn't want to stay in Yazoo City, Catherine. I *couldn't* stay there."

"Why not?" Catherine heard the shrillness in her voice, but she couldn't stop herself. "People don't just pick up and run off whenever they have a setback, Della Boyd! What makes you think you can just show up on our doorstep and expect us to make room for you without the slightest bit of warning? You're just not thinking straight, Della Boyd. That's not the way things are done! Why didn't you call Blake if you had a fire at your house? Why didn't we ever hear the first word about it?"

"Where is Blake?" Della Boyd asked suddenly. "I want to see Blake. I need to talk to him."

"Yes, I need to talk to him, too!" Catherine said. "In fact, I'm going to call him right now." She turned to leave the room, then wheeled back around. "Who let you into our house?" she asked.

"The front door was unlocked, and I came on in," Della Boyd said. She pointed to her raincoat again with one hand and fingered her bangs with the other. "My hair must be a sight. It was raining hard yesterday when I left Yazoo City. It was pouring down. I had to wear my raincoat."

"Yes, yes. I know all about that. And you had to carry your umbrella, too, didn't you? And you hung it outside on our mailbox!"

"Oh, it's not really mine," Della Boyd said. "Somebody left it on the bus I guess. I waited till everybody was off and nobody claimed it." Della Boyd looked briefly penitent. "I even asked the bus driver if—"

Catherine cut her off. "Well, don't go unpacking anything in here!" she said. "This is Blake's little problem, and he'll just have to come home and solve it. I'm going to call him right now." And with that, Catherine closed the door behind her and charged down the hallway to the telephone in the kitchen.

She quickly jabbed the buttons of the telephone and waited impatiently for the receptionist at Blake's office to answer. When she did so, Catherine interrupted the woman's business greeting with "Yes, yes, Tiffany, I need to speak to Blake right now." There was a moment of silence, and Catherine could picture Tiffany, one shoulder hunched to brace the receiver against her ear, batting her eyelashes as she tried to process the information. Tiffany had the most ridiculous drawl Catherine had ever heard and a big, toothy Dolly Parton smile. She wore her dark hair swept up, but Catherine was sure the part on top was mostly a hairpiece. "Did you hear me, Tiffany? Get Blake on the phone. I need to talk to him now!"

"He's . . . uh, he's . . . just a minute. Is this Catherine?"

"Well, of course it's Catherine!" Catherine said. "Where is Blake?

Isn't he in the office?" She looked down at the toe of her red Bandolino flat and realized she was tapping her foot. Finally, after months and months of checking up on Blake, she had caught him—just when she needed him at home for a crisis, unfortunately.

"Well, he should be . . . he's . . . uh, could I have him call you back, Catherine?" Tiffany's voice was on the breathy side, so combined with the syrupy drawl and all the upward inflections, it was one of the most irritating sounds Catherine had ever heard. Catherine shook her head with exasperation as she heard a clunk on the other end. No doubt Tiffany had dropped the receiver again. She had a bad habit of shuffling papers and trying to continue working on the computer while she answered the telephone. Oddly, in spite of her ditzy ways and her silly name—Tiffany Suzette Tribble, of all things!—Blake had often said she was a surprisingly competent receptionist, that underneath the fluff there was something solid. At times he laughed about Tiffany's quirks, of course, but Catherine often wondered if he just did that to throw her off, so she wouldn't suspect anything between the two of them at the office.

"Sorry, Catherine." Tiffany had evidently reclaimed the receiver. "I can have him . . . oh, wait a minute. I think . . ." Catherine heard her ask a question, but her words were muffled.

"Where is my husband?" Catherine shouted. "Quit giving me the runaround and tell me where he is! I need to talk to him right this minute!"

Tiffany tittered. "Well, all right, Catherine. I think he's in the restroom, if you really want to know. Velma Kay said she saw him just a minute ago, but he's not at his desk now. We think he went around the corner to the men's room, but . . ." She broke off again, and Catherine heard her ask plainly, "Hey, Jimbo, will you check the men's room? Blake's got a phone call from his wife." Catherine would be willing to bet anything that Tiffany had rolled her eyes and made a face when she said those last two words. "Hold on—I've got somebody checking for me, Catherine," Tiffany said.

Catherine heard Velma Kay's laughter in the background followed by a muted chime, probably triggered by someone's opening the door of the front office. "Hey there, girls!" Catherine heard a male voice boom, and she heard Tiffany reply, without even covering the mouth of the receiver, "Why, hi there, Mr. McCormick! How're you liking retirement? Boy, we sure miss you around here!"

Catherine thought about lashing out at Tiffany about telephone etiquette, asking her if she didn't know how to put people on hold instead of carrying on other conversations right in their ear. But the truth was that she really didn't want to be cut off. She liked to hear all the office sounds. They always seemed to be having such a good time over there at the Forrest Bonner Tool and Die. She often felt jealous of Blake, getting to escape to such a busy, happy place every day.

Right in the middle of Mr. McCormick's account of a recent trip he'd made to see his grandson in Albuquerque, New Mexico—most of which Catherine could make out—there was a click and Blake came on the other line.

"What is it, Catherine?" he asked. His voice was hard and tight like a thin steel wire.

"Well, I'm sorry to have to interrupt your busy schedule this afternoon," Catherine said, taking a defensive tone, "but I thought you'd like to know about a little problem that was waiting for me when I got home about fifteen minutes ago."

"Catherine, I've got an interview scheduled in five minutes," Blake said. "The guy's already sitting out in the lobby. What is it this time?"

"You might like to know," Catherine said in clipped syllables, "that your sister is sitting on the bed in the guest bedroom right this very minute. And she says she intends to stay here. According to her story, her house in Yazoo City caught on fire, and she's hightailed it out of Mississippi with her insurance money—sold her car and everything and just walked right into our house while I was gone and made herself at home! If you want to know my opinion, something sounds fishy to me."

"Della Boyd is there now?" Blake asked.

"That's what I just finished telling you, isn't it?" Catherine said. "She's sitting back on the bed, acting like she's lost her wits. I can hardly make heads or tails out of what she's saying. She keeps staring around like she's not all there and repeating everything. Of course, that's nothing new. She's always done that. But she looks awful. It makes me wonder if she set fire to her own—"

"Stop it, Catherine!" Though Blake had lowered his voice, it was more caustic now, full of anger. "Just stop it," he said again. "What did you say to her? Did you say that to her?"

"Believe me, it wouldn't faze her if I did," Catherine said. "But I didn't call so we could have this long friendly chat. I called to let you know that you need to get yourself home right now and take care of this."

"Is she okay?" Blake asked.

Catherine heard, and resented, the concern in his voice. She couldn't help wondering what he would say if somebody called and told him that she, Catherine, had turned up incoherent in a distant city, claiming some disaster back home. She couldn't imagine that he'd ask, "Is she okay?"

He'd probably say something like "Oh no, what has she gone and done this time?" She had recently accused him of showing more regard for their dog, Kinko, than for her, to which he had replied icily, "And vice versa,"—one of his typical riddlelike remarks. She had suspected, however, that he meant Kinko paid more attention to him than she did, so she had responded, "I don't recall the last time I saw Kinko in the kitchen cooking your meals," to which he had shot back, "Such as they are."

"Well," Catherine said now, "if you call acting half-cracked and looking like death warmed over *okay*, then yes, by all means she's just doing hunky-dory. Like I just finished explaining, if you were listening to anything I said."

Neither one of them spoke for a moment. Then Blake said, "I'll come home as soon as I can. This interview's important, though. If we can get this guy to . . . oh well, never mind. What do you care? Just leave Della Boyd alone till I get home, Catherine. Don't say another word to her."

I'll say whatever I feel like saying!" Catherine shouted. "And don't act like I'm the bad guy. I live here, remember." And even though she knew Blake had already hung up, she added, "Your sister's the one who turned up out of nowhere and walked right in like it was her own front door."

As she glared at the receiver in her hand, her last words hovered in the air, and a childhood memory swept over her—one she hated, one she still had nightmares about. She didn't want to think about it, but she had no choice. "Her own front door . . ."

Catherine couldn't have been more than eight or nine when she came home from school that day to find the front door locked. Her sister had gone to a friend's house, so she was by herself. She rang the doorbell and knocked, but nobody came. She threw all her weight against the door, but it wouldn't budge. She went around the house and saw her mother's car in the garage, but the back door was locked, too. It was a big house, so the windows were too high off the ground. They were all closed tight anyway.

Catherine tried to think. They had two different housekeepers and a man who came to do yard work on Mondays and Fridays, but . . . what day was this? Thursday—it was Thursday because she and Patricia had their ballet lessons on Wednesday, and that was yesterday. Catherine started to panic. Thursday was the day neither one of the maids came to clean or cook.

She pounded on the back door and screamed. It was the same word over and over and over. "Mother! Mother! Mother!" But nobody came, and then she lay on the steps sobbing for a long time. A horrible thought seized her. What if her mother had died in her bed? What if she were lying cold and still upstairs right now with all the doors locked?

. She was terrified. She didn't want to go for help. She didn't want people coming to see her mother's dead body. She got up and launched herself at the door again, kicking at it. She could hear the doorbell inside, but then she stopped ringing it. Dead people couldn't hear doorbells. If she could only get inside, she could call her father. But she couldn't, of course, and she fell down on the steps again, sobbing.

She couldn't remember exactly, but it seemed that she must have stayed there for two hours. Every few minutes she would get up and try again, hoping somehow she was mistaken, that the door really wasn't locked after all, that all she needed to do was turn it a certain way and it would open. It didn't, though, and she fell down again each time and cried some more. She didn't want her mother to be dead. Would they blame it on her? There would have to be a funeral, of course, and she had heard awful things about funerals.

She always hated this part of the memory especially. How stupid she must have looked in a heap on the back steps! Not that any of the neighbors could see her since their house was on a huge lot and the backyard was enclosed by high hedges. But how stupid she must have looked to—now came the absolutely worst part of the memory—to her mother. Her mother's bedroom was on the back side of the house, and as Catherine got up from the steps a few minutes later to try the door again, she looked up, and what she saw made her heart turn to ice. There stood her mother at her bedroom window, looking down at Catherine.

"Open the door!" she called to her mother, but her mother just stood there shaking her head, and then she disappeared from the window. Catherine wondered later if she could have imagined that part, but she knew she hadn't. It must have been another hour after that when her father came home and found her on the back steps and let her inside. Catherine remembered him charging upstairs, and she heard voices drifting down the staircase. When he came back down, he went straight to the front door and turned the knob. The big door swung open.

"See, Catherine, your mother said the front door was open all along," he said. He patted her head and called her a silly goose as he walked past her, back to his study. But Catherine knew the door hadn't been open. She knew it had been locked when she came home.

She realized all of a sudden that she was still standing in the kitchen, holding the telephone receiver in her hand and breathing very hard. "Silly goose," she whispered to herself, and very slowly she hung up the phone.

Thin Air

4

Catherine had no sooner hung up the telephone than she heard Hardy's footsteps coming up the basement stairs. He hadn't turned his music down, of course, so when he opened the door leading into the kitchen a great blast of noise—it was hard for Catherine to think of it as *music*—flooded the room. Catherine immediately put two fingers to each temple and pressed. She closed her eyes and out of habit adopted an expression of martyrdom. This had long been her method of dealing with Hardy—with all three children for that matter—and in the early days it had seemed to have a softening effect on them, although now she was sure it was usually counterproductive. It was a hard habit to break, however, and she often had no idea how else to respond. Sometimes, of course—in fact, fairly regularly—she did let loose and shout at them.

These days Hardy seemed to think that every encounter between the two of them was some kind of sport. Lately he had begun mimicking her. He would stagger about the room with the back of his hand against his forehead, moaning and pretending to swoon, gasping in a silly Scarlett O'Hara falsetto: "I am not appreciated in my own home! Why do my children torment me so? My heart is just on the verge of explodin' with grief!" Olivia and Philip thought it was hilarious, of course, and last time Olivia had even chimed in with a couple of lines herself: "After all I do for you around here, and this is the thanks I get!" and "Someday when I'm gone, you'll regret how you treated me!" Of course, they overdid it. She never carried on so outrageously.

Catherine stood now with her eyes closed, still applying pressure to her temples, and said, "Your father is on his way home, so I'd go right back downstairs and turn down that racket if I were you."

She heard Hardy approaching her, and she heard him laugh deep in his throat, a cartoonish cackle he had learned as a child and never dropped.

"*If you were me,*" he said. "Now, there's an interesting thought."

He spoke directly into her ear. She could feel the warmth of his breath. She smelled him, too—a metallic, sour smell like a mixture of vinegar, sweat, and greasy hair. She didn't move, hoping he would leave her alone, but he stayed there for what must have been a full minute breathing hotly into her ear, blowing hard each time he exhaled—on purpose, she could tell. She thought of her new hairstyle and imagined it going limp on that side from his foul breath.

At last he said in a low, menacing voice, "There better be something to eat around here, 'cause I was checkin' earlier, see, and all I saw was a pile of—"

"Hardy? Is that Hardy? Can it be?"

Catherine's eyes flew open at the words. For just the shortest moment she had forgotten all about Della Boyd. Hardy stepped back away from her quickly, and both of them turned to stare at the figure standing in the hallway just outside the kitchen.

From this perspective Catherine noticed how exceedingly tall and thin Della Boyd looked. She had always been tall, of course, but never this thin, Catherine was sure. She looked brittle, as if she could snap right in two if she twisted the wrong way. It irritated Catherine to look at someone that thin. Why, Della Boyd probably didn't even work at it! She probably went around saying things like "I sure wish I could put some meat on these skinny old bones of mine." Well, she'd better not say anything like that around me, Catherine thought. It was hard enough to keep trim without someone like that around.

Della Boyd walked into the kitchen in her stocking feet and stopped a few steps from Hardy, her arms outstretched and a smile of delight on her face. "Hardy?" she said again. "This can't be little Hardy. Such a thing just can't be. Why, the last time I saw you, you were just a little boy, and now you're . . . why, you've got to be almost as tall as your daddy! You remember your aunt Della Boyd, don't you, Hardy?"

Catherine couldn't remember the last time she had seen Hardy at a loss for words, and the sight amazed her now. He sucked in his cheeks and stared at Della Boyd, ignoring her outstretched arms. He slid his fists into the pockets of his baggy shorts, pulling them down even further. Catherine felt like saying, "Nobody wants to see three inches of your underwear!" but she didn't. She was just glad to see that he had his underwear on today since he didn't always. As usual, he wasn't wearing a shirt, and she found herself staring at the dark patch of hair growing on his chest. Nobody wanted to see that either, she thought, but she didn't dare say so. The last time she had objected to his bare chest, he had plucked out a hair without flinching and put it into his mouth, then made a great show of ecstatic chewing and swallowing. "It's so handy for snacking this way," he had said.

Della Boyd didn't bat an eye at Hardy's lack of enthusiasm about her being there, didn't even seem to notice that instead of rushing into her arms he had taken a step backward, that his nose was wrinkled up like he couldn't stand even being in the same room with her, that he was still scowling at her with a mixture of dread and disgust. Catherine was tempted to intervene, to try to say something to defuse what seemed to be building up into a nasty little scene, but the truth suddenly hit her that if Della Boyd could see Hardy's true colors right here at the beginning, she'd be more likely to want to get back on the bus and head straight back to Yazoo City as soon as she could.

Della Boyd, evidently catching on that Hardy wasn't the hugging type, lowered her hands and put them on her hips, then tilted her head in a coquettish sort of way. "You remind me so much of your daddy!" she said to Hardy, and then she laughed a high twittering little laugh. "When your daddy was about your age," she said, looking off toward the kitchen window now, "he used to look at me that same way, and the things he'd *say*! Why, the most extreme things you ever heard, just trying to get a rise out of me. But he was always a sweet boy, really, underneath it all."

She paused to laugh again in a halfhearted way, her eyes still turned to the window. "He vowed and declared one day," she continued, "that men could beat women at anything physical—*anything*, mind you—and when I disagreed, he puffed himself up and said, 'All right, Sister'—that's what he always called me, of course: Sister—'all right, Sister,' he said, 'you pick three things, and we'll go head to head, and so I . . .'"

Della Boyd trailed off, craning her neck forward a little as she looked at the kitchen window, frowning. Catherine couldn't see a thing except the children's old swing set and the enormous lopsided magnolia tree that looked like some kind of botanical freak in the backyard, the branches growing right down to the ground so that the trunk wasn't even visible. It looked like a bush that had gone haywire and didn't know when to quit growing, and if it weren't for the big showy blossoms it kept producing every year, Catherine would have had it taken out years ago.

Hardy cut a puzzled glance at Catherine and, in a rare moment of partnership, twirled a forefinger in the air beside his ear, jerking his head in Della Boyd's direction. Catherine nodded.

"Is that what I think it is out there in the backyard, Catherine?" Della Boyd said, her voice full of wonder. She took a few steps toward the window.

"I don't know what you *think* it is, Della Boyd," said Catherine.

"Why, it looks like a magnolia tree, but I wasn't expecting to see any of those here in South Carolina," Della Boyd said.

"Well, Mississippi doesn't hold the franchise on magnolias, Della Boyd," Catherine said. "We've got cotton and boll weevils in this part of the South, too."

"Is that so?" Della Boyd turned back and smiled at Catherine and Hardy. "Well, I ought to feel right at home if that's the case."

"Well, I wouldn't start putting down any roots if I were you," Catherine said. "Blake is on his way home right now, and we'll get all this cleared up. I'll just tell you right now that we can't figure out what in the world's going on, but it all sounds suspicious—like you're imagining things. People just don't pick up and leave home on a whim."

Della Boyd cocked her head and studied Catherine with puzzlement. "Imagining things? I thought you understood," she said. "I thought I told you my house burned down and I had to leave."

"Oh yes, *that*," Catherine said. "Well, people don't just turn up out of thin air with a story like that. People's houses don't just burn down to the ground without their families hearing something about it, Della Boyd."

"But you did hear about it," Della Boyd replied. "I just told you."

Hardy suddenly snorted with laughter. Catherine shot him a withering look and before she could stop herself said, "It's not in the least bit funny, Hardy!"

At this, Hardy cranked his laughter up several notches, holding his sides and lurching to the counter to lean against it for support. Catherine studied him as he continued to laugh, wave upon wave of what anybody could tell was fake hilarity. She felt like screaming and stamping her feet but knew that nothing would please Hardy better, so she tried to concentrate on keeping her expression neutral. Just breathe nice and slow, she told herself. Don't give him the pleasure of losing your cool.

Della Boyd looked back and forth between Hardy and Catherine, a slight smile playing about her lips, as if she wanted badly to catch onto whatever the joke was. She took a few steps toward Hardy, then stopped, laying one hand across her heart. Still Hardy carried on, clutching the edge of the counter with both hands now and pretending to be convulsed with enormous, shrieky hiccups as he laughed.

Catherine could have predicted the next part of the routine. She watched with narrowed eyes as Hardy's knees began to wobble, then buckle. She had seen it all before. He appeared to be trying desperately to maintain his hold on the countertop, but inch by inch he collapsed further and slowly slid to the floor, his laughter subsiding into whimpers, until he lay stretched out on his back like a dead man, silent, his tongue lolling out the side of his mouth. A tiny shrill hiccup sounded, and one leg rose and twitched with an exaggerated flourish, then fell again.

It was clear that Della Boyd didn't know what to think about the performance. She looked uncertainly at Catherine, as if searching her face for clues. "Is he—?" she said, then stopped.

"Hardy just has a warped sense of humor, that's all," Catherine said tightly, enunciating each word clearly. "He doesn't put on these little shows for just anybody, so you should feel real honored, Della Boyd."

At that Hardy's entire body jerked, and both arms flailed wildly before falling limp once more.

Della Boyd's face brightened, and she gave a timid laugh. "Well, he sure could have fooled me," she said to Catherine. "He must have gotten his acting ability from you. I sure never saw Blake do anything like that." She stepped closer to Hardy and bent over him, cupping her hands to her mouth. "I'm going to clap my hands for you, Hardy!" she called out. "That was as fine a job as anything I've ever seen on the TV set!" And she actually started applauding.

Hardy opened his eyes and forced a loud, rolling belch, prolonging it with a series of ratchetlike grunts at the end. The smile on Della Boyd's face never faltered, though Catherine felt her own mouth pinch in at the corners. Evidently Della Boyd's five-year teaching stint in a Yazoo City junior high school had acquainted her with all the obnoxious habits of boys. Of course, playing mother to Blake all those years had probably taught her a thing or two about boys, too.

In what seemed like one quick movement, Hardy was suddenly on his feet again. Catherine wasn't sure, but it almost looked as if he was embarrassed by Della Boyd's applause, though she couldn't imagine such a thing. He flung open the refrigerator door and stuck his head inside. "What you got to eat in here?" he called. "All I see is stuff that looks like road kill or pig puke." Catherine heard him knock something over as he shoved things around on the shelves.

"Oh, that reminds me of Blake so much!" Della Boyd said. "I never saw the likes of how that boy could eat! Why, I remember one day I broiled a hen for our supper and left it sitting on the top of the stove . . ."

At that moment the doorbell rang. "Good grief, who in the world can that be?" Catherine said aloud. "The last thing I need is somebody ringing the doorbell right when everybody's in a tizzy around here!" As she marched off toward the living room, she heard Della Boyd pick up her story as if nothing had happened.

". . . and it was the prettiest little golden brown hen you ever saw, broiled up so nice, with its chest sticking up so proud and juicy. And anyway, I left it in the roasting pan on the stove and went outside to plant some marigolds around the cucumbers to help keep the bugs away—marigolds are good for that, you know—and when I came back in . . ."

When she got to the front door, Catherine stood on her tiptoes and peered out the fanlight window onto the front porch. There she saw Barb Chewning from across the street, her toddler balanced on one hip. She heard her say, "What'sa matter wif Sammy Wammy?" in the high, silly voice women always use with young children. Catherine felt a sharp tug inside. She wished Hardy were that little again and she could start all over with him. She saw Barb Chewning bump noses with Sammy and then say, "Mama's gonna get that baby, yes, she is!" It had been years since Catherine herself had used such a voice, but she knew that if a baby were to be thrust into her arms, it would all come back in an instant.

Catherine set her jaw and flung the door open. A tiny bud of dried baby's breath fell from the eucalyptus wreath to the wood parquet floor, and Catherine sighed as she bent to retrieve it. "Yes?" she said, pushing the storm door open a few inches.

Barb Chewning shifted Sammy to the other hip, and her face dimpled into a smile, a slow, leisurely smile, which clearly indicated to Catherine that she had no unwanted relatives or lazy teenaged children cluttering up the inside of her house. The baby turned his fuzzy head and fixed Catherine with a pair of the biggest eyes she had ever seen on a child. They were a deeper blue than the ordinary color of blue eyes, almost a cornflower blue, and combined with the size of them, they made Catherine feel like Sammy Chewning harbored some grave knowledge about her. So strong was the sensation that she even felt relieved for a fleeting moment when the thought flashed through her mind that her secrets were safe, since surely he was too young to put many of his thoughts into plain sentences.

Catherine opened the storm door another inch and said a little louder, "Yes?"

Barb Chewning craned her neck so as to direct her words through the slender crack Catherine had provided and said, "Well, I guess this is the typical question a neighbor asks," and she laughed as if she had said something witty. Catherine made no response. Why didn't the woman just come out with whatever it was she wanted? she thought. She didn't feel like standing here playing guessing games while a family crisis was brewing right here in her own home.

Barb Chewning was pretty in an outdoorsy, natural kind of way. Catherine had noticed that the first time she had met her, a week ago when the Chewnings had hailed her from their front yard on the day they were moving in. Now that she had a closeup view, Catherine decided that her looks were probably more cute than pretty, although she could imagine men calling her "pretty" without realizing the difference. Nothing glamorous or stylish by any stretch, but she had that smooth, unfrazzled, fresh-faced look like the mothers on those old TV programs—Timmy's mother on *Lassie* or Kate on *The Real McCoys*. She was even wearing a pair of cotton pedal pushers printed with little sprigs of yellow flowers like somebody straight out of a farmhouse kitchen.

Barb held up her hand and wiggled it. It was then that Catherine noticed she was holding a plastic measuring cup. "I'm right in the middle of mixing up a cake, and I just discovered I don't have enough sugar," Barb Chewning said. "I was wondering if you could lend me a cup."

Catherine wondered if this was just a trick of some kind to get inside her house. Why would you need a cup of sugar if you used a cake mix like most women nowadays did? She knew for a fact there were women who would do that—go to neighbors' houses on a pretext, just so they could size things up inside.

Catherine considered snatching the cup and leaving Barb outside on the porch to wait, but when she opened the door farther, Barb took it as an invitation to come inside and stepped forward immediately.

"I sure appreciate this. I'll send one of the boys to the store tonight so I can pay you back right away. I thought I had another bag of sugar somewhere, but I guess I lost track of things in the move. I've looked everywhere and can't find it. Of course, I'll admit I'm not the most organized person in the world, so there's no telling where it might show up. I might have packed it in with a box of old shoes somewhere." She laughed happily.

Catherine took the measuring cup and turned on her heel. "Well, I'll tell you one thing," she said. "A cup of sugar is the last thing in the world I'll be thinking about tonight, so you can wait till tomorrow to bring it back!"

As she marched back to the kitchen, she could hear Barb following her. Sammy emitted a squeal, and Barb said, "We've still got boxes everywhere, and I keep starting on one thing and then getting sidetracked. It takes so long to get things in place after you move, doesn't it?"

They were in the hallway now, and Catherine stopped abruptly at the kitchen doorway, not bothering to answer the question, which in her opinion wasn't really a question anyway. Not only did disorganized people irritate her, but she couldn't understand why Barb Chewning would talk so openly about her shortcomings. Whenever things fell apart on Catherine, she tried to find an excuse and then not think about it anymore. She certainly didn't go around admitting the problem to other people.

Della Boyd was at the window again, looking into the backyard, but Hardy was standing at the table now, spreading butter and jam on a Pepperidge Farm roll. He had apparently opened the plastic bag and turned it upside down, dumping all the rolls right onto the table. They lay scattered like pale pincushions. He hadn't bothered to get out a plate or even a paper towel, and now he was setting his roll and the used knife down on the solid oak tabletop. Catherine noticed dark smears of jam in the open butter tub.

Hardy licked his fingers and wiped them on his shorts, then picked up the roll, smashed it between his palms until the jam oozed out the sides, and took an enormous bite.

"Those rolls are for supper tonight," Catherine announced. Della Boyd turned around from the window and Barb Chewning chuckled, but neither of them spoke. The kitchen was silent except for the soft tocks of the clock on the wall as it marked the seconds. Even the baby seemed to be waiting for permission to make a noise.

Hardy gazed at Catherine darkly as he chewed, then stuffing the other half of the roll into his mouth, said, "Yeah, so? I'll eat the rest of 'em, then."

Catherine set her mouth and headed for the sugar canister. She wouldn't get into a shouting match with Hardy now, not with Barb Chewning and her saucer-eyed toddler standing right there. She jerked the lid off the canister and grabbed the scoop.

Behind her she heard Barb say, "Hi there, I'm just a begging neighbor from across the street. I don't see where you teenage boys put it all!" She paused to laugh and then added, "I have two of my own, and it never ceases to amaze me." Hardy made no comment. Catherine could imagine him staring with open disdain at Barb, not bothering to disguise his contempt for her cheerfulness. Either that or he was ignoring her altogether.

Sammy made a happy, shrill sound and said quite clearly, "Have some? Have some?"

Catherine glanced back and saw him leaning out of his mother's arms, pointing at Hardy, who was holding another roll.

"No, you can't have a roll, you little moocher," Barb said, but she let him down nevertheless, and Sammy headed straight for Hardy, still pointing and saying, "Have some, have some?"

Catherine misjudged the amount of sugar in the last scoopful and overran the cup slightly. She shook a little back into the canister and then swept the spilled sugar into the sink. When she turned around, Sammy was clutching the edge of the table, and Barb, who had followed him, was trying to pry his fingers loose and pull him away.

"Now, Sammy, you're acting like a two-year-old," she said, laughing. As she picked him up again, Sammy wailed, "Want some!"

Hardy shrugged his shoulders and handed Sammy a roll. Catherine wanted to tell Hardy not to be giving their expensive rolls away, wanted to rush forward and grab it back, but the baby had already seized it and stuffed it partway into his mouth.

"Oh, now, you didn't need to give him that," Barb said to Hardy. "He loves bread, but we're trying to teach him he can't have things he whines for." But she made no move to take it away from him. Then Barb turned again to Hardy, furrowed her brow, and said, "You never really enjoy something you've whined for, you know. I've always been disappointed in everything I've gotten that way." Without waiting for a response, she added, "That's a rule of life."

This woman was sure a strange duck, Catherine thought, to go from talking about bread to disappointment in one short breath.

To Catherine's surprise, Hardy quit chewing for a second, nodded at Barb, and said, "Yeah, I know."

"Doesn't look like he's one bit disappointed, though, does it?" Barb said as they watched Sammy gnaw contentedly at the roll. "Looks like he's already developing the characteristic of all boys when it comes to food."

Della Boyd had been watching the scene silently but now advanced toward Barb shyly, one hand extended.

"Hello, I'm Blake's sister, Della Boyd Biddle," she said.

Della Boyd had a soft, musical voice. It had always irked Catherine that some people were just born with a pretty voice when they didn't even *need* such a voice, while she had had to work like a Trojan in college to get any kind of range, or "melody of expression" as one of her drama teachers had called it, out of her own voice. "Let it go," Mrs. Yarborough had been fond of saying in her own tuneful, well-inflected tones. "Pretend that your words are riding the waves of the ocean or wafting through the air like a feather, lifting and falling. Pretend they're like colorful balloons ascending up, up, then POP! You make your point, and they float back down." Mrs. Yarborough had been given to flowery descriptions, and

Catherine had often imitated her to the other girls in the dormitory.

"I was just telling Hardy the same thing a few minutes ago," Della Boyd said to Barb. "I remember so well how Blake used to eat me out of house and home when he was a youngster. Why, he could . . ."

Catherine quickly crossed the kitchen with the cup of sugar, speaking right over Della Boyd's words. "Here's your sugar," she said loudly. "Now you can finish your cake." Barb took it with a startled smile, looking back and forth between her and Della Boyd, who had continued to talk as if nothing had happened.

". . . anything you could think of, and he'd just devour it like those swarms of locusts on the frontier that you used to read about that came in like a black cloud and . . ."

"You know," Catherine said, raising her volume another level, "sometimes when I've run short of sugar, I've gotten some from my sugar bowl. Did you ever think of that? Most people keep at least a cup or so in their sugar bowl."

". . . like a bottomless pit, that boy was!" Della Boyd concluded.

Barb laughed again. "Well, I'm pleased to meet you, Della Boyd, and I appreciate the advice, Catherine. Isn't it funny how people's minds work so differently? I never would have thought to check the sugar bowl. Of course, I doubt if I could find it even if I had thought of it since I have no idea which box I packed *that* in. But it's still a good idea. Knowing me, I probably packed the sugar bowl with the sugar still in it." Then she looked at Sammy and said, "Well, we'd better scoot, Sambo, and get that cake in the oven." Sammy was still happily absorbed with his roll. He *should* be enjoying it, Catherine thought. Those rolls weren't cheap!

"Thanks again, Catherine," Barb said, lifting the cup of sugar like a toast. "I'll pay you back."

Blake chose just this moment to walk into the kitchen through the back door. With all the commotion, Catherine hadn't even heard him pull into the garage. He looked around at everyone, his brow creased as if confronted by a great mystery.

Della Boyd murmured a cry of joy and came forward at once. "Oh, Blake! It's so good to—why, you look thin, Brother. Have you—and your hair is shot through with gray. You'll be as gray as me one of these days!" She reached up to touch his hair, and Blake took her hand almost reverently, it seemed.

If Catherine didn't know better, she could have believed Blake and Della Boyd were husband and wife greeting each other after a long separation. She couldn't recall the last time Blake had greeted her so affectionately after one of his business trips.

"Well, bye everybody," Barb called. "I'll close the front door on my way out!" She and Sammy left the kitchen, and a few seconds later Catherine heard the front door close. She hoped Barb didn't pull it shut too hard. She sure didn't want any more of the baby's breath to come loose.

Still holding her hand in both of his, Blake looked past Della Boyd to Catherine. "I hope everything's all right around here," he said. "You're all right, aren't you, Della Boyd?"

Della Boyd sagged a little bit and leaned into Blake, who put one arm around her shoulder. "Oh, I'm okay, Blake, just tired is all," she said.

Catherine cast a quick look at Hardy, hoping for his support in what she sensed was going to be a difficult situation. But Hardy seemed oblivious to everything except the slathering of another roll, which he then crammed into his mouth whole.

"Well, why don't you go lie down and rest awhile," Blake said to Della Boyd. "Here, let me take you to the guest room, and you can get a nice long nap before supper." He took her gently by the hand and led her from the kitchen.

"Oh, she already knows where the guest room is!" Catherine called after them as they disappeared down the hall. "She found it all by herself without a bit of trouble!"

Hardy held up both hands, palms out. They were splotched with raspberry jam. He lurched forward, gasping, his mouth still stuffed with the roll, his words barely intelligible. "Help, I'm bleeding to death!"

"Oh, stop it, Hardy!" Catherine said, putting her hand to her forehead. "This is no time for that. Go wash that sticky mess off your hands."

To her surprise he merely laughed, cackled really, and went to the sink. Another time he would have done something infuriating like wipe his hands on a clean white dish towel without even washing them. Catherine heard Blake's footsteps returning down the hall. Her hand still against her brow, she walked over to the table and sat down.

"She must have been through a terrible shock," Blake said, sighing. He took a glass out of the cupboard and set it on the counter, then opened the refrigerator and took out the milk. "She asked for a glass of milk," he added. "I don't think she's had anything to eat since yesterday."

"Yes, well, I've had a terrible shock, too," Catherine said, "coming home to find her in our house, bag and baggage, acting like she's here to stay, like she's been invited to move in and take over our guest room! Acting crazy and mumbling some half-cocked story about a fire." She saw that Blake had finished filling the glass with milk and was holding it in one hand, staring at her.

"Don't you ever think of anyone but yourself, Catherine?" he said.

"Don't you ever?" And he walked out of the kitchen and down the hall-way.

"I might want a glass of milk, too!" Catherine shouted. "Did it ever cross your mind to offer me one?" But Blake was gone, and he didn't answer.

She looked up to see Hardy drying his hands with a paper towel and looking at her with an expression very close to loathing.

Slow Circles

5

Propped against two pillows in bed later that night, Catherine leafed idly through her most recent issue of *Vogue*. Part of her wanted to laugh hysterically at the thought of one of these glamorous, long-legged models coming down here to Berea, South Carolina, to live, and another part wanted to scream at the sound of Blake running water in the bathroom sink. More and more these days he had been using the hall bathroom that Olivia and Philip shared, waiting until late at night when it was vacated. But tonight after supper she had seen him take Della Boyd's arm and escort her down the hallway. "Why don't you put your things in this hall bathroom, Sister?" he had said.

Then he had called to Olivia in the den. "Olivia, come in here and make room for your aunt to put some of her things out!" Catherine had heard Olivia utter a murmur of protest at the interruption, but she had nevertheless lifted herself off the sofa and sauntered back toward the bathroom. One thing she'd say for Blake: The kids didn't mess around with him when he told them to do something. The only problem was he didn't tell them often enough to do something. Half the time he wasn't even home to speak to them at all, and then when he was, he didn't seem to notice anything they did or said for long stretches at a time until he blew up over some trifling matter.

So now it looked like he'd be sharing the master bath with her for a while, no doubt getting in there just when she wanted to—as was the case right now. And splashing water all over the vanity and mirror and steaming up everything with his hot showers. She could hear him now, rapping his toothbrush against the side of the sink, and she wanted to shout, "Don't do that! You're splattering little drips of water everywhere!"

This issue of *Vogue* featured fall fashions that Catherine thought were the most bizarre things she'd ever seen. One model was wearing a short white sweater dress that was so loosely knit you could see right through to her skin, and another one had on filmy pink silk trousers and a black sequined halter top of all things! These wouldn't exactly be the warmest clothes for chilly fall days, Catherine thought, but then, these models probably stayed indoors all day under hot camera lights and never even felt the change in temperature outside.

She tried to imagine what the people around Berea would think if she wore such an outfit to the opening PTA meeting this September. She thought of the narrow-minded principal at the middle school where Philip attended—a woman named Sterling Gunderson, of all the ridiculous names. What would the straitlaced Miss Gunderson say if Catherine sashayed into the school auditorium in, say, one of these clingy purple spandex bodysuits with the large diamond-shaped cutout in front? Catherine placed a hand over her heart, assumed the look of Victorian surprise that would undoubtedly appear on Miss Gunderson's face, and gasped, "Mrs. Biddle, you are absolutely indecent! Why, I have *never* in all my born days . . ."

Her little charade was ill timed, for Blake chose that minute to exit the bathroom, a towel wrapped around him like a skirt. "You have never in all your born days what?" he asked.

"Nothing," said Catherine. "I wasn't talking to you." She slapped the magazine shut and threw the sheet off. "I've been sitting here in bed waiting for you to get through so I could get in the bathroom," she said.

"Well, help yourself," Blake said wearily. He leaned forward and shook his head, then ran both hands through his thick hair as if to dry it. Catherine wished he would do that in the bathroom, although she didn't like the idea of his leaving dark hairs strewn over the cream tile floor anymore than over the mint green carpet in the bedroom. No, she just wished he wouldn't shake out his hair at all. All it did was leave a mess for someone else to clean up. She didn't dare say anything, though. He'd be sure to fire back something like "Why should it matter to you? Sparkle does all the housework around here anyway, doesn't she?"

Hiring Sparkle Flynn had been a source of contention between them, for it had been Blake's opinion that Catherine should orchestrate a housecleaning schedule involving the three children. "They need to learn some responsibility!" he was always saying. "When I was their age, I was helping with everything—laundry, vacuuming, cooking, the works!" And when Catherine had invited him to put his long-dormant skills back to good use again, he had looked as if he wanted to take her by the shoulders and shake her. "You're forgetting one little detail," he had said. "I happen to work ten or twelve hours a day already, trying to support a family that treats money like it's the air they breathe." That was another one of his favorite soapbox themes—her loose spending habits, which he claimed had rubbed off on the children. And he wouldn't even listen when she pointed out that she really was quite thrifty, always buying day-old bread, never tipping hairdressers or bag boys, and rarely paying full price for her new clothes.

Catherine flounced into the bathroom and glared at the mirror, which was fogged up from Blake's shower. Sighing, she rummaged quickly through a drawer for the shower cap she kept for such occasions and yanked it onto her head to cover her new hairdo. She wasn't about to spend good money at Dottie Puckett's hair salon only to have it all go flat in a steamy bathroom. Then she grabbed a hand towel and began fanning it through the doorway as if to drive out the moisture. Blake made no sign of catching her hint even though she saw him glance at her indifferently. She gave it up after a few seconds and turned to start her bath water, first adjusting the mix of hot and cold, then dispensing two capfuls of foaming bath oil under the faucet.

The sight of the bubbles billowing up under the running water made Catherine think of that stupid song Della Boyd had sung after supper a few hours ago as she was clearing off the table and running a sinkful of soapy water in the kitchen. "I'm forever blowing bubbles," it started, and Della Boyd had laughed gaily after singing those first words and had said to Blake, "Do you remember how I got those old men to play that song at your high school dance that time?"

She had deposited a stack of dirty plates on the countertop beside the kitchen sink, turned off the water, then scooped up a handful of soapsuds and stared at them with a look of transcendental euphoria. It was odd how Della Boyd had gotten up from her nap that afternoon refreshed and full of good spirits and had taken over in the kitchen as if she had come here expressly to make Catherine's life easier—mixing up corn bread from scratch and peeling potatoes like it was the joy of her life. Not that her little ploy was going to make her any more welcome, but Catherine sure didn't mind letting her help out tonight since she was already here. Cooking—and kitchen work in general—wasn't at the top of Catherine's list of favorite things to do.

Catherine replayed the whole supper scene in her mind now. Blake, finishing up a wedge of corn bread, had smiled over at his sister and nodded. "How could I forget that song?" He had then turned to Olivia, who was sitting on his left—if such atrocious posture could be called sitting—

and said, "She not only got these gray-headed geezers to play this hokey old song, but she stepped up to the microphone and *sang* it as they played it—right there in the gymnasium in front of practically the whole school."

Della Boyd held the puff of white suds aloft in one hand, then caught hold of the hem of her dress with the other hand, and closing her eyes, she began swaying as if getting ready to take off and dance across the kitchen floor. Catherine, who had been unloading the dishwasher so it could be refilled, had slammed the silverware basket down on the counter and said, "Well, for crying out loud, let's not go off the deep end here! Who cares about a high school dance almost thirty years ago?"

And out of pure meanness, Catherine was sure, Hardy had piped up with feigned childish glee and, clapping his hands, said in a high-pitched voice, "Oh, sing the whole song for us, Auntie Della Boyd. Pwease do, pwease, pwease. We all want to hear it!"

Blake had flashed Hardy a warning look, but Della Boyd turned toward the table with an expression of pleased acquiescence and bowed slightly, as if granting one last curtain call to an adoring audience. Catherine saw Hardy and Olivia exchange smirks while Philip buried his head in his arms and snorted. Blake scowled fiercely at all three of them. Without any shade of self-consciousness, however, Della Boyd blew lightly into the soap suds in her palm and began singing. Her singing voice, like her speaking voice, was prettier than Catherine liked to admit, especially for someone in her sixties.

Della Boyd sang it slowly, savoring each note and smiling wistfully the whole while, right through to the last line: ". . . pretty bubbles in the air." She held out the last note, extending one arm upward, her gaze wistfully following all the imaginary bubbles she had blown toward the ceiling, as if watching all her dreams float away. When she had finished, Della Boyd curtsied briefly and, as if she was totally unaware that she had just made a complete fool out of herself, started picking up more dishes from the table and carrying them over to the counter. "You know, that was probably the best dance they ever had at that school," she said.

No one said anything for a few seconds. Catherine was making a clatter as she slung the silverware into the right slots in the drawer. She couldn't figure Della Boyd out. She was several bricks shy of a full load, that was certain, not even catching on that the kids were making fun of her. And for someone who had supposedly just lost everything she owned in a house fire, she wasn't acting the least bit sad. A little daffy maybe, off in la-la land, but not sad. In Catherine's opinion, that was the biggest giveaway that her story was bogus. You didn't just watch all your earthly possessions go up in smoke and then take off to visit relatives and make corn bread and sing songs about blowing bubbles.

At last Olivia said to her father, "How come you had a bunch of old guys playing for a high school dance, anyway? Didn't you know any better back then, or was that all they had in Mississippi?"

"Oh, that's another story," Della Boyd said. "The young people had a rock and roll group from Jackson all lined up to drive to Yazoo City and play, but they had a wreck on the way, and they all ended up being taken to the hospital an hour before the dance was supposed to start."

"The Gladflies," Blake said.

"The *what?*" Philip asked.

"That was the name of the group that got canceled," Blake said. "The Gladflies."

"Catchy name," Hardy said in a nasal voice, for he had shredded his paper napkin, rolled up two long tubes, and inserted them into his nostrils.

"So Della Boyd saved the day for us," Blake said, "by getting these retired men she knew about down at the veterans' club to come fill in at the last minute. What was it—a few trumpets, a couple of clarinets, and a tuba?"

"I remember a saxophone, too," Della Boyd said. "Which all worked out fine, except they didn't know anything but old songs like 'Yellow Bird' and 'Moonglow' and things like that."

"The liveliest thing they knew was 'Chattanooga Choo-Choo,' "said Blake. "But I guess they really weren't half bad for a bunch of old coots."

"They were better than nothing," Della Boyd said.

"I guess," Blake said, smiling.

"Everybody talked about that dance for months."

"Oh, they sure did. We were the laughingstock of the whole state." Della Boyd laughed. "Well, it was something different for the sixties."

"And what were you doing there?" Philip asked her.

"Well, I was helping Blake," she said. "He was on the student committee that planned the dance, and when everything fell through an hour before it was to start, I thought of the veterans' group and offered to call them up and get them all over to the school gym."

"Which she did," said Blake. "Hardy, act your age and take those things out of your nose right now." Hardy complied by blowing through his nostrils so that the tissue tubes ejected themselves into his lap.

"Then I stayed around to see how things were going," Della Boyd said, "and somehow the songs they were playing put me in mind of a song I remembered our mother singing. Blake wouldn't remember it because she died when he was born. But she used to sing it a lot when I was a little girl, and I'd sing along sometimes." She stopped and hummed a few notes, staring up at the ceiling fan, her eyes following its slow circles. "We'd sing it together," she said softly and hummed another couple of bars. "So anyway"—she looked back to those seated at the table—"I asked them if they knew the song, and you know what? They did!"

"And you sang it," Olivia said.

Della Boyd nodded. "And I sang it."

The table was cleared off by now, and Della Boyd started scraping off the plates and rinsing them. She had already set the pots and pans in the soapy water to soak, and Catherine noticed that she had even removed the placemats from the table, shaken them out, and wiped the table down. Her procedure of supper cleanup was totally different from Catherine's, but Catherine wasn't about to say anything. Let her do it however she wanted to. Let her run the whole business. If someone was going to help out in the kitchen, Catherine sure wasn't going to fuss about methodology.

Hardy burped, pushed his chair back, and stood up. He raised his arms and extended them toward the ceiling, at the same time emitting a sound that was half grunt and half yawn. He had put on a T-shirt for supper, but as he stretched, he exposed a narrow strip of his stomach and a larger one of his underwear above the waistband of his shorts. Catherine could feel Blake's disapproval without even looking at him. Actually, she was surprised that there hadn't been an eruption before now, with all three children sitting at the supper table for an entire meal. She couldn't remember the last time they had sat together as a family for supper. But Blake had insisted on it tonight, and everybody must have sensed that it wasn't up for discussion.

"Sit back down," Blake said to Hardy.

Catherine heard Hardy take in his breath in preparation for an argument. Well, Della Boyd was going to hear it all sooner or later, Catherine thought, so it might as well be now. She was still counting on getting rid of her sister-in-law before another day had passed, and a knockdown–dragout might help move things along.

"Oh yes. Sit down, sit down," Della Boyd interjected, turning again toward the table with a smile. "We haven't had dessert, and I just remembered I haven't given out my presents yet, either."

Hardy's eyes shifted quickly to Della Boyd, and Catherine thought for a minute that he was going to light into her. But then his face relaxed just slightly and he said, "Dessert? What's that?" He scrunched up his face in fake concentration, then snapped his fingers, and adopted his squeaky little-boy voice again. "I wemember! I wemember! Mommy made bwownies for dessert one time, and Owivia bwoke her tooth on hers and Bubba Phil put his in his wock cowection."

"Very funny," Catherine said.

"Well, this is about the simplest dessert in the book," Della Boyd said, rinsing the last pan and setting it in the dish drainer. "Now sit back down, Hardy, or you won't get any."

Remarkably, Hardy sat down. Della Boyd dried her hands, then went to the refrigerator and took out the glass mixing bowl, which contained the vanilla pudding she had whipped up that afternoon. Catherine hadn't even known you could make pudding without a box of pudding mix, but Della Boyd had made it without looking at a recipe and then had peeled and sliced a couple of peaches and stirred them up in the pudding. She watched now as Della Boyd scooped a serving of pudding into each dessert bowl then crumbled a graham cracker over each one. Catherine carried them to the table as Della Boyd finished them, and in no time seconds had been served, the glass bowl was empty, and dessert was over.

"Now stay put everybody," said Della Boyd, rising from her chair. "I've got presents to pass out." At the doorway she turned back around. "I don't know why I'm so nervous about this, but I am. I just don't know how you're going to like them, but . . . well, I'll go get them. There's a present for everybody."

Catherine rolled her eyes and crimped one corner of her mouth. Della Boyd acted like such a little girl half the time, and Catherine was sure she did it on purpose—to wear down people's defenses.

When Della Boyd had disappeared down the hallway, Blake looked around the table sternly and said, "Whatever they are, *act nice*—all of you." And it seemed to Catherine that his frown lingered on her even longer than on the children.

Della Boyd had apologized when she came back in carrying a brown grocery sack. "I guess I lost track of how old you children were," she said. "I'm afraid these presents aren't right at all, but . . . well, here they are anyway." From the top of the bag she pulled out a small stuffed raccoon with a tag around its neck that read, "Hi There! My Name Is Ringtail!" She handed it to Philip, who smiled weakly and cut his eyes at Hardy.

"Hey, hey, hey. A new pet!" said Hardy. "Maybe he won't kill this one."

Catherine felt a small pang of sympathy for Philip even though she was the one who had ridden him the hardest about all the small animals that had died under his care—or lack of it. Most recently a salamander had starved to death in his bedroom. Last year he had rolled over on his baby rabbit in his sleep and smothered him. Blake had laid down an ultimatum after that: no animals in bed. Catherine made a mental note now to ask Philip sometime tonight if he'd fed his gerbil recently or cleaned its cage in the last month. She shuddered as she remembered the smell that had assaulted her when she had opened his bedroom door this afternoon. She'd have to get Sparkle to tackle Philip's bedroom one of these Fridays, and she'd have to pay her extra. Usually she just told her to skip it.

Della Boyd reached inside her brown sack again and pulled out a bright fluorescent orange Frisbee, which she offered to Hardy. "The rim glows in the dark," Della Boyd said, and Hardy whistled with mock awe, then balanced the Frisbee on his index finger and twirled it expertly. "Way cool," he said in a whispery voice.

Olivia's present was a set of barrettes and ponytail clamps. "When I first saw you today, I was so glad to see you were still wearing your hair long," Della Boyd said. "I guess you can use these . . . if the girls still wear this kind of thing, that is. I don't really keep up with the young people's fads these days."

Olivia stared at the card of plastic barrettes blankly. They were arranged in perky pairs—five of them, shaped like bows, in bold crayon colors.

Hardy pounded the table with his fist and cried with exaggerated feminine inflections, clicking his tongue after every few words, "Those are *just* the thing! I was telling Olivia just the other day that she needs to *pin her hair back* because she looks downright *sloppy and unkempt*, and it's a shame we spent *all that money* to pay for her contacts and braces when nobody can even *see* her face half the time because of all that *stringy hair* hanging down!"

Though he never once looked at her, Catherine knew, of course, that Hardy was satirizing her, quoting almost verbatim a speech she had delivered to Olivia only days earlier.

"This is awfully nice of you, Della Boyd," Blake said, staring pointedly at the three children.

"Yes. Oh yes, it is!" squealed Hardy, hugging his Frisbee. "And we all wike our pwesents! Thanks ever so much, Auntie!"

"Thank you," Olivia mumbled.

"Yeah, thanks," Philip said, mindlessly patting his raccoon's head.

Blake's gift was a shoehorn with a long handle so he wouldn't have to stoop over, and Catherine's was a bibbed apron in green gingham with huge gaudy sunflowers appliquéd all over it. Catherine didn't know whether to laugh or be insulted—as if she'd ever wear anything like that!

As he left the table, Hardy balanced his Frisbee on top of his head.

"Hey, look, I'll wear this at night, and when it glows people will think I have a halo."

"Oh, right," Olivia said. "They'll all say, 'There's that nice Boy Scout, Hardy Biddle, on his way to do another good deed.'"

At which point Hardy reached over suddenly and grabbed a handful of her long blond hair, twisting it tightly. The Frisbee fell off his head and rolled across the kitchen floor. "Whatsa matter?" he said. "Is poor little Olivia jealous that her barrettes don't glow in the dark?" Olivia slapped at him, and Blake ordered him from the table, to which Hardy replied, "I was going anyway." He flew off, cackling down the basement stairs, slamming the door behind him.

Catherine closed her eyes now and settled down farther into her bubble bath. She suddenly felt very tired, as if she'd been mountain climbing or running a marathon. This day had certainly not followed its expected course. Maybe tomorrow things would get back to normal, whatever that was in a house like this.

She felt a whoosh of air as the bathroom door opened, and there was Blake standing above her as if about to say something. He was wearing an old pair of gym shorts and a tattered undershirt, his standard nightwear in spite of the fact that he had a drawer full of brand-new pajamas with matching tops and bottoms. Catherine sank down deeper into the bubbles and reached up to slide the shower door closed, but Blake held it open.

Catherine snatched her washcloth off the towel rod and primly laid it over her chest. "Well, are you going to just stand there staring?" she said. "What do you want?"

Blake laughed—almost derisively. "Don't worry," he said. "I'm not going to get any ideas."

"I don't know what you're talking about," Catherine said. She had the uncomfortable sensation that hundreds of tiny bubbles in her bath water were popping and that soon there would be none left at all. "I wish you'd just get out!" she snapped. "If you've got something to say, you can wait till I'm finished or else talk to me through the door."

"I do have something to say," Blake said, "and I'm going to say it right now—right here where I'm standing."

Catherine closed her eyes and laid her head back. If he was going to act so high and mighty, she sure wasn't going to give him the pleasure of her attention. She adopted a bored expression.

"Della Boyd is going to stay here until I find out what happened back in Yazoo City," Blake said evenly. "And even after I find out, she's going to stay here as long as I think she needs to. If you dare act ugly to her or make her feel unwelcome in any way, I'll . . . I'll make you wish you hadn't. And that's a promise I'll keep." Catherine knew he was probably waiting for some kind of response from her, but she had no intention of accommodating him. He could wait till the cows came home before he'd see her give in. Della Boyd was perfectly capable of taking care of herself. She was just taking advantage of her brother's silly, overblown sense of family loyalty by showing up here and acting all traumatized.

A sudden fanciful notion seized Catherine. Della Boyd was running from the law! She had committed a series of heinous crimes back in Yazoo City, and her picture was plastered on Wanted posters all over the country. She had set fire to her own house to destroy the evidence and had hopped town under a pseudonym. The idea amused Catherine. She even smiled and began humming, her eyes still closed. Della Boyd Biddle alias Big Moll Rathbone.

"What are you smiling about?" Blake said.

"Nothing," Catherine said with a little laugh.

"You're a sick woman," Blake said. "I don't know what kind of perverted idea is going through your head right now, but I'm warning you, Cat, you better watch your step around my sister. I mean to help her through this, whatever it is. And I won't have you pulling any of your tricks on her."

"Oh, you don't have to worry about your precious sister!" Catherine said, opening her eyes and slapping the water petulantly with both hands. "And if you want to know what I think, I think *she's* the one you need to worry about pulling tricks! She knows you'll believe anything she tells you, and she's come running here with some half-baked story, trying to squeeze some sympathy out of—"

"Shut your mouth," Blake said, enunciating each syllable slowly.

Catherine stopped talking, though she knew her mouth was hanging open. It struck her like a hammer blow that not once during all their arguments over the years had Blake ever told her to shut up. Until right now.

As if he were thinking the same thing, he seemed to soften for just a minute. "I just wish—" He broke off and lowered his eyes, shaking his head. "I wish you wouldn't talk about her that way," he said. "She's not that kind of person, and you know it." And without saying anything else, he turned and left the bathroom.

Not able to think of a single biting retort at the moment, Catherine sat very still and heard the echo of those three words over and over again. *Shut your mouth. Shut your mouth. Shut your mouth. Shut your mouth.* . . .

Blake had stepped over a line, one that he himself had drawn years ago. On their honeymoon in Florida, in fact. They had stopped by a grocery store in Coral Gables to get some snacks to take with them to the beach, and they had gotten behind a middle-aged couple in the check-out line. Catherine remembered it as if it were yesterday. The woman wore a silver turban on her head, white capri pants, and a sheer blouse the color of orange sherbet. The hair that stuck out around the bottom of her turban was an unnatural shade of red with a maroon cast to it, wispy and dried out. Her skin was leathery, the color of a walnut shell, as if baked hard in the sun. The man was tall and distinguished looking, even though he was wearing Bermuda shorts and a Hawaiian print shirt. He had a full head of salt-and-pepper hair, Catherine remembered, and eyes as blue as Paul Newman's.

Catherine had noticed the couple right off because they looked like such a curious mixture of classy and tacky, of local and tourist. It was funny how she could still picture them so plainly after all these years. She hadn't thought of them in ages. It wasn't their looks that had made the biggest impression, though. It was what they said. One minute they were standing quietly in front of Blake and Catherine like civil human beings, and the next they were engaged in the most acrimonious duel of words Catherine had ever heard. And right out in public! It had been touched off by the smallest thing, too—the man had accidentally stepped on the woman's heel as they moved forward in line.

Catherine recalled how everyone—customers, cashiers, stock boys—had frozen in disbelief at the words that were hurled back and forth at such volume and with such venom. A little child in someone's buggy nearby had broken the silence after the altercation had subsided. "Why are those people mad, Daddy? Are they going to hit each other?" The father had stuck a Tootsie-pop in the child's mouth, and no one else had spoken a word.

Catherine had forgotten most of what the couple had said, except for one repeated phrase: *"Shut up!"* The man must have said it a dozen times or more, along with plenty of other things.

After it was over and Catherine and Blake were back in their car in the parking lot, Blake had taken her hand in his and said, "We'll never talk to each other that way."

And Catherine—how naïve they both were, she thought now—had shaken her head and said, "Never."

"I wish we hadn't heard it," Blake had said. "It's going to be hard to forget something like that."

And as a joke, Catherine had said, "Oh, shut up, and let's get to the beach!"

But Blake hadn't laughed. "Don't tease like that, Catherine," he said with such an injured look on his face that Catherine thought he must be pretending. Evidently he wasn't, though, for his next words were just as serious. "I hate to hear anybody say 'shut up,' but when it's a man saying it to a woman, I hate it even worse." Catherine hadn't known how to respond. She was ready to go to the beach. She sure didn't want to sit in a parking lot talking in a hot car. Blake must have sensed her impatience, for he let go of her hand and touched the tip of her nose, then started the car. "I'll never tell you to shut up," he had said.

Catherine thought of his promise now, over twenty years later. "Oh, sure you won't!" she said right out loud. If Blake heard her from the bedroom, he didn't reply.

As she wondered if there had ever been a time when that couple in Florida had thought they would never speak a harsh word to each other, she noticed that her foaming bath bubbles had evaporated to only a few scattered patches now, and her bath water had cooled considerably.

An Empty Room

6

Two days later, on Friday morning when Catherine stepped outside to check the mailbox, she heard someone call her name. It was Barb Chewning from across the street. She was sitting in a folding lawn chair beside a child's plastic pool, inside which Sammy was splashing and squealing. Catherine wondered why the Chewnings hadn't bought a home with an in-ground pool. She knew they could afford it. Curtis Chewning was a doctor—a pediatrician, actually. He had recently moved his office from nearby Derby to Berea, which was closer to the hospital. These were nice houses, of course, but surely the Chewnings could do better than Brookside Drive. Caroline Burkett down the street had told Catherine that Curt and Barb Chewning were very "down to earth," whatever that was supposed to mean. Caroline's daughter-in-law took all of her children to Dr. Chewning and thought he hung the moon.

Barb pointed to an empty chair beside the one in which she was sitting and motioned to Catherine. "Do you have a minute to visit?" she called. "I've got an extra chair!" She stood up and walked toward the front curb, shading her eyes. She was wearing a pair of faded denim jeans and an oversized T-shirt with a big red heart on it. "I'll even offer you a glass of iced tea!" she said.

"I can't," Catherine said. "I've got someone cleaning my house inside, and I need to check up on her." The truth was, Sparkle Flynn didn't need a bit of supervision, but the last thing in the world Catherine wanted to do was to sit in a lawn chair under the blazing sun in Barb Chewning's front yard and play the friendly neighbor game. She had already figured out that this woman was not her type at all. They were on totally different wavelengths.

"Maybe you can come over after she leaves," Barb said. "Sammy's going down for a nap in a little while, and we could talk inside if the sun bothers you."

Catherine didn't say anything for a moment. She was thinking. Della Boyd was inside helping Sparkle. In fact, the two of them were knee-deep in Philip's bedroom right now, dragging trash out from under the bed, throwing stuff out into the hallway, sorting through the junk piled in his closet. Her instructions to them had been simple. "If it doesn't look useful, just clear it out!" Philip was spending the day down at the pool where Olivia worked, so by the time he discovered the transformation in his bedroom, it would be too late. Catherine intended to haul all the junk off to a trash bin somewhere before he and Olivia got back at suppertime.

She had heard Della Boyd talking to the gerbil as she walked past Philip's door a few minutes ago. "You are sure a cute little fellow!" she was saying. She was bent down with her nose almost touching the cage. "Look at those little whiskers and those sweet little ears! And your little paws— why, you're about the cutest little thing I've seen in my whole life!"

Catherine had been tempted to say, "Well, why don't you open the cage and give him a big wet kiss on his dear little lips?" Della Boyd had been here only two days now, and already Catherine was sick and tired of her sweetness. Maybe she *should* go over and sit in Barb Chewning's yard for a few minutes to get away from it all. Looking across the street at Barb's smiling face, though, she knew she would be in for another overdose of cheerfulness if she accepted the invitation.

"Or I could come visit you if you'd rather not leave home," Barb suggested. She laughed. "Nothing like inviting yourself over to somebody's house, huh?" When Catherine didn't answer, she added, "Sarah could watch Sammy for me. You know, I've found that there's nothing like a good visit. A good book is close, but it doesn't quite measure up to a visit. A good visit always seems to refresh your spirits and give you a new outlook."

Catherine felt like saying, "Look, I don't want to come to your house today or any day, and I don't want you to come to mine, and I don't need to have my spirits refreshed or my outlook renewed, so let's just keep to our own side of the street!" But she couldn't quite bring herself to be so rude, especially after Barb had sent over six pieces of cake yesterday, along with the borrowed cup of sugar.

It was one of her twin sons who had appeared at the front door before lunch yesterday—a tall, good-looking boy of about fifteen or sixteen, Catherine guessed. He looked a lot like his mother, with an open face and light hair, and he had her same friendly manner.

"Hi! My mom asked me to return the sugar she borrowed," he said, extending a measuring cup. "And here's the hard part," he continued, holding out a plate covered with aluminum foil. He took a deep breath and said in a shaky voice, "She wanted me to give you this cake, too."

Catherine hadn't known what to say. She had a feeling the boy was teasing, but she didn't see his point. As she took the plate from his hands, the boy's lip quivered and he pretended to sob.

"Good-bye," he said, waving at the plate. "We could've had such a good time together, you and my stomach."

Catherine had stared at him for a moment, then said, "Wait here and I'll bring your cup and plate back."

Before he turned and leaped down the front steps a minute or so later, he had flashed her a wide smile and said, "Thanks a lot, ma'am!" It didn't occur to her until he was already halfway across the street that she should probably be the one saying thank-you. The cake had been quite good—chocolate with pink frosting. They had eaten it for dessert last night. Frankly, it surprised Catherine that someone as disorganized as Barb Chewning seemed to be could make a cake from scratch.

Catherine looked back across the street now to where Barb stood by the curb. "I guess . . . I can come over for just a minute," she said. This way, she decided, she could take her leave after a few pleasantries had been exchanged. If Barb came over to her house, there was no telling how long she would stay. Some people just didn't know when their welcome had expired. "Let me go inside and check on things first, and I'll be over," she said. "I can't stay long, though. I've got a million things to do!"

"I understand!" Barb called. "The train never stops, does it? But sometimes I just make up my mind to jump off and catch a later one." She laughed again and waved, then went back to sit beside the pool. Catherine heard her coo to Sammy, "Mama's little boy is gonna wrinkle up like a raisin if he stays in here much longer—yes, he is!" And Sammy let out an ear-piercing shriek of glee.

As she approached Philip's bedroom, Catherine heard Sparkle Flynn say, "That boy been livin' in a pigsty!" and she saw an empty pizza box fly through the doorway and land beside the other trash in the hallway.

Catherine stalked to the door, put her hands on her hips, and said, "When I want your commentary on my son's bedroom, I'll ask you for it!" Sparkle was on her hands and knees at the moment, peering under Philip's bed, but she slowly swung her head around and looked toward the door. With her sad, droopy eyes and baggy clothes, she reminded Catherine of a basset hound.

Della Boyd was sitting on the floor over by the closet, matching up shoes, but she also paused and gazed at Catherine silently. Even the gerbil was poised motionless on its hind legs against the side of its cage, its little nose pointed toward the doorway, sniffing the air. The room already looked much better, Catherine noticed, even though they had been at it less than an hour. At least there was room to walk across the floor now. The curtains were pulled back for the first time in ages, she was sure, and someone had opened the window. The smell of Pine-Sol lingered in the air.

"Well, what's everybody just sitting there for?" Catherine said. "Time's wasting! The meter's ticking!" And she wheeled about and headed back down the hallway. Passing the door to the basement, she felt the bass throb of music. She'd have to send Sparkle and Della Boyd downstairs with a couple of shovels to clear out Hardy's room sometime in the next week or two. Maybe rent a bulldozer, gas masks, and an industrial-strength fumigator, too. If they thought Philip's room was a pig-sty, they should just wait till they saw Hardy's. Catherine herself hadn't been down there for months. The bathroom was probably home to entire colonies of mold and fungi by now. She supposed some people would consider it strange that she was so particular about certain parts of her house but was willing to let the boys' rooms go for months on end.

It dawned on her as she crossed the living room to exit through the front door that she was already assuming Della Boyd would still be here at least another week. Two days ago she had thought she'd go stark raving mad if her sister-in-law didn't get out of her house, and now here she was planning cleaning projects for her in the upcoming weeks. Catherine couldn't deny that Della Boyd was a hard worker—capable and uncomplaining. At the front door she cupped her hands and shouted back toward the hallway, "I'll be across the street for a few minutes!" Then she stepped outside and closed the door behind her, taking a moment to admire the new wreath once more.

Barb started talking to her before she was out of her own yard. "Isn't it nice for August? They say it's supposed to get back to the nineties in a few days, but I wouldn't mind if it stayed like this, would you?"

Catherine noticed a little girl on the Chewnings' front porch, changing the clothes of a life-sized baby doll. She had three or four other dolls of varying sizes arranged beside her, propped up with their backs against the wrought-iron porch railing. A little table nearby was spread with miniature teacups and a tiny pitcher.

Catherine walked across the Chewnings' grass, sat down beside Barb, and sighed. "I couldn't care less about the weather, one way or the other," she said. "These people who keep track of every raindrop and the exact percentage of humidity drive me crazy." She crossed her legs and swung her foot, admiring her sleek new leather thongs. She was glad she had given herself a pedicure last night.

Barb laughed heartily. "Well, I like an honest person. So now I know to skip the trivial talk about weather with you and get right to the serious stuff." She called to the little girl. "Sarah, pour a glass of tea for our neighbor, will you, sweetie? Do you like lemon?" she asked Catherine.

"Not especially," Catherine said.

"Just put some ice in it, honey," Barb said, "and remember—"

"I know, Mom—wash my hands first," said the girl, who set her doll down and disappeared through the front door.

Sammy turned his enormous round eyes on Catherine and lit up with a magnificent smile. "I swim!" he said, smacking the water vigorously. He then flopped over on his tummy and set about kicking for all he was worth. Water flew in all directions, and Catherine emitted a small cry of dismay, put her hands to her hair, then quickly moved her chair back a couple of feet.

"Sorry," Barb said. "I should have warned you." She moved her chair back also and addressed Sammy. "Don't splash us, Sammy. This nice lady's hair will get all wet."

The toddler stopped splashing and sat up, regarding Catherine soberly. He looked for all the world as if he were weighing the truth of the label "nice lady." After a moment he stood up and pointed to her. "Wet hair," he said plainly.

"No, she doesn't want wet hair," Barb said, then turned to Catherine. "Speaking of hair, I really like the way you wear yours. And of course, the color makes it all the prettier."

"Thanks," said Catherine, reaching up to finger the hair along the nape of her neck. She knew Barb was probably dying of curiosity about her hair color, wondering if it was natural, but she wasn't about to tell her that she got occasional henna treatments to bring out the red and cover the tiny bit of gray she had.

"When Sammy gets a little older," Barb said, "I'm going to find a style like that and keep my hair fixed up." She took hold of her ponytail and gave it a shake. "Right now, though, this is the easiest thing I can think of." She smiled. "Do you do your own hair?"

"Heavens, no!" Catherine said. "I wouldn't have the patience." She didn't intend to go around advertising Dottie Puckett, however. If everybody found out about her, Dottie might get so busy it would be hard to get an appointment.

"There's a woman who goes to our church who does hair," Barb said.

"I keep meaning to go to her for a trim, but I never seem to get around to it. I hear she's good." Catherine didn't say anything. She was watching Sarah Chewning, who was coming toward them with a tall glass of iced tea. She grasped it firmly with both hands, as if afraid of spilling it, and took little mincing steps. The girl was probably around eight or nine, and Catherine couldn't help remembering when Olivia was that age and wore little shorts sets and sandals and pulled her hair back neatly with a headband as Sarah did. She wondered if Barb was so naïve as to think her little girl would always be this compliant and eager to please. "Just wait a couple of years," Catherine wanted to tell her. "She'll turn into a little hellcat overnight!"

"Did you want a glass of tea, too, Mom?" Sarah asked.

Barb shook her head. "No, sweetie, but thanks for asking."

Catherine took the glass, and Sarah skipped back to the front porch. "I usually drink tea only at supper," Catherine said, but took a sip nevertheless and found it quite good. Not everyone could make good tea.

"She has a shop out on Highway 11 in that turquoise house," Barb said, and when Catherine frowned, she added, "My friend from church who does hair."

"Oh, she does?" Catherine said, and since it was evident that Barb already knew about Dottie, she continued, "Well, that's a coincidence, I guess, because it must be your friend who did my hair this time—Dottie Puckett."

"Well, imagine that!" Barb said, and looked at Catherine again approvingly. "She really does do a good job, doesn't she? I'll have to tell her on Sunday that one of her customers is my new neighbor."

With a sudden jolt Catherine realized something that almost made her slosh her tea onto her new white cotton knit romper. So *that's* why she had a funny feeling about Barb Chewning! If she went to the same church as Dottie Puckett, Barb must be a religious fanatic, too! And here Catherine sat in her front yard drinking her iced tea. She took several hasty gulps. She'd just finish up this visit as soon as possible and get on back to her side of Brookside and stay there.

Sammy was presently occupied with pouring little bucketfuls of water from the pool onto the ground, and Barb had just started telling Catherine her plans for landscaping their front yard when Sarah called out, "The phone's ringing, Mom!" The little girl ran inside and reappeared a minute later with a portable telephone. "It's Caleb," she said and handed the phone to her mother.

Barb cocked her head against the phone and listened for a few moments, then said, "Sure, I guess you can do that." Then, "Right, right."

Then finally, "Yep, it'll be okay, but let's don't make this a regular thing, all right? You know how your dad feels about that. Right. Bye, honey."

By the time Barb had pushed the button to conclude the phone call, Catherine had set the empty glass on the ground beside her chair and was on her feet. "I've got to get back now," she said. "Thanks for the tea."

"Hey, hold on a minute," Barb said. "Surely you're not going already. Can't you stay a little longer?" She was shading her eyes and looking up at Catherine. "You just got here," she added. She glanced down at Sammy. "It's past time for Sammy's nap, and he'll be out like a light when I put him down. We could talk inside."

"No, I need to keep an eye on my cleaning woman," Catherine said. "You know how some of them can be if you're not right there checking up on them!" She tightened her lips and shook her head as if cleaning women had been the curse of her life.

"Wasn't it your sister-in-law I met the other day when I came over to borrow the sugar?" Barb asked. "Is she still here?"

"Oh yes, she sure is," Catherine said with a sigh.

Barb stood up. "Well, I was wanting to ask you both if you'd come to a meeting at my house this Monday night. I was planning to tell you a little about it before you left," she said wistfully. "Are you sure you can't . . ." but Catherine was already inching toward the curb.

Sammy began whimpering. "Mama, Mama," he said over and over, holding out his arms for Barb to pick him up, which she did after wrapping him in a big towel. He immediately laid his head on her shoulder and put his index finger in his mouth.

Barb followed Catherine to the street. "It's a poetry club, and we've been meeting once a month," she said, trailing along behind her. "I signed up for August before I knew we were moving, but I think I can have the living room presentable by Monday. We can always sit on boxes." She laughed, then continued, "I don't even know if you like poetry, but Loretta Whittington next door told me you do some stage acting in the area, and that made me think you might be interested in our group. I believe she also said you were on some library committee, so I figured you must like literature." Barb chuckled. "Loretta just laughed when I invited her—said if it was a cooking club or something about home decorating or fashions, she might come, but she'd fall asleep if it was poetry."

They were at the curb now, and Catherine turned back to face Barb. The very fact that Loretta Whittington had spurned the idea was almost enough to make Catherine embrace it, no questions asked. Loretta Whittington had to be one of the most provoking women she'd ever met—always trying to make everybody think she was the next Martha Stewart, bragging up and down the street about the most preposterous new recipes she had tried, for things like Crabmeat Mornay or Zucchini-Eggplant Ratatouille or Shad Roe Omelet. She sometimes brought by little samples on a tray for her neighbors to try and then stood there bright-eyed, with her wild blond hair flying out in all directions, waiting for compliments.

Loretta thought she was the last word on interior decorating, too—had even presumed to tell Catherine one time that the floral fabric she had chosen for a wing chair could use a brighter dash of red, maybe even orange, which could be expected from someone with Loretta's flamboyant tastes. Just the way she dressed told you to take her decorating advice with a grain of salt. She put some of the strangest colors together. And her *jewelry*! Why, she practically clanked when she walked! Sometimes when Catherine caught a glimpse of Loretta going out to get in her car, she wanted to laugh out loud at her ensemble. "Where's the gypsy convention?" she felt like yelling.

Barb smiled and shrugged her shoulders. "But then, I guess everybody's entitled to his own preferences," she said. "Anyway, we've only been meeting a few months, but it's been wonderful so far. Our leader is very—well, let's just say Margaret's an unusual person. Very smart and a natural-born teacher. She's really the only one of us who knows much about poetry, but we're all learning. I feel as if there's an empty room inside my soul that's opening up." She paused and looked up at the sky with a faraway expression, as if slipping into a reverie. "It's slowly getting filled up with furniture," she added, "and decorated, too."

Catherine feared that Barb was about to start quoting a poem, but then she snapped out of it, looked back at Catherine, and said, "You know, years ago women used to have these literary clubs all over the country, but I guess everybody got too busy and then a lot of women started getting jobs. That's one reason we have our meetings at night—so more women can come. They only last about an hour and a half or so, and the time goes so fast! I think you'd enjoy it a lot. And your sister-in-law is welcome to come, too. Oh yes, and we call our group Women Well Versed."

Catherine had never heard anything so corny in her whole life. She wished she had something to use as a ready excuse, but she couldn't think of anything right off. If only it were the second Monday of the month instead of this one, she could tell Barb she had a Friends of the Library meeting. "Well, I don't know," she said aloud. "I'll think about it—but I wouldn't hold my breath if I were you."

"Okay," Barb said, nodding. "I'll get back with you on Monday. But I won't hold my breath, I promise—I'll just keep right on breathing."

Catherine looked at Barb sharply. She wasn't making fun of her, was she? But Barb's face was as pure and innocent as Ivory soap. She rubbed Sammy's back gently and looked up at the sky.

"My boys will sure be disappointed if it rains tonight," she said. "They've got big plans for camping out." Looking back at Catherine, she smiled and added, "Oops, I forgot. I promise not to mention the weather again." Then she raised one hand in a brief wave. "Thanks for coming over, Catherine. Say, does anybody ever call you Cathy?"

"No!" Catherine answered quickly. "I can't stand that name!" What she didn't tell Barb was that she *used* to like it. That was what her father had sometimes called her. But the last time he had promised to come to something and hadn't shown up—it had been a one-night community production of *The Importance of Being Earnest* the summer she was nineteen—she had suddenly grown to hate the name Cathy.

"I'm sorry, Cathy," her father had said late that night, after the performance was over. "Something big came up and . . ."

"I know," she had interrupted. "Something far more important than a dumb play your daughter had a lead role in."

"Now, Cathy, don't . . ."

"My name is Catherine!" she had shouted. "Not Cathy!" And she had hated the name ever since, for no good reason. No good reason other than it stood for one too many disappointments, one too many times her father had tried to sweet-talk her into forgetting a broken promise.

"Okay," Barb said now. "I'll remember that. Well, Catherine, maybe next time we can talk longer. I bet we'd never run out of things to talk about. 'Of shoes—and ships—and sealing wax—of cabbages—and kings—' Who was it that said that?" Apparently she didn't expect an answer, for she turned and started back toward her house. Sammy shifted his head so that his large blue eyes were peering at Catherine over his mother's shoulder.

"Hi there, Catherine!" she heard someone call, and there stood Trixie Thorndike two doors down, sprinkling her bed of pink impatiens. "Cute romper!" Trixie said.

"Thanks!" Catherine shouted, making a beeline for her front door before Trixie could strike up a conversation. That woman would talk your ear off once she got started, and Catherine had had enough neighborly chatter for the day.

"I was telling Chuck this morning that . . ." she heard Trixie saying, but Catherine got inside and closed the front door before she could hear more.

The sound of the vacuum cleaner let her know that Sparkle and Della

Boyd were progressing with Philip's room, and she walked down the hallway to check on them. The pile outside the doorway was even larger now.
Catherine stopped and scowled at it for a moment. She could hardly believe that all this stuff had been in Philip's bedroom. Where had it all
been crammed? She counted seventeen empty pop cans, most of them
riddled with small, ragged holes. An old metal trash can imprinted with
baseball pennants had been similarly punctured. Had Philip been shooting his BB gun *in his room*?

The pile in the hallway was a conglomeration of some of the most
unlikely objects Catherine had ever seen lumped together—a rusted hub-
cap, an old rotary telephone half disassembled, a broom handle sharp-
ened to a deadly point, a mutilated kite, an electric clock with a smashed
face, a velour bathrobe with one sleeve ripped off, a set of fan blades bent
at odd angles, a small dented washtub with a swastika spray-painted on
the inside, a piece of garden hose with what looked like knife slashes
along its length, a lampshade with the words *Bloody Guts* scribbled on it
in red crayon, and a stop sign that appeared to have been beaten with a
sledgehammer. Catherine remembered clearly when the sign at the corner
of Brookside and DeLaney had disappeared several months ago. As she
stared at the objects, which were only the ones she could see on top of
the pile, Catherine wondered why so many of them looked as if they had
met with violence. Surely Philip wasn't developing an abusive streak, was
he?

Catherine knew Blake would skin Philip alive if he saw some of these
things, so the sooner they could get rid of them, the better. She could just
imagine Blake's reaction about the stop sign especially. He'd probably go
stratospheric and haul Philip down to the courthouse for a lecture from
the juvenile judge! As if kids hadn't been snitching stop signs for years
on end. Why, thousands of kids did things like that and still turned out
to be normal, decent adults. She turned quickly and went out to the garage to find some cardboard boxes.

In Catherine's opinion, for a man living on the brink of the twenty-
first century, Blake sure had his head in the sand a good bit of the time.
He hung onto some of the most old-fashioned ideas that plain old common sense told you just wouldn't work in today's society. Some of his
standards were absolutely absurd! Not that he enforced them with his
own children, of course—at least not most of them. He was terribly in-
consistent in his dealings with the children, mainly because he was out
of town so much of the time, a fact that Catherine frequently pointed out.
No, he didn't have many rules for his own kids, although there were a few
that he treated like stone tablets from a holy mountain.

Catherine still remembered the big blowup after Hardy had said a swear word—screamed it, actually—to his father's face one day back in the spring. It had taken place in front of Olivia and Philip, too, which had made it worse for Hardy's ego. They all happened to be in the kitchen at the time—passing through or in various stages of eating something before bedtime. Olivia was doing homework at the table. Catherine remembered that all her books and papers had gotten scattered across the floor by the time it was over.

All three children knew Blake's opinion about bad language, and though they made smart cracks about it behind his back, they weren't willing to risk his wrath by stepping over the line at home—especially when Blake was around. Except for that one day back in—it must have been May, Catherine decided, because it had happened right after Hardy had been suspended from school for two days, and that was only a couple of weeks before school was out for the summer. It was the suspension from school that Blake was commenting on, in fact, when Hardy had let loose and shouted the bad word.

There had been a blinding instant of dead silence before Blake turned on Hardy with the look of a madman, and Catherine had yelled at him, "Stop! Don't touch him! He didn't mean it!" And she had run to stand in front of Hardy, her arms extended as if ready to stop a locomotive.

To which Hardy had replied, "Yes, I did" from between clenched teeth, and then he had purposely shouted the word again very distinctly.

As Blake had barreled toward her, he had looked her straight in the eye and spat out the words "Get out of my way right now!" He was so angry she wouldn't have been surprised to see him foaming at the mouth. When she had hesitated, he had taken her by the shoulders, picked her up, and set her aside as easily as if he were moving a floor lamp. She gave a final imploring screech—"Don't hurt him!"—and flattened herself against a wall.

Even today Catherine couldn't figure it out. Hardy had known exactly what he was doing and how Blake would respond, yet he had done it anyway. Had he actually thought he could overpower his father? He had always been quick and good in sports, though he probably held the record for having been kicked off the most teams for temper flare-ups. Why, even his T-Ball coach had made him sit out a game when he was only five!

Now, at sixteen, he was already six feet tall and filling out fast. Catherine knew that was one reason he liked to go shirtless—to show off his muscles. She knew he worked out in the basement as he watched TV and listened to his loud music. She had seen him grab hold of a doorframe any number of times and do a dozen or more chin-ups. "You're going to pull the house down!" she had said once and then added, "Besides that, you're leaving your filthy dirty fingerprints all over the place!" He had laughed his trollish cackle and said, "And I sure feel bad about that," after which he had proceeded through the whole house to every single doorway doing chin-ups.

So he must have viewed the incident as a showdown of male strength. He must have thought he was ready to establish his dominance at 117 Brookside Drive. Though she still cringed at the memory of the scene in the kitchen that night, and of other similar scenes, Catherine hated to think of what things would be like at home when it got to the point that Blake couldn't put Hardy in his place anymore.

At forty-five, Blake was a powerful man. Besides having been a wrestler and a distance runner in high school and college, he still jogged regularly and played racquetball with some of the men at work. Not to mention that he had a good two or three inches of height and at least thirty pounds on Hardy. Catherine knew it must have taken Hardy only seconds to realize he had bitten off more than he could chew. The whole thing hadn't lasted long, thank goodness, and when Blake had Hardy practically throttled, lying flat on his back across the kitchen table and making horrible choking noises, he spoke with menacing softness. "If you ever utter another word like that in this house, I will throw you out in the street—literally." And for over three months now Hardy hadn't tested him to see whether he really meant it.

"Miz Biddle?" Sparkle Flynn was standing in the doorway between the kitchen and hall, her brow furrowed. "What you wantin' us to do with all this rubbish out here?" She jerked her head back toward the hallway.

"Whatever can be thrown in the garbage, toss it!" Catherine said. "I can't find any boxes, so we'll just have to use trash bags. Stuff them as full as you can, then put them in the trunk of my car. I'm going to get rid of it all before Philip gets home and has a hissy fit."

"Some of it's too heavy and big for a trash bag," Sparkle said.

"Well then, just put it in the trunk loose! I'll go out and unlock it. Get Della Boyd to help you." She removed a box of large plastic garbage bags from the cupboard under the sink. "Here, use these—but only as many as you need. They don't give those things away free, you know."

Sparkle took the box, then turned and plodded back down the hall, grumbling to herself.

"If you've got something to say, say it out loud where everybody can hear you!" Catherine shouted.

The Same Hand

7

It was true. Della Boyd's house had burned to the ground. Blake had spent hours on the telephone, tracking down different people, trying to get to the bottom of it all. It peeved Catherine that he didn't seem the least bit concerned about their phone bill, which would no doubt be sky-high after all this.

"Well, so what did you find out?" she asked him on Friday night, but he didn't say anything at first. It was late, and Catherine had just finished her bath. The scent of Honey Peach Body Splash wafted from the bathroom. She was sitting up in bed now, filing her fingernails. She had chipped a nail that afternoon when she and Della Boyd had unloaded all the junk from Philip's bedroom into a trash bin over behind the bank, and now she was having to trim them all to match that one. It was so aggravating—she had gotten them all just the right length, and now this! She would have to do a touch-up on her nail polish, too.

She had made sure she got in the bathroom first tonight so she didn't have to wait for Blake to finish his steamy shower. While she was bathing, she had heard Blake through the bathroom window out on the patio talking to Kinko and bouncing the basketball. At least she had *thought* it was Kinko at first because he was using that same affectionate tone of voice he always used with the dog, but a little later she had heard Della Boyd saying something, and she realized Blake and his sister were outside together having a late moonlight chat. If she could have raised the window without attracting their attention, she would have done so, just to know what they were talking about, but the bathroom window always made a terrible racket, so she didn't even try.

The voices had finally stopped, and she had seen the patio light click off and heard the sliding of the glass door into the den. Several minutes later, after Catherine was out of the tub, Blake had come back to the bedroom and was now pulling off his shirt. At her question, he took in a big breath, then balled up his shirt and threw it into the open hamper. He then stepped out of his khaki walking shorts and made an elaborate deal out of rebuttoning and zipping them, straightening the waistband, lining up the legs, and folding them neatly.

"Well, Mr. Sherlock Holmes, are you going to tell me what you found out or not?" Catherine said after several long moments when he still hadn't spoken. "Or is it some deep dark secret?" She stopped filing her nails and fixed Blake with a stern look. "Or are you afraid to tell me because you found out she made the whole thing up just like I said?"

There was a plush, low-backed maroon velvet chair beside Catherine's dresser, mostly for looks, and Blake sat down in it. She wondered if he had any idea how ridiculous he looked sitting in a velvet chair in his boxer shorts. "Okay, I'll tell you," he said.

It was actually a fairly simple story. Things had happened pretty much as Della Boyd had reported them, only Blake had dug up a lot more details than she had furnished. She had been away the afternoon of the fire, volunteering as a receptionist in the intensive care unit at the hospital, something she had done every Thursday for years and years. Della Boyd lived on the outskirts of Yazoo City with two empty lots between her house and the nearest neighbors, a feeble couple in their eighties. Some kind of big electrical generator occupied a tract of land on the other side of her property. By the time someone had noticed the smoke and called the fire department, the house was too far gone to save.

It was just a little cracker box of a house, as Catherine remembered it—three small bedrooms and one bath, no dining room, no den, only the sorriest excuse of a kitchen, with the dinette table sitting out at one end of the living room! But Della Boyd hadn't seemed to realize how inadequate it was, had lived there for nearly her whole life in fact, had it chock-full of oddly matched furniture, stacks of books and magazines, and cheap bric-a-brac of all kinds.

It was the house Blake had lived in, too, during his school days—a fact that was clearly evident to anyone who stepped foot inside, since Della Boyd had dedicated practically every room as a shrine to Blake's youthful accomplishments. His certificates for everything from grade school penmanship to membership in the National Honor Society were plastered all over the walls. Why, she had even framed a picture he had drawn in first grade of an orange polka-dot ferris wheel and had it hanging in a prominent place by the front door! High school trophies cluttered up the mantel in the living room, along with clay sculptures and model cars he had made as a child.

Catherine had been there only three or four times in the early years of their marriage. She had hated the place more each time she went. It seemed that every time she turned around she was bumping into something or somebody. She also hated the way Della Boyd had always made such a fuss over Blake. It was downright weird in her opinion for an older sister to act so dotty about her little brother, as if he were her own child, and it didn't make a bit of difference when Blake reminded her that Della Boyd *had* been like his mother for all practical purposes since she had been seventeen when he was born—that must have been some little surprise!—and their parents had both died by the time he was only two. Della Boyd had raised him, he kept telling Catherine, so it was only natural that their relationship was more like mother and son than sister and brother. None of that mattered to Catherine, though. All she knew was that Della Boyd and the whole town of Yazoo City got on her nerves, and she finally refused to go there anymore.

When they had finally gotten word to Della Boyd at the hospital about the fire, she was right in the middle of consoling a woman whose father had just died minutes earlier and who had no other living relatives in town. Coincidentally, it was a woman with whom she had taught during her few years as a teacher. The two of them had renewed their acquaintance during the past few weeks at the hospital. Della Boyd had her arm around the woman's shoulder, and the woman had just said something like "He was all I had," speaking of her deceased father, of course, when one of the hospital personnel had approached Della Boyd and told her there was an urgent phone call for her at the nurses' station.

According to what Blake had been able to piece together, this woman whose father had just died—a woman named Helena Ludwig—had come with Della Boyd to the telephone and then proceeded to comfort *her* over her loss and even rode with Della Boyd to her house, or what used to be her house, and stood out in the street with her, watching the firemen hose down what little remained. From the reports, the house must have gone up in flames like a cardboard box, all the books, old letters and diaries, certificates and papers acting like kindling. The official conclusion was, as Della Boyd had said, that it had been caused by an electrical short from an old window unit in the living room, which she had left on during her absence to keep the house from heating up during the hot summer day. As it turned out, it had heated up quite a bit anyway, Catherine thought.

The fire had happened over four weeks ago, in late July, and Della Boyd, who always had a habit of keeping to herself and therefore didn't have an abundance of close friends, had hooked herself up on the spur of the moment with this Helena Ludwig, the woman from the hospital, and had even, at Helena's invitation, moved into her house with her after the fire. Not that she had anything to move, really, but Helena took her in, gave her the spare bedroom, shared some clothes with her, and the two of them set about bearing each other up during their mutual losses. Della Boyd helped Helena with the funeral arrangements for her father, even helped her write thank-you notes to friends and neighbors who sent flowers and casseroles, and Helena guided Della Boyd through the dealings with the insurance company.

When Helena had told Della Boyd several days after the funeral that it was her intention to move back to the town in Louisiana where she had grown up, Della Boyd had helped her get her house on the market, show it to prospective buyers, and start packing boxes. All this time she had pretended to Helena that she was in daily contact with her brother in South Carolina and that he was pressing her to come live with him as soon as all the insurance matters were settled.

"I didn't want her worrying about me," Della Boyd had explained to Blake after he had finally located Helena Ludwig by phone and heard her side of things. "And I didn't want *you* worrying about me, either," she had said, "so that's why I didn't call. I just decided it would be . . . well, it would work out better to get on the bus and come. I didn't mean to lie to Helena, but I didn't want her feeling responsible for me. She had already done so much."

Blake told all of this to Catherine in their bedroom that Friday night, and after he finished, he said, "You know why she didn't want to call, don't you?" His tone sounded accusing.

"How should I know?" Catherine said irritably. She held out her left hand to see if all her fingernails looked even.

"She didn't want to take the chance of being turned down," he said.

Although he didn't have tears in his eyes or anything that drastic, Catherine could have sworn that his voice was on the verge of quivering. "Good grief," she wanted to say, "get hold of yourself. You're a grown man. We're not talking about the end of the world here!" Still, she wondered about his underlying meaning. Was he blaming *her* for the fact that Della Boyd hadn't called before she showed up on Wednesday? That's sure what it sounded like.

"So what are we supposed to do now?" Catherine asked. "How long is she going to be here? She's got her insurance money. She told us that. So why can't she just get another house back in Yazoo City and start over?"

Blake looked up at the ceiling and shook his head. "No, not now she can't. She's not . . . she's not strong enough. I don't think she's even accepted it all yet. Or it hasn't sunk in or something. Della Boyd isn't . . . well, I'm worried about her." He sighed deeply. "I should have gone back home to check up on her more. You can't tell anything from phone calls." He let his eyes travel to the Monet print above the bed, behind Catherine's head. "She needs to be here with us for now," he said. "She's . . . I don't know . . . maybe *fragile* is the word."

Catherine pursed her lips scornfully and blew out a puff of air. "Fragile? She seems pretty strong to me—and perfectly happy, too," she said. "She's no different than she's always been as far as I can tell—off in her own little dreamworld most of the time. She acts just fine to me, like she's on vacation without a care in the world!"

"Some vacation," Blake said, glancing sharply at Catherine. "Listen, that reminds me. I don't want you treating her like a housemaid, Catherine. I know she helped Sparkle most of the day today and then cooked supper tonight. She'll do whatever you ask her to, you know that. I don't want you taking advantage of her. She's my sister, and she's our guest."

"I didn't ask her to do a thing!" Catherine said, aware that her voice sounded shrill and much too loud for a private conversation. "She volunteered! She *asked me* where the dust rags were and where I kept the glass cleaner and if it was okay with me if she waxed the parquet by the front door and a million other things! She got in there with Sparkle *of her own free will* and cleaned out every nook and cranny in Philip's room, and she *hummed* while she worked! And I didn't ask her to cook supper either— she just up and did it. Nobody's taking advantage of your sister, Blake!"

"Well, shall we open up the doors and windows and make an announcement to the whole neighborhood?" Blake said.

Catherine clamped her lips shut and filed furiously, suddenly realizing that she had whittled one fingernail down much farther than she had intended to. She stopped all at once and threw the file down on the comforter. Blake didn't budge from the velvet chair. He had his arms up, with his hands clasped behind his head, and out of the corner of her eye she could tell he was looking at her. She also knew it wasn't a look of adoration.

"And what are you staring at?" she snapped.

"I want you to take Della Boyd downtown tomorrow and help her pick out some things she needs," Blake said.

"Like what?"

"Personal things—whatever she needs. She lost everything she had in the fire, in case you've forgotten."

"So what does she have in those satchels and paper bags?"

"Not nearly enough," Blake said. "Think about it, Catherine. Put yourself in someone else's shoes for a change. How would you like to be down to whatever could fit into a few satchels and grocery sacks?"

"And who's going to pay for these things?" Catherine demanded.

"I am," Blake said.

"She's got money! There's no reason we should have to replace everything for her! She got a settlement from the insurance company!"

Blake rose suddenly from the chair and moved swiftly to the side of the bed. He leaned over and spoke intensely, not four inches away from Catherine's face. "You spend my money all year long on things you want, but this time, Catherine, *this time* I'm spending it the way I want to, and that happens to be buying some new things for my sister!"

"I spend my own money half the time, and you know it!" Catherine cried.

"Yes, but your little extra allowance isn't enough, is it? You can't stretch your thirty thousand out over a whole year, can you? You always run short, don't you?"

He was so close that his features were a blur. Catherine could tell his eyes were bright with anger, though, and he held her gaze without flinching. Slowly he backed away, then stood up straight and came into focus. Catherine refused to look away. It would be like giving him the upper hand, and she wasn't about to do that.

"It still amazes me," Blake said slowly, "that you can even spend your father's money. It amazes me that he didn't change his will at the end and cut you out completely. Tell me, Catherine, doesn't your conscience ever hurt you just a little bit when you get that check every year? Don't you ever think about how you treated him during that last year?"

"No, I don't! I didn't do a thing wrong. I *couldn't* go. Daddy knew that! I wasn't feeling well, and I was all stressed out trying to coordinate those fundraisers for the library, and besides, there wasn't a thing I could've done anyway. I just wasn't up to it. Seeing him like that would have sent me over the . . . oh, never mind! You'll never understand. But Daddy did—I know deep down in his heart he understood."

"Too bad your sister didn't. Too bad Patricia was stuck with arranging all the details for the nursing home. Too bad she was the only visitor your father had for all those months. Too bad she didn't have her only sister there to help her bear the load." He paused briefly. "Too bad she won't speak to you anymore."

"Daddy didn't want to see me anyway!" Catherine cried. "He always loved Patricia more—just like Mother did. They both made that very clear."

"Your mother was a sick, deluded woman, Catherine. You can't hold somebody like that responsible. And your father sure acted funny for somebody who didn't love you. Why did he keep begging you to come see him that last year?"

"Well, he never gave me the time of day before he found out he was dying. The whole time I was growing up, he lived like a hermit, holed up in his study. You don't have any idea what it was like! He hardly even ate with us. One of the maids took his meals to him on a tray. You don't know *anything*—I haven't told you half of it!"

"So he made mistakes when you were a kid. Don't we all?"

"Yes, *don't we?*" Catherine said. "I saw about as much of my father growing up as your kids see you!"

Blake clamped his mouth shut and turned away from her. When he finally spoke, the fire had gone out of his voice, but somehow that was worse. "Well, I know one thing," he said. "At least my kids would come to my funeral if I died."

Catherine put her hands to her ears. "Stop it! I won't listen to another word!" she said. But inside her head she kept hearing her father's last words to her over the telephone, his voice so weak she could hardly hear him. "I want to see you before I die, Cathy," he whispered. Somehow she had managed to keep from saying what she wanted to: "And what about all those times you didn't have time for me, Daddy?"

Blake walked toward the bathroom door. "Getting back to the subject," he said, turning back for a moment, "I already told Della Boyd you'd be taking her shopping tomorrow. I don't care whether it's morning or afternoon, but just make sure you set aside a couple of hours. I need to get her in sometime soon to see a doctor, too."

"And what if my schedule's full?" she challenged.

"Clear it," he said, then went into the bathroom, leaving the door open. She saw his shadow against the bathroom wall as he finished undressing and stepped into the shower.

A funny thing happened in the minutes that followed as Catherine applied a light coat of Frosted Chantilly Pink to her nails—or *started* to. She never actually got past uncapping the bottle of polish. She had experienced things like this a few times before—and she knew the French term for it, of course—but it had been so long ago that she had almost forgotten about the other times.

She paused for a few seconds at the onset of the feeling, the tiny tip of her Frosted Chantilly Pink brush poised a fraction of an inch above her thumbnail. It started with a sudden sensation that she had done all of this before—that it wasn't *now* but some earlier time and that everything that was about to happen in the next few minutes was something that had already happened. So before she even fully heard the horrendous thump in the bathroom, she had already set the brush back inside the bottle of polish and was out of bed and halfway across the floor, as she had been that other night when Philip was barely a year old and both he and Hardy, who was not quite five at the time, were taking a shower with Blake. That time it had been Hardy who had slipped on the soap and fallen, gashing his head open against the side of the tub.

Catherine had been polishing her nails that night, too, had already finished one hand, in fact, when she had heard the commotion, run into the bathroom, and opened the sliding glass shower door to see her wet, naked husband and sons, one of whom was bleeding profusely, flailing about while the shower still pelted them in a steady stream.

She had been so shocked she couldn't figure out what to do first. She recalled standing on the tile floor, feeling the spray of water on her feet as she surveyed the scene. She wasn't sure, but she thought Blake was probably the one who had finally turned off the water. She couldn't begin to remember how they had managed to get Hardy to the emergency room of the hospital to have nine stitches in his scalp. Memory was a strange thing, though—she *could* remember that her nail polish, which hadn't had time to dry, had gotten badly smudged in all the confusion.

But Hardy and Philip weren't showering with Blake this time, and she knew as she flew toward the bathroom that she would see only one body in the bathtub. She could tell through the shower door that Blake wasn't standing, and almost in one motion she slid the door back and twisted the knobs to turn off the water. One good thing about déjà vu, she supposed, was that you could maybe improve on the parts you had bungled earlier.

Blake was lying partly on his side, his legs bent at the knees. The tub, which always felt nice and roomy when Catherine took a bath, looked terribly small now. As Blake struggled to sit up, Catherine could see a large egg-sized lump already forming just above his left temple. A thought sprang to her mind, something she used to hear her father say when he read about scandals in the newspaper: "Lo, how the mighty are fallen." She didn't say it out loud, although she was tempted to, but instead said, "Well, what in the world have you gone and done?"

"What does it look like?" Blake said, touching the lump gingerly. He didn't say it angrily, though, and Catherine could tell he was embarrassed. She felt a small surge of satisfaction that the tables were turned—that she was standing on the outside of the tub this time and he was trapped inside, looking up at her. Of course, he didn't have a layer of bubbles to hide under as she had, so he was at a double disadvantage.

Catherine pointed to the rubber mat hanging over the towel rack above the tub. "If you had been using that . . ."

". . . but I wasn't," Blake said. He sounded as if his embarrassment might be giving way to irritation.

Catherine couldn't resist. "That's why I bought it," she said, "so nobody would slip getting in or out."

"I wasn't getting in or out. I was already in. I was standing here taking a shower when—"

"But you don't stand perfectly still to take a shower. You have to turn around, and that's why—"

"Are you going to stand there and lecture me or do something helpful?" Blake interrupted. "Like go get some ice?" He took hold of the side of the tub and slowly stood up.

Catherine pinched in the corners of her mouth and studied him a few more seconds, after which she yanked his towel off the rod behind the door and threw it at him. "Here. Dry off," she said and then, as if it were her idea, added, "I'll go get some ice."

As she opened the bedroom door into the hallway, she saw that Della Boyd stood in the doorway of the spare room in her stocking feet, a look of fear on her face. One hand was raised, three fingers against her mouth.

"Is anything the matter, Catherine?" she asked. "I heard . . . loud voices and things . . . and then a sound like something fell or . . . somebody got hurt."

"Everything's just fine," Catherine said, closing their bedroom door firmly behind her. "Blake just had a little slip in the shower, that's all. I'm going to get some ice."

Della Boyd uttered a small gasp. "Is he all right?"

"Of course he's all right," Catherine said. "It's just a little bump on the head. People get them all the time, Della Boyd. Now go on to bed." She turned and breezed down the hallway toward the kitchen, her pastel blue peignoir flowing out behind her.

"Sometimes those bumps on the head are more serious than people think," Della Boyd called after her. "Sometimes people find out later that what they thought was just a bump was really a concussion."

"Well, this one isn't!" Catherine said.

As she was filling a Ziploc bag with ice cubes, Della Boyd came into the kitchen. "I hope I'm not going to . . . well, be a burden to you while I'm here, Catherine," she said. "I really don't want to make it—"

"Well, it might have helped if we'd had some preparation for all this!" Catherine interrupted.

Behind her, Della Boyd made a sound that started out like a laugh but ended up more like a moan. "Nobody ever seems to have the luxury of preparing for things, do they?" she said. "Things just happen, don't they? Life is—"

"Oh, don't go giving me a speech about *life*!" Catherine said. "I know plenty about life, believe me!" And she turned and whipped past Della Boyd, down the hallway, and back to the bedroom. As she passed the den, she called to Olivia and Philip. "You two need to turn off that TV and get to bed!" But neither of them made any sign of having heard her, and she didn't stop to push the matter.

Blake had already gotten into his shorts and T-shirt and was lying flat on his back, eyes closed, on his side of the king-sized bed. The lump looked even bigger to Catherine now and was already turning faintly purple.

"Here," Catherine said, and as she laid the ice pack on the bed beside him, he groped for it with one hand. For the briefest instant his hand touched hers, covered it really, before he realized it and lifted it away as quickly as if he had been bitten by a rattlesnake.

Catherine went into the bathroom to do her teeth. She bared her teeth and got up close to the mirror to examine them. She had perfectly straight teeth. She was almost as proud of them as she was of her auburn hair. She glanced back out into the bedroom. Blake had the ice against his temple now. A vague, troubling thought began to gnaw at her and continued to do so as she flossed, brushed, and gargled. It took her a while to identify it, first to shape it and then stand back and study it, so to speak.

It had to do with Blake. And she finally put her finger on what it was. It must have been the touch that triggered the thought. It came to Catherine as she looked at herself in the bathroom mirror that Blake's feelings for her had at some point progressed past the common annoyance or exasperation that husbands and wives frequently display toward each other. She knew it happened all over the world. You couldn't be repeatedly exposed to your spouse's shortcomings and keep on acting as if you were on your honeymoon, for heaven's sake.

The fact that Blake showed no outward evidence of *loving* her wasn't really what troubled her, for she had grown used to that and didn't expect flowers and boxes of candy and verbal endearments anymore. But it was something else, something that could alarm a person if she wasn't careful. It wasn't so much that Blake neglected to do or say anything to demonstrate his love, but rather that he didn't seem to have any love to demonstrate, that whatever love he used to have had turned into something much different—like the total opposite!

She looked back out into the bedroom. He was lying absolutely still, pressing the ice against his temple with the same hand that had touched hers, the same hand that had drawn back like it had touched a red-hot skillet. She tried for a moment to remember the last time he had touched her on purpose, besides the time he had picked her up bodily and moved her away from Hardy. How long had it been since he had touched her gently? She did remember a time—it must have been months ago now—when he had *tried*, but she had been exhausted from the fashion show she had been helping to plan to pay for renovations to one of the library branches, and she had resisted. Actually, she had given his hand a slap and said, "You've got to be kidding!"

She removed the lid from her jar of Night Balm and began applying the cream to her face in small circular motions. The more she thought about it, the angrier she grew. Who did Blake think he was, recoiling from her the way he had a few minutes ago—especially after she had gone to the trouble of getting ice for him? Something was definitely suspicious here. He was a red-blooded American male, and yet he hadn't touched his wife for months! Catherine felt like charging in, pounding on his chest, and yelling, "Okay, buster, who is she?"

She looked back out into the bedroom. He had shifted slightly and was holding the ice pack with his other hand now, his left one. He had big hands, with broad palms and powerful fingers. For no reason at all Catherine suddenly remembered how tiny Olivia had looked when she was just a newborn, lying curled up in Blake's hands. They had a picture of it in an album somewhere, a close-up that one of the nurses at the hospital had taken.

She remembered the jewelry store calling her after she had ordered Blake's gold wedding band over twenty years ago. The woman had wanted to confirm the ring size. She was afraid one of their new employees might have misunderstood and written down the wrong number. "No, it's right," Catherine had said. "Size *sixteen*." It almost made her laugh now to remember how she had bragged about his ring size and told everybody about the phone call.

Again she looked back at Blake lying on the bed. She could see the glint of his size sixteen wedding band on the hand pressing the ice against his head. At least he still wore his wedding ring—but she knew some men did that just to keep their wives from getting too curious.

She didn't know why, but suddenly she wished Blake would take her hands in his large, strong ones and hold them there—not for long, but just for a minute or two.

A Little Taste

8

Three days later, on Monday afternoon, Catherine went outside to move the sprinkler and found Della Boyd on her hands and knees at the side of the house digging up a narrow strip of ground alongside the fence.

"Della Boyd! What do you think you're doing?" Catherine said.

Della Boyd looked up, startled, and then sat down with her back against the fence and pointed with her trowel toward a brown sack. Catherine noticed she was wearing the cheap pair of black slacks she had insisted on buying at Wal-Mart when they had gone shopping on Saturday afternoon, and the knees of them were already dirty. She was also wearing an old straw hat of Blake's.

"Oh, Catherine," Della Boyd said, "I was hoping you wouldn't . . . well, you see, I wanted to surprise you come spring."

"Well, you've surprised me all right!" Catherine said. "People don't usually go around digging up other people's yards whenever they feel like it."

Della Boyd waved the trowel toward the house next door and said, "He told me it was a little late for planting them but said it shouldn't really matter that much. And since there wasn't anything along here, I thought it would be such a nice surprise for you to come out here in the spring and find them growing all along the fence—this is where he suggested I plant them—and you know the good thing about them when you pick them and put them in water is that new blooms keep opening up all along the stem, and—"

"Wait a minute! Hold on!" Catherine said. "What in the world are you talking about? What is it you're trying to plant, and who gave you all these instructions?"

"Mr. Abernathy next door," Della Boyd said. "He said his brother had dug up all these iris bulbs from his yard and brought them over, and he didn't know what he was going to do with them all. Said his brother—Dennis is his name—had bags and bags of them. You see, Dennis sold his farmhouse out on the old highway, Mr. Abernathy said, but before he did he dug up all the irises to give them away to people he knew. But Mr. Abernathy said his yard was already so full of flowers there was hardly room to turn around, and he asked if I thought we could use some, and he said I could have as many as I wanted, so . . ."

"And since when have you and Myron Abernathy become such good friends?" Catherine demanded.

"Oh, we talked a long time across the back fence on Saturday morning while you were out, and then this morning when you took Olivia to the pool he brought the bulbs over, and we talked some more." Once again Della Boyd pointed to the brown paper sack with the trowel. "He's a real nice man, Mr. Abernathy is. He gave me that whole sackful there and told me where I should plant them. We thought they'd be nice along the fence."

"Yes, well, maybe he should have talked to me first!" Catherine said. "After all, it's our yard, not *his*!"

Della Boyd didn't even seem to hear her but got back on her knees and started digging again. "He told me all about his eye surgery and said his wife, Sylvia, has to have a knee operation sometime coming up. And his brother in Charlotte, North Carolina, has been on dialysis for almost a year now. And their little granddaughter was born prematurely with some kind of birth defect, so of course the whole family—"

"Did he tell you about his great-aunt's liver condition, too?" Catherine asked.

"No," said Della Boyd, stopping and looking up. "How long has she had that?"

"Oh, never mind!" Honestly, she thought, Della Boyd was as dense as a concrete block.

"So anyway, the whole family's real upset about the little grandbaby," Della Boyd said, "and the Abernathys might try to go out there to see them. But it's such a long trip, and Mr. Abernathy said Sylvia's afraid to try to make it since neither one of them is feeling up to par right now. It's out in Iowa . . . or maybe he said Ohio."

"Yes, well, the world is full of problems," Catherine said.

"Or it could be Idaho. I'll have to ask Mr. Abernathy again."

"You be sure and do that," Catherine said. "And next time you decide to plant something in my yard, ask me about it first."

Della Boyd stopped digging and turned around, squinting up at Catherine from under the brim of the straw hat. "Oh, did you have something else planned for here, Catherine? Because if you did, I could sure dig these back up and plant them somewhere else."

"No, no. Go ahead now that you've gotten started," Catherine said. "But just *ask* next time, for heaven's sake." Actually, Catherine liked irises a lot and had even badgered Blake several years earlier about planting some. He had never gotten around to it, however, and she had finally hired a landscape man to come plant a few things in the front yard. He had charged an arm and a leg, though, so she had dismissed him before they got around to irises.

"I sure wish it could have been a surprise for you, but it can't be helped now," Della Boyd said, resuming her digging. "This will be the perfect place for them with all the sun they'll get. You know, I had irises all over my backyard in Yazoo City, and they were the prettiest things!" She stopped suddenly, her trowel poised motionless. "I wonder if the fire got all my iris bulbs. You know, I never thought about that. I wonder if being underground helped protect them. Maybe when springtime comes—"

Catherine interrupted her. "Well, it doesn't look like you're planting those deep enough to me."

Della Boyd looked up and down the row she was planting. "Drakes on a lake," she said.

"What? What's that supposed to mean?"

"That's what Mr. Abernathy told me. You plant them shallow, with part of them showing, you see—so they look like drakes on a lake."

"Well, isn't Mr. Abernathy just the source of all kinds of fascinating gardening tips?" Catherine said.

"Oh, he sure is!" Della Boyd agreed. "Mr. Abernathy *thinks* the ones I'm planting here will be mostly purple, but there might be a few yellow ones mixed in, he said, and in the spring they. . ."

Catherine was just about to cut her off and tell her not to count on still being here in the spring to see whether the irises bloomed purple or yellow when suddenly she was aware that someone had walked up behind her. She turned around to see Barb Chewning standing there in a pink sundress. "Well, if it's not Rebecca of Sunnybrook Farm," Catherine felt like saying.

"Hi, I wanted to check with you again about the poetry club that'll be meeting at my house tonight," Barb said, then smiled broadly. "There, how was that? No small talk about the weather—just straight to the point." Catherine couldn't think of a response, and Barb didn't wait for one. "I don't know if I told you the time, but it starts at seven," she continued, "and I'd love to have both of you come." She cocked her head and smiled down at Della Boyd on the ground. "Some of the ladies bring notebooks and pens with them to take notes, but I'll leave that up to you. We'll have refreshments at the end."

"A poetry club!" Della Boyd exclaimed. She set the trowel down, then got up from the ground and brushed her gloved hands together. Catherine had already noticed that she was wearing an old pair of her gardening gloves, which she must have found in the garage along with the trowel and Blake's straw hat. It didn't surprise Catherine one bit. Why should she expect Della Boyd to ask about minor details like borrowing a pair of gloves or a hat or a trowel when she hadn't even bothered to ask about digging up a twelve-foot strip of her yard? Or about moving in with them, for that matter?

"Do you like poetry?" Barb asked.

"Oh yes, I do!" said Della Boyd. Then to Catherine's great amazement, she clasped her hands together in a melodramatic pose, looked up at the sky, and began to recite:

> *I wandered lonely as a cloud*
> *That floats on high o'er vales and hills,*
> *When all at once I saw a crowd,*
> *A host of golden daffodils;*
> *Beside the lake, beneath the trees,*
> *Fluttering and dancing—*

"Okay, okay, okay, Longfellow!" Catherine said. "We get the point."

"Oh no. It's not by Longfellow," Della Boyd said. "It's by William Wordsworth."

"I knew that," Catherine said. "It was just a joke, Della Boyd."

Barb laughed. "Well, I sure hope you can come tonight, both of you. We'll have to get you to recite that poem for the whole group sometime, Della Boyd."

Catherine could imagine Della Boyd doing just that and not feeling one ounce of embarrassment. Why, she'd probably follow it up by singing "I'm Forever Blowing Bubbles" and then asking if anybody had a request!

Barb glanced back over her shoulder, then said, "Well, I'd better get back home. My kitchen's turned upside down. The floor's all sticky where a carton of orange juice got spilled, and I've got to finish making cookies for tonight, and Sammy's due to wake up any minute." She lifted a hand in farewell and said, "Nitty-gritty details—they can wear you out, but I guess they make life interesting. Well, I hope to see you both tonight."

Catherine had a sudden troubling thought. "Say, this isn't a *church* meeting of some kind, is it?" How horrible if she were to get stuck in the middle of a bunch of religious women trying to act like they were cultured! "What kind of poetry do you study?" she added.

"Oh, all kinds," Barb said. "And no, it's not a church meeting. I know a poetry club sounds a little strange for this day and age, but I really think you'll like it, Catherine. I think I told you our leader is really . . . well, she's just really unusual. But in a good way. She really makes us think, and we have some pretty lively discussions sometimes."

"So it's not sponsored by your church or anything like that?" Catherine asked.

"No, no. Not at all," Barb said. "A few of the ladies do go to my church, but more than half of them don't. Margaret Tuttle, our leader, is our church organist, but she'd never mention it. She's teaching us *poetry*, I promise. These aren't disguised Sunday school lessons. We call our group Women Well Versed. Did I—?"

"Yes, you already told me that," Catherine said.

"Why, that's a nice name," said Della Boyd. "You know, there was a reading club in Yazoo City—a relic of local history, it was. They called it the Married Ladies Literary Society, but since I wasn't married, I didn't qualify." She looked briefly regretful and sighed softly. "All the members were rich society ladies, too, so I couldn't have gotten in anyway, but I always wondered what it would have been like to belong to the Married Ladies Literary Society. That was always a dream of mine."

Catherine lifted her chin slightly. She was sure *she* would have been invited to join the club if she had lived in Yazoo City, even though that was the last place on earth she'd want to live.

"Well, you don't have to be married or rich to come to our club," Barb said with a smile, "so I'll be looking for you tonight at seven." She pointed across the street to her house. "Right over there—the house with the blue shutters."

"I'll be there," Della Boyd said.

"Well, I'm not making any promises," Catherine said. "I might and I might not. I don't have a lot of extra time to squander."

Barb looked at her for a moment, nodding, then said, "Time sure goes fast, doesn't it? Like water through a sieve. And the older I get, the faster it seems to go." She sighed and smiled. "Then when it all runs out, our turn is over. Our time here on earth is so short."

"Isn't that the truth?" Della Boyd said, which seemed to Catherine like a pointless reply.

That night at seven o'clock Catherine took her seat in Barb Chewning's living room, more out of curiosity than anything else. It sure wasn't out of a burning love of poetry. Not that she *hated* poetry exactly, but it just never had been her thing. It had always seemed like such a lot of trouble in high school and college to read a poem and tear it apart line by line and look for hidden meanings and symbols and all that. But the idea of any kind of club aroused her interest. She wanted to see who all came. This one should be entertaining if nothing else. A group of women from this part of the state trying to have a serious discussion about poetry should be good for a laugh! Plus, she wasn't about to let Barb Chewning think her sister-in-law from Yazoo City, Mississippi, cared more about literature and such than Catherine herself did.

She was immediately disappointed in the women seated around her. Not that she had expected anything different, really. From their dress and manner she could tell at a glance that nobody of any real importance belonged to the Women Well Versed, so Catherine crossed her legs and swung her foot as she turned her attention to Barb Chewning's living room decor.

The room was painted a rather startling shade of brick red. She wondered if that had been Barb's idea. There were several attractive antiques mixed with a wide assortment of newer pieces. It didn't appear to be terribly planned or coordinated, and there were things still missing—like draperies and pictures—but the eclectic effect was really quite pleasant. The lamps were of good quality, and the large Persian rug was clearly authentic, not one of those tacky orlon imitations with colors that were too bright and patterns that were too distinct and bold. A stack of cardboard boxes stood in one corner, and Catherine wondered what Barb had been thinking. It looked like she'd have had a little more pride than to leave them out in plain sight.

Barb was in and out of the room for several minutes, answering the door and showing women into the living room, but finally she stood in the doorway and said, "Well, I think we can go ahead and get started. Jewel called earlier and said she and Eldeen would be a little late, so we'll let them have these two seats when they get here." She pointed to the two chairs next to Catherine. "We have a few visitors here tonight," she continued, "and I want to start by introducing them."

Besides Catherine and Della Boyd, there were three other visitors, but none of them amounted to much in Catherine's opinion. One worked at the H&R Block in Derby, one was a retired kindergarten teacher, and the other one, a pale woman named Michelle somebody, was a stay-at-home mother with six children between the ages of two and ten. Catherine wondered how Michelle had the energy to put one foot in front of the other after running around after six children all day. She looked frail, as if a stout wind would carry her right off. Catherine bet there were days when Michelle *wished* for a stout wind to carry her off!

After taking care of the visitors, Barb introduced the leader, a woman named Margaret Tuttle, who sat in a ladder-back armchair directly across the room from Catherine. Catherine hadn't even noticed her when she first scanned the group, but now she saw that the woman was quite pretty even though she was probably fifty if she was a day. She had thick, curly hair, dark with silver streaks, and she sat very tall and straight with her ankles crossed and her eyes fastened on Barb. She wasn't exactly smiling, but she looked—*calm* was the word that came to Catherine's mind. She wore a dark blue dress that sure wasn't anything special, but Catherine noticed she was also wearing a necklace with what appeared to be a real diamond pendant, although it was probably one of those Diamonique things ordered from the QVC shopping channel.

Barb then went around the circle and had all the regular members say their names. Catherine couldn't have repeated them all afterward, but she did remember several: Shirley, Nina, Belinda, Joan, Carrie Sue, and Lois. It struck Catherine as odd that the women were of all different ages, anywhere from late twenties to late sixties or so.

When Barb turned things over to the leader, everyone started rustling around, opening spiral notebooks and clicking ball-point pens. Margaret Tuttle waited for things to settle down, and then she spoke. "After our good discussion last month concerning the use of irony, I thought we might take up the role of emotion in poetry tonight, for I believe it is an emotional experience, far more than a purely rational line of thought, which we seek in poetry. That is not to say that a poet cares nothing for the mind and its reasoning powers, but . . ."

As Margaret Tuttle continued, Catherine wondered if the woman always talked this way. Good grief, how strange. She sounded like an encyclopedia. Catherine stared at her intently, trying to figure out whether she was reading from notes she had taken or had maybe memorized this little opening speech. She had a book open in her lap but hadn't looked down at it a single time.

" . . . and he was also the one who said 'a poem is never a thought to begin with' but starts with 'a lump in the throat,' " Margaret said, and for just an instant Catherine wished she had been listening more carefully so she could have heard who it was who said that. She glanced over at Della Boyd to see if she had written anything down, but Della Boyd was sitting there like a statue, staring at Margaret Tuttle with an awed look, as if she had never before heard anyone speak the English language.

Just at that moment a little disturbance occurred out in the entryway. The front door opened, followed by a loud "Shh!" and then the sound of something dropping and a solid thunk as if someone's elbow had hit a wall. All this was followed by an audible whisper: "Now looka there what I went and did—dropped my notebook and my pocketbook all in one! Here, Jewel, can you pick up my Clorets and my little fingernail doojigger under that little bench? They must've rolled out of my pocketbook." Barb Chewning jumped up and headed to the front door, and Margaret Tuttle stopped in the middle of a sentence while everyone turned to look out into the entryway.

"I believe our last two members have arrived," Margaret said. "We will resume after they are seated."

Catherine noticed that most of the other women were cutting glances at each other and smiling. At this point a woman's head peeked around the corner into the living room. Catherine had never seen such a funny-looking old woman and wondered for a moment if this was some kind of prank. Maybe whoever it was had on a mask. Then the woman came on into the living room nodding and smiling at everyone, talking the whole time in a thick, low voice. "I told Jewel we was going to tiptoe in quiet as a little mouse, but no, sir, I had to go and make a great big ruckus droppin' all my paraphernalia and attractin' ever'body's attention. I'm sure sorry to barge in and interrupt the flow of things, Margaret, but we'll just get ourself sat down here by this cute little carrot-top lady in the yellow britches—I don't think I've ever met you before, have I, honey?"

She sat down next to Catherine and turned to her, scrunching up her face in a smile that looked more like she was gritting her teeth in pain than smiling. Staring at the old woman's teeth, too white and too straight for her age, Catherine wondered for an instant why people didn't order dentures with slight imperfections so it wouldn't be so evident that they had false teeth.

Barb quickly stepped in and introduced them. "This is a neighbor of mine across the street named Catherine Biddle, Eldeen. And most of you already know this is Eldeen Rafferty and her daughter, Jewel Scoggins, but I'll be sure everybody gets introduced properly after Margaret finishes our lesson tonight, all right?"

"That'll be just fine, Barb honey," Eldeen said. "Me and Catherine here, we'll get along like two peapods, settin' here next to each other." She reached over and patted Catherine's knee. "Now, Margaret, old Eldeen has stopped the show long enough. You go right ahead, and I'll keep as still as a little bug in a corner."

Catherine could hardly stand to look at the old woman next to her yet couldn't take her eyes off her either. Eldeen Rafferty was big all over, not fat really, just big. She wore her straight gray hair in a short, ragged cut. It was fairly obvious, in Catherine's opinion, that the woman was her own hairstylist. In fact, it didn't even look like she used a mirror for her haircuts but just whacked here and there in a haphazard way. Her eyebrows were thick and overgrown, and Catherine noticed that she even had a faint mustache.

But the most bizarre thing of all was her clothes! Why, it looked as if she had reached into a grab bag at the Salvation Army store and put on whatever she pulled out! She had on a bright purple short-sleeved rayon dress that she must have thought was a jumper, because underneath it she was wearing a long-sleeved pink polyester blouse. She wore a double string of fake pearls around her neck and large silver earrings studded with pearlized beads. On her feet she wore white socks and a pair of huge black rubber-soled sandals.

Catherine watched Eldeen dig around inside her big straw purse for a pen and test three different ones before she found one that would write. Then she opened the three-ring binder she had on her lap and proceeded to flip through the pages until she came to the divider labeled in bold letters *NOTES FROM POETRY CLUB MEETINGS—WOMEN WELL VERSED—MARGARET TUTTLE—MONDAY NIGHTS*. She opened the metal rings and switched the order of two pages, then closed the rings again with a loud snap. Glancing over at Catherine, she pointed to her hand-scrawled notes and whispered, "My handwritin' looks like chicken scratch!" She wrote the date and then added, "I got arthritis!"

Catherine was aware that Margaret had begun talking again, but she was so distracted by the spectacle of Eldeen sitting next to her that she could hardly concentrate on a word that was being said. Over the next few minutes she watched Eldeen write down several phrases in a childish, labored script: "mixed feelings," "not enough," "too much," "sentimentality—a disease!" This last one she underlined several times. Catherine couldn't help wondering if Eldeen had any idea how the phrases tied together with what Margaret was saying.

When Margaret started talking about favorite subjects of sentimental poets, such as soft kittens, ragged teddy bears, rosy-cheeked toddlers, and Grandma's rocking chair, Eldeen raised her hand. "All them is mighty *nice* things, though," she said when Margaret had paused to acknowledge her. "Do you mean to be sayin' poems about them things can't be *good* poems?"

As Margaret inhaled to answer, Eldeen added, "I wrote a poem one time about settin' on a old porch swing with my little girl—it was Jewel here next to me when she was only six years old—and she had a ribbon in her hair and was swingin' her little legs that had bad patches of poison ivy all over 'em, and she was a'squeezin' her doll baby she'd got for her birthday, and our old one-eyed boxer dog named Sinbad was a'layin' on the front steps, too, and it was summertime, I remember, and rivers of sweat was pourin' off me! The butterflies was a'flittin' and the snapdragons was a'bloomin' and I was just flooded all of a sudden with a happy feeling of bein' alive and havin' my own little girl and breathin' in the fresh summer air, and so I wrote me a poem tellin' all about it, and . . ." She paused and looked puzzled. "So that was a . . . what you call it? A *sentimental* poem 'cause it had a little girl and a doll baby and a porch swing and butterflies and flowers in it? And that makes it *bad*?"

Margaret smiled slowly and leaned forward to address Eldeen. "I would never judge a poem based on its subject alone," she replied. "So much depends upon a poet's tone and style. But I will say that in your poem the poison ivy, the one-eyed dog, and the perspiration have excellent potential as a counterbalance for sentimentality." There was a ripple of laughter among the other women, and then Margaret continued. "As a general rule, I believe we can say that the best poems avoid excess, whether of tender emotions or of cynicism. Honesty and realism are hallmarks of fine writing."

And as if Eldeen's question had been planned, Margaret used it as a springboard to illustrate how a risky subject for poetry—the death of a child—could be handled in two entirely different ways. She read aloud two poems, one titled "Papa's Letter" and the other "Bells for John Whiteside's Daughter," and then asked a simple question. "Which one is true and which is false?"

This led to a discussion in which almost everyone participated. Even Catherine herself contributed a comment: "Whoever wrote that first poem obviously doesn't know the first thing about little boys or he wouldn't have had the kid talking like such an imbecile! I mean, a lisp is one thing, but that little kid has a major speech impediment!" Several women smiled, and Eldeen laughed so hard she almost choked.

When they got home a few minutes past nine o'clock, Blake was in the kitchen drinking a can of 7-Up and eating one of the caramel bars Della Boyd had baked that afternoon. "Well, how was it?" he said.

"Oh, nothing to write home about," Catherine said, heading for the telephone. She had remembered at the end of Margaret's lesson, while they were discussing a poem by Tennyson called "Tears, Idle Tears," that she had forgotten to call Arlene Babcock, the woman in Derby who did all of her sewing and alterations, and tell her she wanted the new window treatment for the dining room by this weekend at the latest. Catherine had taken her the fabric two whole weeks ago, and Arlene still wasn't finished!

"How did you like it, Sister?" Blake asked Della Boyd.

Della Boyd walked right up to him, held her hands in a prayerlike pose under her chin, and said, "Oh, it was just wonderful! I've never heard anything like the way that woman can teach! I feel like I've had a little taste of heaven tonight. She read the nicest poem about a cat, Blake, just to show how you could write about animals without being sentimental. You should have heard it. It was so real it made me feel like I *was* a cat!"

Catherine picked up the receiver of the telephone to dial Arlene's number. "We talked about the dangers of overstatement, too," she said to nobody in particular. Actually, it had peeved Catherine just a little that Della Boyd had seemed so *connected* to everything Margaret Tuttle was saying. Why, she had even asked a couple of halfway intelligent questions. It was funny, Catherine thought, how a person could be so slow in some things yet get really tuned in on others.

One thing that *had* pleased Catherine about the meeting was when Margaret Tuttle had asked her during refreshment time if she had ever played the role of Amanda Wingfield in *The Glass Menagerie* over in Abbeville. She had been to one of the performances with friends, she told Catherine, and had very happy memories of the evening. "I recognized you the instant you walked in tonight," Margaret had said, smiling. "My husband still quotes some of your lines from time to time. He is especially fond of the phrases 'Christian martyr,' 'gentlemen callers,' and 'little silver slipper of a moon.' "

Catherine had given Margaret what she considered a gracious smile, then, as if bestowing a favor, had adopted her Amanda Wingfield voice, which wasn't really all that different from her own, and said, "Horrors! Heaven have mercy! You're a Christian martyr, yes, that's what you are, a Christian martyr!" Catherine didn't know why, but suddenly she remembered that neither of her parents ever saw her play Amanda Wingfield. Her father had been involved in another big trial when she first played the role in college. They had meant to come to one of the performances but had never made it, as Catherine had known they wouldn't.

Now, as she punched the last number on the telephone, Catherine said aloud, "Of course, everyone knows that most poets are nut cases." And that, she thought, is probably why Della Boyd is so attracted to their poems.

As Arlene's phone rang, Blake finished the last bite of his caramel square and looked back and forth between Della Boyd and Catherine. "Two different ways of looking at the same thing," he said. Then he gave Catherine a long look over the rim of his glass as he drank the last of his 7-Up.

The Right Words

9

Something Margaret Tuttle had said the night before was repeating itself in Catherine's mind when she woke up on Tuesday morning. At some point in her lesson, Margaret had used the phrase "cheap emotions grabbed off the bargain table of sentimentality," and this was the phrase that kept going through Catherine's mind. Catherine couldn't remember ever really *thinking* very much about the subject of emotion before, and certainly not the difference between cheap and genuine emotions. And she had never stopped to consider how thoughts and feelings linked up in real life. They had always seemed totally separate to her.

"*Cheap emotions*"—the words played over and over in Catherine's mind as she peeked at Blake, watching him get dressed to go to work, and as she remembered the way he had jerked his hand away from hers last Friday night. She knew perfectly well that if she put forth the least bit of effort, she could work up a regular geyser of tears about that little incident. But she still felt too stunned to cry about it, and then there was that phrase to consider—"*cheap emotions*." Was that what it would be if she "turned on the faucet," as Blake used to call it whenever she'd start crying? "There she goes again," he'd say. "Stand back, folks, she's turning on the faucet!"

Which was all rather odd, considering that Catherine hadn't cried much as a child. When your mother didn't love you and your father didn't notice you, what was the use? It was better to hold your head up, she had learned early on, and act as if you didn't care. You could shoot words like bullets to protect yourself.

But in her teens she had found that tears were easy and sometimes fake crying could get you out of trouble. When she had gone to college and had taken Acting Techniques as part of her theatre arts major at Ole Miss, she was the best in her whole class at producing tears on cue. JoBeth Montgomery, one of her chief rivals in her drama classes, had once told her out of pure spite that although Catherine might win the prize for quantity of tears, JoBeth herself would win for quality. And it was true that JoBeth *had* gotten the lead in a play for which both of them had tried out and for which Catherine had cried copiously at the audition, while JoBeth had managed only a few paltry sniffles. Catherine had been offered a secondary role, which she had flatly refused, and she had told everybody that JoBeth had gotten the main part because she and the director were having a little fling together.

As she lay very still now and watched Blake move around the bedroom, she couldn't get the phrase out of her mind: *"Cheap emotions grabbed off the bargain table of sentimentality."* She knew she could cry about Blake's changed behavior toward her, but would it be *real* crying? He was buttoning his shirt now—a Tommy Hilfiger in a tiny navy-and-white check that she had bought him last year for Christmas. She remembered what pleasure it used to give her when they were first married to watch his huge fingers handle small shirt buttons so easily. She also remembered how he had opened the box last Christmas, looked at the shirt indifferently, and then put the lid back on without comment.

"Cheap emotions." Catherine's mind went back to the poetry meeting, and after Blake finished dressing and left the bedroom, she remembered something else that had been said last night, this time by Barb Chewning. Catherine had been keeping an eye on Eldeen Rafferty so closely—the old woman had just taken a small package of Kleenex out of her purse and tossed the whole thing across the living room to a young woman named Belinda, who had had a sudden sneezing fit—that she almost missed the question a woman named Joan had asked: "Do you think thoughts and emotions are always interdependent, or is there such a thing as pure emotion and pure thought without any of the other mixed in?" Catherine remembered frowning at the question. She thought it was pretty far off the subject of poetry. What did it matter anyway?

Margaret had given an answer, which Catherine hadn't heard because Eldeen had leaned over just then and whispered, "That poor little Belinda has a terrible time with her allergies! It's a cross she has to bear ever' day. I just bet you there's somebody settin' close to her that's doused theirself with perfume." A few seconds later she had added, "I sure wisht people'd be more considerate thataway," and then, "You're not wearin' any perfume, are you, honey? I sure can't smell it if you are, so at least you know the meanin' of the word *moderation!*"

When Margaret had finished her answer, whatever it was, Barb Chewning had said something that struck Catherine as completely wrong, even though not one soul challenged her on it. "I agree with you, Margaret," Barb had said, "and I also believe you can make up your mind to feel a certain way because it's *right*, and if you start acting that way, sooner or later you can really start feeling that way."

Clearly Barb Chewning didn't know the first thing about acting. Catherine had done enough stage work to know that *acting* was something you stepped into and "became" only in a temporary way. As soon as your part was over, it was over. That was it. The curtain came down, and you went right back to being yourself. As she threw off the covers and got out of bed, Catherine decided that if she ever got a chance, she'd have to set Barb straight about that. You felt your way into acting; you sure couldn't act your way into feeling!

She got her chance to talk to Barb two hours later, after she had gotten out of bed and dressed to take Olivia and Philip to the swimming pool. It had not been a happy ride. Philip had flung himself out of the car before Catherine had even brought it to a complete stop. He had hardly spoken to her since Friday, when he had come home to find his bedroom stripped of everything he considered precious. That Friday afternoon when he had gotten home, he had stormed out onto the patio, where Catherine was taking a late afternoon sunbath and talking to Elaine Berryhill on the portable telephone about one of the other library committee members, whose husband had been in Florida for the whole summer.

Elaine had just said, "I think he's planning to *stay* in Florida for good if you ask me" when Philip descended like a holy terror.

"Where's all my stuff?" were the first words out of his mouth, and before it was all over, Catherine had been forced to tell Elaine that she'd have to hang up and call her back.

As she pulled into the driveway, Catherine was still seething over her altercation with Olivia before she had gotten out of the car a few minutes ago in her hot pink two-piece bathing suit. After Philip had slammed the door and dashed off to the pool, Olivia had said, "Oh, by the way, Scotty's bringing me home after I get off," and she flipped her hair back from her face and looked Catherine right in the eye as if daring her to object.

"Oh, by the way, that's very funny," Catherine had replied. "And what time was he planning to have you home this time? Two in the morning like that other time?"

Olivia had rolled her eyes and said very slowly, as if she were talking to a dimwit, "Get over it, Mom. Scotty's picking me up when he gets off work today."

"Oh no, Scotty is not!" Catherine had replied.

"He'll be here at six," Olivia had said. "He's planning on it. We already talked about it."

"Well, change your plans!" Catherine said. She could hear the tight, shrill edge to her voice.

"I can't," Olivia said. "There's not a phone out there where he works."

"Well, then either send him a carrier pigeon, or else I'll tell him myself when he gets here!"

They had glared at each other for a long tense moment, and finally Olivia had curled back her top lip in a sneer before reaching for the door handle. "You're not fooling me," she said. "The only reason you don't want me having any fun is because you're *jealous*. You're jealous of your own daughter."

"Ha! Jealous of *what*?"

"Everything."

"Look here, Miss Know-It-All, maybe you don't remember what happened last month, but I sure do. And so does your father! In fact, maybe we should just swing by your father's office right now and ask him what *he* thinks about Scotty Brooks bringing you home tonight. I'm sure he'd have an opinion." Catherine even took her foot off the brake pedal and let her Buick Park Avenue roll forward a little. But Olivia opened the door, grabbed her tote bag, and leaped out. She said something as she slammed the door shut, but Catherine couldn't tell what it was except that it started with "I hope you . . ." There were countless directions that sentence could go, but from Olivia's tone of voice, Catherine was certain it hadn't ended with "have a nice day."

So as she opened the garage door and pulled in, Catherine was still fuming over Olivia's accusation of jealousy. As if a good-looking grown woman like herself would stoop to being jealous of a straight-haired teenager! Of course, Olivia *was* pretty—whenever you could catch a glimpse of her face through that sheet of blond hair—and she was young and she had developed quite a nice figure and she could make good grades when she wanted to and seemed to have a lot of friends, at least judging from the amount of time she spent on the telephone and the number of parties she was invited to. Catherine had once told Olivia, "If I could get back all the money I've spent on birthday presents for your friends, I could buy a condo and move to Hilton Head!"

But jealous? How ridiculous. Catherine did remember one time earlier this summer when she had watched Olivia run out the front door and climb into a Jeep crowded with five or six of her friends. She had watched her through the living room window. Olivia was wearing a pair of frayed denim shorts and a short yellow T-shirt that barely covered her navel. Catherine had heard someone in the Jeep whistle and yell, "Hey, hey, hey. Here's Liv! Now we can start!"

Start *what*? Catherine had wondered. She remembered feeling a swift pang of longing. What did Olivia talk about when she was with all those other teenagers? What did they do? She thought back to her own high school days in Biloxi and the heady freedom of riding around in a car with her friends. Not that she had had that many close friends, but it was easy enough to get up a carful when your father was generous with his keys. She had stood at the living room window that night watching the Jeep speed away, knowing Olivia was in it, laughing and having a good time, and she had felt . . . *wistful* was what she guessed it was. But jealous? No, that was taking it way too far.

After pulling into the garage, Catherine walked back down the driveway toward the front sidewalk to pick up the morning paper. Hardy was just coming out the front door with his skateboard. He was wearing a pair of baggy green-striped shorts and one of those ribbed undershirts that old men wear. Catherine wished that he would wear something normal in public just one time.

She set her mouth in a thin line as she watched him come down the steps. His hair, which he finally seemed to have washed recently, was parted in the middle and hung down below his ears on both sides. Hardy had Blake's coloring—dark hair and deep-set brown eyes—and clear skin, which always amazed Catherine, since she was sure he didn't wash his face like he should. He could be a handsome boy if he dressed right and kept himself clean and neat, but if she were to see him at the mall, not knowing who he was, Catherine was sure she'd turn up her nose and wonder what kind of upbringing he'd had. But what could she do? A parent was totally helpless in a case like Hardy's.

Catherine sighed and picked up the newspaper from beneath the azaleas. If that paper boy ever threw the paper in the same place two days in a row, she'd faint from the shock of it. Hardy was headed down the sidewalk now, balancing his skateboard on the end of one finger.

"Are you planning on going somewhere?" Catherine called to him.

"What was your first clue?" Hardy said, not even turning around. At the curb he paused to look all the way down Brookside Drive to where it met DeLaney Street. Then he set his skateboard down and pushed off. In a flash he was gone, and Catherine watched him weave in smooth curves away from her, both hands clasped behind his head as if relaxing for a nap.

"Where's your helmet?" Catherine called, but even as she said it, she knew she wasn't going to get an answer.

"Hi, Catherine!"

She looked across the street to see Barb Chewning in her carport holding two empty boxes by their cardboard flaps. Catherine wished the Chewnings' kitchen window didn't face the street. She had the feeling that Barb was always going to be on the lookout for any little chance to rush out and start up a conversation. She couldn't help wondering if Barb had observed the scene with Hardy just now.

"I got two more boxes emptied!" Barb called, lifting one of them and shaking it. "I'm getting there slowly but surely."

The first thing that popped into Catherine's mind to say was "Really? Let's call the newspaper and have them send out a reporter." But she didn't say it aloud. Instead she nodded and said curtly, "Well, that's good." Barb Chewning was sure taking her time getting unpacked and settled in, and it didn't seem to bother her a bit. She kept saying things like "I don't let myself get ulcers over housework" and "All those boxes will wait—they aren't going anywhere." Then she'd sit outdoors for two solid hours watching Sammy and Sarah play.

Barb had told Catherine that she found herself getting less and less particular about neatness as she got older, whereas Catherine felt she was the very opposite. She couldn't stand disorder—except for the boys' bedrooms. She had given up that battle years ago and had found that she was able to pretend those rooms weren't even part of her house. She could seal them off and forget about them for long periods of time, although she did have occasional bad dreams about some television crew sneaking into her house and taking pictures of Hardy's and Philip's rooms, then showing them in living color on the evening news. She had never forgotten the telecast featuring a filthy, roach-infested apartment in Chicago in which a social worker had found young children living. The mother's name and picture had been splashed across the screen, too.

Catherine glanced back down the street. Hardy had already disappeared from sight. She wished she knew where he was going. DeLaney was a busy street. He really should be wearing his helmet. Only last month a boy on a bike had been hit on DeLaney and thrown against another car's windshield.

Barb set the boxes against the carport wall and started down her driveway toward the street. She was barefoot, Catherine noticed, and had on a pair of loose slacks in a bright floral print. Barb could look really good if she knew how to dress and fix her hair, Catherine thought. She was a nice size and had that all-American, Cheryl Tiegs kind of face. But it was completely wasted because of the wrong clothes and that silly ponytail.

"I was wondering how you liked the poetry meeting," Barb said, stopping at the curb on her side of the street.

Catherine remembered something she had been curious about. "Fine. It was fine. Say, where did you get that little round green vase I saw on your mantel last night? It looked just like one Blake brought me back from Korea years ago, before we had Philip, who was the world's worst child for breaking anything valuable he could get his hands on!"

Barb laughed. "Why, I think it might have come from Korea, as a matter of fact. I think they call it celadon. My husband's parents travel a lot, and they're always bringing us things from other countries." She paused, then asked, "But I really did wonder how you liked the meeting itself—the lesson and all."

"Well, yes, it was . . . well, it was fine," Catherine said. "That woman who sat next to me was sure a piece of work!"

"Yes, isn't she something?" Barb said, smiling. "I guess I should have warned you about her. Eldeen comes on a little too strong for some people's tastes, but she's sure got a big heart." Barb shook her head, still smiling. "How did you enjoy Margaret's lesson?" she asked. "Isn't she a good teacher? You'd think she'd been teaching her whole life, but actually she's been taking some courses in poetry over in Greenville just in the last several months and is teaching us what she's been learning. Of course, she's read and studied poetry on her own since she was a little girl."

"Well, I can't say I agreed with everything I heard," Catherine said. She suddenly remembered what she had been thinking earlier that morning and by way of illustration added, "For example, I think it's really stretching it to say you can make yourself feel a certain way just by *acting* that way." When Barb looked a little puzzled, Catherine continued. "You said that. You said you could make up your mind to be a certain way, and if you started acting that way, that's what you'd be."

Barb's face cleared. "Oh, that," she said. "Well, yes, I guess I did say that. And I believe it, only it's not quite that simple." She stepped off the curb and started across the street, walking gingerly on her tiptoes. "I was talking more about things you know you ought to change. You know what I mean—things like . . . well, here, let me get real specific."

She stopped talking for a few moments until she had walked right into Catherine's yard and stood only two or three feet from her. "I used to get really irritable when Curtis got emergency calls at home," she said, "and I'd take it out on everybody. The last thing he'd remember me saying as he headed off to his office or to the hospital didn't have anything to do with the poor kid who was going through some kind of trauma—or the kid's parents, who were probably in even worse shape. It was always about how much I needed him at home to do this or that or how I'd counted on being able to go out for dinner or a hundred other things I wanted. I knew it wasn't the right response, but I kept on doing it. And I'd get grumpy with the children and go around feeling sorry for myself for hours because my plans had been ruined."

Catherine hadn't expected Barb to launch off into a True Confession story, but at the same time she found it interesting. She enjoyed hearing about other people's problems, and, besides that, she'd always wondered what it was like being a doctor's wife. In fact, whenever people asked her what her husband did, Catherine always wished she could say breezily, "Oh, he's a doctor" or "He's a lawyer" instead of having to say he was the training supervisor at a tool and die company. It didn't matter that Blake knew every job at Forrest Bonner inside and out from design to production, that next to the owner and president, he held the highest position in the whole operation. It still wasn't what Catherine considered a prestigious job, and she always cringed whenever she sensed that someone was about to ask her where her husband worked.

"Then one Wednesday night," Barb continued, "when our pastor was teaching a series about living with your spouse's limitations, he really stepped on my toes. I even accused Curtis of telling him what to preach about. See, I knew Curtis was going to be a doctor before I married him, and I knew doctors had to make room in their schedules for accidents and all, and I knew it wasn't anybody's fault when he got an emergency call, so I *knew* all the right things in my head, but I kept letting my emotions get in the way. Anyway, Brother Hawthorne said a person couldn't use his feelings as an excuse for doing something wrong. He said, 'Show me a person who lets his emotions rule him, and I'll show you a person who has shoved God out of his life.' And he said a good way to stop being selfish and start correcting a fault was to use your head instead of your feelings and just start *doing* what you knew was right. So I started praying about it and really working on it, and I think I just about gave Curtis a heart attack the next time he got an emergency call at home."

All this talk about preaching and praying might have gotten on Catherine's nerves at any other time, but since Barb was telling it all so good-naturedly and like a story, it wasn't as annoying as it could have been. As Barb paused to smile, Catherine noticed for the first time that her hair, which was light brown with blond streaks in it, appeared to be not so much blonde at the temples as *gray*—or at least graying. If she didn't wear it pulled back on the sides that way, it wouldn't show up nearly as much.

Catherine watched her ponytail swing back and forth as she shook her head.

"It must have been two or three years ago now," Barb said. "It was at our other house in Derby, and Curtis was outside with Josh and Caleb staining the deck when his beeper went off. After he came inside and returned the call, he came to tell me, and I could see it in his eyes how much he dreaded it." Barb folded her arms and looked down at her bare feet for a second. "But I had made up my mind that I was going to respond the right way this time, and when he told me, I gave him a big hug and told him how proud I was that he could be the one to help this other family. And I told him I'd be waiting for him when he got home." Barb laughed. "Like I said, he almost keeled over."

"And I guess when he came home you met him at the door with his slippers and bathrobe and a big piece of apple pie," Catherine said.

"No, I think it was cherry," Barb said, smiling. "That's his favorite."

"Well, that's a real sweet little story," Catherine said. "But I still think you're going overboard to say you can change just by putting on an act."

"No, you can't put on an act for very long," Barb said. "You're right about that. I think everybody would see right through you. But my point is that you can *act right* until it becomes second nature. See, I didn't *feel* happy about him leaving home that day, so nothing had changed about that, but I decided to say the right words and do the right thing anyway. And the next time I did the same thing, and the next and the next, until pretty soon it wasn't so hard anymore. And I actually started putting myself in the mother's place whose kid was sick or hurt, trying to feel what she was going through. And one day I realized that I was responding the right way almost automatically. So in that one little area, you see, I had rerouted my feelings and changed my behavior. Not that it was easy. There was a lot of thought and prayer that went into it. And I'm not saying I haven't slipped a few times."

She sighed. "It gets awful tiresome sometimes trying to keep supper warm when his appointments run late because some woman brought in her four other children instead of just the one she'd made an appointment for. Or when your anniversary has to be postponed or one of your own kids needs a father's firm hand, if you know what I mean. Or something needs to be fixed, and he can't get around to even looking at it." Barb wrinkled her nose. "I can't begin to count how many times we've had to cancel plans for the evening because something came up. We've gotten to where we hardly ever make evening plans anymore. It's easier that way."

Catherine stared hard at Barb's friendly face. There was something about this woman that definitely rubbed her the wrong way, yet she couldn't bring herself to really *dislike* her altogether. She seemed to be so honest and open about everything. And she wasn't really pushy, which was definitely in her favor. If there was anything Catherine hated, it was a pushy woman.

"Curtis and I have been Christians only about five years," Barb added, "so we're still learning. I hope I don't sound like I'm patting myself on the back, because for every little thing I fix with the Lord's help, I see umpteen others I need to work on!"

"Yes, well, anyway," Catherine said, but she didn't know what else to say. She didn't want Barb to get started talking about *the Lord*, like Dottie Puckett was so fond of doing at the Be-Beautiful Style Shoppe. And she sure wasn't going to start telling her own story of "My Problem and How I Solved It." In fact, she couldn't even think of a problem she had solved lately.

"Do you and your husband go to church anywhere?" Barb asked.

Catherine's answer was a single, emphatic syllable. "No!"

"Well, maybe some Sunday you could—"

Catherine cut her off and said tersely, "No, we don't go in for that kind of thing." She took a step back, fanning herself with the folded newspaper. "I've got to go now. I've got a stack of things to do inside."

"Believe me, I understand perfectly," Barb said. "I've still got boxes to go through and unpack. And then with school starting in just a few days, I don't know when I'm going to find time to get the kids ready for that. My boys have outgrown almost every stitch of clothing they have, and I've just got to break down and take them shopping. Are your sons in the same fix?"

"The way boys dress nowadays, I don't see how they could ever really outgrow anything!" Catherine said. "Hardy buys clothes that practically fall off him!"

Barb smiled. "How old is Hardy anyway?"

"Sixteen," Catherine said.

"What grade?"

"Tenth," and then, worried that Barb would think he had failed a grade, she added, "We started him a year late in kindergarten." Catherine didn't tell her that after two weeks in kindergarten when he was five, the teacher and principal had called Blake and her in and asked them to consider keeping Hardy at home for another year—"until he's more socially mature" is how they had put it. Catherine still remembered the glazed look on the face of the teacher as Blake had asked her what the problem was. And she still remembered the inept woman's answer after all these years: "Hardy upsets the other children." "Well, they probably upset *him*, too!" she had wanted to scream. Here she had looked forward all this time to sending Hardy off to school for the whole morning, and now they were telling her she had to keep him home for another whole year!

"I thought he looked like he was about the same age as my boys," Barb said. "They're sixteen, too. We didn't let them start kindergarten until they were six, and if Curt had had his way, it would have been even later. He thinks boys shouldn't start school till they're seven or eight." She laughed. "Say, maybe they can get together with Hardy sometime. Does he like sports? Joshua and Caleb love basketball and soccer."

"Oh, sure, he likes them okay, especially basketball, but his favorite sports are TV, loud music, and video games! Oh, and skateboarding."

Barb tilted her head, and her smile faded a little. "I guess he goes to Berea High?" she asked.

Catherine nodded. She suddenly remembered that she still hadn't told Blake about the trouble Hardy had gotten into a few weeks ago and the phone call from Morton Hollings, the principal of Berea High.

"Was he on the JV basketball team last year?" Barb asked.

"Yes."

"Then he probably played against my boys," Barb said. "They were at Derby High last year." Catherine saw no need to tell her that Hardy had been benched and then kicked off the team after the third game of the season.

"You have another son and a daughter, too, right?" Barb asked.

Catherine nodded again and sighed. "Oh yes, and the three of them keep me going in circles!" She twirled her finger in the air.

"Being a mother is sure a full-time job," Barb said.

"You can say that again!" said Catherine.

"Being a mother is sure a full-time job," Barb repeated, but Catherine didn't smile. "My boys aren't too excited about switching schools," Barb said. "They liked Derby High a lot. They'll be in tenth grade, too. Do your kids drive yet?"

Catherine was getting tired of all these questions. She sighed and shifted her purse to the other shoulder. "No, they don't," she said curtly. She sure wasn't about to go into all the battles they had fought over *this* subject. While Olivia regularly whined about not having her driver's license, she refused to practice parallel parking so she could go take the driving test. And Blake kept telling Hardy he wouldn't even consider letting him get his driver's license until he showed some improvement in his grades, which would be a cold day in July as far as Catherine was concerned. The idea of Hardy behind the wheel of a car sent cold chills down Catherine's spine. "Well, I really do have to go," she said to Barb.

"Me too," said Barb. "Anyway, I'll tell the boys about Hardy, and maybe they'll come over and kidnap him someday and make him play some basketball with them out in the driveway."

"They're welcome to try," Catherine said. She imagined Hardy getting mad over a missed shot and laying one of the Chewning boys out flat on the driveway as he had done to that other boy a year ago in the last game he'd played. She almost added, "It'll probably be the last time they ask him to do anything!" but she decided not to.

"Don't kids change your perspective?" Barb said. "When I think of who I was before the kids came along, well, I don't even know that person. Isn't motherhood interesting?"

"Oh yes, enthralling," Catherine said. She couldn't help thinking of the multitude of ways her children frustrated her. Yet she knew that if anything happened to one of them, she would curl up and die. Sometimes she found herself almost resenting her own children because she loved them so much. It didn't seem fair. They had all this love they didn't even seem to *want*—love she would have given anything for at their age. Not that anyone would have ever guessed, for she had learned very early how to cover up her emotions. In fact, that's probably where her acting ability started. You could lift your chin, set your jaw, and act like nothing bothered you.

All Those Wrinkles

10

It was a conversation that Catherine overheard between Della Boyd and Philip several days later that made her stop and wonder whether she might have given her sister-in-law a little less credit than she deserved as far as intelligence went. Of course, anybody could tell after meeting Della Boyd for the first time that she didn't exactly carry a membership card for Mensa in her billfold, but then, there were different kinds of intelligence also, Catherine reminded herself.

It was Saturday afternoon, and Catherine had come home after an exhausting shopping trip with Olivia to the mall over in Derby. She had been tempted to just give her a charge card and tell her to buy her own school things and then meet her by the mall entrance at a certain time, but she knew that would never work. Not only would Olivia have bought totally impractical things but she would also have bought six times as much as she needed. As if she really *needed* anything!

During the whole shopping trip, Catherine had harped on the fact that Olivia should be buying her own things the way other kids did who had jobs, and Olivia had kept saying, "I'm saving my money for Myrtle Beach," which was where the cheerleaders were going next April for a national competition. And every time she said it, Catherine thought, Oh, sure you are! She knew for a fact that Olivia had spent most of her life-guarding money this summer on clothes and CDs and movies. And she knew that when it came time for the cheerleaders to go to Myrtle Beach, Olivia would go to Blake for money, and he'd give her any amount she asked for.

It had taken three trips from the car to get all the purchases back to Olivia's room, and the two of them hadn't even spoken to each other the whole time they were going back and forth. Four and a half hours in Olivia's company had put Catherine in a rotten mood, and she had the distinct impression that the feeling was mutual. How could you love your children so intensely, she wondered, yet dislike being with them so much? But she'd rather go on fifteen shopping trips with Olivia than one with Hardy! She had already told Blake that she wasn't having any part of *that* little excursion, that he could take his son out to buy whatever he needed for school. In fact, she decided that's where Blake and Hardy must be now, since Blake's car was gone and she didn't hear Hardy's music downstairs.

When Catherine came into the kitchen a few minutes later to put away the cinnamon rolls she had stopped to get at the bakery, she saw a pie cooling on the counter. She paused to inspect it. It had meringue piled on top, perfectly swirled and browned just right, but there was no way to tell exactly what kind of pie it was. The crust was perfect, too, frilled all around the edge like a picture out of a cookbook.

If Della Boyd had ever once acted the least bit proud of her cooking, Catherine wouldn't have eaten a bite of it. But for the whole ten days she'd been at their house—which felt more like ten weeks to Catherine—Della Boyd had acted like it was a complete miracle that anything she made turned out right, and if Blake complimented her on anything, she'd always change the subject and talk about how *her* biscuits or *her* cake couldn't hold a candle to so-and-so's back in Yazoo City. Why, *that* woman could cook with her eyes closed and her hands tied behind her back. Of course, her modesty sometimes rankled Catherine more than if she just accepted the praise, and twice already she had said, "Oh, Della Boyd, just say thank you and be done with it, for crying out loud!"

Catherine saw that Della Boyd had also ironed several of Blake's shirts while she and Olivia had been gone and had hung them over the top of the pantry door. Blake had told her a couple of times already not to bother doing that since he always sent them to the cleaners, but she had said she didn't mind one bit, that there was actually something about ironing that made her feel satisfied. "All those wrinkles just disappearing like magic," she had said with a look of delight on her face, "why, it makes life's problems seem unimportant. If only everything could work out so smoothly!"

And when Blake had objected again, Catherine had said, "Oh, let her do it if it makes her happy!" She could sure think of better ways to spend that fifteen dollars every couple of weeks than shelling it out to the Clean and Crisp Laundry Service! Besides, in spite of what Blake said, she thought it only right that Della Boyd should pitch in around the house if she was going to be camping out in their spare room for who knew how long.

Something caught Catherine's eye through the kitchen window, and looking out into the backyard, she was surprised to see Della Boyd sitting under the magnolia tree in a lawn chair that she had obviously moved from the patio. At least she guessed it was Della Boyd. She was facing the trunk of the tree so that Catherine could see her only from the back. The magnolia was so big its branches reached all the way to the ground. Della Boyd wasn't really sitting under it as much as she was sitting inside it. On the side facing the house there was a gap in the branches, which looked like a little doorway or a cave opening, and there sat Della Boyd in the lawn chair. For the life of her, Catherine couldn't figure out what she'd be doing a thing like that for on a hot August day.

She walked into the den, quietly slid back the glass door to the backyard, and stepped out onto the patio. Kinko, who was lying against the house in a little hollow place he had dug, raised his head and stared at Catherine. If it had been Blake standing there instead of her, she knew Kinko would have bounded up joyfully and cavorted about in a frenzied greeting. And Blake would have carried on just as enthusiastically, as if he hadn't seen the dog only a few hours earlier. The whole family knew Kinko was Blake's dog even though he had supposedly brought him home for the children several years ago. They had tried other names before Blake had suggested the name of the duplicating chain store, pointing out that the puppy was an exact copy of its father, a shepherd-chow mix. Kinko had finally learned to leave Catherine alone after she had repeatedly whapped him on the nose with a rolled up magazine and said things like, "No, no, no! Stay down! I don't want dog slobber and muddy paws all over my new white pants!"

The air conditioning unit had just kicked on, so she couldn't be sure about it, but she thought she heard Della Boyd talking to someone. Or maybe she was talking to herself—that would be more likely. Or maybe to the birds! It wouldn't surprise Catherine one bit to find Della Boyd carrying on a make-believe conversation with an animal. She walked out into the yard a little way. Yes, she was certain Della Boyd was talking. Changing her angle of approach so she couldn't be seen through the opening in the branches, Catherine kept walking softly until she was only a few feet away from the magnolia tree. It wasn't really that she was intending to eavesdrop, she was just planning to find out what was going on.

". . . if only I'd stopped to think about it," Della Boyd was saying. "And I keep telling myself I should have *known* how you'd feel because I used to be your age, believe it or not, and I had things that anybody else would have considered worthless, but to me they were my own special things, and if anybody had taken them away, I would have lost all desire to live." She stopped for a minute, and Catherine thought she heard something rustling in the branches. Was Della Boyd talking to a squirrel?

"I remember this one thing I had," Della Boyd continued, "and you're not going to understand how I could have been so attached to anything like this, but then I was a little *girl*, you have to remember. It was an old sock I had stuffed with little bits of fabric my mother had left over from her sewing, and I sewed on little eyes and a nose and mouth and stitched up the open end nice and tight and made a little doll out of it. I named her Opal for some reason, and I put clothes on her, even though she didn't have much of a shape at all—and no arms, of course. She was just a tube with a bend in the middle where the heel of the sock was." Catherine heard more rustling and a low-pitched noise that sounded like a soft growl. Maybe the Thorndikes' tomcat was up in the tree.

"And one day a man came over to see my daddy about a crop-dusting job," Della Boyd said, "and he had a goat in the back of his pickup truck. For some reason I wanted a closer look at that goat, and I climbed up on the back of his truck while he and Daddy were talking inside, and I accidentally dropped Opal over the tailgate. Quicker than anything, that old goat snatched up my doll and started chewing on her, and I ran inside screaming like I'd been shot." Della Boyd paused reflectively, then said, "Of course, I guess you don't go running anywhere after you've been shot, do you?" She stopped again for several moments. "That goat snatched Opal right up and was *chewing* on her," she said quietly. Then she paused again.

Well, go on, Catherine thought irritably. Finish the story—did you get the stupid doll back? She was beginning to feel hot standing out in the sun, and she wanted to get back inside where it was cool. She found herself not caring much anymore who it was Della Boyd was talking to. She could be talking to the Jolly Green Giant for all she cared.

But she caught her breath in surprise a second later when she heard a voice from the branches overhead say, "So what happened? Did the goat eat it up?" Catherine knew exactly whose voice it was, but she thought Philip had given up climbing trees years ago. She remembered how much time he used to spend up in this tree when he was younger, but all he seemed to want to do now that he was almost thirteen was play Nintendo or watch television or hang around the pool where Olivia worked. Yet here he was up in the magnolia, listening to Della Boyd ramble on and on about an old sock doll that got mutilated by a billy goat! Catherine had no idea how that had come to happen.

"He shredded it to bits," Della Boyd said. "When I got back out there to the pickup truck, Opal was . . . well, she was past repair. I grieved over that doll for weeks, and it didn't even help when my mother tried making me another one, which was nicer in a lot of ways than Opal ever was. This one had arms, I remember, and Mother even glued yarn all over her head to look like hair. But you see, she wasn't Opal—and I never did take to her." Catherine heard Della Boyd sigh. "I've never liked goats," she said, then repeated, "I never did take to that new doll."

Catherine felt like charging in, waving her arms, and crying, "Okay, okay, enough! Great day in the morning, it's too hot to be outside in the middle of the day!" But she was glad she kept quiet or she would have missed out on what came next—the thing that made her reassess Della Boyd's intelligence.

"But it's different," Philip said. "Your mom didn't sneak into your room and take your stuff without asking you." Catherine was startled at how angry he sounded. She had expected the initial temper tantrum when he had first seen his clean bedroom, of course, and she had known he'd probably not speak to her for days, but frankly, that part didn't much bother her. She was used to her children's sullen silences. One of them was always mad about one thing or another. What surprised her now was how fresh Philip's anger sounded. Good grief! It had all happened over a week ago!

"That's not the point," Della Boyd said. "I'm just saying that I know how you feel, because all my life, starting when I was younger than you, I've lost things that meant a lot to me. It hurts to lose special things, and it doesn't matter how you lose them—it still hurts. That's all I'm saying right now. That's my first point, and if you don't understand that, then I can't go on to the next one, but if you do understand, then I'll keep going . . . if you don't mind, that is."

Catherine heard something drop to the ground, like a stick or rock, and after a little pause Philip said, "Yeah, okay, okay." She could hardly believe it. She couldn't begin to count the number of times Philip had walked out of the room while she was talking to him, yet here he was sitting in a tree listening to his aunt talk up a blue streak, telling her he was ready for her next point!

"All right, number two," Della Boyd said. "If you're going to be mad at your mother, you'll have to be mad at me, too, because I was the one who helped throw all those things away. It was these hands right here that pulled things off your shelves and out of your closet and set them in the hallway and then helped your mother take them to the . . . to dispose of them. And I'm sorry about it, I surely am. I do remember hoping that nothing we were throwing away was anything important, but I kept thinking how much you were going to like your nice, clean room, and I just went ahead and kept piling things in the hall."

"But *she* told you to do it! And she doesn't even care! At least you're sorry, but she's not! She's just mean and . . . ."

At the same moment Catherine felt a shudder come over her from Philip's words, she heard Della Boyd catch her breath, and she must have stood up suddenly because when Catherine leaned sideways to peer through the opening in the branches, she saw that the lawn chair had been knocked over backward and Della Boyd was standing and looking straight up into the branches above her. "Don't say that!" Della Boyd's voice sounded shaky all of a sudden. "Don't ever say things like that about your parents, Philip!"

"But it's true. She doesn't—"

"I don't want to hear it!" Della Boyd was breathing hard. She busied herself for several moments picking up the lawn chair and getting herself reseated. Then in a low voice she resumed. "People have different ways of showing their feelings, Philip, and you're old enough to know that. Your mother *does* care, and she didn't clean out your room to be mean. If you can't see how much she loves you, well, then you . . . well, just the way she looks at you children sometimes, why, anybody can tell she . . . she just can't . . . ."

". . . can't stand us," Philip said.

"No, no. Hush now. She just can't . . . find a way to say how proud she is of you. I think she's especially proud of you because you . . . well, you're the youngest, of course, but also you learn things so fast, and you've always been a cheerful boy and such a good-looking one, too. And I know she's tickled to pieces that you got her red hair. I just wish you could see the way she looks at you sometimes. Then you'd know how proud she is. It's written all over her face."

Philip grunted as if in disbelief but didn't say anything. Catherine wasn't sure she liked the idea of Della Boyd observing the expression on her face when she looked at the children, and she wondered when it had happened. Della Boyd always seemed so out of touch with the present that such a thing didn't even seem possible.

"There's all kinds of parents, Philip," Della Boyd continued. "Some of them go around saying things like 'I love you' and 'You're so smart' and 'You sure did a good job' so much that it all sort of loses its meaning after a while. And then others hardly ever say those things even though they feel them. It could be they feel them a lot more than those other parents, but it's just not their way to go around talking like that."

"She's always on my case about something," Philip said.

"But it's just not their way to go around talking like that," Della Boyd repeated. "And if that were your mother's way, you'd probably be sitting up there grumbling about how you wish she wouldn't gush all the time, about how embarrassing it is the way she always carries on over you. There's all kinds of different parents, Philip."

"Well, why can't she just be in the middle?" Philip said, and then, as if getting his argument back on track, he raised his voice and said, "Why'd she have to throw all my stuff away?"

"She didn't *have* to," Della Boyd said. "In fact, I'm going to be real direct with you, Philip. If you kept your room like your father used to keep his at your age, your mother wouldn't have had to set up an all-day cleaning session the way she did last week. My advice is, if you want to keep your treasures from getting tampered with, then keep things picked up and in order in your bedroom so your mother doesn't feel ill every time she passes your door. There, that's my advice. And that was my third point. I'm sorry it had to be so blunt, but it's the truth." And then, as if wrapping up a school lesson, she summarized, "Number one, I understand exactly how you feel. Number two, I'm sorry for my part in it. And number three, if you keep your room neat, I don't think it will happen again. There now."

Catherine was filled with surprise. She hadn't thought Della Boyd capable of organizing a three-point outline and delivering it with such boldness. And it all made perfect sense—that was the real shocker. It was clear that she had underestimated her sister-in-law. Della Boyd had a few more active brain cells than Catherine had assumed.

Philip didn't say a word in response, but Della Boyd didn't seem to expect him to, for she added immediately, "I'm going inside now," and Catherine heard a soft metallic scrape as she folded up the lawn chair. Realizing all of a sudden that she couldn't make it back to the house without being seen, Catherine walked quickly to the other side of the magnolia tree to hide from view. Della Boyd paused to say one more thing before heading back to the house. "And tonight at supper, Philip, why don't you tell that interesting story you told me the other day about what the man at the swimming pool said? I think it would make your mother happy for you to start talking again at the table." Then she turned and left.

Catherine listened until she heard Della Boyd open the sliding door by the patio and close it again. After waiting a few more seconds to be sure Philip wasn't coming down right away, Catherine quickly made her way to the side yard, past the fence where Della Boyd had planted the iris bulbs, and went into the house through the front door. All the way from the backyard into the house, Catherine tried to sort through what she had overheard. She never would have expected Della Boyd to stick up for her like that, and she didn't really know if she approved of everything she had said, but still, she couldn't help feeling a small flash of gratitude. Della Boyd might be irritating in a lot of ways, but she had sure taken Philip down a notch or two. And wonder of wonders, he had actually seemed to listen to her!

One thought troubled her, though. Philip had said she was mean, and even though it had come from the mouth of a twelve-year-old, it still bothered her, especially since the twelve-year-old was her son and he had been talking about her. Of course, Blake had told her she had a mean streak before, but that was different. Blake was just naturally critical, and she had grown used to his unflattering comments. But it was a whole lot worse overhearing your son calling you mean than having your husband say it to your face in the heat of an argument. Philip just didn't know what *mean* was. He had never heard his own mother tell him she wished he'd never been born. He had never been locked out of his own house or been accused of pretending when he came home early from school with the flu. He had never been ignored or called stupid by his own parents. The only thing *he* had suffered was a clean bedroom!

"Oh, Catherine, you're home!" Della Boyd was putting the pie into the refrigerator as Catherine walked into the kitchen. "How did the shopping trip go?"

"Well, the best thing about it is it's over!" Catherine said. "Did Blake take Hardy out? I don't know why he didn't go ahead and take Philip, too." Then, hoping Della Boyd hadn't noticed her slip, she asked, "Or did he?"

"No, he said he'd wait till Monday for Philip," Della Boyd said. "I don't think he and Hardy will be gone long, though. The only place Hardy wanted to go was the Salvation Army store."

"Oh, I might have expected that!" Catherine said. "And I imagine Blake will just stand by and let him get as many of those tacky old clothes as he wants."

"Aren't teenagers curious?" Della Boyd laughed, then repeated, "Blake said he'd wait and take Philip out on Monday."

"Well, nothing like putting it off till the last possible day," Catherine said. "School starts on Tuesday!"

"He said he'd better not try taking them both at the same time," Della Boyd said. "He said he did that last year and regretted it." She disappeared down the hall to the laundry closet and came back a minute later carrying a load of towels to be folded. "You know, it's the strangest thing," she said, emptying the towels onto the kitchen table, "but I can't remember taking Blake shopping for school clothes every year." She picked up a yellow towel and held it against her cheek. "I always like the way warm towels feel straight out of the dryer, don't you?"

Catherine watched her fold towels for a while with a slow, dancelike grace. When she was working at anything, Catherine had noticed that Della Boyd always seemed to retreat into another world. A faraway look would settle in her eyes, and Catherine knew if she snapped her fingers in front of her and said, "Quick, tell me who the president of the United States is!" Della Boyd would probably respond dreamily with something like "Claude Debussy."

"Maybe Blake never got any new clothes," Catherine said. "He wasn't exactly the best-dressed boy on campus at Ole Miss, you know." Catherine remembered vividly trying to educate Blake about clothes. She had finally been forced to take a ratty old blue sweater he loved to wear and sneak it into a trash bin.

Della Boyd stopped folding and looked briefly confused, as if trying to process Catherine's remark. "Oh no, he got new clothes," she said at length. "I used to take him to the JCPenney store in Jackson, I remember. Daddy had set up an account down there before he died because he knew the manager of the store. They had been in the service together. And that man was always so nice to us after we lost Daddy—Mr. Gurvritch was his name. He was Jewish, which was funny because he wasn't at all stingy like some people say Jews are. He would mark down the things we bought and slip in a little something extra every time." She folded one of the beach towels Philip took to the pool and then repeated, "Oh yes, Blake got new clothes, but not many. And not *every* year before school started." She looked straight at Catherine. "I'll never forget how nice Mr. Gurvritch was after we lost Daddy. Such a kind man."

Catherine remembered Della Boyd's words to Philip out in the backyard: *"It hurts to lose special things, and it doesn't matter how you lose them— it still hurts."*

"How old were you, Della Boyd, when you lost your father—seventeen, eighteen? What was it?" Catherine knew Blake had told her the story time after time when they were dating, but she couldn't recall all the details now.

"Nineteen," Della Boyd said. "And seventeen when Mother died."

"And how old were the two of them?"

"Mother was only thirty-eight. The doctor had warned her about trying to carry another baby with all her physical problems, but she was so thrilled about it that she wouldn't listen. I remember how happy she was the whole time she was carrying Blake. But she had a lot of trouble when he was born." Della Boyd set another folded towel on top of the stack and pressed the whole stack down with both hands. "She only got to hold him one time before she died," she said, then added, "It was a hard time. He cried almost solid for the first few months." She picked up another towel to fold. "He had colic."

"And you took care of him."

Della Boyd nodded and smiled. "Oh yes, I took care of him. It was like having a baby of my own in a lot of ways, I guess."

Catherine thought back to when she was seventeen, living in Biloxi, Mississippi. She was in the eleventh grade and had a lead role in *The Pirates of Penzance* that spring, another performance her parents hadn't made it to. She tried to imagine what she would have done if someone had told her she had to drop out of the play and quit school to take care of a colicky newborn brother. But, of course, her mother never would have had another baby. "I should have stopped after I had Patricia," she had told Catherine more than once.

Della Boyd picked up the stack of towels to take back to the bathroom. "And then Daddy died when he was forty-one, and Blake was only two," she said. "So it was just Blake and me left. Just the two of us."

Catherine watched her walk out of the kitchen. She heard her still talking as she made her way down the hallway. "Just the two of us, Blake and me. He was only two, so he was into everything, and . . ." Her voice grew fainter until Catherine couldn't make out what she was saying. She wondered briefly if it was her imagination, or if she really did keep missing the ends of what people said. In Della Boyd's case, though, it wouldn't matter since she was probably just repeating something she'd already said.

Catherine had a sudden vision of Blake in his mother's arms only moments before she died. She saw him then as a toddler holding Della Boyd's hand trustingly. And as she stood in the empty kitchen, she wondered if *her* mother had even wanted to hold her when she was first born. She couldn't remember that she had ever sat in her mother's lap or held her hand. She wondered if her mother had ever helped her get dressed or comb her hair.

The Very Tip

11

That night at supper, which was later than usual, Philip did talk. So much, in fact, that Hardy finally said, "Okay, Flip, let's play the Quiet Game. How about if you count to a hundred trillion in your head?" Philip hated to be called Flip, and Catherine saw him move in such a way that she was sure he had tried to kick Hardy under the table. Hardy leaned forward and said, "Sorry, Flip. It takes coordination, which you're a little short on. But then, you're a little short, period."

Catherine wasn't sure how much of Philip's change of mood was due to Della Boyd's talk under the magnolia tree that afternoon and how much was due to the excitement in the neighborhood just two hours earlier when a small airplane had crashed in the open field behind the Partridges' house three blocks down the street. Philip's friend Andy Partridge, who was shooting his BB gun out in his backyard, had seen the whole thing and called Philip as soon as it happened. A whole parade of ambulances, fire trucks, police cars, and news vans raced up and down Brookside after that, as did half of Berea's population, who just wanted to gawk.

So that's what they were talking about around the table at supper while they ate the ham Catherine had heated up and the macaroni and cheese and green bean casserole Della Boyd had made. They had all walked down the street at various times to take a look, except for Della Boyd, who said she was afraid she couldn't get to sleep that night if she saw a tragedy up close. And it didn't matter that they told her nobody was killed, that before the plane caught on fire both the pilot and his wife had gotten out and were taken to the hospital fully conscious, apparently with only minor bumps and scratches.

"But they lost their plane," she had said. So she spent all afternoon in the kitchen instead, cooking and reading old issues of *Reader's Digest*, which was her favorite reading material. The morning a week ago when Della Boyd had discovered the whole shelf of *Reader's Digest* back issues in the den bookcase, she had carried on to such an extent that Catherine had finally said, "Well, for pete's sake, calm down. It's just a few little magazines, not the hanging gardens of Babylon!"

It was really the fire she didn't want to see. Catherine had heard Blake explaining it quietly to Philip out in the hall when Philip had come running home, shouting for everyone to come down to the Partridges' to see the crash. Of course the fire trucks had come right away and put out the fire, so that part didn't last all that long. "But it would still remind her of her house burning down," he had told Philip, then added, "And of course, our father was killed in a plane crash, so she'd be thinking about that, too."

"And they were on their way from like *Saluda* to—where?—*Landrum* or somewhere for *supper?*" Olivia was saying now. "Weird."

"I heard somebody say it was their anniversary," Blake said. "That's what the pilot told somebody before they took him off in the ambulance. He was taking her out for dinner."

"Weird," Olivia repeated.

Catherine agreed. She could sure think of nicer places to go for an anniversary dinner than Landrum, South Carolina! She wondered where they were planning to eat—at Burger King? Or maybe Taco Bell?

"Well, I still can't believe the two of them were really married," Catherine said. "The woman didn't even look like an American, and she was a lot younger than the pilot. She looked like she was from Pakistan or India or one of those countries around there."

They all stared at her for a few moments before Hardy broke the silence. "Personally, I think she was from Sri Lanka," he said, clicking his tongue in a womanish way and laying an index finger against his chin. "Or maybe Nepal. But definitely not Burma—her forehead wasn't right for Burma. Bangladesh is a possibility. Yes, the earlobes looked like Bangladesh."

Catherine shot him a withering look. "No need to be a smart aleck just because I happen to be a lot more observant than the rest of you."

Blake looked annoyed. "How could you tell anything about her? She was lying flat on a stretcher, and we were standing thirty or forty feet away!"

"Oh, I could tell," Catherine said. "Anybody with eyes could tell."

"Well, even if it were true, who cares?" Blake said. "You think they're going to put that in the headlines—'American Man and Foreign-Looking Wife Crash in Berea'?"

Olivia laughed out loud, and Catherine fumed silently. Olivia knew how to get on her father's good side, always laughing at things Blake said, most of which weren't even remotely funny.

For a while no one spoke. Catherine saw that Philip had separated the mushrooms out of his green bean casserole and was now scrutinizing a forkful of macaroni and cheese.

"Just eat your supper, Philip," Catherine said. "Don't dissect it."

"This macaroni is different from what you usually make." Philip put it in his mouth hesitantly and chewed slowly. Catherine took it as a compliment and smiled.

"That's because Aunt Della made it," Olivia said. "And she didn't use a box like Mom does. She grated real cheese and everything."

"I like it," Philip said. "It's good. This is the kind Andy's mom makes."

"Well, Andy's mom doesn't have any outside interests!" Catherine snapped. "I think Wilma Partridge sets up a cot and *sleeps* in her kitchen."

"Maybe that woman in the airplane was from another country but considered herself an American," Della Boyd said. "I knew a man in Yazoo City who was from Cyprus, but he was an American, too—Mr. Charalambous. He'd gone through all the steps to be a citizen and could vote and everything. He ran a little restaurant downtown."

Hardy gasped, his fork poised in midair with five large bites of ham speared on it. "Did he have *dark skin*? And they let him run a *restaurant*? And *vote*?"

"Not so very dark, no," Della Boyd said. "But the blackest hair and a thick handlebar mustache. He had an accent and talked real fast, I remember that. Yes, I'm quite sure he voted. He really liked Ronald Reagan, as I remember."

"Never mind, Della Boyd," Catherine said. "Hardy's just trying to make fun of me. I happen to think the nationalities were intended to be kept *separate* instead of all mixed up like a big pot of goulash! Foolish me, I'm of the mind that white people should marry white people and Negroes should marry Negroes and Orientals should marry Orientals."

Hardy nodded vigorously. "And Swiss mountain climbers should marry Swiss mountain climbers, and Russian spies should marry Russian spies, and Siamese twins should marry Siamese twins, and . . ."

"Okay, that's enough," Blake said. "Don't talk with your mouth full."

"Andy's mom said she didn't see why those two people weren't killed," Philip interrupted, eager to get back to the subject of the crash itself. "The plane ripped right through some trees in the field and ended up sideways. Andy saw the wing get torn off—this one up here, the right one." As he talked, Philip stretched out his arms and imitated the movement of the plane. "And Andy's mom said if it hadn't landed where it did, it could have smashed into some houses or cars and killed some people."

"Ooh, that's scary," Hardy said. "Say it all again."

Philip made a face at Hardy, then said, "Hey, Dad, what kind of plane was it your dad was killed in? Was it a little one like that one?"

Blake looked quickly at Della Boyd, but she seemed absorbed in chewing her last bite of food. She was gazing pensively at her empty plate.

"No, Flip, he was crop dusting in a Leer jet," Hardy said.

Della Boyd shook her head and looked up. "No, no. It was what they called a Stearman," she said. "Daddy sure loved that little airplane. Of course, it looked pretty big to me back then. But everything looked big back then—why, I thought Mississippi was the whole world. I had never been more than twenty miles away from home. I had never even been to Jackson or Vicksburg until after Daddy died."

"Pour me some more tea, would you, Olivia?" Blake handed her his glass. "Well, didn't I see a pie around here somewhere? Anybody besides me want dessert?"

Della Boyd got up and walked to the refrigerator.

"And he hit a power line?" Philip asked. Catherine knew Philip didn't need to ask. He had heard the story a hundred times.

"Yes," Blake said. "Here, Philip, help take some of the plates over to the sink."

"It was a new power line," Della Boyd said. "That's the way it was back then. New lines popping up every few days it seemed. It made it real hard for crop dusters."

"You going to make coffee, Catherine?" Blake asked. "Olivia, you could get some clean forks for the pie."

"But wouldn't it just break the line?" asked Philip. "How come it made the plane crash? Wouldn't a plane just go right through?"

"Philip, we'll talk about it some other time," Blake said. "Say, did you buy those steaks to grill on Monday?" He addressed this question to Catherine. "Almost time for the old Labor Day cookout, you know."

As if it were a family tradition, Catherine thought. Last year Blake had played golf all day, and the children were off in three different directions, having their last fling before school started the next day. Catherine had ordered herself a takeout chicken sandwich at Wendy's on her way home from shopping in Greenville, she recalled.

"Yes, I got the steaks for the old Labor Day cookout," she said. "So why *would* it make a plane crash?" she asked, directing her attention to Della Boyd. "Since Blake doesn't seem to know the answer, maybe you do." She had never thought about it before, but Philip's question made her curious. She couldn't remember Blake ever explaining that part before.

"I know the answer, Catherine," Blake said, "but I'd rather not talk about it right now." He was tapping his fingers against the tabletop, and Catherine could tell that his teeth were clamped tight by the way his jaw muscles were working.

"Well, I don't know why not," Catherine said. "Della Boyd doesn't mind talking about it. Do you, Della Boyd?"

"New power lines had sprung up all over the Delta," Della Boyd said, making a wide sweeping motion with her left hand. She had set the pie on the kitchen counter and was looking out the window above the sink, her back to the table. "The crop dusters had to keep an eye out for the poles," she said, "and then they could usually figure out where the wires were before they could even see them. That way they could duck down under and miss hitting them. Some of the time they could miss hitting them." She leaned closer to the window and looked up into the sky. "They couldn't always miss hitting them."

Blake looked at Catherine angrily as if to say, "See what you've done?" Hardy was slumped down in his chair with his eyes closed, though Catherine knew he was following everything that went on. He never missed a trick. Philip was carrying dishes from the table to the sink, one at a time, looking cautiously from Blake to Catherine to Della Boyd. Catherine could tell he wanted to ask more but was afraid to push it.

Catherine handed Della Boyd a knife and pie server. "Here, I guess we could just set the pie in the middle of the table and *look* at it, but if you ever decide to cut it so we can eat it, you might need these." Della Boyd took the knife and looked at it as if she'd never seen one before. Then she glanced over at the pie and seemed to come back to earth. Laying the knife against the meringue, she made a firm, straight cut across the pie. As she lifted out the first piece, Catherine saw that it was a lemon pie.

"Oh, make mine just a small piece," Catherine said. "I would never eat a piece that big unless it was a flavor I really liked."

Olivia gave a sudden yelp of laughter for no apparent reason and said, "I can't believe I belong to this family!"

"Yeah, it gives me a tingly feeling all over, too," said Hardy, his eyes still closed.

After Della Boyd cut three slices of pie, she set the knife down and said, "Oh, I just remembered something," and she left the kitchen abruptly.

Blake spoke almost immediately, in a low, urgent voice. "Okay, no more questions about our father's plane crash. I tried to drop a hint, but nobody seemed to catch on." He looked directly at Catherine when he said this. "It always used to upset her to talk about it, and I don't want that to happen. So let's just change the subject and—"

"But she's *fine*!" Catherine burst out. "It's not bothering her one bit to talk about it! You're the one who's hyperventilating over it. Della Boyd's a big girl now, Blake, and you need to stop tiptoeing around her like she's made of glass!"

"Look, Della Boyd is different from a lot of people," Blake said. "She's more . . . more sensitive or something. I don't know what it is, but she never could even talk about Dad without crying."

"Well, maybe she's gotten over it," Catherine said. "And if she hasn't, she *should*. And maybe she *would* if she didn't have a brother who catered to all her little idiosyncrasies! I mean, good grief, it happened what?— over forty years ago? If she can't talk about it now, then . . ."

Just then Della Boyd came back into the kitchen holding an old snapshot, which she took over to Philip. "Look at this," she said. "I've carried this picture in my billfold for years and years. All my photos got burned up except the ones in my billfold. See, there's Daddy standing by his airplane. My mother took that picture in 1949. I still remember the exact day she took it because they had just bought the camera and both of them wanted to try it out. See, the date's written on the back. June 4, 1949. I would have been thirteen." Della Boyd showed no signs of breaking down, and Catherine looked at Blake smugly. "I don't have but just a few photos left," Della Boyd said again, "and they're the ones I keep in my pocketbook."

Philip sat back down at the table, took the picture, and studied it closely.

"That was a Stearman plane?" he asked.

"It was a Stearman," Della Boyd said, returning to the counter to finish cutting the pie. "I don't know if Blake ever told you or not, but after the war our daddy did some stunt flying in his spare time, but mostly he was a crop duster. There was a big demand for those in Mississippi." She stood for a moment looking at the six pieces of pie she had cut as if she couldn't remember what to do next. "It was a dangerous job," she said, gently laying the pie server in the sink. "Crop dusting was a very dangerous job."

"Well, here, what are we waiting for?" Catherine said, grabbing two saucers and taking them to the table. Della Boyd followed her with two more.

Philip, who was still looking at the photo, said, "So this was the plane that hit the power line? This same one here in the picture?"

Hardy reached over and snatched the photo out of Philip's hand. "Pass it around, Pip," he said. Pip was another name Philip hated, which was why Hardy used it so frequently. Philip squealed with rage and would have lunged for Hardy if Blake hadn't intervened and taken the snapshot himself.

"Ooh, listen to the Pip squeak," Hardy said. Then he picked up his fork, sectioned off half of his slice of lemon pie as a single bite, and stuffed it into his mouth. Hunched over his plate that way, he looked so uncouth that Catherine wondered what other people must think when they saw him eating. She knew he had been taught at some point in the past how to hold a fork, but you'd never know it now.

Della Boyd spoke as she placed her own piece of pie on the table and sat down slowly. "Yes, that was the plane. That was the one Daddy was in the day he hit the power line. You see, sometimes crop dusters would hit a wire before they even knew it, and it might break off part of the propeller or a wing or the tail, and then the plane would start shaking and stall out. And then sometimes when they saw the wire too late to miss it, they'd try to give the engine extra gas so they could just cut through. Broken lines were a real inconvenience for the electric company, of course, but at least they could be fixed up as good as new." She paused and shook her head. "A power line could be fixed up, but a plane that crashed couldn't always be." As Della Boyd talked, she gestured gracefully with her hands.

Catherine watched her with a twinge of envy. She knew Della Boyd had never had an acting lesson in her life, and yet there she sat moving her hands so freely—and naturally! Of course, she wasn't *thinking* about her hands, and that made the difference. And she wasn't sitting in a classroom with a picky teacher waiting to pounce on any false move nor standing on a stage with an audience full of critical people watching her.

Getting the gestures right had always been hard for Catherine, though she would never have admitted it aloud. She'd had a teacher at Ole Miss, a tiresome old codger named Dr. Harold Mulligan, who had often complained about what he called her "formulaic gestures" and her failure to "dig for the motivation" of the feeling she was trying to portray. "Your hands are an extension of your heart," he was always saying, and "Quit acting prettily and act *sensibly*." His favorite word was *sensibility*, and he loved to quote from some ancient, obscure textbook he carried around under his arm like a Bible.

Catherine could still remember the sentence that seemed to come out of Dr. Mulligan's mouth every time he opened it: "Sensibility combines with intelligence to take possession of an actor so that even his slightest movement is an authentic accent of his emotion." All the theatre arts majors had to memorize that sentence by the end of the first week of Dr. Mulligan's class. Catherine thought it was a stupid sentence and was fond of saying things like "It sure would be nice if that man had even the faintest little glimmer of a sense of humor!"

The ironic thing was that when she had mimicked Dr. Mulligan in college, it was his gestures more than his tonal inflections that she had captured most accurately—his habit of holding both index fingers straight up in front of him like two little candles when he was stressing something he thought was important, his making fists of both hands and bumping his knuckles together when he gazed off to the corner of the room in contemplation, his crisscrossing the air with his right hand as if drawing an *X* when he bellowed, "No, no, no. You cannot do it that way!"

"So the wire broke his propeller?" Philip asked. Catherine saw him glance uncertainly at Blake, who sighed but said nothing.

Della Boyd set her fork down. She had eaten only the very tip off her slice of pie. "When it was too late to miss the line," she said with great deliberation, "the pilot would try to gain full speed to break through."

"You already said that," Catherine said. Why Della Boyd thought she had to repeat everything was beyond her.

Della Boyd continued slowly, as if weighing every word. "The way it was told to me, Daddy increased his speed, trying to break the wire, but it wouldn't break. The plane kept straining forward and the line kept on stretching and stretching, but it wouldn't break. It just wouldn't break. Then finally I guess the power line won and the engine just had more than it could take because according to the report—you see, there were three or four men who witnessed it—the plane all of a sudden shot backward." Della Boyd rearranged her napkin in her lap, then added, "They said it looked like a giant slingshot."

There wasn't a sound at the table for several seconds as everyone stopped eating and tried to absorb this information. They all stared at Della Boyd. "Daddy landed in the top of a pecan tree," she said.

Then Catherine heard a brief hack of laughter and realized it had come from her. She covered her mouth to smother another burst of laughter and saw Olivia looking at her in disgust. But she couldn't help it. The scene in her mind was like a cartoon. Daffy Duck—that was it. Daffy

Duck was the pilot, wearing goggles in an open cockpit. His little plane rammed into a power line, which kept stretching out for miles and miles like a giant rubber band, and then with a mighty BOING! the little red biplane whizzed backward and Daffy went flying up into the air, somersaulting over and over until he landed with his goggles all cockeyed amid an explosion of stars in the branches of a pecan tree, jarring the tree so much that a whole truckload of pecans dropped to the ground like hailstones.

Catherine put both hands over her mouth in an attempt to stifle her laughter, but she couldn't get the picture out of her mind. But even while she was laughing, it made her a little mad that she was the only one who seemed to find it funny. Even Hardy sat there looking at her poker-faced. Normally he'd be the first one to crack a joke about such a story as the one Della Boyd had just told. And the look on Blake's face as he scowled at her was so close to hatred that she didn't know what else to call it.

Strangely enough, it was Della Boyd who came to her rescue. And for the second time that day Catherine was amazed at the good sense her sister-in-law sometimes displayed. "You know, I can see how it must sound funny to anybody who wasn't involved," Della Boyd said. "In fact, this is going to sound . . . well . . . odd, I guess, but I used to wake up in the night sometimes and realize I had just dreamed about Daddy's accident, but instead of seeing it like a spectator, it had all happened to *me*. I was the pilot, but I didn't know how to fly an airplane! Nobody had ever taught me, and here I was trying to control a plane that had run into a power line. And here's another really odd thing—in the first part of the dream I wasn't myself but some kind of little comedian, but not really a real person like Charlie Chaplin, but something make-believe, like . . . like . . ."

"Daffy Duck," Catherine said.

"Well, maybe that's it. Yes, maybe one of those characters in the cartoons. It's hard to explain, but it wasn't real, any of it, and I wasn't a real *person*. And when I'd land in the top of the tree in my dream, I'd hear people laughing."

Catherine took her hands away from her mouth. She wasn't laughing anymore, but even if she were, it wouldn't matter. "See," she wanted to say to Blake and the others, "Della Boyd can see the funny side to it, so why can't you?" She saw Hardy studying Della Boyd thoughtfully as he jammed another huge bite of pie into his mouth.

"I'd be in the top of the tree," Della Boyd said, "and I'd hear them laughing and laughing. At first it sounded real happy and innocent, but then they'd keep laughing so hard and so long until it finally turned real ugly and crazy, like something in a horror show, and that's what would wake me up—the crazy laughter." She picked up her fork again and prepared to cut another bite of her pie. "I sure didn't like that dream," she said, then looked at Catherine. "But I can see how it sounds when you hear it for the first time. I really can see it—it doesn't sound like something that could really happen, does it? An airplane getting thrown backward that way."

Catherine almost started laughing again until Della Boyd added, "Daddy's neck was broken when he landed in the pecan tree." Suddenly the whole thing didn't seem nearly so funny to Catherine as it had a minute earlier.

"You never told me about all that, Sister," Blake said. "I just thought his plane hit a power line and crashed. I didn't know about the rest."

"Well, I never saw the need to tell you," she said. "You were only two when it happened. And when you got older, well, I just never saw the need. There are some things a child doesn't need to know."

As Catherine took another bite of her pie, she saw that Hardy's slice was now gone, even the crust, which she had never known him to eat before. She watched him scrape his fork across his saucer to pick up the last few crumbs. And she nearly fell off her chair a few seconds later when she heard him say, "Good stuff, Auntie Deeb." Catherine couldn't remember the last time Hardy had paid somebody a compliment. And she couldn't help resenting it, along with the tone of affectionate teasing Hardy had begun to use with Della Boyd. Catherine wished he would just call her plain Aunt Della Boyd, but for several days after her arrival, he had called her Auntie Della Boyd, then Auntie D. B., and now it had turned into Auntie Deeb.

"Why, thank you, Hardy, honey," Della Boyd said, waving her hand in a self-deprecating way. "That's mighty sweet, but I sure wish you could taste Jeanine Callahan's lemon meringue pie. She used to bring one to the potluck the hospital volunteers would have every year back in Yazoo City. Now *that* was a lemon pie."

"Yeah, well since I don't know this Jeanine Callahan babe, can I have another piece of your crummy imitation?" Hardy asked, and Della Boyd laughed as if she'd never heard anything so funny in her whole life.

The Middle of the Day

12

On the following Monday morning, Labor Day, Catherine heard Blake calling "Della Boyd? Della Boyd? Sister?" as he went through the house. And she heard Della Boyd's voice, distant yet pleasant, replying, "I'm out here, Blake."

She was out in the garage, of all places, and when Blake asked her what she was doing, she said, "Oh, nothing much. Just straightening things up a little." When he told her it was too hot to be out there, she said cheerfully, "Oh no, it's not bad at all, really. See, I raised the garage doors and plugged in this little box fan I found out here. And you'll never guess what I just ran across up here on one of these shelves!"

Hearing both Blake and Della Boyd laugh, Catherine got up from the den sofa, where she was looking through her notes from the previous year's Tour of Homes that she had helped to organize as a fundraiser for the new branch library over in Filbert. As chairman of the Friends of the Library, she needed to get going on this year's tour and start contacting the right people so she could give a report at the next meeting of the library board.

She had already decided that she was going to insist they drop some of the homes they had used in past years, such as the Driscolls'. Joyce Driscoll hadn't even bothered to have the chandelier in her foyer polished before the tour last year! And no one could have missed seeing the cracked pane in the French doors between the sunroom and courtyard. Joyce had said it happened the day before the tour when her grandchildren were visiting, but Catherine had her doubts about that. She would have to find a replacement for the Driscoll home, and that wasn't going to be easy. The homes in this part of South Carolina weren't exactly regular features in *House Beautiful* or *Southern Living*. Now, if she were organizing a tour of trailer parks or a pickup truck show, it would be a cinch.

She walked into the kitchen and over to the door leading into the garage. "Della Boyd, I'm not sure I want all those shelves rearranged," she said, stepping out into the garage. Actually, she couldn't care less how the garage shelves were arranged because she hardly ever touched anything out there, but she wanted to see what Della Boyd was up to and what she was showing Blake.

And there stood her sister-in-law halfway up a stepladder—a grown woman!—holding a bright blue plastic jar in one hand and a little plastic wand in the other, blowing clusters of shimmery bubbles out through the open garage doors into the driveway, right in plain sight of anyone who happened by. And there stood Blake with his hands stuffed in his pockets watching her as if blowing bubbles on a September morning was the most natural thing in the world for a sixty-something woman to be doing!

Della Boyd climbed down from the stepladder and waved the plastic wand at Catherine. "See what I found on this shelf up here, shoved behind all those clay pots?" she said. "Would you like to try it, Catherine?"

"No, I would not," stated Catherine.

Della Boyd stepped out into the driveway and blew another dozen or so bubbles, then looked back at Blake delightedly. "You probably don't remember it, but you used to love doing this when you were a little boy. We'd go out on the porch during rainstorms and blow bubbles and watch the rain pop them." As if that little front stoop of their house could be called a *porch*, thought Catherine. She didn't have a bit of trouble imagining Della Boyd standing out in the rain!

Catherine had a vague memory of hiding a jar of bubbles on one of the garage shelves a few years back when Philip had brought them home from a birthday party and then proceeded to torment Olivia for days by blowing them through the crack under her bedroom door. But surely the solution would have evaporated by now, wouldn't it? Why, that must have been three or four years ago. Yet there stood Della Boyd dipping the wand into the jar and pulling it out over and over to blow mounds of bubbles that floated off in all directions.

Catherine watched one especially big one that wobbled as it floated across the driveway, then rose skyward. In the brief instant when it popped, Catherine formed an analogy which both pleased and irritated her. The analogy was simple enough, too simple in fact. She was sure it had been around for eons. It was this: Life is like a bubble. It's pretty for only a little while before it gets shaky and then poof!—everything nice disappears. It pleased her because only a week earlier that speaker at the poetry club—that Margaret Tuttle person—had said that the ability to form analogies was characteristic of a poetic mind. But it irritated her also because it was such a bleak analogy. It reminded her of fleeting time, dashed hopes, old age, and all those kinds of annoying things, and she didn't like to think about things like that.

To make the situation worse, Della Boyd started singing that silly song again. "I'm forever blowing bubbles," she sang. She'd blow a big string of bubbles, then add a line of the song, then blow more bubbles.

Catherine couldn't believe she stood there and let Della Boyd go on for so long before she finally cut in. "I'm sure the Chewnings across the street are enjoying the show!"

Della Boyd just nodded and went right ahead and finished the rest of the song. "Are you sure you wouldn't like to blow some?" she asked Catherine again, turning to hold the wand toward her. "I haven't used it all up yet."

"Oh yes, of all the things in the world I want to do," Catherine said, "blowing bubbles in my driveway in broad daylight is right up there at the top of the list." Della Boyd frowned ever so slightly as if she was't sure whether that was a yes or no. "I'm sure Sammy Chewning would take you up on your offer, though," Catherine added.

"Why, I bet he would," said Della Boyd, smiling. "Blake was about his age the first time we blew bubbles in the rain. Here, Blake, do you want to do it? I sure don't want to monopolize the fun."

"No, Sister, you go right ahead." Blake walked around and leaned against the fender of his black Lexus. "I don't feel like doing much of anything today."

"Well, I sure wish you'd paint the shutters one of these days like you keep talking about," Catherine said. "They're getting to be an embarrassment."

Blake didn't even look at her as he answered. "Labor Day is a day *off* work, not a day *of* work. Those shutters can wait. They aren't going anywhere." He was sounding like Barb Chewning now, Catherine thought. "Anyway," Blake said, "I already talked to those boys across the street about doing it. One of them told me they were looking for Saturday jobs. He said they painted the shutters at their other house earlier this summer."

"And what are *you* going to do—play racquetball or golf while you pay a couple of *kids* to paint the shutters?" Catherine said, wishing just as soon as the words were out of her mouth that she could take them back.

Blake turned and looked at her for several long seconds before he answered, and in that interval Catherine knew exactly what was coming.

He spoke quietly, but she heard him distinctly across the two cars. Della Boyd had started her song over and was engrossed in her bubble blowing out in the driveway once again, so Catherine wasn't sure whether she heard what Blake said or not, but she almost didn't care. Della Boyd had to know by now that theirs wasn't one of those lovey-dovey marriages.

"That reminds me of something I've been wondering about," Blake said. "What exactly is it that *you* do while you pay Sparkle Flynn to clean the house every week?"

Catherine wheeled around and flounced back inside the house, closing the kitchen door more firmly than necessary. She returned to the den and tried to get her thoughts back on the Tour of Homes, but she kept hearing Blake and Della Boyd out in the garage. She couldn't tell what they were saying, but she could hear the rise and fall of their voices. She put a check mark beside the name of Paul and Anne Marie Darlington on her list of tour homes. She would definitely call them again, even though she had used them several years in a row. The Darlingtons loved seasonal tours, and since this one was going to be in early December, she knew Anne Marie would go all out for Christmas as she had done with spring-time decorations for the April tour three years ago and the July Fourth tour last year.

She paused when she came to the next name on her list: the Fitchners. Trina Fitchner was so tiresome with all her arts and crafts. Their house wasn't the least bit elegant, but it was a popular home on the Tour because of its novelty. A stone cottage, it looked like something out of a fairy tale, and Trina was always adding some quaint new touch—like the octagonal stained glass window she had installed in the kitchen last year. She had designed and tinted the glass herself, of course, and made sure everybody knew it. There wasn't anything Trina Fitchner couldn't do. Why, Catherine wouldn't be surprised if the woman didn't start raising sheep so she could produce her own wool and make braided rugs from the yarn she spun and dyed with crushed berries.

Catherine was just writing a note to herself to recommend raising the cost of tour tickets from seven dollars to eight when she heard the door from the basement open. The next thing she knew, Hardy was standing out in the hallway staring into the den at her. She didn't look up, but she knew he was there. She stopped writing and glanced through last year's brochure, frowning and tapping her pen as if in deep concentration. She was hoping that by acting busy maybe Hardy would go away. She sure didn't feel like dealing with him right now.

"She sat on the couch pretending to read something," Hardy said in a deep voice like a radio announcer, "as she tried hard to ignore her son standing in the doorway."

Catherine took a deep breath and looked up. "What do you want?" she said, and then for some reason she couldn't have explained, she added, "Your father is out in the garage."

"Well, now, that's sure an interesting bit of info," Hardy said.

Catherine frowned as she noticed the shirt he was wearing. It was one of those ugly olive green shirts that gas station attendants used to wear. It had an oval patch on the right pocket with the name *Buck* stitched on it in cursive.

"But I wouldn't want to bother Dad on his day off, would I?" he said. "So here's my idea, see. You give me thirty bucks, and I'm outa your hair."

"For how long?" Catherine asked. She didn't mean it the way it sounded. She really did want to know how long he'd be gone because Blake had said he would grill the steaks around noon instead of waiting until suppertime. He wouldn't like it if Hardy was gone.

"Her heart was filled with grief at the thought of her son leaving," Hardy said, using his radio voice again. "But when he told her he'd be back by midnight, she managed to get her emotions under control and give him the money he'd asked for, plus ten dollars extra."

"That's not amusing," Catherine said. "In case you've forgotten, school starts tomorrow. There's no way you can stay out that late. Besides, we're cooking out for lunch, and your father expects everybody to be here."

"Oh, fun in the neighborhood," Hardy said. "A family barbecue on the patio. And I guess Dad's gonna make us play croquet and badminton in the backyard, too." Then before Catherine could prepare herself, he swiftly bounded across the room to the sofa and put his face two inches from hers. "Hey, I got plans for today, and I ain't changin' 'em, see," he said through clenched teeth.

Before Catherine could catch her breath to reply, Blake appeared in the den doorway. "What's going on?" he said.

Hardy whirled around quickly to face his father. "Nothin'. We were just having us a little talk is all."

Blake frowned and took a few steps into the room. "Well, sorry to interrupt your little talk, but somebody wants to see you out in the driveway," he said to Hardy.

"Who?"

"Go out and see." As Hardy passed him on his way out of the den,

Blake added, "And by the way, don't count on going anywhere today. We have plans here at home."

Hardy mumbled something as he started down the hall and then made a gagging sound like Kinko made when he got something stuck in his throat. Blake pretended not to hear.

"I'm leaving right now to take Philip to Wal-Mart to get his school stuff," Blake said. "When we get back, I'll grill the steaks. I'm saying one o'clock at the latest." Catherine didn't answer. "If you think you can manage it, you could put some potatoes in the oven to bake," he said. "And see if you can find that bag of charcoal. I know it's somewhere out in the garage, but I can't find it."

When she glanced up, he was already gone, and a minute later she heard his car start and back out of the garage.

Catherine sighed and put her papers down. She got up and went into the living room to look out the front window. Hardy was standing on the grass by the driveway, staring down at his bare feet, his thumbs hooked through the belt loops of his baggy shorts. Catherine could see the rip across his backside where his underwear showed through. Why he liked to wear such disgraceful-looking clothes she couldn't begin to figure out. In front of him stood the Chewning twins, both of whom appeared to be talking at the same time, making wide, sweeping gestures with their arms. She wished Hardy would look at them. If she had told him once, she had told him a million times to look people in the eye when they were talking to him. She saw Della Boyd approach them. The Chewning boys smiled politely and said something, and even Hardy looked up and smiled—or maybe he was just squinting into the sun.

"I need a ride." Catherine almost jumped out of her skin at the sound of Olivia's voice right behind her.

"Good grief, don't sneak up that way!" Catherine said, turning around.

"What way?" Olivia said. "All I did was walk in. Can I help it if you're deaf?" She paused a second, then added loudly, "I said I need a ride."

"Where to?" Catherine demanded, although she could have guessed from the fact that Olivia was wearing her swimsuit. "You said last Saturday was your last day at the pool."

"I said it was my last day *to work* at the pool. I didn't say it was my last day to *go*."

"Well, you can't," Catherine said.

"What do you mean, I can't?"

"Just what I said. Your father says everybody's staying here. He's cooking out as soon as he gets back, and he wants everybody here."

"Cooking out?" Olivia's eyes darted to the clock on the mantel. "In the middle of the day?" She put her hands on her hips and said, "Well, I'm going to the pool. I'll eat something later. Besides, who knows when Dad will be back? If he's with Philip, it might take all day."

"He said it wouldn't be later than one," Catherine said.

"He *said*." Olivia laughed a short derisive laugh. "Dad's never on time for anything."

Catherine couldn't believe her sudden urge to defend Blake. "You're one to talk about running late!" she said to Olivia.

Olivia dropped the argument and pretended to look contemplative. "Well, okay, one o'clock," she said, folding her arms and letting her eyes settle on the clock. "That's a little over two hours from now." She chewed on her lip a moment. "I'll just have to leave the pool earlier than I had planned. Two hours isn't much, but it's better than nothing, I guess. I'll go get my stuff, and you can take me right now."

"I'm not taking you anywhere!" Catherine said. "I'd have to turn around and go get you right in the middle of something else. Has it ever occurred to you that I don't exist for the sole purpose of chauffeuring you around?"

"And how else am I supposed to get places?" Olivia asked.

"Well, if you would practice parallel parking like I've tried to tell you to, you wouldn't have failed the stupid driving test for the second time!"

"That dumb woman who gave the test wouldn't have passed me anyway," Olivia said. "She *smiled* when she told me I'd failed. She was, like, 'Sorry, you'll have to try it again after you've practiced some more.' She was a witch." She paused, then added, "Besides, you'd never let me drive your precious car anyway even if I did have my license." She gave a fake gasp. "Why, I might get a *fingerprint* on the steering wheel or something!"

Catherine felt like slapping her and wondered what might have happened if Della Boyd hadn't wandered in just then.

"Oh, Catherine, guess what?" she said. "That nice Barb Chewning sent her boys over to ask us all to come eat homemade ice cream with them tonight. I told them I'd come in and ask you." When Catherine just stared at her, she added, "They're out in the driveway right now, waiting for an answer." She glanced toward the window. "They sure are nice boys. And funny, too—why, you should hear them talk. They're out there trying to get Hardy to come over and play some basketball with them. I think he's going to."

"I need a ride right now," Olivia repeated. "I'm already late."

"Late?" Catherine knew she was practically shrieking, but she couldn't help it. "Why is everybody always demanding things around here? Hardy wants money! Blake wants me to bake the potatoes and find the charcoal! Olivia wants a ride! And now the Chewning boys want an answer!"

Della Boyd looked bewildered. "Catherine, honey, here, why don't you sit down?" She attempted to take Catherine's arm, but Catherine pushed her away.

"I don't need to sit down!" she said. "I just need to be left alone!" She turned and stomped into the kitchen. She jerked open the pantry door and pulled several potatoes from the bag on the floor, then took them to the counter beside the sink. She dumped them onto the counter and turned the water on full force.

Behind her came Della Boyd's gentle voice. "I saw the charcoal out in the garage, Catherine. It was hidden behind those two big bags of dog food. Blake probably just thought it was another bag of Gravy Train."

"Well, good for you!" Catherine said. She started scrubbing a potato so hard with her vegetable brush that part of the skin came off.

"I could take Olivia wherever she needs to go. If you trust me with your car, that is. My Mississippi driver's license is still valid. It doesn't expire until next year."

"Olivia doesn't *need* to go anywhere!" Catherine said.

"Oh, well, all right," said Della Boyd. "I just thought . . . well then, how much money does Hardy need? I could . . ."

"Quit trying to be helpful, Della Boyd. Nobody needs anything." Catherine picked up another potato and washed it off. She closed her eyes and let the cool water run over her hands. She took several deep breaths.

She heard the door from the garage open and bare footsteps slap across the kitchen tile into the hallway. "No need to invite us in, Hardy—we'll just wait out here," a voice called from the garage. There was laughter and then, "Yeah, we'll blow some of your aunt's bubbles while we wait."

She heard Della Boyd go to the kitchen door. "Oh, did Hardy forget his manners?" she said. "Here, come on inside a minute, boys, unless you really do want to blow bubbles. Do you? You're welcome to, although I've just about emptied the bottle I'm afraid. I was just telling Hardy's mother about your nice invitation. You're probably wanting an answer, aren't you? Is Hardy going to play ball with you?"

Catherine turned around to stare at Della Boyd. She sounded like a flustered schoolgirl!

The Chewning boys stepped inside the kitchen from the garage, and both of them flashed a smile at Catherine. They had identical smiles—

kind of cockeyed, with one side of the mouth stretched out farther than the other. Catherine could tell they were going to be handsome men. In fact, they weren't bad looking right now—blond and blue-eyed and lanky.

"Does she do that all the time?" one of them asked Catherine.

"Do what?" Catherine said. She wondered how in the world anyone could tell these two boys apart.

"Ask so many questions at one time," the boy said. "How do you answer them—in order, or do you go in reverse?"

"Let's see, if you go in order, it would be yes, no, yes, yes," said the other boy.

"So in reverse, it's yes, yes, no, yes," said the first one. "Yes?"

"Yes!" said his brother.

Della Boyd laid her hand across her chest and laughed. "These boys are the cleverest things," she said to Catherine. "When one of them stops, the other one picks up, and . . . well, you should just hear them."

"Stereo effect," said one of them.

"Surround sound," said the other.

Catherine studied the boys for a moment, then turned around and started scrubbing another potato.

She heard one of them whisper loudly to the other, "Hardy's mom thinks we're really funny."

"Yeah, I know," said the other one. "We always have that effect on women."

Della Boyd laughed again. "Oh, you two boys just never quit, do you?"

"Energizer Bunnies," one of them said.

Evidently Hardy came back into the kitchen just then because one of the boys said, "Hey, here he is, the guy all the NBA scouts are dreaming about—Hardy . . . hey, I forget, what's your last name?"

"Har Har," quipped his brother, jabbing him with an elbow. "Hardy Har Har. Get it?"

They finally left the kitchen, to Catherine's great relief, but not before one of the Chewnings walked up behind her and said, "So can we tell our mom you can come for ice cream, ma'am? She said anytime around seven or seven-thirty would be fine."

There was a moment of silence before Catherine answered tersely, "I'll check with my husband when he gets home and let her know."

"She'll let us know, Mush Head," said the other. "Quit bugging her."

As they left, Della Boyd was laughing again. "You boys take good care of Hardy now." She closed the door behind them and leaned against it.

"They sure are likable boys, aren't they? Wouldn't it be nice if Hardy could make friends with them?"

The kitchen seemed very quiet to Catherine now that the Chewnings were gone. It was strange how two skinny boys could fill up so much space in a room. Catherine finished washing the last potato and started pricking the skins with a fork. When she stopped to turn on the oven, she noticed that Della Boyd had already done so.

Bits and Pieces

13

That evening when they came back home from the Chewnings' house, it seemed to Catherine that they had been away for weeks. Her head was spinning with thoughts. They had eaten ice cream, yes, as the original invitation had stipulated—but there had been so much more to the evening than just eating ice cream!

She could still hear Barb Chewning's chatty farewell as she had walked with them to the end of the driveway only minutes ago: "I sure hope we can do this again sometime. We made quite an interesting twelvesome, don't you think?" Then she had called out to Olivia and Hardy, who were making for home as if they had just been released from a torture chamber, "Hope you kids have a nice day at school tomorrow."

Neither of them responded, and Catherine saw Blake's jaw tighten as he watched the two of them disappear inside the house. But Barb didn't show any signs of taking offense. She shook her head and laughed a little. "Kids," she said. "It's sure a different world today than when we were growing up, isn't it?" She turned to Philip, who was executing one last layup in the driveway. "If Philip's anywhere near as good at schoolwork as he is at basketball, I know he'll have a good year." She spoke loud enough for him to hear.

Without missing a step Philip said, "I'm not." He took one more shot, then walked toward the curb, where the rest of them stood.

"Well, he *could* be," Catherine said. "If he put forth the least little bit of effort, he could make straight A's."

Barb patted Philip's shoulder and said, "Well, keep your chin up, Philip. It's a new year, and seventh grade will probably be a lot more interesting than sixth."

Philip shrugged. "Maybe."

"Hey, thanks for playing with the little kids tonight," Barb said. "That was sure nice of you."

Philip looked at Barb—right in the eye like Catherine was always telling Hardy to do when he talked to people—and said, "That's okay." Then, "Where'd you get all those LEGOs in that closet?"

"Oh, here, there, and everywhere," Barb said. "Josh and Caleb must've collected every set they made, up until a couple of years ago. Come back sometime and I'll show you the rest. We've got lots more still packed in a box somewhere. The boys saved all the instruction sheets, too, I believe."

Catherine wondered if Barb had any idea *which* box they were in. She felt like asking her, "Would that be one of the boxes stacked up in the den or one of the ones in the hallway? Or one of those in the living room maybe?" She couldn't believe how many boxes were still sitting around inside the Chewnings' house! And there were probably dozens of others piled up in rooms she hadn't been in. But it didn't seem to bother Barb one bit—nor Curtis either, for that matter. Catherine couldn't imagine inviting company to your house, as Barb kept doing, when things were still so helter-skelter. Good grief, they'd moved in three weeks ago now, and Barb stayed home all day—so what was the big holdup?

Philip lifted his eyebrows at the mention of more LEGOs. "Yeah, sure, okay," he said. "Thanks."

There, thought Catherine, at least she had one child who could be counted on to be halfway civil to adults. With a brief wave, Philip stepped off the curb and ambled across the street toward home.

Blake thanked Barb again for her hospitality, which Catherine thought was unnecessary since he had already said the same thing inside just a few minutes earlier. And Della Boyd started up again also, adopting the old-fashioned way of speaking she liked to use at times—"My, what a gracious hostess you've been this evening" and "The refreshments were delightful" and so forth—until Catherine broke in and said, "Well, let's don't stand around out here in the dark all night! Tomorrow's a school day!" She gave Barb a nod and a quick word of thanks, then took off across the street.

Behind her, Barb raised her voice. "Bye now. Maybe next time we play Guesstures, we'll let the men get a few more points so they won't feel so bad. Poor things. They take it so hard."

Curtis Chewning, who was thumping around in the carport putting the lawn chairs away, called out, "I heard that!" and Barb laughed.

"Good, I meant for you to," she said.

"You're asking for trouble, lady," Curtis said.

Barb laughed again. "Oh, you and your threats. They don't scare me a bit!"

Tonight was the first time Catherine had ever seen Curtis Chewning up close, and she still didn't quite know what to make of him. She had watched him all evening and had listened to him—though he didn't really talk all that much—but she still couldn't decide whether to feel sorry for Barb or envy her.

Passing by Philip's bedroom door on her way down the hallway, Catherine gave a sharp rap and said, "Don't lollygag now! You need to get to bed." Philip didn't say anything, but Catherine heard a single swift, solid bump as if he had kicked something.

As she proceeded down the hallway back to the master bedroom, she thought about Curtis Chewning. Feature for feature, he wasn't nearly as handsome as Blake. Anybody with eyes could tell that at a glance. And even though he was a doctor, Catherine doubted that he was any smarter than Blake, at least in a general sense.

Sure, as a pediatrician, he could diagnose a case of whooping cough or rubella, could put a splint on a broken finger, prescribe antibiotics for ear infections, treat burns, and check the reflexes of a newborn—things like that. But then there were probably parts of Blake's job that Curtis Chewning wouldn't know the first thing about, so that wasn't really any test of intelligence.

He was exceptionally bright, though—no doubt about that. Catherine thought of the intense look on his face as Blake had described the 3-D CAD drafting system they used at Forrest Bonner Tool and Die to design parts. He had asked questions, too, so he must have been following along. He had nodded with understanding when Blake mentioned things like tolerances and specs and calibrations, and out of the blue he had asked Blake to explain what a jig grinder was. He'd heard the term somewhere, he said, and wasn't sure exactly what it was.

When Blake had pulled a couple of tiny metal parts—"doodads," that's what Catherine called them—out of the pocket of his jeans, Curtis had examined them minutely and had listened attentively to Blake's boring explanation of what they would be used for.

Catherine herself had long ago lost interest in Blake's work. Only a few days earlier, before bed one night, she had scooped up four or five doodads from the top of Blake's bureau and flung them in the wastebasket. She remembered now that one of them had looked like a miniature biscuit cutter, though the likeness had escaped her at the time. They were all different shapes—tiny disks, tubes, cylinders, rectangles, all sorts of unidentifiable little thingamajigs made out of stainless steel or copper. "I'm sick and tired of seeing these silly little bits and pieces all over the house!" she had said. "Everywhere I look there's another one! Can't you leave them at work instead of bringing them home to clutter up everything?"

Blake hadn't answered right away but had given her a long look of disdain before stooping down to pick the parts out of the wastebasket. "These silly little bits and pieces," he had said after he had found them all, "are what pay for the roof over your head and the food on your table."

Catherine remembered glaring at him as he stood there gazing down into the palm of his hand affectionately, as if he were holding gold nuggets instead of silly little scraps of cheap metal. It was the same lingering look he often gave to Kinko out on the patio every evening. He would fold up the newspaper neatly, then reach down and pet Kinko gently. The dog would lift his head and nuzzle Blake's hand, and Blake would usually talk to him while the two of them looked at each other as if they were saying good-bye before a long separation. Catherine couldn't recall the last time Blake had looked at *her* so fondly.

Catherine walked into the bathroom and picked up her hairbrush from the vanity. She ran it through her hair, fluffing it up here and there, then turning from side to side to admire the way it feathered back on the sides. She had told Dottie Puckett last Wednesday that she wanted a hair appointment only every other week from now on instead of every week since she planned to experiment with blowing it dry and styling it herself with a curling iron. There certainly wasn't any sense in paying Dottie Puckett to do what she could do herself.

She swept the hairbrush back across the sides again, watching the way every hair fell right into place. Barb had commented again tonight about what pretty hair Catherine had. Catherine couldn't remember now how the subject had come up, but she had tossed her head and laughed lightly at the compliment, then reached up and fingered the hair around her ears. Blake had looked away as if annoyed, fastening his eyes on something on the ceiling. Della Boyd had spoken right up, though, and said, "Yes, I don't know of anybody that can hold a candle to Catherine's pretty head of red hair," which was just another example of Della Boyd's odd way of putting things at times.

One of the Chewning boys had picked up on it right away, of course, and said, "Oh, I bet I could." And he had made a motion as if to grab the blue candle right out of the small hurricane lamp in the middle of the kitchen table. "Here, somebody hand me a match."

Catherine had noticed Curtis Chewning studying his wife as she sat there at the kitchen table complimenting Catherine for her pretty hair. She wondered if he ever wished Barb would do something with her hair besides wear it in a ponytail. She tried to imagine him complaining to Barb tonight as they got ready for bed: "Hon, why can't you get you a nice hairstyle like Catherine's?" But the thought wasn't very convincing.

It dawned on Catherine suddenly that Barb surely didn't wear her ponytail at night, and she tried to imagine what she looked like with her hair down around her shoulders. In spite of the tackiness of the ponytail itself, anybody could see that Barb's hair had real potential. It looked shiny and healthy. At least it was a thick, bouncy ponytail rather than a sparse, limp one—but then Catherine gave a brisk shake of her head and smiled. As if one kind of ponytail were superior to another. A ponytail was a ponytail!

She kept seeing Curtis Chewning's face as he looked at Barb. There was something about him that made Catherine wonder if he was a normal man. Not that he wasn't masculine—no, not at all. He was a man in every physical sense of the word, of course. He was about as tall as Blake, though not nearly as filled out. His shoulders drooped just slightly, but it didn't make him look slovenly really, only a little tired. Maybe it was just a result of having to bend down all day to listen to wheezy coughs and peer down sore throats.

Although no one would describe him as a weakling, it was easy to see that he probably didn't go in for pumping iron in a gym. It wasn't hard, though, for Catherine to picture him with his shirtsleeves rolled up doing farm work. He was probably in his early forties, but he had the look of an adolescent—that lean, angular look. She could imagine him in a white doctor's coat, his stooped shoulders and hard, slender frame lost inside all that fabric like a pole in a tent.

Catherine put her hairbrush down and walked back into the bedroom. Slipping out of her sandals, she tried to figure out what it was that interested her about Curtis Chewning. It sure wasn't his looks. His sandy brown hair was clearly starting to thin, and his forehead had already begun to crease along habitual lines. He was fair skinned, probably the type that would burn in a second if he got too much sun, and it was clear to Catherine, judging from his paleness, that he hadn't gotten too much sun in a long, long time. Not that he was a homely man exactly, but you could never call him *handsome* by any stretch of the imagination. There was something else about him, though, something in his eyes, she thought, that would make women look twice at Curtis Chewning. And the funny thing was that Catherine couldn't even remember what color his eyes were!

But it was definitely in his eyes. *Soft*—that was the word that kept coming to her mind. Not the kind of soft that suggested somebody with a delicate constitution or somebody you could push around, but softhearted. Yes, that was it. He seemed softhearted and gentle. She supposed that came from all the years of tending to sick babies and children. Or had he been that way before he decided to become a pediatrician? Was it his gentleness that had led him to devote his life to the well-being of children, or had the gentleness come afterward? Though he had smiled only a few times the entire evening, he had a steady way of looking at a person that spoke of kindness. He looked like a man you could trust.

Blake walked into the bedroom and pulled off his bright yellow Ralph Lauren polo shirt, messing up his hair in the process so that it stuck out above his ear on one side. He had been quite talkative over at the Chewnings' house, had joked around with the twins and teased Sarah until she blushed bright red. He had even held Sammy Chewning on his lap and patiently explained his fall in the bathtub when the toddler pointed to the fading bruise on his temple. And he had chuckled good-naturedly when Sammy had dribbled ice cream onto his yellow polo shirt. She guessed it was easy to chuckle at drips and spills when you weren't the one who had to wash the clothes!

Catherine could see the stain now as Blake tossed the shirt onto the end of the bed. He had made it worse by smearing it with a paper napkin instead of blotting it, had even laughed and said, "Oh well, don't worry, it's sure not the first time," which wasn't exactly right since it *was* the first time for a stain on that particular shirt, a new one Catherine had bought him at the mall in Derby a few weeks earlier at an end-of-summer clearance sale. Of course, Blake didn't appreciate its quality. He hadn't been one bit impressed when she had told him it was originally a $68.00 shirt but she had gotten it for $12.99. All he had said was "No way would I ever pay sixty-eight bucks for that."

Catherine watched him now. Apparently unaware that his hair was sticking straight up on one side, he slowly emptied his Chap Stick and the loose change from one pocket of his jeans and the metal doodads from the other pocket. He set them all on top of his bureau. He looked as though he was deep in thought.

The idea flashed across Catherine's mind that maybe he was thinking about Barb Chewning, trying to figure out what it was that made her so different, just as she herself had been thinking about Curtis. Was it a common thing, she wondered, for husbands to study other men's wives the same way she so often studied other women's husbands—not in a promiscuous way, but just out of curiosity, as a sort of comparison or a point of interest? No, knowing what she did about the way men's minds worked, she doubted that they ever did that. The only thing they ever wondered about was who was going to make it to the World Series in the fall or win the next NFL game on Monday night.

But even though Blake's list of faults was a mile long, Catherine had always found plenty to criticize in other men, too. And in spite of the fact that Blake was light-years from being perfect, she had never known another man she would want to trade him in for—not really. Nobody specific, that is. Of course, there had been hundreds of times she had been so mad at him she had wished he would drop off the face of the earth, and she hadn't hesitated to tell him so either. More than once she had even flung the word *divorce* at him at the height of an argument, but she knew that saying the word and actually going through with the act were two different things.

"Philip needs to get to bed," she said now, hoping Blake would go to his room and tell him so. But Blake didn't answer nor did he make a move toward the hallway. "If he doesn't, he's going to be impossible in the morning," she continued, then added, "I can't believe school is starting already!" and sighed peevishly as if the whole idea of school starting was a conspiracy aimed directly at her. Blake still said nothing but pulled off his jeans and laid them across the back of the chair beside his bureau. He acted as if he hadn't heard a single word she had said.

Catherine pressed her lips together and watched him disappear into the bathroom. She remembered how interested he had seemed to be an hour or two earlier when Barb Chewning had been talking about the various surfaces of tennis courts—of all the subjects she could have chosen to talk about!—and which one she preferred.

"Clay is a lot slower than asphalt," she had said. "The only real tournament I ever won was on a clay court when I was fifteen or sixteen. I still have the trophy somewhere, don't I, Curt?"

Curtis had nodded. "I think the last time I saw it, it was in Sarah's toy box."

"Yeah, Mom's real proud of that trophy," Josh said. "I saw her use it one time to pound a nail in the wall."

"I play tennis, too," Catherine had said.

"Well, sort of," Blake had said, and although she felt like throwing her bowl of ice cream at him, Catherine had forced a laugh.

Barb had gone on to talk about how her father had been a grounds keeper at a private golf club in a suburb of Memphis, Tennessee, when she was growing up. When the club had expanded to include tennis facilities, it had become her father's job to learn about the upkeep of clay courts. Catherine could still see Blake, leaning forward across the kitchen table as Barb talked, latching on to every word she said. And she could still picture Barb, sitting there totally unconcerned that she didn't have on a stitch of makeup and that she was wearing a shirt and slacks that were two entirely different shades of navy blue, laughing freely as she talked, her ponytail swinging, her eyes crinkling into dark dashes.

"I helped him in the summers from the time I was old enough to push a broom," she had said. "I still have dreams about sweeping those clay courts. There was a certain pattern to it, and you had to be real methodical to please Daddy, or he'd make you do it again. Now they have little riding machines that pull these big brushes behind them, so all you have to do is sit there and steer, but when I was . . ."

"But when Mom was a kid," Caleb chimed in, "she had to get up at four in the morning and walk barefoot twenty miles uphill on a gravel road, then wade out in the marshes to cut reeds and then lay them out to dry so she could make her own brooms to sweep the courts with, and . . ."

"Okay, kiddo, zip it," Barb had said. And she had reached over and punched Caleb in the arm playfully. Catherine couldn't imagine punching Hardy in the arm like that. He would probably haul off and knock her unconscious.

In Catherine's opinion, Barb Chewning's mind had a kink in it. She came out with some of the most unexpected comments at times, one of which Catherine remembered now. It was right after Barb had told about her father's job as grounds keeper. She had grown pensive, then looked around the table at all of them, opened her eyes wide, and said, "Do you ever wish you could make time go backward and see your parents when they were your age? Wouldn't it be interesting, for example, if all our fathers could suddenly be our age right now and be right here in the room with us? I wonder how they'd all get along."

What was the use, Catherine thought irritably, of wondering something like that? What did it matter? She knew exactly what her father would do, though. He would excuse himself and head straight for the door, saying he had to go work on the most important case of his whole life. That's the way he had always described every case he ever worked on—as "the most important one" of his life.

Hardy and Olivia had sat on stools at the Chewnings' kitchen counter, glowering into their bowls of ice cream, both of them in a private sulk over their spoiled plans for the day. Every now and then one of them would mutter something to the other, and they would exchange glances of mutual disgust at being trapped in the middle of all this tedious family stuff with a couple of severely uncool twins who acted as if they were enjoying every minute of it.

Catherine wanted to shake them both. Not that she was having the time of her life, really, and not that she had been exactly thrilled when Blake had jumped at the Chewnings' invitation, but for pete's sake, Hardy and Olivia needed to learn one of these days that the world didn't revolve around what *they* wanted to do. Sometimes you just had to do things you didn't want to do. Oh yes. Couldn't I write a book on that subject? Catherine thought.

The twins, Joshua and Caleb, didn't seem to notice anything amiss with Hardy and Olivia. At any rate, they didn't let it dampen their spirits in the least. They also sat on stools at the counter, across from Hardy and Olivia, but they turned to face the adults and younger children at the table. They were sweaty, both of them, their hair plastered against their foreheads, their T-shirts darkened with perspiration.

In fact, Catherine could smell them all—Philip, Hardy, Blake, Curtis, the twins. *"Boy sweat,"* she used to call it. The six of them had played a vigorous game of three-on-three basketball out in the driveway in the fading light while the ice cream was finishing up inside. Della Boyd had sat in a lawn chair in the Chewnings' yard, hooting enthusiastically and calling out inane remarks like "That's a boy, Hardy! Shoot it! Whiz it right over their heads! Don't let them thwart you, Philip! Get in there and scramble! That's it, swish it, Brother! Oops, get the rebound, Philip—now pass it to Hardy! That's the way! Teamwork!"

Catherine had sat in a lawn chair, too, alternately sighing and fanning her face with both hands until Barb finally asked her if she'd like to go inside, at which point Catherine said, "I sure would! It feels like I'm sitting in a barbecue pit out here!" When she had gotten up from her chair, she had felt her chambray shorts sticking to the backs of her thighs. Olivia had remained outside, sitting on the grass Indian style, her head drooping as she plucked at the grass, looking as if her whole life had been ruined.

The Chewnings had two ice cream makers and had made two different kinds of ice cream: vanilla custard and Butterfinger. Catherine had expected something besides just ice cream, but that's all there was—that and paper cups of ice water. Barb pulled an ancient set of pastel plastic Tupperware bowls out of a cupboard, the kind of bowls women had thirty or forty years ago. Curtis helped her dish up the ice cream, and then she grabbed a handful of spoons from a drawer and just plopped them into the middle of the kitchen table along with a stack of paper napkins. "Dig in, everybody," she said.

"Oh, this is all so lovely!" Della Boyd said, cupping both hands around her pale pink plastic bowl. The only thing in the least bit lovely about it in Catherine's opinion was that the spoons were a good quality of Oneida stainless—the Dover pattern she herself had almost bought twenty years ago for her everyday flatware and had even wished at times that she *had* bought instead of the fussier Michelangelo pattern.

Catherine had told Elaine Berryhill on the telephone just a few days ago that she firmly believed every bride should wait at least ten years to buy her china and silver so that her tastes would have time to develop. "What does a twenty-year-old know?" she had said, and Elaine had laughed. "You're absolutely right. I got tired of my china pattern even before I got tired of Darren." Catherine had changed the subject quickly, for Elaine loved to talk about her two ex-husbands and would do so for hours if she found a willing ear.

The Chewnings' ice cream had tasted good—better than Catherine could remember homemade ice cream being—and she even asked for another helping. "Only a smidge," she said to Curtis, who was taking orders for second servings. "I try not to eat many sweets."

It was Barb who suggested the game of Guesstures after the ice cream, and Blake agreed right away and let Hardy and Olivia know with a pointed look that they would all stay for the game. They all moved into the den then, and that's where they were when Della Boyd had gone and embarrassed everybody with a ridiculous display of emotion right before they started playing the game. Seeing an open box on the floor next to the piano bench, she had caught her breath and reached down to pick up a photo album. "Oh, look at all these!" she said.

"I imagine they'd rather unpack their own boxes, Della Boyd," Catherine said.

But Barb spoke up quickly, shaking her head. "Oh, that's okay—really. It's just a box of old family pictures and scrapbooks. I started to unpack them earlier and then never got back to it."

And the next thing anybody knew, Della Boyd was standing there looking down at a photo album in the middle of the Chewnings' den crying her eyes out! Blake went quickly to her side and attempted to comfort her while everyone else stood around awkwardly. Catherine said, "Well, what in the world?" right out loud, but nobody bothered to respond.

Within seconds it was over. Della Boyd wiped the tears off her face and apologized to everyone in a whispery voice. "Oh, I'm so sorry. I don't know what came over me all of a sudden." Barb urged her to sit down on the sofa, and after she was seated, still clutching the photo album, Della Boyd said, "I guess it all came back to me how I lost all my pictures in the fire."

Blake explained briefly about the fire, and the Chewnings shook their heads in sympathy.

"I was thinking about it again just yesterday," Della Boyd continued, her voice stronger now. "Of all the things I lost, it's the pictures I mourn the most. You can't replace things like that—those, and all the scrapbooks of Blake's school achievements. His awards and ribbons and certificates and artwork and . . . well, they all burned up." She paused a moment and lifted her hands in a helpless gesture. Catherine was afraid she was going to cry again, but thankfully she didn't. "The wind carried them away," she added. "All those treasures just turned to ashes." She swept one hand back and forth in front of her, her fingers fluttering. "I can never get them back. They all burned up."

Catherine was just about to open her mouth and say sensibly, "Well, you've just got to get on with life, Della Boyd, because there's no sense dwelling on something that can't be changed" when she had a sudden vision of her own collection of photo albums on a high bookcase shelf in her den at home. She hadn't thought of them in ages. She couldn't even remember now when they had last used their camera at home. But there had been a time, and not so very long ago, when they had taken pictures of everything.

Many of her favorite snapshots came back to her now in a sudden surge—a whole collage rushing at her from nowhere. Hardy as a toddler with a purple Kool-Aid mustache banging two pan lids together like cymbals. Olivia riding the bumper cars at Six Flags. Philip crouched behind home plate in his catcher's getup at a Little League Baseball game. She and Blake sitting on a stone bench at Ole Miss before they were married. Blake holding Olivia in his big hands only minutes after she was born. Philip as a baby lying sprawled across Blake's stomach, both of them fast asleep. On and on they came, in no particular order. Hardy at four in his first Halloween costume as Darth Vader. Blake standing beside a lighthouse on their honeymoon. Olivia in the Miss Junior Berea Pageant at the age of ten.

Catherine realized that the moment for commenting aloud on Della Boyd's little scene had come and gone, that someone else had filled the void with something kind and understanding, and Josh and Caleb Chewning were now in the process of getting the Guesstures game out and explaining the rules. She had only an instant to consider the question that popped into her head. "What if all *our* photo albums suddenly went up in smoke?" And though she didn't allow herself to answer the question, she knew in her heart that it wasn't something she would get over right away. She knew she wouldn't be able to tell herself to "get on with life and quit dwelling on something that can't be changed." She gave Della Boyd a long look and watched her trace a finger over the gold letters P-H-O-T-O-S on the album cover before Blake gently took it from her lap and returned it to the box.

The game didn't take all that long, maybe forty minutes or so, and the women had won quite easily. "You can sure tell Catherine took acting classes in college, can't you?" Della Boyd said afterward, and Barb agreed heartily.

"Didn't you say you graduated from Ole Miss?" Barb asked.

And as Catherine began to nod, Blake said tersely, "She didn't graduate."

"Well, all I lacked was two silly semesters," Catherine said.

Olivia and Hardy sat gloomily, declining to participate in the game, but the twins played on the men's side, acting out their words with goofy abandon. Once, Catherine thought she actually saw Olivia smile at one of their antics, but when she looked more closely, the smile, if that's what it was, had vanished. Sarah had taken Sammy back to her room earlier to play and had shyly asked Philip if he wanted to see her Marbleworks game and her LEGOS. Catherine knew Philip would die of humiliation if anyone told his friends that he had played with an eight-year-old girl and her two-year-old brother for almost a whole hour. And she knew that Hardy would no doubt make a point of mentioning it to Andy Partridge the next time he had a chance.

Blake was out of the bathroom now. He was wearing his baggy cotton sleeping shorts and an old T-shirt, and he didn't even look at Catherine as he walked to the bedroom door and headed down the hallway. She heard him say something to Philip in the hallway, and then a few seconds later a cupboard door in the kitchen opened and closed with a bang. She imagined Blake standing by the refrigerator, barefoot, pouring himself a huge glass of milk as he did most nights. As if he needed it after eating three bowlfuls of ice cream at the Chewnings' house!

When Blake came back into the bedroom several minutes later, however, Catherine couldn't resist calling out from the bathroom, "I sure hope you left enough milk for breakfast! There are five other people living in this house besides you."

His reply from the other side of the door was immediate and intense. "Don't get started on that, Catherine. Just don't even get started."

Catherine turned on the tub faucet and poured a capful of bubble bath into the water. A sudden, giddy thought seized her. What would Blake say, she wondered, if she laughed like Barb Chewning and called out cheerily, "Oh, you and your threats. They don't scare me a bit!" Feeling hot all at once, she bent down and adjusted the temperature of the bath water. A lukewarm bath—that's what she needed tonight.

Missing Items

14

It was almost ten o'clock the next morning when Blake called from work. He had left with all three children shortly after seven-thirty that morning, and the house had been blessedly quiet now for over two whole hours. For the first day of school, things had gone surprisingly smoothly, the only minor setbacks being a brief altercation between Blake and Hardy when Hardy showed up at the kitchen table wearing a green T-shirt with the sleeves ripped off and the faded words *DO WHAT FEELS GOOD* emblazoned across the back, followed by Philip's insistence that he couldn't carry the same old backpack this year that he had used all last year in sixth grade.

"I thought you took him out for new school stuff yesterday," Catherine said to Blake, who shrugged.

"He never mentioned a backpack yesterday," he said.

Hardy stormed back downstairs after a few heated words and reappeared wearing a pink T-shirt—pink the color of strawberry sherbet!—imprinted with *MOTHERS LOVE JOHNSON'S BABY POWDER* on the front. Blake pretended not to notice, but Catherine clicked her tongue loudly and muttered, "Oh, huge improvement!"

There was absolutely no accounting for Hardy's taste in clothes. His two favorite places to shop were the Salvation Army and Goodwill stores over in Derby, and the more Catherine protested over a garment, the more he seemed to like it. Why, he had even brought home a pair of brown corduroy bell-bottoms from the '70s last year and had worn them to school practically every other day! "You ought to be mortified to be seen in public like that," Catherine had said on more than one occasion, at which Hardy had thrown back his head and laughed like a lunatic. The truth was that Catherine was the one who was mortified over his clothes, and they both knew it. She had finally given up buying him nice things from regular department stores. It was a waste of money when he wadded them in a drawer and refused to wear them.

Della Boyd calmed Philip down by promising to buy him a new back-pack—any kind he wanted—for his birthday, which was coming up in November, and finally everyone finished breakfast and cleared out, after which Catherine took the newspaper and went back to bed for an hour.

Della Boyd stayed in the kitchen all morning, having decided after breakfast to make two loaves of homemade bread. "I used to make bread all the time," she had said to Catherine as they cleared the dishes off the table, "and it was so relaxing!" She pursed her lips in thought. "I don't know why I haven't made any in so long," she continued. "Why, it must be, oh, five or six months, no, probably more like eight or nine now, since I've made bread." She stood there a moment counting on her fingers. "Even before the fire threw me into such a spin, I wasn't making bread like I once did. My, how I used to enjoy it—kneading the dough and watching it rise and punching it down and rolling it out and . . . oh, it was all so satisfying and . . . well, *relaxing!*" She rummaged in a cupboard and found three packages of yeast, which Catherine had bought a while back, intending to try a recipe Elaine Berryhill had given her, then concluding that it was too much trouble.

"Well, go ahead and relax to your heart's content," Catherine had said before heading down the hallway with the newspaper. Later, after getting out of bed again, she puttered around getting dressed and going through her closet to take out some things that needed to go to the cleaners. Then she went to the den to jot down a couple of new ideas in her notes about the Tour of Homes.

She had remembered a complaint from one of the hostesses of last year's tour that the new linoleum in their kitchen had been damaged by high-heeled shoes, and although Catherine had come close to telling the woman that they shouldn't have tried to skimp by laying down that spongy, low-budget linoleum instead of ceramic tile, she had promised to make a note requesting that only flat shoes be worn on next year's tour. She had also decided to call Nathaniel and Danette McQueen, whose home had been advertised in the Tour of Homes brochure in past years as "an antique lover's dream overlooking the eighteenth green of the Verdant View Golf Club," to see if they would be willing to host the Library Patrons' Reception this year, which was always the closing event of the tour.

For some reason the McQueens' phone number had a question mark beside it on her list, and Catherine was just in the process of checking it in the phone book when the telephone rang. Catherine glared at it and let it ring three times. She was tempted to ignore it, but she had forgotten for the moment about Della Boyd, who picked up the receiver in the kitchen after the third ring.

"Oh, hello, Brother," Catherine heard her say. Then, "Yes, she surely is. I'll go tell her." And instead of raising her voice and calling to Catherine from the kitchen like any normal person would do, Della Boyd came padding silently down the hallway in her black velour slippers, stopping at the doorway of the den when she saw Catherine seated on the sofa.

"Oh, there you are, Catherine. Blake is on the telephone."

"So I heard," Catherine said, not looking up. She underlined the McQueens' phone number in the phone book and then proceeded to copy it down very deliberately on her list.

"He wants to talk to you," Della Boyd said.

"You don't say," Catherine said, knowing the sarcasm would be lost on Della Boyd. She paused to yawn before reaching for the telephone. "I'll wait until you hang up the phone in the kitchen," she said, covering the receiver with one hand. "Oh, and close the door there before you go."

Della Boyd nodded and pulled the door shut, then hurried back to the kitchen as if charged with a life-or-death mission.

When Catherine heard a click on the line, she uncovered the receiver and said, "What do you want?"

There was a moment of silence so long that Catherine thought Blake may have stepped away from the phone. She was almost ready to repeat the question when he finally spoke.

"What do I want? Well, several things come to mind."

She could tell from his tone that this wasn't going to be a quick, simple phone call nor a friendly one. "Look, I'm too busy to play games," Catherine said. "Why did you call?"

"I just heard from Morton Hollings," he said, then added with emphasis, "You know, Morton Hollings, the principal."

Catherine felt sick. When she didn't answer, Blake continued. "You know, the principal of Berea High. That's where two of our children attend school, you might remember." Still Catherine said nothing. "Hollings gave me a call here at work a few minutes ago," Blake said.

Keeping her voice cool and even, Catherine replied, "And. . . ?" She should have known Morton Hollings and Blake would meet up sometime. She had kept meaning to tell Blake about Hardy's run-in with Mr. Hollings a few weeks ago, but the right time had never come. She had kept it from him at first out of spite for his having been absent so long on his most recent business trip, but then it got lost in all the hubbub of Della Boyd's arrival, and frankly, with each passing day, it seemed less and less important.

"He said he talked to you several weeks ago about Hardy."

"So. . . ?"

"He said he was sure you had told me about Hardy's probationary status at school this fall, but he wanted to remind us—and he thought about it in particular this morning because of a little incident that happened within ten minutes of Hardy's arrival at school."

Catherine sighed. "So what did he do that was so awful this time—pass a note in class?" Honestly, it looked to her like the teachers at a high school could make the students behave without running to the parents about every little infraction.

"Wait a minute," Blake said, his voice tense with anger. "Why don't you back up and tell me what he did this summer? I should have admitted to Hollings that I had no idea what he was talking about, but I didn't. I should have told him that my wife had somehow forgotten to mention that little detail to me when I came home from—"

"Oh yes," Catherine broke in, "when you came home from your gazillionth trip of the year to honor us with a few days of your presence before you found some other excuse to go trotting off somewhere else! I never have figured out why you seem to be the only one at that place who takes all these business trips. If you had been at home when Hardy played his little prank this summer, you'd have known all about it when Morton Hollings called you this morning. So don't go trying to blame it all on me."

"Catherine, I can't believe it's come back to this again. Anytime anything goes wrong, you land right back on this square, don't you? Look, I *have* to travel. It's part of my job, as if you didn't already know that."

"Well, it's funny that you've somehow managed to stay home now for two whole weeks in a row since your sister's been here. How did that work out so conveniently?"

She could hear Blake breathing hard into the phone, and he was silent for a moment before answering. "I rearranged some things," he said at last.

"Well, maybe you need to try rearranging things more often. If you'd stay home more, maybe your children wouldn't get into these little scrapes. And if you'd pay more attention to them when you *are* home instead of going around in a daze ninety percent of the time and then blowing up over some little piddling thing that doesn't amount to—"

Blake interrupted. "Well, at least they listen to me when I tell them to do something, which is more than I can say—"

"*When* you tell them!" Catherine snapped. "Now there's the trick, believe me. *If* you happen to be in town and *if* you happen to be paying attention to anything that's going on at home during your rare guest appearances, then yes, maybe they do listen to you. But that's only because they're afraid of you, and in my opinion that's nothing to brag about!"

Blake replied slowly. "What a stirring speech on parenting skills, delivered by the Mother of the Year." While Catherine was trying to think of some appropriate comeback, he added, "Now, if you don't tell me what this thing with Hardy is all about, I'm going to get in my car and come home and . . ."

He trailed off, and Catherine didn't say anything for a few seconds, knowing that the silence would weaken the effect of his threat and make it sound foolish.

"It wasn't all that big a deal," she said after what she considered a suitable interval. "He and that idiot friend of his, Jordan Baxter, got a can of spray paint and wrote some words on the back steps of the school one night."

"What words?" Blake asked.

"Oh, who knows? Just the same old stuff kids have always written." But she knew that was hardly the truth. When it had happened back in July, Morton Hollings had asked her to come down to the school to see the writing, and what she had seen had almost knocked her over.

But she hadn't given Morton Hollings the pleasure of shocking her. Instead, she had turned on him indignantly. "And how can you prove Hardy had any part in this?" she had demanded. "Just because somebody accused him doesn't mean—"

"Mrs. Biddle, I caught him in the act," Hollings had said. "I ran by my office to pick up something late last night, and I thought I heard something as I was leaving so I walked around the building and saw Hardy writing words with the can of paint while the other boy stood there holding a flashlight."

"Well, I can bet the other boy did more than just stand there holding a flashlight the whole time!" Catherine said.

"Rest assured that I have called his parents also," Hollings said. He had gone on to lay out Hardy's penalty—three days of janitorial duties at the school the following week, a notation of the incident on his permanent school record, and disciplinary probation status when school began in the fall. "One wrong move," Hollings said, "and he will be expelled from Berea High. We've given your son many second chances, Mrs. Biddle, and he's been uncooperative at every turn." He had told her they would have to have the steps sandblasted to get rid of the painted words. "And that's not my favorite way to spend the taxpayers' money," he had ended. At that, Catherine had turned abruptly and left his office, largely out of fear that he'd suggest she fork over the money to pay for it.

Hardy had served his three days while Blake was still out of town and had come home after each day dirty and angry. After the first day Catherine felt like calling Morton Hollings and saying, "This is the stupidest idea in the world," but she was fairly sure from the look on his face when she had left his office that such a call wouldn't help a bit. Morton Hollings seemed like a hard-nosed man. It was easy to see how he could incite a rebellious attitude in an independent-minded boy like Hardy.

Blake sighed on the other end of the telephone. "So now we have a son with vandalism on his record." He grunted, and Catherine could imagine him shaking his head ominously as he thought of the whole list of Hardy's misdemeanors. Truancy, shoplifting, disturbing the peace, trespassing, and no telling how many other things he hadn't gotten caught for. "I wish I had been here when it happened. Oh, I wish I had," he said through clenched teeth, then, as if warding off another tirade from Catherine about his absences, added quickly, "But of course we both know if I had been here, he wouldn't have done it. Just like Olivia and that Brooks boy. When does she come sneaking in at two in the morning? Not when I'm in town. No, of course not. She waits till I leave town so you can call me up at some motel in Timbuktu at two o'clock in the morning to tell me my daughter hasn't come home yet. Honestly, they must think they can get by with anything when I'm gone."

"Hey, one plus one equals two," Catherine said. "Congratulations on figuring it out!" She felt she had gained a small victory, but not a satisfying one. She didn't like the way the conversation seemed to be headed.

"You let them run all over you, Catherine," Blake said. "The world is full of kids whose mothers can make them behave. I won't let you lay it all in my lap."

Just then Catherine heard Della Boyd drop something in the kitchen. It sounded metallic, like a mixing bowl. It reminded her of a bell signaling the end of something, and she suddenly realized that she was tired of arguing with Blake. She knew from long experience that she'd never win—at least not decisively. Trying for a bored, indifferent tone, she yawned and said, "Well, we can make two columns and divvy up all the blame later." She couldn't resist one last dig, however. "Funny, isn't it, that he got into trouble at school today, considering what you just finished saying? He must've forgotten you were in town. What happened anyway? Tell me quick so I can get back to work."

Blake gave a scornful laugh, as if ridiculing the idea of Catherine doing anything associated with work. If he only knew how much she did! Men acted so condescending about the concept of work. She'd like to see *him* stay home and keep things organized and running for just two days. She'd like to see him plan a Tour of Homes almost single-handedly!

As if he were also weary of arguing, however, Blake summarized the report in a single sentence. "According to Hollings, it seems that Hardy showed up at school this morning with a certain article of feminine lingerie that ended up hanging from the eagle at the top of the flagpole in his first-hour class."

"Well, of all the silly things!" Catherine said. Out in the kitchen she thought she heard Della Boyd laugh and say something. Or was that someone else's voice? Even as she was wondering whether Della Boyd was talking to herself again or whether someone else was in the kitchen with her, she was also wondering exactly what article of lingerie Hardy had taken to school and where he had gotten it. She intended to check her lingerie drawer for missing items before the day was over.

"Yes, of all the silly things," Blake said. He sounded dispirited. "Well, I've got to go. I have work to do."

He might as well have said *real work* the way he added a little extra weight to the word *work*.

As soon as she had hung up, Catherine heard more laughter from the kitchen and knew exactly whose it was. What in the world was Barb Chewning doing in her kitchen at ten o'clock in the morning? Was that woman going to be showing up at her house every time she turned around? Was she here to borrow more sugar? Or was it flour this time? Well, Della Boyd could take care of whatever it was. Catherine didn't intend to waste away her morning chitchatting around the kitchen table.

She walked over to the den doorway and quietly opened it a crack. As she did so, she heard Barb Chewning say quite plainly, "Yes, isn't that the truth? And haven't you wished there weren't so many things you wanted to do at the same time? Take last night, for instance. I was sitting on the sofa in the den reading a book about life during the Civil War, when all the men were off fighting and the women had to keep everything going back home, and it was all so interesting. I was reading about this one woman in North Carolina who raised hogs and kept bees and lived in a covered wagon, of all places, and then right in the middle of that chapter this program came on television about the exploration of Lewis and Clark. It was part of a documentary series, and they were telling all about that Indian girl named Sacajawea and how so much of the success of that whole expedition depended on her help. I never knew she had a baby during that time, did you? Anyway, there I was torn between wanting to read more about the hog woman and wanting to listen to what the television was saying about Sacajawea! It was awful—and yet what a nice problem to have, huh?"

Catherine screwed up her face into a fake, squint-eyed smile and mouthed a silent imitation of Barb, complete with exaggerated hand-clapping gestures. "Oh, isn't life just wonderful? There are so many nifty things to do and just not enough time to enjoy everything!" At that moment Catherine thought that nothing would please her more than to hear Barb Chewning break down sobbing and say, "My husband beats me, my kids are on drugs, I have cancer, and we're filing for bankruptcy!"

As she flung herself back onto the den sofa, Catherine heard a high-pitched squeal, followed by "No, no you don't, Sammy. You know better than that."

She tried to get her thoughts back on the Tour of Homes, but she kept seeing the strangest concoction of images—Hardy with a can of spray paint in his hand, an old woman with bees swarming about her head, a lacy undergarment dangling from a flagpole, an Indian girl with a papoose on her back, Sammy Chewning's startling blue eyes, Hardy's pink Johnson's Baby Powder T-shirt, a herd of hogs grazing around an old wagon. She kept hearing the murmur of voices and laughter from the kitchen.

Finally she gave up and tossed her folder aside. She might as well run her errands now as later. She checked them off mentally. There was that hand-painted porcelain lamp at the mall over in Derby she wanted to check on, then take the things to the cleaners, run by Arlene Babcock's for the window treatment that she had promised—finally!—to have finished by today, stop by the bank, and drive by Olga Marsden's new house out on Harper Bridge Road to see if it was finished yet. If it was, she was going to figure out some way to approach Olga about including it on the Tour of Homes, although she had no idea how she'd go about it because, as everybody knew, Olga Marsden was totally antisocial. A lot of people called her Ogre Marsden. It was rumored that Olga had slapped her gardener one time for wishing her a happy birthday—had told him her birthday wasn't any of his blankety-blank business. Catherine thought it was a great story. She felt a certain kinship with Olga Marsden.

Stepping out of the den into the hallway, she heard Della Boyd say, "Well, she was on the telephone with Blake a minute ago, but I think she's done now. You want me to go see?" And before Catherine could escape to her bedroom and lock the door, Della Boyd was in the hallway.

"Oh, there you are, Catherine. Guess who's here and wants to see you?"

Catherine sighed and turned around. "Let's see . . . is it Hillary Clinton?"

Della Boyd clutched her throat and laughed gaily. "Oh, my goodness, no, not Hillary Clinton!" She called back over her shoulder, "Did you hear that, Barb? She guessed Hillary Clinton!" Turning back to Catherine, she could hardly speak for laughing. "No, it's Barb Chewning from across the street. And she's got little Sammy with her. I gave him a few marshmallows, and you should see how excited he is about them. Come on out to the kitchen a minute. Barb wants to see you."

"Well, I haven't changed a bit since she saw me last night," Catherine said. But she followed Della Boyd into the kitchen nevertheless, announcing to Barb as she entered, "What can I do for you? I was just getting ready to run out for a couple of hours."

Barb was seated at the table with Sammy on her lap. The toddler lifted a sunny face to Catherine, held up a marshmallow out of which a bite was already taken, and said plainly, "Powder." Then he patted his neck and shoulders with the sticky side of the marshmallow and emitted a happy shriek. Catherine frowned at the half-dozen marshmallows lined up in front of him. The open bag was lying in the middle of the table.

"It's supposed to be a powder puff," Barb explained. "He's seen me use bath powder. Here, Sammy sweetie, now eat it. You're getting yourself all sticky."

Sammy held the marshmallow firmly in his plump fist and stared at Catherine, his wide eyes a deep hydrangea blue. Solemnly he pointed at her and said, "Wet hair."

"He must be remembering that day you sat by his little pool in the front yard," Barb said, laughing.

For some reason that day seemed like months ago to Catherine. "Yes, he must be," she said. She wished Sammy would stop staring at her, but even as he took another bite of his marshmallow, the toddler kept his eyes fixed on her. Well, he could stare all he wanted. She wasn't about to let a two-year-old get the best of her. She picked up the bag of marshmallows from the table and secured it with a twistie-tie. "What was it you wanted to see me about?" Catherine asked Barb.

"Well, Curtis and I have a little proposition for you and Blake. It's kind of short notice, I know, but we hope you can help us out."

"With what?" Catherine asked. Though Barb had pulled out the chair next to her, Catherine remained standing. What kind of help could Barb Chewning be wanting? Catherine sure wasn't in any mood to be doing favors for anybody with school just getting started and so many things on her mind right now. She sure hoped the Chewnings didn't need to borrow one of their cars, and if it had anything to do with keeping their children, forget it. She was seized with a sudden dread. What if Barb wanted her to baby-sit for Sammy? She wrinkled her nose at the thought of changing a diaper. Or what if they wanted to form a carpool for school? Catherine had tried that once with Wilma Partridge down the street, and it had gotten terribly inconvenient and complicated. What if Barb was going into the hospital and they needed somebody to cook meals for a while? What if she wanted help unpacking boxes and getting organized? No, thank you—Barb could finish that little job all by herself!

Catherine glanced over at Della Boyd, who was standing at the counter stirring something in a bowl. Whatever this was all about, maybe she could pawn it off on Della Boyd.

November 22 - December 29

BARB

Too Much Trouble

15

Barb Chewning couldn't believe she had waited so long to start assembling things for their Thanksgiving dinner. Before this year she had always managed to get going at least two or three days in advance, but here it was the day before Thanksgiving, and she hadn't even bought a turkey yet. And all because of a poem. A short poem at that—only twelve lines. When she thought of all the time and energy she had spent wrestling with those twelve lines, it was little wonder to her that so many poets teetered on the brink of insanity and often fell in. But ever since Margaret Tuttle had challenged them the month before to try writing a poem of their own, Barb had been determined to have something ready for this month's meeting.

Balancing Sammy on one hip, Barb opened her pantry door in hopes of finding that some miracle of restocking had occurred.

"One itsy-bitsy can of sweet potatoes won't do it, will it, Sammy boy?" she said, holding the can up.

"Oranges!" Sammy said, pointing to the picture on the can.

"No, they're sweet potatoes," Barb said, laughing. "But hey, I just remembered something." She set him down. "Here, you hold the can for Mama very carefully." Then she bent to poke around in a mesh bag of potatoes on the floor under the pantry shelves. "Yep, I was right!" she said triumphantly, pulling several large sweet potatoes from among the white ones. She had almost forgotten about picking these up at the grocery store a few weeks earlier.

"Yep, I was wight!" Sammy mimicked, shaking the can he was holding.

Barb took the sweet potatoes over to the counter, and Sammy toddled after her with his can. "Yep, I was wight!" he repeated.

"They're past their prime for sure," Barb said, examining the potatoes, "but I guess it won't matter if all I'm going to do is boil and mash them." She got out a large pan and began filling it with water.

"Mash them!" Sammy shrieked excitedly, shaking the can so hard that he lost his grip on it. "Uh-oh. I drop," he said. The can rolled across the kitchen floor and under the table, and Sammy immediately fell to all fours to retrieve it.

"Get it and bring it back to Mama," Barb said. She put the pan of water on the stove to boil, then turned back to the sink. Holding a potato in both hands, she let the cool water run over it as she lifted her eyes to scan the sky through the window. "Looks like it might rain again this morning," she said. "As if we need any more rain."

From her kitchen window, she had a clear view of the Biddles' house across the street. It was one of the things she had liked most about this house when she and Curt had first looked at it five months ago. Every house she had ever lived in from the time she was a little girl had had a kitchen on the back side of the house, and not a single one of them had looked out on anything interesting. The fact that this kitchen faced the street had endeared the house to Barb from the moment she first saw it. Of course, the fact that it had five bedrooms and three baths didn't hurt either. But it was the kitchen she had fallen in love with.

"Finally!" she had told Curt. "Something to look at besides an empty lot or a bunch of trees!" He had teased her about wanting to spy on her neighbors, and she had laughed and said, "Well, I might as well get some reward for all the time I spend in the kitchen. Anyway, I can keep my finger on the pulse of the neigborhood this way."

As she picked up another potato to wash it, she saw a most amazing thing. The sky suddenly darkened with what appeared to be hundreds of big, black, cawing birds. They swooped down en masse and landed on the Biddles' front yard across the street. Just as she opened her mouth to exclaim over the sight, she heard a loud thump behind her, and Sammy let out a yelp of pain, followed by an outbreak of lusty crying.

Barb dropped the potato into the sink and whirled around. "Oh no, did you bump your head on the table, sweetie?" She crossed the floor quickly, wiping her hands on her denim jumper. "Come to Mama." She swung Sammy up into her arms and kissed the top of his head. "Just a little owie," Barb said, examining it. "It'll be all right." Then to divert his attention, she carried him to the kitchen window. "Mama's got something to show you! Look—they're all over the ground!" And she pointed to the Biddles' front yard, where the birds were still congregated. Their raucous cries had subsided, and they seemed to be occupied with eating, although Barb couldn't imagine what they might be eating. Catherine Biddle wasn't the type to set out birdseed or morsels of bread.

Sammy stopped crying at once and stared intently. "What's it?" he said in a hushed tone. He pointed at the birds. "What's it?"

Barb squeezed him. "You know what they are, you silly Sammy boy," she said, laughing. "They have feathers and fly and go 'chirp chirp tweet tweet.' You tell *me* what they are."

Still Sammy pointed and stared transfixed. "Tweet tweet," he whispered. He was so absorbed in the sight that he was barely breathing.

Then it struck Barb what they must be eating: worms. With all the rain lately, there must be plenty of worms trying to escape their little flooded underground tunnels. "Bet the poor worms hadn't counted on a whole flock of hungry blackbirds coming by for a visit!" Barb said aloud. But wasn't it odd, she thought, that they'd all crowded into a single yard—as if there weren't worms in every other yard along Brookside? They must be traveling together, heading south for the cold months. She wondered how they all got together. Was there some blackbird meeting place where they all gathered on a certain day before taking off?

"They're eating worms," Barb said.

"Eating worms," breathed Sammy.

As they stood at the window watching, the Biddles' front door suddenly flew open and out came Catherine Biddle, waving her hands and crying, "Get away! Shoo! Scat!" The birds rose in a great black wave, cawing loudly, and settled themselves in various trees nearby.

Sammy threw back his head and gurgled with laughter. "Shoo! Shoo!" he cried. "Birds all gone!"

"See them sitting up in the trees?" Barb said. "They're waiting for a chance to come back down."

Sammy's big blue eyes widened as he scanned the treetops. "Birds in trees!" he said happily. "Birds in trees!"

Across the street, Catherine stood on the top step of her front porch, hands on hips, glaring up into the trees. As usual, she was dressed in what Barb called a matchy-matchy style—slacks, blouse, vest, shoes all color-coordinated in shades of moss green and rust red. Barb could see her lips moving. Heaven help those birds, Barb thought, if Catherine Biddle got hold of them. She smiled as she imagined a revised version of Alfred Hitchcock's famous movie *The Birds*, with Catherine taking over Tippi Hedren's role. The whole plot would have to be changed, for Barb couldn't imagine Catherine being intimidated by a flock of birds. Instead she saw visions of Catherine grabbing up birds by the handful and flinging them against walls while the rest of the flock knocked themselves sense-less trying to get out of her way.

Catherine suddenly turned and went back into the house, closing the door behind her. Within seconds the birds began to float down from the trees one by one, and soon the Biddles' yard was again blanketed with them. Once more Catherine came charging out of the house, shouting and waving her arms. This time Barb joined Sammy in laughing at the sight of the great host taking sudden flight.

"Let's go outside and look at them up close," she said to Sammy, and she carried him through the hallway into the living room. Stepping out onto the front porch, she looked across the street at Catherine and, as she always did, offered up a quick prayer that this contact with her neighbor might forge another small link in their friendship, which was a mighty short chain at present. At least Catherine was beginning to open up to her more, though. "Hi, Catherine! What is this?" she called. "The great blackbird migration?"

"I have no earthly idea!" Catherine called back. "But they'd better be on their way if they know what's good for them! I don't want them poking holes all over our yard. If there's anything I hate, it's crows! They're such disgusting, ugly birds!"

Behind her, Della Boyd stepped out of the Biddles' house and waved to Barb. She was wearing a green apron over a bright fuchsia sweatsuit, and her silver gray hair was curled close to her head.

"Hello, Barb," Della Boyd called, cupping one hand to her mouth. "How's our sweet little Sammy this morning?"

"Wave to Della Boyd and Catherine," Barb told Sammy, but he cried out, "I see birds!" and flung both arms around as he looked up into the trees.

Della Boyd laughed. "Oh, look at him. Isn't he just the limit?"

"I'm trying to get myself in gear for Thanksgiving dinner," Barb called, descending her porch steps. "I let myself get sidetracked working on my poem the last couple of days, and now I'm paying for it. I'm run-ning way behind this year!"

"Why, that's just what we're doing!" Della Boyd said.

"She means working on Thanksgiving dinner, not writing poetry," Catherine interjected. "We're not running behind, though."

"Well, I did write a little piece of verse I haven't shown anybody yet," Della Boyd said. "It's not very good, but I might read it Monday night if other people read theirs." She shook her head. "It's just a little thing, and it's not at all what I hoped it would be."

Barb wondered all of a sudden what kind of poem a woman like Della

Boyd would write. "I've not been writing any poems today, though," Della Boyd added. She paused, as if the next thought were too joyful to express. "We just finished cutting up a *pie pumpkin*," she said, forming the shape of a pumpkin with her long, slender fingers. "We've got it cooking in Catherine's Crockpot right now, and I'm going to make the pies tonight!"

"Which is all a big waste of time in my opinion!" called Catherine. "I had some canned pumpkin in the pantry, but do you think she'd hear of using that? Oh, no-o-o, it has to be *real* pumpkin, she says! As if what's in the can is some kind of soybean product!" She shook her head in exasperation, but Barb noticed that she was smiling. At first she had thought it was her imagination, but now she was sure that Catherine had actually begun to mellow in small ways over the past couple of months. For one thing, she seemed to be treating Della Boyd with a little more respect now.

Sammy lifted both hands to the sky. "No, no, birdies! No! Come back, birdies!"

Sure enough, the birds were rising from the treetops, as if having passed around a message from their leader, saying, "Okay, troops, if these people are going to stand here yapping all day, let's move on to quieter pecking grounds!"

"Well, good riddance is all I have to say," Catherine said, turning abruptly to go back into the house.

"I sure hope you're talking to the birds and not me," Barb said, laughing.

Della Boyd hooted merrily. "Why, you know Catherine wouldn't say anything like that to you!" she called.

Barb smiled, actually finding it quite easy to imagine Catherine saying such a thing. Although Catherine might have begun to mellow in a few ways, there were lots of other ways that she was still her same old self.

"Say, Catherine, wait a minute," Barb said, walking down her front sidewalk toward the street. "You're still on for next Monday night, aren't you?"

"Well, of course we are," Catherine said, turning back around. "I wouldn't volunteer to have something at my house and then back out at the last minute." She frowned as Barb reached the curb and stepped out into the street.

"Just checking," Barb said. "Dottie Puckett told me on Sunday that you'd invited her to come. That was nice of you. I had asked her once, right before Bonita's accident, but she said her evenings were pretty full, and she really wasn't very interested in poetry. Then after she lost Bonita,

I guess I just figured she still wasn't interested."

"Well, I didn't really *mean* to invite her," said Catherine, "but whatever it was I said, she took it as an invitation and snapped it right up." Her frown deepened. "I think she needs to get out more, if you ask me. It sounds like the only places she ever goes are church and Thrifty Mart. I don't see how she keeps from going stark crazy cooped up in that little beauty shop of hers, smelling permanent solution and sweeping up loose hair all day long."

"I went to the beauty shop with Catherine this morning," Della Boyd said, patting her hair. "Can you tell? Dottie gave me a permanent."

"I noticed it right away," Barb said. "It's very becoming."

"It ought to be," said Catherine. "It cost a fortune."

"Well, Dottie was tickled over the invitation to the poetry meeting," Barb said. "I guess she's looking for things to take up her mind. That was really nice of you. I should've thought of asking her again, but—"

"Down, down!" Sammy said, trying to wriggle out of Barb's arms. "Want down!" Barb pulled up the hood of his little sweat shirt and set him down on the Biddles' sidewalk. He immediately trotted off and began mounting their front steps.

"We can't go inside Catherine's house, Sammy," Barb said.

Still frowning as she regarded Sammy's ascent up the steps, Catherine sighed. "I sure hope we can round up enough chairs to seat everybody on Monday night. I think we're going to have to break into two groups if we keep on growing! Of course, I imagine we'll have a slimmer crowd this time because of Thanksgiving and all." She was visibly relieved when Sammy turned toward the glider on her front porch and scrambled up into it. "I guess we could have the meeting upstairs," Catherine continued. "There would be plenty of room up there! We could just sweep up the sawdust and sit under the beams in a big, happy circle!"

"How's the project coming along up there?" Barb asked.

"Well, Blake sure isn't winning any prizes for speed, believe me," Catherine said. "He should've just gone ahead and hired somebody to do the whole thing like I told him. I don't know why he's insisting on doing the whole thing himself. At the rate he's going, we'll be lucky if it's done before Philip graduates from high school!"

"But it's going to be awfully nice when it's finished," Della Boyd put in. "He's dividing it into two big rooms, you know."

"I swing!" Sammy announced proudly from the glider.

"Here, I'll swing with you," Della Boyd said, sitting down beside him. "Isn't this fun?" She beamed at Sammy and clapped her hands like a child. "It's going to be two big rooms," she said again to Barb, spreading her hands far apart. "And Hardy's going to move up to one of them when they're finished. We're going to bring him up out of the pit—that's what Blake is always saying now because it's so dark down there in Hardy's basement room. Up out of the pit and into the sunlight is what he says. My, my, it sure will be nice when it's all done. And Blake is going to put in a bathroom up there also. My brother can do anything when it comes to remodeling!"

Catherine made no comment, but Barb saw her study Della Boyd sternly.

Barb smiled. "Well, I wouldn't worry about places to sit on Monday night," she said to Catherine. "Your living room is every bit as big as mine, probably even a little bigger."

Catherine shrugged. "Well, it's bigger than that place we met *last* month, that's for sure. I've never seen so many people squashed so close together in all my whole life! Why, Della Boyd might as well have been sitting in my lap. And *hot*—I thought I was going to pass out!"

Barb laughed. "I think everybody was glad when you spoke up and suggested turning the heat down."

"Well, somebody needed to!" Catherine said, fanning her face as if remembering the occasion. "They had that heater cranked up like it was the middle of January and thirty degrees below!"

That was the thing about Catherine, Barb thought. You could count on her to speak her mind. You always knew right where you stood with Catherine Biddle. She recalled clearly the look on Margaret Tuttle's face when Catherine had interrupted her reading of a poem about the sunrise. It had been only minutes after their last poetry meeting had gotten underway.

"Excuse me, Margaret," Catherine had said, "but speaking of the sun, I feel like it's sitting right over there in that corner." And she had gestured toward the gas heater in Jewel Scoggins' small living room. "I feel like I'm going to have a heatstroke!"

Margaret, having broken off in the middle of a word, stared in surprise at Catherine. But then she had smiled, and so had everyone else. "It is a mite warm in here," a woman named Nina said, and several others murmured agreement.

"They keep it turned up for Eldeen," said Della Boyd from the glider. "Poor old Eldeen has bad circulation in her feet. Did you hear her telling about—"

"Did I *hear* her?" said Catherine. "You'd have to be stone deaf not to hear Eldeen!" Then in a perfect imitation of Eldeen Rafferty, Catherine lowered her voice and said thickly, " 'I've tried ever'thing I can think of, but my feet still stays just as cold as blocks of ice.' " Switching back to her normal voice, she added, "That woman sounds like she's got a fog-horn stuck in her throat when she talks!"

Della Boyd laughed again. "Oh, Catherine, how can you do that? You sounded just like her!" She looked at Barb and shook her head in wonder. "Didn't she sound just like her? Catherine can copy anybody's voice."

"Well, I'm not dressed warm enough to be standing out here gabbing all day," Catherine said. "I've got to get back inside." She looked at Della Boyd. "We have things to do."

"I've got the refreshments already planned for Monday night," Della Boyd said to Barb, rising from the glider. "They're called toffee crescents."

"And they're entirely too much trouble, if you ask me," Catherine said, "but you can't tell her a thing." She rolled her eyes toward Della Boyd. "She gets her jollies out of doing things the hard way!"

"They call for those little toffee candies," said Della Boyd. "I'm going to use Catherine's food processor to crush them up."

Sammy squealed and patted his hands together. "I swing!" he said.

"Maybe we can swing again tomorrow," Della Boyd said, then addressing Barb, she added, "That food processor is just a marvel! I'd sure like to shake the man's hand that invented it!"

"Come on down now, Sammy," Barb said. "We've got to get back home." She gestured for Sammy to come, but he scooted farther back onto the glider and tried to get it rocking harder.

When he saw Barb coming up the steps toward him, he began crying, "No! I swing! I swing!"

Barb picked him up firmly and tapped his leg lightly. "Stop fussing, Sammy, or Mama will have to spank." Sammy's mouth opened wide, and he emitted a single brief wail before burying his face against Barb's shoulder.

"Poor little fellow," Della Boyd said, her face melting with sympathy, but Catherine's mouth was a thin line. Barb knew that Catherine was watching her carefully these days. In fact, ever since she and Curt had invited the Biddles to the parenting seminar back in September, she had felt that Catherine was observing everything she did, just waiting for her to slip up and make a mistake with one of the children. And Barb knew she had made more than her share. There was so much about being a mom that you couldn't learn from a parenting seminar or a book.

After telling Catherine and Della Boyd good-bye, Barb headed back across the street with Sammy still whimpering softly on her shoulder.

"Sammy want to swing," he kept saying. "Sammy want to swing."

"We'll swing again later," Barb said. "But right now Mama has to get those sweet potatoes—oh, my goodness! I forgot about the water! I hope it's not all boiled out!" She ran up the sidewalk to the front steps, remembering all the other times she had gone off and left water boiling. She had ruined one pan for good and almost caused a fire.

The front door was still standing open. She set Sammy down as soon as she got inside and raced to the kitchen. She didn't smell anything burning, so that was a good sign. Sammy followed her, calling, "What's it, Mama? What's it?" She whisked the pan off the stove and sighed with relief. Thankfully, there was still a half-inch or so of water in the bottom of it, and she set the pan in the sink to refill it.

Sammy was looking up at her wide-eyed. "It's okay," Barb said, kneeling down in front of him. "The pan didn't burn. Mama caught it in time." She squeezed him and planted a kiss on his cheek. "Say, why don't you listen to your tape recorder, okay? You can listen to your Toby Tugboat tape before nap time." She touched the end of his nose with her finger. "Want to?"

"Okay," Sammy whispered. Barb hugged him again tightly, and he scooted off toward the hallway. Barb marveled once again that he was so easygoing for a two-year-old. The twins had kept her hopping every minute of every day when they were Sammy's age—and not only because there were two of them instead of one. They had been what Curt called high-maintenance kids, fired up from the crack of dawn until bedtime, going like a tornado the whole day long, rarely giving in to afternoon naps. Compared to them, Sarah and Sammy had been a breeze. But it was like Benjamin Webb, the leader of the parenting seminar, had said: Every child is different. You can't cut out the pattern for your second child based on the behavior of your first.

The invitation to the parenting seminar had been awkward, Barb recalled—both the giving and receiving of it. It had actually been Curt's idea to invite the Biddles, but Barb had been the one to approach Catherine about it first, then Curt called Blake later that day to follow up.

Barb thought back to that first day of school in September, almost three months ago now, when she had gone over to the Biddles' house to invite them to the Benjamin Webb seminar. She had gone grocery shopping after delivering Josh, Caleb, and Sarah to their new schools, then around ten o'clock had run across the street with Sammy.

Catherine had let her know right away that she was on her way out and didn't have much time to spare, so Barb had launched right into the dinner invitation, telling Catherine they had a proposition for her and Blake and apologizing for the late notice. "Curt and I would like to take you and Blake out for dinner tonight if you have the time," she had said. Catherine had looked startled—and distrustful. "We thought about that place over in Derby called the Purple Calliope," Barb said. "Have you ever been there?"

"Yes, I have."

From the way Catherine said it, Barb got the feeling that it wasn't an experience she wished to repeat. But maybe she was wrong. Though Catherine was totally transparent at times, it was hard to read her at others. Maybe she was just waiting to find out more.

Della Boyd, who had been stirring something in a bowl at the time, said, "Why, that's a real nice idea, and don't you worry yourself one bit about the children, Catherine. I can whip up something easy for them for supper. You and Blake go on and enjoy yourselves. We'll get along just fine." She stopped stirring for a moment and looked back at Barb. "I'm making bread this morning. I've already got one kind rising." She smiled as she looked toward the covered loaf pan on the stovetop. "I used to make bread regularly back in Yazoo City, but I stopped doing it for some reason. I told Catherine this morning, though, that I was in the mood to pick it back up, and I decided I might as well go ahead and use the other package of yeast while I was at it, so I found this recipe for oatmeal bread in Catherine's Betty Crocker cookbook, and so . . ."

Catherine heaved an audible sigh, and Della Boyd trailed off. She smiled over at Sammy, who was struggling vigorously to get down from Barb's lap. "What's it?" he said over and over, pointing at something. He waddled toward a tall stool at the end of the counter.

"Why, look what he's found," Della Boyd said. "That's the Frisbee I bought for Hardy." Sammy lifted it in one hand and waved it like a tambourine, then dropped it and jumped on top of it.

"Oh, let's don't jump on it, Sammy," Barb said. "It might break. You don't want to break Hardy's nice Frisbee, do you?"

"Fizzbee!" Sammy squealed. "I not bweak Fizzbee!" He sat down at once and picked up the bright orange Frisbee with the chartreuse ring around the edge, then flung it across the floor. It slid across the ceramic tile with the speed of a hockey puck on ice and hit the baseboard with a whap.

"Careful, sweetie, let's not throw it in the house," Barb said.

"I didn't think it was a very good present at first," Della Boyd said, "but then Hardy started taking it out in the backyard a week or two ago and started teaching Kinko to catch it, and you know, it's really amazing how that dog can learn. You wouldn't think a dog that big could jump so high, but . . ." She suddenly caught her breath. "Oh my, what am I thinking? You might not want Sammy playing with something Kinko's had in his mouth."

Barb waved a hand and smiled. "Oh, he's played with lots nastier things, I'm sure. Anyway, germs die in forty-some seconds, you know."

Della Boyd's mouth dropped open. "Forty seconds?" she said. "Is that a fact? I'll have to remember that. Well, it's been a lot longer than forty seconds since Kinko played with it. You should see that dog jump! He's big, but he sure can jump high."

Sammy picked up the Frisbee again.

"That thing shouldn't even be in the house, Della Boyd," Catherine said. "I sure didn't know Kinko had been slobbering all over it."

Della Boyd tapped her wooden spoon against the mixing bowl and smiled. "Did I tell you it glows in the dark?" she said to Barb. "I bought it at a toy store in Yazoo City called The Whirligig—isn't that a clever name for a toy store?—and Mr. Arnett, the man that owned the store, said it was real popular with the young people nowadays, but then after I got here and saw what a big boy Hardy had grown to be, I was a little worried that it wasn't the right gift. But he's started taking it out in the backyard with Kinko now and . . ."

"Okay, Della Boyd!" Catherine said. "I'm sure Barb didn't come over here this morning to hear you give the life story of Hardy's glow-in-the-dark Frisbee, for heaven's sake! Now, why don't we let her get back to whatever it was she was saying? I've got lots of things to do this morning."

"Oh, all right," Della Boyd said pleasantly.

With both Catherine and Della Boyd looking at her expectantly, Barb took a deep breath. Now came the hard part. Suddenly all of this didn't seem like nearly as good an idea as it had when Curt had suggested it the night before. "Well, the invitation's not over yet," she said. "Dinner's only the first part."

Catherine pinched in the corners of her mouth and nodded knowingly. "All right, what's the rest of it?" she said. "Are you selling Amway, or is it some kind of insurance deal?"

"Neither," Barb said. She couldn't help laughing at Catherine's bluntness. "You don't have to spend a penny, I promise."

Catherine stared at her in icy silence. "Well, then, what is it?" she asked.

"Well, we were hoping you'd come to a meeting with us, is all."

"A meeting?" It was clear from the tone of her voice that she would just as soon step into a snake pit. "What kind of meeting? If it has anything to do with religion or politics, forget it!"

"Nope, no revivals or town hall meetings," Barb said, laughing. "And it lasts only an hour and a half, so we'll be home before nine unless we stop somewhere for dessert afterward, which we might do if you don't mind. The speaker is really good. I can promise you he won't be boring. We heard him once before, maybe eight or ten years ago when we used to live up near Asheville." She paused, then said again, "He's really a good speaker."

"Well, it seems like I'm getting all the details except for one," said Catherine. "What is this really good speaker that you heard eight or ten years ago when you used to live up near Asheville going to be speaking *about*? What *kind* of meeting is it?"

Barb suddenly wished she had stayed home to unpack her groceries instead of coming over here to the Biddles' house. She knew there was no way to answer Catherine's question without making it sound like she thought Catherine *needed* to attend a lecture on this particular subject. She should have thought through all of this beforehand.

But now that she had gotten this deep into it, she'd just have to brace herself and get it over with. "It's a series called 'Good Kids,' " she said, then rushed on. "Benjamin Webb is the speaker. You've probably heard of him. He's a child psychologist and family counselor who lectures all over the country. He's written several books about kids and parents, and he has eight children of his own, so he—"

"Eight? Is he a Roman Catholic?" Catherine asked. "Or a Mormon?"

"No, no, but he sure knows kids firsthand. The man is amazing! I wish I had just a thimbleful of his wisdom when it comes to dealing with kids. He tells some of the most interesting stories about cases he's worked with." Barb wondered if she sounded as nervous as she felt. Catherine was staring at her as if she'd like to chew her up and spit her out.

She decided she'd let Curt break the news to Blake that the meeting was to be held at their church, the Church of the Open Door over in Derby. Maybe it was a little deceptive not to mention the fact that besides being a child psychologist and family counselor, Benjamin Webb was a born-again Christian, but she wasn't about to get into that now. Rising to take her leave, Barb clenched her hands together and said brightly, "Well, you might want to talk it over with Blake. Curt's going to try to give him a call later today. We sure hope you can go with us." She scooped up Sammy from the floor. "I've got to get back home now," she said quickly. "Just stay where you are—I know the way out. Bye! Talk to you later."

As she headed through the hallway toward the front door, she heard Della Boyd's voice from the kitchen. "You know, there was plenty of that spaghetti left over from Sunday. I could heat that up for the children's supper. And then the bread I'm making now, plus a tossed salad—why, don't you worry one minute about the children and me, Catherine. You go on and accept that invitation. We'll be just—"

"I know, I know, Della Boyd!" Catherine cried out. "I know you have everything all planned out!"

Barb had been astonished in the end that the invitation had been accepted, but she was sure it was Blake more than Catherine who had wanted to go. And she was also sure that something had happened that very day to make Blake so open to attending a lecture about parenting. He as much as told them so during dinner at the Purple Calliope that night.

"You gotta wonder sometimes," he had said at one point, staring at a piece of steak on the end of his fork, "how a kid in your own house gets so far gone." He had glanced over at Catherine, who was stabbing at her salad greens with a vengeance. "I was wondering about that just this morning, as a matter of fact," he had said.

A Truth of Life
16

At half past two on Thursday, the Chewnings had finished their Thanksgiving dinner, which by Barb's calculation had probably taken more than ten hours to prepare and less than thirty minutes to consume. She took the last bite of her pumpkin pie and told Curtis she was going to lie down with Sammy, who had fallen asleep in his high chair, clutching a half-eaten crescent roll in one hand.

"That's fine, we'll get the table cleared," Curtis said as she gently pried the roll from Sammy's fist and lifted him from the high chair.

Caleb yawned loudly and put his head down next to his plate. "I suddenly feel really sleepy, too, Dad," he said, and, following suit, Joshua rolled out of his chair, flopped his lanky form down on the carpet, and began snoring loudly. Fighting a smile, Sarah watched her brothers' antics, glancing from one to the other and then back to her father.

Barb stooped to kiss the top of Sarah's head as she carried Sammy out of the dining room. She often worried about Sarah and wondered if she was overlooking something obvious as a mother. Sarah was so quiet and docile it was easy to forget she was around half the time. Wasn't this the kind of child she had read about—who often erupted at some point and committed some shocking act of violence?

Sarah didn't seem to mind solitude. No, that wasn't right. It wasn't that she didn't mind solitude—she actually seemed to *prefer* it. She would spend long hours in her bedroom with her dolls and books, talking softly to herself, and Barb often found sheets of paper on which Sarah had written brief fanciful stories with tiny, intricate illustrations all around the margins. She had discovered one of them just this morning, in fact, stuck between the pages of a magazine in the den and had shown it to Curt.

The written part was only five short sentences, a simple little story about a girl named Gilda Oxrent who lived in a cottage in the forest and ate wild berries and honey, but the drawings along the edges were astonishing in their detail. Curt had studied the paper for several long moments before saying, "Wow . . . special kid, huh?"

That was just like Curt. While Barb sometimes had thoughts like "Should we look into counseling?" he took everything in stride. No deviation from the norm seemed to alarm him. When the twins were younger, there were days when Barb was positive that somebody in their house should be institutionalized—either the boys or herself. But then when Curt would come home and she'd start describing the day, the boys' rambunctious energy and nonstop escapades never translated into the exhausting reality they had been. More often than not he had ended up chuckling, and, of course, she usually ended up laughing, too, though the day's events had been anything but funny at the time. Barb supposed it was a combination of being a man and a pediatrician that made Curt so broad-minded about children and their individual differences.

As Barb carried Sammy out of the dining room, Curtis said, "Okay, guys, suit yourselves, but no turkey sandwiches and leftover pumpkin pie tonight for anybody who doesn't help with the dishes. Come on, Sarah, we'll do it by ourselves."

"Here, Dad," Josh said brightly, springing from the floor, "let me carry that for you."

"You boys better be careful with my good dishes," Barb called back over her shoulder. "I still haven't replaced that platter you broke a year ago messing around."

"Yeah, Josh, you klutz," Caleb said, "be careful."

Barb smiled as she passed the framed pictures of her children in the hallway on her way to the bedroom. She knew every mother thought her kids were the best, which was odd since it was generally the mother who saw her kids' faults so regularly and at such close range. She wondered if every mother was seized with sudden surges of love as powerful as the ones she felt. Or moments of paralyzing fear when imagining all the different kinds of harm that could come their way.

She remembered a recent conversation she and Catherine had been having less than a week ago when they were interrupted by a telephone call. She smiled again now as she thought of the humorous irony of it all.

For all her own complaints about her three children, Catherine Biddle was fiercely defensive of them when it was someone else who was doing the complaining. They had been in Catherine's kitchen in the early afternoon. Barb had run over to ask for an egg, which she had forgotten to buy at the grocery store because she had forgotten to write eggs on her list. Catherine always seemed to have whatever item she needed to borrow, but she never let an opportunity pass to instruct Barb about how to keep from running out of things.

After telling Barb for at least the tenth time about her method of writing an item on her grocery list *as soon as* she opened a new box, jar, bag, or carton of something, Catherine had begun talking about her son Hardy's terrible organizational habits. "Too bad an organized mind isn't hereditary," she said, "especially with boys. Both of my sons are just walking disasters. You wouldn't have believed the chaos in Hardy's bedroom when Sparkle and Della Boyd finally got up their nerve to go downstairs and clean it out like they did Philip's. Why, it looked like those pictures you see on TV of homes ripped apart by tornadoes—things just thrown around and heaped up all over the place! Of course, knowing Hardy, I wasn't a bit surprised. He can just *look* at something and mess it up!"

She had gone on to describe his empty closet—empty because all the clothes and shoes were strewn about the floor. "And the *bathroom*," she said, waving her hand in front of her nose, "well, I don't want to make you sick to your stomach, so I won't go into all the sordid details, but let's just say it would have kept a biology class busy for a whole semester classifying all the different things growing down there!" She shook her head. "Of course, he was *supposed* to have been cleaning his own bathroom every week, but his idea of cleaning a bathroom is to flush the toilet every now and then."

It always surprised Barb that once Catherine got started on a subject, she never seemed to care that she was telling things that might best be kept secret. "And then Blake had to go and throw an all-American classic fit when he saw all the junk they brought upstairs in garbage bags to throw away," she continued. "Of all the days for him to come home right in the middle of the day for no good reason. He saw all those bags and down the stairs he went, ranting and raving, to see for himself. Della Boyd tried to keep him from doing it, but he wouldn't listen. Coming when he did, though, at least he didn't see the worst of it, thank goodness, or there's no telling what he would've done. That was the day he put his foot down and said Hardy couldn't stay in the basement anymore, that he was finishing the attic and moving him upstairs, though I told him it's just going to be the same story all over again up in the attic—if he ever even gets the bedrooms up there finished, that is! Hardy will probably get married and leave home before Blake gets done with the attic." She lifted her hands in a dramatic pose of mock horror and added, "Married! I pity the poor girl who ends up with Hardy!"

Then with hardly a breath, Catherine forged ahead, freely criticizing Hardy for what she called his "animal behavior" and Blake for his "hobbyhorse lectures to the kids," which according to her never did the least bit of good, although Barb herself thought she had seen small signs of improvement in Hardy's behavior over the past couple of months.

She knew that Blake was making a real effort to turn some things around at home. He had bought all three of Benjamin Webb's books about parenting and had asked Curtis several times for his opinion about things involving one of the children. He had even come to their church twice on Wednesday nights, by himself, to hear Pastor Hawthorne speak on family unity. He told Curtis not long ago that he knew he had "a lot of damage to undo" with the children, that he had let a lot of important things go over the years and now they were all paying for it.

Catherine kept talking. "It's a wonder Hardy's not flunking every subject he's taking," she said. "If he wasn't so smart, he would be. He never has the first clue about what he's got for homework, or at least he *acts* like he doesn't, and studying for tests is a totally foreign concept to him." Sighing heavily, she summed it all up: "He has absolutely *no gumption* when it comes to anything important!" It was at this point that the telephone had rung, and from a back room, Della Boyd had called out, "I'll get it, Catherine!"

Barb, egg in hand, had moved toward the doorway into the living room. "Well, I need to run. Sammy will be waking up from his nap pretty soon."

"It's for you," Della Boyd said to Catherine, walking into the kitchen with the portable telephone. "Oh, hello, Barb, I didn't know you were here. Say, I want to show you something if you can wait just a minute. I'd like your opinion." And she headed back down the hallway after handing the phone to Catherine.

"Hello," Catherine said into the receiver. She said nothing else for several long seconds but appeared to be listening intently, frowning all the while. Barb walked out into the hallway so as to give her some privacy. She needn't have bothered, however, for Catherine suddenly exploded, apparently unconcerned about Barb's overhearing.

"Well, what do you expect?" she said. "He's a *boy*, for crying out loud! So he doesn't bring his book to class—I'll bet half the boys in your class don't bring their books. And if he's passing the tests, then why is the homework such a big deal? He probably knows more about algebra than anybody else in the whole class. I mean, isn't it just finding *x* and *y*?"

Catherine paused to listen for another few seconds, then said, "Well, maybe if the classes were more interesting, the students wouldn't get distracted and act up so much! Hardy's probably bored stiff. He's actually got a lot of self-motivation, but you've got to meet him halfway. When I was in high school, my teachers always . . . ."

"Here it is," Della Boyd said, coming toward Barb from her bedroom at the end of the hall. "Here, can you come into the den and sit down a minute?" She handed Barb a sheet of notebook paper. "It's that little bit of a poem I told you about that I've been working on for our next meeting. I'd sure appreciate it if you'd read it and tell me what you think. It's a villanelle. Remember that villanelle Margaret showed us about that man's father dying?"

Barb nodded. " 'Do Not Go Gentle Into That Good Night.' "

"Yes, that's the one," Della Boyd said. "Of course, mine doesn't come close to that one."

Seated on the edge of the den sofa, Barb studied Della Boyd's poem, penciled neatly in a small, graceful script. She liked the title: "Burning the Edges." She began to read, but from the kitchen she kept hearing Catherine's voice. "Well, *you're* the teacher! What can I do about it when I'm not even there?"

"Oh my," Della Boyd said, cocking her head, "it sounds like somebody's got Catherine upset, doesn't it?"

Barb had stayed only another minute or two after that, for Della Boyd's nineteen-line poem didn't take long to read. She seemed greatly pleased at Barb's comment of "Wow, how interesting. I can tell you spent a lot of time on this," which really could have been taken a number of different ways. Frankly, Barb wasn't completely sure what Della Boyd was driving at in the poem, but she knew a good villanelle wasn't easy to write. She also knew that her own poem was coming mighty slow and was a long way from perfection.

"I keep tinkering with those repeating lines," Della Boyd said as she walked Barb to the front door. "They still don't seem to be just right."

Catherine's telephone conversation seemed to be over now, for the only sounds from the kitchen were the running of water and the slamming of a cupboard door.

Barb had returned home with the egg she had borrowed and a renewed vow to keep knocking at the Biddles' door. What a houseful of unique people they were, and they all desperately needed something. Even though they invariably closed up at any mention of God, Barb knew that the gospel was powerful. Over and over she had seen the most unlikely people accept Christ and turn their lives around. Still, she often felt that her faith was weak concerning the Biddles—their worldly perspective and self-sufficiency seemed so deeply rooted—but God was still in the business of working miracles. She firmly believed that. Quit doubting, she told herself.

She had prayed for Hardy that day. Anybody could tell he was a bright kid. And funny, too—a real individual. But, as Curtis said, he had a lot of loose wires that needed grounding. She prayed for Josh and Caleb that day, too, that they could make friends with Hardy. They had gotten him to shoot baskets with them in the driveway a number of times, but as soon as they invited him to any kind of youth activity at church, he made a joke out of it and found a quick excuse to leave. He still seemed to regard them with a mixture of suspicion and loathing, though at times he almost forgot himself and actually laughed at something one of them said.

"But hey, it's two against one," Josh had told Barb recently. "We'll keep wearing him down. He can't resist our wit and charm forever."

After the visit at the Biddles' house that day, one of the lines of Della Boyd's poem kept going through Barb's mind. "The clearing broadened when the edges burned." The poem's tone was curious in that while she had been reading it, the lines seemed very quiet and the meaning obscured, but when she had finished, she felt a ringing in her ears as if she had heard a deafening roar. She hardly knew what to think of it. She thought the poem had potential, but she didn't trust herself enough to say definitely.

Two months ago she never would have thought Della Boyd capable of writing a poem, but she was beginning to realize that there was a lot more to Della Boyd than most people guessed. She seemed so unaware so much of the time that you assumed she wasn't terribly bright. Then she went and wrote a villanelle titled "Burning the Edges" that made your ears ring. True, Barb didn't catch it, except that she thought it must have something to do with Della Boyd's house fire, but she had read it only once and was more willing to lay the blame on her cursory reading—which Margaret Tuttle had stressed repeatedly was *not* the way to read a poem—than on the poem itself.

Barb laid Sammy down gently on their bed now and spread a light blanket over him. She loved Thanksgiving Day. Tonight they would have a fire going in the den and watch their video of *It's a Wonderful Life* together. She pulled down the window shade and slipped off her shoes. As she slid under the blanket with Sammy, she smiled again at Catherine's heated defense of Hardy on the telephone that day. How funny it was that in one breath a mother could say her son had "absolutely no gumption" and in the next that he had "a lot of self-motivation."

We mothers are a curious lot, she thought to herself. She looked over at Sammy and watched him breathe. Would the day come, she wondered, when a teacher would call her about his behavior at school? Would she take his side as Catherine had done? She began to pray, first for Sammy, then for Sarah, then for Joshua and Caleb, then for Curtis. She then progressed through the Biddle family, and at last she fell asleep.

She wasn't sure exactly what it was that woke her up. So many things intersected at about the same time that it could have been any one of them. She did remember glancing quickly at the bedside table. The digital clock read 3:56. She had been in the middle of a dream during which Curt had shouted something, but she couldn't make it out and kept asking, "What? What did you say? What?"

At some point before, during, or after the dream, the telephone had rung, and she had heard Sarah's voice saying "Daddy? Daddy! It's for you!" She could tell from the darkness of the room that it had clouded up outside—more rain on the way, as predicted for Thanksgiving weekend. Almost simultaneously she heard an ominous roll of thunder, a distant train whistle, and a dog barking nearby. Probably the Biddles' dog, Kinko, since she knew of no other dogs on this street. A solid thump against the back of the house was followed by silence. She thought she heard the boys' voices in the backyard.

Barb slipped out from under the blanket and sat up on the edge of the bed. She felt dazed and wondered for a moment if she were still dreaming. She saw that Sammy was still fast asleep, one fist balled up under his chin. Everything was quiet now, almost too quiet. She rose slowly and headed toward the hallway. As she pulled the door open, she almost fell over Sarah, who was standing right at the threshold peering up at her. Barb wondered how long she had been standing there. She pictured Sarah stationing herself in front of the door, staring intently at the doorknob, determined to wait as long as necessary for her mother to emerge.

"Daddy's across the street at the Biddles' house," Sarah said. "He said to tell you."

Something in Sarah's gray eyes made Barb ask quickly, "What's wrong?"

"Philip got hurt," Sarah said. "They called Daddy to come over."

"Where are Josh and Caleb?" Barb asked.

"They're out in the backyard. Joe Leonard came over, and they're playing soccer."

"You stay here, sweetie," Barb said. "When Sammy wakes up, you can give him some juice and play with him, okay? I need to go see if Daddy needs any help." She started down the hallway, then turned back.

"Do you know how Philip got hurt?"

Sarah shook her head. "Mrs. Biddle called. She was talking fast, and then Daddy came to the phone, and then he left." Sarah took a deep ragged breath and pressed her lips together. "Oh, Mommy, you don't think Philip died, do you?"

Barb came back to her quickly and bent down to hug her. "I don't think so, sweetheart. Why don't you pray and ask God to help Philip? Now, can you be brave and stay here in the house by yourself while I go check on things?" Sarah nodded. "Thank you for being my big girl," Barb added, taking Sarah's small, earnest face between her hands. "Your brothers are out back if you need anything."

The Biddles' front door was partly open. Barb didn't even bother to ring the doorbell but went on in, calling, "Catherine? Blake? It's Barb." She thought she heard muffled voices in the kitchen, but she found that they were actually coming upstairs from the door that led to the basement. From the top of the stairs she could see that Philip was lying on the floor at the bottom of the steps, one leg bent at an odd angle. Curtis was on his knees, leaning over him, and Blake, Catherine, and Della Boyd were all kneeling around them. Catherine, a hand to Philip's forehead, kept repeating, "Oh, Philip, Philip, baby, please open your eyes," in a voice that sounded nothing like her own. Barb didn't see Hardy anywhere, but Olivia was standing behind her father, one hand across her mouth.

It was Olivia who first looked up at the top of the stairs and saw Barb. By now the sounds of an approaching siren could be heard. "Did he fall?" Barb asked, addressing her question to Olivia, who nodded.

"Philip, Philip honey, don't go. Please don't go," Catherine moaned. "Open your eyes, Philip. Open your eyes, baby. Stay with us."

Curt looked at Blake and said something. "The ambulance is coming, Catherine," Blake said. "Let's go outside and meet them." He even tried to take her arm to help her up, but she flung him off.

"I'm not leaving Philip!" she cried. "I'm his mother!"

It was Barb who met the ambulance outside and led the attendants to the basement. She stayed upstairs in the kitchen, watching the scene below. As the paramedics eased Philip onto a stretcher, she suddenly became aware of someone else in the kitchen, and she turned to see Hardy standing behind her. For once his swagger was gone. His eyes were hard, but he had a vulnerable look about his mouth that Barb had never seen. It was his mouth that made Barb go to him and, without meaning to, enfold him in an embrace. "Oh, Hardy, I'm so sorry," she said. She halfway expected him to jerk away from her and say something sarcastic, but he didn't. He didn't say anything at all. She released him but stayed at his side, and together they watched as the paramedics negotiated the stretcher up the narrow stairway.

Catherine came up the stairs right behind the stretcher, still chanting, but in a near whisper now. "No, Philip, don't go, don't leave us, open your eyes! Oh, Philip, baby, don't go!" She was dressed in a teal sweater and gray wool slacks, a picture of stylishness as always, but the silver earrings dangling beneath her shiny bob of red hair somehow seemed inappropriate to Barb at a time like this. She couldn't help thinking back to earlier in the day, wondering what had been going through Catherine's mind when she had gotten dressed this morning. No doubt she had been looking forward to a bountiful Thanksgiving dinner with her family. Spearing the tiny sterling silver posts into her earlobes, she never could have dreamed that the day would unfold like this. How swiftly disaster could descend, Barb thought. The longer she lived, the more she saw that this was a truth of life.

As the paramedics carried Philip through the doorway and turned to go through the living room, Catherine caught sight of Barb and Hardy in the kitchen. In a flash her pretty face, which had been crumpled with despair, completely changed. Her eyes glinted, and her mouth tightened. Pointing straight at Hardy, she raised her voice and, to Barb's utter amazement, said to him, "If anything happens to Philip, I never want to see your face again."

Barb knew that at any ordinary time this kind of comment would have invited a lewd retort from Hardy. He might have started listing various body parts, asking his mother if she'd be willing to see *those* instead. Barb knew what he was capable of. She had heard him on more than one occasion. Now he inhaled as if to reply, but he clamped his lips together and said nothing. In a moment he had wheeled around and disappeared through the kitchen door into the backyard.

Barb followed the others through the house and into the front yard. Outside, neighbors were gathered all along the street, huddled in groups along the curb, watching the house. Barb looked across the street and saw the living room drapery pulled to one side and Sarah's face against the windowpane. The twins were standing in the driveway with their friend from church, Joe Leonard.

In no time Philip was borne away, with Catherine beside him in the ambulance. Curt rode in the ambulance, too. He had assured Blake and Catherine that he'd keep a close eye on Philip and take care of all the details in the emergency room. Blake, Della Boyd, and Olivia followed shortly in Blake's car, none of them apparently giving any thought to Hardy.

"I'll close up your house and then come down later," Barb said to Blake in the front yard before they left, and Della Boyd, looking as if she were in a trance, said to Blake, "My pocketbook. Let me just run back to my bedroom and get my pocketbook. Wait for me to get my pocketbook." She was gone for only the briefest time, then reappeared clasping her black purse. "I found my pocketbook," she said distractedly. "Let's go see Philip now." As she got into the car, Barb heard her say, "It was on the chair beside my bed. I always keep my pocketbook there."

After they left, Barb explained to all the neighbors that Philip had taken a fall down the basement stairs. When they asked her how serious it was, all she could say was what Curt had told her when she had asked the same thing. "Time will tell." Barb had heard him say that more times than she could remember. Anyone could see that Philip's leg was broken, of course, and it was evident that he had struck his head during the fall, but Curt had learned a long time ago to be cautious when predicting the outcome of head injuries. Barb looked around at her neighbors apologetically. "Wish I could tell you more," she said, "but I just got here a few minutes ago myself, and I'm not sure exactly what happened."

"I had a cousin who died falling down the stairs," said Loretta Whittington. "Broke his neck." Several people shot disapproving looks at her.

"Kids are supple," Trixie Thorndike snapped. "They can bounce back from a fall better than adults."

"Well, it sure is a sad thing to happen on Thanksgiving Day," Caroline Burkett said.

An idea suddenly came to Barb. "If nobody would be offended," she said, "I'd like to offer up a word of prayer for Philip on behalf of his neighbors."

There was an audible murmur of assent, and Myron Abernathy said, "Go ahead, Mrs. Chewning. We're all with you on that."

As Barb prayed, she heard Wilma Partridge whispering, "Yes, Jesus. Yes, oh please, dear God," and when she finished, Wilma said loudly, "Amen, may the Lord see fit to answer our prayers!" Barb made a note to walk down the street to visit the Partridges soon. She didn't know Wilma Partridge except to give her a neighborly wave. She lived several houses away from the Chewnings, down toward the cul-de-sac, so Barb rarely had reason to drive past her house. She had heard Wilma was a single mother, and she knew that the Partridge boy, Andy, was a friend of Philip's. He stood beside his mother now, his arm wrapped around her waist. Was it possible, Barb wondered, that this kid was a Christian? Had he ever shared his faith with Philip?

As the neighbors began to disperse after the prayer was over, Barb told Josh and Caleb to go check on Sarah and Sammy and then come back over to the Biddles' house. "I'm worried about Hardy," she told them. "I'm going to look around for him."

The twins looked puzzled. "Hardy?" Caleb asked. "Did he get hurt, too?"

"No, I don't think so," Barb said. "But he left the house right after they took Philip away, and I haven't seen him since. He was pretty upset." A nagging thought kept returning to Barb's mind. She hoped she was wrong about it, but she couldn't shake the fear that Philip hadn't fallen down the stairs by himself. If Hardy had had something to do with it, that would explain Catherine's comment to him in the kitchen.

Barb closed her eyes. She couldn't forget the look on Hardy's face in the kitchen. Nor could she get Catherine's words out of her mind. What must he be going through? What must Catherine be going through?

Barb went out into the Biddles' backyard first and called Hardy's name. Kinko came slinking toward her with his tail tucked but still wagging, as if uncertain of his reception. He stopped a few feet from her, flopped down on his stomach, and looked up at her hopefully. Barb reached out her hand and spoke softly as she approached him. "Wish you could talk, buddy," she said. "You could tell us if you saw Hardy." As she stroked the dog's head, he nuzzled her hand.

"Here we are, Mom," Josh said. He, Caleb, and Joe Leonard were standing on the patio. "Sarah's okay, and Sammy's still asleep. We'll help you find Hardy."

But they couldn't. They searched the entire backyard, even the big magnolia tree, and every room of the house, but there wasn't a trace of him.

"He probably climbed over the back fence there," Caleb said as they returned to the backyard and stood together on the patio.

"He could've gone through the woods and come out over near the highway," Joshua said. "No telling where he is now."

Barb sighed. "Well, let's go back home. I need to get down to the hospital." She dreaded telling Blake and Catherine that Hardy wasn't at home. She hated to add to their worries.

"Maybe Hardy's on his way to the hospital," Caleb said as they went back into the Biddles' house, but Barb didn't believe it for a minute.

"Here, let's put some of this leftover food away before we go," she said, looking around the kitchen.

At any other time one of the twins would have responded with a joke, like "Yeah, give me a fork and I'll put it away!" But today neither of them said a word. Barb thought she had never seen anything gloomier than the turkey carcass sitting on the counter. A small pile of meat and a long knife lay beside it.

As they headed across the street to their own home several minutes later, Barb saw that Sarah was still at the living room window. She felt something similar to guilt at the sight of her daughter's sweet face. She thought of Sammy and the way he so often smiled when he was sleeping. She looked up at the twins, walking on either side of her, their faces still flushed from the exertion of their earlier soccer game. Her children were safe, but Catherine's weren't. Behind her, from the Biddles' backyard, she could hear Kinko howling mournfully.

That Small Gesture

17

Fifteen minutes later Barb was ready to walk out the door on her way to the hospital when she received a phone call that Philip was being transported by ambulance from the Dickson County Hospital Emergency Room to Greenville Memorial Hospital. She was grateful that Curt had thought to send word so she wouldn't make an unnecessary trip to the wrong hospital.

As she drove to Greenville, she thought back to the happy beginning of the day. After pancakes and bacon that morning, Curt had gone to the hospital to make rounds and check on a newborn, but he had been home shortly after noon and had been seated at the head of the table when they sat down at two o'clock for their Thanksgiving dinner. That alone was reason for rejoicing, for Barb could remember many Thanksgivings when he hadn't been there. Turning off Highway 11 onto 385, she glanced at the clock on the dashboard. It seemed impossible that only two hours ago she had taken the last bite of her turkey dinner and gone back to her bedroom with Sammy to take a nap. What enormous changes could take place in the blink of an eye.

It was close to four-thirty when she arrived at Greenville Memorial and found Curt and the Biddles sitting in a waiting room on the pediatric floor. Philip's broken leg had been set, they told her, but he was still unconscious. A neurologist was examining him now and would talk to them as soon as he was finished. Philip would then be taken to a pediatric intensive care unit, where they could be with him, Blake said, "until something happens one way or the other." Catherine glared at him fiercely, then looked away quickly.

"We just have to wait now," Curt said quietly. "Wait and pray." He turned to Blake. "They'll let you and Catherine go in to see him as soon as they get him settled in the intensive care unit. I've seen people wake up from falls like this and snap right back in no time. It just all depends."

"And sometimes they don't ever wake up, do they?" Catherine said, turning to stare at Curt for several long moments.

Out in the hall they heard the sound of something heavy rolling by and a woman's voice plainly called out, "Your shift over at eleven, Vicky Sue?" Another voice answered. "Yes, and I'm counting the hours. It's been one of those days." Catherine scowled at the doorway. Barb knew she must be wishing that her own shift here at the hospital would be over at eleven like Vicky Sue's and that all her troubles would be ended by then. "One of those days" was an extreme understatement for a day like today.

As gently as she could, Barb told them about Hardy's disappearance. "It's probably nothing," she said, "but I figured you'd want to know."

Catherine's shoulders sagged. "This is all we need right now," she said. Within minutes, Blake had called everyone he could think of who might know where Hardy was, but nothing had turned up. He called the police station in Derby also, but they said they couldn't do anything yet since he had been missing such a short time. Barb had told the twins before leaving for the hospital to keep a close eye on the Biddles' house and to let them know at once if they saw any sign of Hardy.

"Hardy's pretty impulsive, but somehow I can't see him running away for good," Blake said. "For one thing, he doesn't have any money."

"He could *get* money," Catherine said. "He's a very resourceful boy when he has to be." She spoke slowly, as if each word were a dead weight.

"He can't be far away," said Blake. "Surely he's wondering about Philip." But he said it more as a question than a statement of fact.

Della Boyd, who hadn't spoken till now, sat up on the edge of the vinyl sofa and said earnestly, "I think Hardy needs to be here."

"I'd be glad to do anything," Curt said. "I could drive back to Berea to look for him and then bring him here to the hospital when I find him." Nobody questioned his use of *when* instead of *if*, and for a moment it was easy to imagine that Hardy had merely gone out for a walk and would be returning any minute.

"You've been such a help already," Blake said. "You don't know how much it means." He paused and looked down as if too overcome to talk. Then he continued, addressing Barb. "This guy is something," he said, motioning to Curt. "The way he took charge over at the other hospital— well, it was something. We didn't know what end was up. He talked with the other doctor in the emergency room, and thirty minutes later here we are in Greenville." He looked around the waiting room, then back at Barb. "Curt said the neurologist who's checking Philip is one of the best."

"It wasn't a hard decision to make," Curt said. "We've got a good hospital, but it can't handle head traumas. Anybody would have had him sent here to Greenville."

Outside the rain had begun again, a steady, cold downpour. The waiting room was brightly lit with large colorful pictures of fairy-tale characters on the walls. Barb wondered briefly whether it was the best choice of artwork for a waiting room outside pediatric intensive care. Would parents want to look at such cheerful depictions of fantasy land when their own children were fighting for their lives in a very real world, when they might never wake up to hear another fairy tale? But perhaps the parents who suffered in this room never even noticed the pictures on the walls.

There were only four other people in the room now, sitting in pairs on opposite sides of the room. One man was sleeping, exhaling raspily with each breath, and the woman next to him looked pale and worn out. The other pair looked dazed—a girl of about ten with a conspicuous scar running across one cheek and a disheveled old woman, maybe her grandmother, wearing a man's coat and a pair of bedroom slippers. They sat side by side, staring at the Biddles with their mouths open. They had the look of people well acquainted with hospital waiting rooms. It struck Barb that most likely none of them in this room had expected to end their Thanksgiving Day this way. She couldn't help wondering about all the other people who had sat in these same chairs in the past weeks and months. What stories of human pain this room could tell.

It was here in the waiting room that Barb and Curt learned the facts about Philip's fall. It was as Barb had feared—Hardy had played a role in the accident. According to Blake, the boys had been in the kitchen when a dispute erupted. Della Boyd was the only other person in the kitchen at the time.

She took up the story from there. "Dinner was over, you see, and I was cutting the rest of the turkey off the bone. Catherine was back in Olivia's bedroom trying to help her with a flower arrangement that's due on Monday for her home furnishings class. That's one of the electives Olivia is taking this year." A troubled look crossed Della Boyd's face. "Home furnishings—schools have changed so much since my time." She shook her head. "Catherine wasn't very happy that Olivia's teacher assigned a project for the Monday after a holiday, and I think she had a good point. I don't think a teacher should require the students to spend their holidays that way." Barb noticed that Della Boyd still clutched her black handbag possessively, as if convinced that she was surrounded by petty thieves. "The flower project was due on Monday," she said again. "That teacher shouldn't have done that."

Catherine, who was watching the doorway as if ready to pounce on any nurse or doctor who walked in, offered a word here, in a weary, grieved tone. "Teachers and their everlasting projects—I could write a book about them."

"Anyway, it was the kind of thing that happens all the time between brothers and sisters," Blake said. "Philip said something, Hardy said something else, Philip said something back, and on and on. I was in the den watching a football game, and I finally called to them and told them to pipe down." He shook his head. "I should have done more . . . but like I said, it happens all the time and then blows over. You know how it is with brothers and sisters." He looked at Barb hopefully, as if for confirmation that she understood such squabbles. She nodded.

"The whole thing was about Mousey, you see," Della Boyd said.

"Mousey?" Curt asked.

"Philip's gerbil," Catherine said bleakly.

"There's a background to all this," Blake explained. "I guess Hardy had hidden Mousey in one of the drawers in the bathroom earlier in the week, and it had really upset Philip. So when he found him missing from his cage again this afternoon, he naturally thought Hardy had done it."

"Which wasn't the case at all," Della Boyd said, leaning forward and raising her voice as if eager to set the matter straight. "You see, I stopped to visit with Mousey when I went into Philip's room before dinner to open the blinds and let in some sunshine." She looked ready to cry. "He never does open his blinds for some reason. But if I hadn't tampered with Mousey, none of this would have happened." She unzipped her purse and found a tissue. "I'm glad I brought my pocketbook along." She dabbed at her eyes. "I always try to keep some Kleenex in my pocketbook."

Sitting in a chair apart from the others, Catherine turned to look at her sister-in-law. "So you mean you took Mousey out of his cage?" she asked. "I didn't know any of this."

"Well, no, I didn't really take him out," Della Boyd said. She blew her nose into the Kleenex and then folded it until it was a tiny damp lump, which she tucked inside her purse. "I just opened his cage," she continued, addressing Catherine now, "and he sniffed my fingers the way he always does. Then I heard you call me from the kitchen, and . . . well, I left Philip's room." Everyone was looking at Della Boyd now. She lifted one hand and fluttered her fingers. "Mousey likes to sniff people's fingers for some reason."

"And when you left his room, you didn't close the door of the cage?"

Catherine asked. She didn't sound angry, as she might have at any other time. She sounded spent and disoriented, as though trying to piece it all together.

"Well, I must not have. I sure don't *remember* closing it." Della Boyd squeezed her eyes shut as if trying to recall the scene.

"But that doesn't mean you didn't," Blake said. "People do things all the time that they don't remember later." He put an arm around Della Boyd. "Don't do this to yourself, Sister. If it hadn't been the gerbil, it would have been something else. You know Hardy and Philip—they're always at each other's throats about something."

Olivia, sitting on the other side of her aunt, reached over and patted her arm. "I think Mousey can open the door all by himself anyway," she said. "He's always getting out."

Della Boyd pressed a fresh Kleenex against her eyes. "I sure wish I had closed the door of Mousey's cage," she whispered, as if she hadn't heard a word Blake or Olivia had said. "But I didn't, and because of that Mousey got out and must have gone and hidden himself somewhere. By the time the argument heated up and I figured out what it was all about, it was too late for me to straighten it out. Everything just happened in a blur." She blew her nose again. "I just wasn't fast enough."

By Della Boyd's account, Hardy, who happened to be in what she called "an especially cordial mood" that afternoon, was sitting on the counter beside where she was working on the turkey, eating the last two yeast rolls from Thanksgiving dinner. He had just reached over and snitched a piece of the white meat Della Boyd was cutting off the bone, put it between one of the rolls, and was preparing to take a bite when Philip came stomping into the kitchen, pointed his finger at Hardy, and shouted, "What did you do with him?"

Hardy had gone ahead and taken a bite, chewed several times, then said calmly, "I knew this was going to happen someday, Auntie Deeb. I knew my little brother Flip was going to . . . well, flip out. I knew that one of these days his little pea brain was going to short-circuit and fry all the connections." He had shaken his head. "It's a sad thing to see it happen in a child." He had taken another bite of his roll, then added, "Especially when he's such a *little* child."

Della Boyd kept asking Philip what was wrong, but he ignored her and launched himself at Hardy, pummeling him as he sat on the counter and shouting all the while, "You did it! I know you did it! What did you do with him?"

"I set the knife down and tried to hold Philip back," Della Boyd said. "I kept asking him *what* was the matter, and he just kept on lunging at

Hardy. Philip's a strong boy, and I couldn't keep him back. I was afraid Hardy was going to get mad and kick him, but he never did. Then Philip went at Hardy again and told him he was going to kill him if he didn't tell him."

Della Boyd went on to say that Hardy treated the whole thing as a joke at first, which made Philip even angrier. "I'd like to fight with you, Pip," he said, laughing his cartoon cackle, "but it wouldn't be any challenge for me. I like some competition when I fight." He hopped down from the counter, dropping the other roll on the floor, then reached out and batted Philip on the side of the head. "I'd be the one killing you if I got much rougher than that," he said. Then he started across the kitchen toward the basement door. "I'm going downstairs, Auntie Deeb. I can't keep standing here watching Pip squeak."

Then Philip shrieked, "Don't call me Pip!"

"That's when Blake called in from the den," Della Boyd said, "and told them to stop arguing."

And that's when Philip hollered back, "But he's got Mousey, Dad, and he won't give him back!"

Hardy had reached the basement door by now and opened it. Before starting downstairs, he turned around. "Mousey? Is that what this is all about? Hey, that was good for a one-time joke, Pip, but I don't repeat my jokes. That's something a junior type might do, but I like variety." Hardy had snapped his fingers. "Hey, I know—maybe he got out in the backyard. I did see some brown fur sticking out between Kinko's teeth when he was catching the Frisbee this morning." And he started down the stairs, cackling mischievously.

"That's when I figured out what Philip was so upset about," Della Boyd said. "And that's when I remembered opening Mousey's cage, and I started trying to tell him it was my fault. 'I did it. I did it. I did it,' I kept saying. But it was like I wasn't even there. He just kept shouting at Hardy, 'Tell me where he is!' over and over again. 'Tell me where he is. Tell me where he is. Tell me where he is!' And then he rushed over and threw something down the stairs at Hardy." She paused, her brow furrowed. "It must have been the roll Hardy had dropped on the floor." She paused again, looking confused. "I never did see Philip pick it up, but that's what it *must* have been." She looked at Blake and spoke softly, almost in a tone of wonder. "I remember seeing a roll at the bottom of the stairs after he fell." She shook her head. "He must have thrown a roll at Hardy."

"All I know is that all of a sudden I heard this *uproar* out in the kitchen," Catherine put in, her eyes still on the doorway. "Della Boyd was yelling and Philip was yelling and—why, it sounded like bedlam had broken loose!"

It was evidently the roll thrown from behind that had sent Hardy into a fit of fury. Catherine had entered the kitchen and cried, "For pity's sake, what in the world is going on in here?" just in time to see Hardy coming back up the stairs toward Philip. Then Blake hurried in from the den in time to see Hardy grab Philip in a standing headlock at the top of the stairs and to hear him shout, "You wanna throw things down the stairs, huh? Okay, now it's my turn!" At the same moment that Blake had commanded Hardy to let Philip go and had rushed forward to separate the boys, Hardy said, "I don't know where your stupid gerbil is!" and he shoved Philip away from him.

"Shoved him down the stairs?" Curt asked quietly.

"No, no. He didn't mean to push him down the stairs," Della Boyd said quickly. "It all just happened so fast." Once again she put the Kleenex to her nose. "It was an accident." She twisted the tissue several times. "Hardy isn't a bad boy," she said. "He never meant for it to happen."

"No, I'm sure it wasn't on purpose," Blake said. "They were standing sideways at the top of the stairs, and when Hardy pushed him away, Philip's back hit the doorframe, and he lost his balance."

Catherine closed her eyes and made a low moaning sound. "Hardy tried to reach for him when he saw him falling. We all did"—she covered her face with her hands—"but it was too late." She rocked back and forth in the chair. "We reached, but he wasn't there." Everything was silent for a moment, and then Catherine spoke again, each word tortured and barely audible. "And then afterward I said the most awful thing to Hardy—the most awful, awful thing."

Blake got up from beside Della Boyd on the small sofa and went over to where Catherine was sitting in a large padded armchair. He stood looking at her, then bent forward and tentatively placed a hand on her shoulder.

Barb had no way of knowing whether she was right, but she suspected that that small gesture was the best thing in the world Blake could have done at that moment. Catherine uncovered her face and looked up to see who was touching her. She immediately closed her eyes again and hung her head but at the same time reached up and laid her hand over Blake's. Neither one of them spoke as Blake eased himself down to sit on the arm of the chair. Barb suddenly realized that this was the first time she had ever seen Blake and Catherine touch each other.

It was at that very moment that a doctor entered the room and said,

"Mr. and Mrs. Biddle?" After he talked with them several minutes, he told them that family members could go back to see Philip. "You can talk to him," he told them. "We never know how much they can hear when they're like this." The last words Barb heard the doctor say were directed to Catherine and echoed what Curt had said earlier. "I can't tell you that, Mrs. Biddle. We'll just have to wait and see."

It was past nine o'clock before Barb and Curt returned home. The twins had already gotten Sarah and Sammy to bed. They hadn't seen any sign of Hardy.

There was no change in Philip the next day, Friday, and still no news of Hardy's whereabouts. Catherine broke down in Barb's arms at the hospital that evening, when no trace of Hardy had turned up after he had been missing twenty-four hours.

"You heard what I said to him," she sobbed. "It's all my fault. Me and my big mouth. I just said the first thing that popped into my head, but, oh, I didn't mean it! I didn't mean it at all."

Barb had tried to comfort her. "Oh, Catherine, I know you didn't. And I can't help thinking Hardy knew it, too. He'll show up. I just know he will. We've been praying all last night and today for him, and I just believe with all my heart that he'll come home. God has His eye on Hardy right this very minute, and He's going to do something good—I really believe that, Catherine."

As if she hadn't heard Barb at all, Catherine cried out, "I knew I shouldn't be saying it! I remember thinking what a horrible thing it was to say to your own son, but it was like I couldn't stop myself. And now I've driven him away, and I'll never see him again!" She cried as if her heart were breaking, stopping only to heap more blame upon herself or to utter sad reflections on life. At one point she said, "Everything can be going along so well, and then all of a sudden the bubble bursts and everything falls to pieces!" Barb let her cry, patting her shoulder the whole time.

Late the next afternoon, on Saturday, Philip opened his eyes all of a sudden and said to Catherine, who was sitting by his bed in intensive care, "Where's Mousey?" Catherine told Barb she couldn't do anything but cry for the next several minutes before she finally got her composure and answered, "Olivia found him under your bed." Then Philip asked another question. "Where's Hardy?" And Catherine started crying all over again.

Saturday passed and Sunday came—another gray, drizzly day. It was strange that no one in the whole area had come forward with any tips about Hardy. No one had seen him. He had disappeared into thin air. "Or else someone knows and isn't talking," Catherine said. She and Blake had paid a personal visit to Jordan Baxter's home and begged him to tell them if he knew where Hardy was, but he swore—literally—that he hadn't seen Hardy since Wednesday at school.

"That boy has some extreme problems," Catherine told Barb afterward. "He gives me the creeps just to be in the same room with him. I'll never understand why, out of all the decent boys in this town, Hardy had to go and pick out somebody with a major personality disorder like Jordan Baxter to hang around with. I have no idea what Hardy sees in him!" An equally disturbing question, in Barb's opinion, was what Jordan Baxter saw in Hardy. Usually kids who hung around together had a lot of things in common. "And his *mother*!" Catherine said. "She just stood in the background staring at us like she was totally out of it. I think she must be on drugs."

Josh and Caleb were the ones who finally tracked Hardy down and helped to bring him home. It wasn't until Sunday, though, three days after his disappearance, by which time Catherine had convinced herself that though her younger son had been spared by some miracle of fate, her older son was lost to her forever.

On Sunday morning Barb and the children went to church without Curt, who had to check on a little girl in the Dickson County Hospital and then wanted to drive back to Greenville to be with the Biddles and talk to the neurologist about Philip's progress. After church Barb had put together a quick dinner of leftover turkey and baked potatoes and then had gotten Sammy settled down for a nap. She was in the den reading the newspaper when Josh came in and announced, "We think we know where Hardy might be."

After sixteen years of watching and listening to them, Barb could read Josh and Caleb easily. They were masters both of deadpan sarcasm and shameless slapstick. Though they didn't always show good judgment in the timing of their humor, of one thing Barb was certain. Neither one of them would joke about Hardy at a time like this. She also knew that both boys had keen powers of observation and logic. Since they were old enough to talk, they had loved figuring out puzzles and riddles and the solutions to mysteries. So she knew immediately to take Josh seriously.

"Where?" she asked, laying the newspaper aside and sitting forward on the couch.

"It was Caleb who thought of it first," Josh said. Just then Caleb walked into the den, pulling a shirt over his head.

"It makes perfect sense, Mom," Caleb said. "I can't figure out why it took me so long to think of it."

"I never thought of it either," Josh said. "I mean, school's not exactly Hardy's favorite place on earth, so we were thinking of every place but there."

"You mean the high school? You think he might be there?" Barb asked. "But school's been closed since Wednesday."

"Exactly," Caleb said.

"So how would he get in?"

"Through a window."

Barb thought a minute. "But those windows don't even open, do they? He'd have to break one out, and that would be a dead giveaway. There's got to be some kind of alarm system at the school."

"We don't mean the main building, Mom," Josh said. "We're talking about the athletic house out back."

"The athletic house?" Barb tried to form a picture of the building. She knew it was on the east side of the football stadium, backed up against the bleachers—a small brick structure to which the football team retired during halftime. She tried to visualize the windows but couldn't.

"Does it even have windows?" she asked.

Joshua nodded. "The old kind. It must've been there when the school was first built," he said. "Somebody said it used to be a garage. Anyway, it must've gotten skipped during the last remodeling 'cause the windows are the regular kind you can open."

"They keep everything in there—football equipment, track hurdles, punching bags, stuff like that," Caleb said. "And here's the part that really makes sense. See, we were in there just a couple of weeks ago talking to Coach Heinrich about getting on the soccer team, and we made Hardy come with us 'cause we had this bet with him and he lost—but that's a long story. Anyway, he was with us, see, and Coach Heinrich wasn't in the gym office, but the secretary said he might be out there, so we checked, and that's where he was—in this little officelike room out there."

"Well, it's not a real office," Josh said. "It's just a little closet kind of room with a desk and a couple of chairs and stuff. The main part of the house is just one big room where they keep everything. There's a big table in there, too, where you can sit—and some benches."

"And a pop machine," Caleb added.

"Another thing about the athletic house," Joshua said, "is there's a bathroom off in one corner."

"Very important detail," said Caleb, nodding.

"And," Josh said, "a *refrigerator*. Now see, that's also very important in Hardy's case. He would need food."

"But how much food could there be in a refrigerator in a storage building?" Barb asked. She knew how the boys loved to theorize, but this one just didn't seem very likely to her.

"Well, funny you should ask," Josh said, raising a forefinger. "After we finished talking with Coach Heinrich that day and he told us about the team and the practices and how many games were scheduled and all, he asked us if we had any other questions. And dum-dum here," he said, motioning toward Caleb, "asked him what was in the refrigerator."

"Hey, it had been three hours since lunch, and I was hungry," Caleb said. "Besides, Coach and me are like that." He held up two fingers close together. "He's my German teacher, you know. And anyway, it helped me figure all this out, didn't it?"

"Well, don't go counting your chickens," Barb said, getting up from the couch and walking over to the telephone beside Curt's recliner. She picked up the receiver. "And what was in the refrigerator?"

"Oh, all kinds of stuff," Caleb said. "Coach opened it up and showed us. Bread and mustard and lunch meat and pickles and orange juice and . . ."

"Yeah, I remember being surprised that it was so full," said Josh. "I was expecting maybe a couple of bottles of Gatorade."

"I think all the coaches use it," Josh said. "They must eat their lunch out there."

"See, Mom, it all fits together, doesn't it?" Caleb said. "It just hit me all of a sudden—I said to myself, okay now, think. Get inside Hardy's mind. Where could you hide if you stayed around here?"

"But I can't see Hardy thinking of all this," Barb said.

"Oh, I can," Josh said. "You should've seen him that day. He didn't say a whole lot to Coach—we think there's some history between them— but he was sure giving the place the once-over. 'Course, he knew about the house already since he played JV football last year."

"Well, part of the year, remember?" Caleb said. "Anyway, as we were leaving that day, Hardy pointed to all the wrestling mats stacked up in the corner and said—now get this, Mom— 'They even got a bed out here.' "

"So, see?" said Josh. "All this would naturally come back to him if he needed a place to stay for a while."

"He could've gotten in through a window," Caleb added.

"Well, don't get your hopes up," Barb cautioned. "For all we know, Hardy could have hitchhiked all the way across the country by now."

"Nah—it's the school, trust me," Caleb said. "It's got to be the school."

"We know Hardy, Mom," Josh said. "We've got him figured out."

"Well, it's worth a try," Barb said. "I'm going to call Blake."

No one was at home at the Biddles', so Barb called Greenville Memorial. By now Philip had been transferred to a private room on the pediatric floor. Blake answered the telephone after the first ring, and when Barb identified herself, he sounded let down. She knew he had been dividing his time between the hospital and the police station these past few days. Every time the phone rang, he must be hoping that it was the police with news about Hardy.

Barb spoke almost apologetically. "Say, Blake, the boys have a hunch that probably isn't anything, but it might be worth checking out."

Josh and Caleb shot her looks of protest, and Josh whispered, "Thanks a lot for your vote of confidence, Mom."

"Hey, we'll try anything," Blake said. "What's their idea?"

"Well, I'm sure someone has already checked the high school, right?" Barb said.

"Yeah," Blake said. He sounded so disappointed that Barb almost wished she hadn't bothered to call. "That was one of the first places the police checked. No sign of anything. No way he could've gotten in anyway with everything locked up over Thanksgiving. Not unless he had a key, which to my knowledge he doesn't." He gave a brief, bitter laugh.

She went on to tell him about the athletic building. "Well, I'm pretty sure they checked the whole school," he said. "At least they said they did." He paused. "But to be truthful, we're not real satisfied with the way they've handled this whole investigation. I think I just might drive over myself and check this out."

In the background Barb heard Catherine's voice. "What is it? Who is that?"

"At least I'd be *doing* something," Blake told Barb. "I hate this waiting business."

"It's probably nothing," Barb said. Again the boys looked offended. "But you never can tell," she added. A thought came to her suddenly. Maybe they would accept defeat better if they could go with Blake and see with their own eyes that Hardy wasn't there. "Say, Blake, would you mind terribly if Josh and Caleb met you there? Maybe they could climb up and look in a window or something."

"Sure, fine," he said. "It'll take me a little while to drive in. Can they meet me there in twenty or twenty-five minutes?"

"Can you be there in twenty minutes?" she asked the boys.

Joshua held out his hand. "Give us the van keys."

Lists of Things

18

Barb heard about it all an hour later, after the twins had come back home. Joshua and Caleb's hunch about Hardy was right, although when they first arrived at the school, they thought for a few minutes that they might have been mistaken. Blake pulled into the parking lot right behind them, and together the three of them walked all the way around the athletic building. The door was locked, of course. That was the first thing they checked. The two windows were higher and smaller than the boys remembered and, from all appearances, painted shut. There were no signs of forced entry—no telltale marks of being pried open, no broken panes, none of that.

Right away Blake was ready to call it off, but the twins stalled, suggesting that they climb up and look through one of the windows. Before Blake could object, Josh pulled the van directly up next to the building.

"Yeah, and he almost sideswiped it," Caleb told Barb.

"Hey, I had a good two inches to spare, no kidding," Josh said. "Bozo here is exaggerating as usual," he said, pointing to Caleb. "I'm up there in the driver's seat sweating it out, and what's he doing? Hopping around down on the ground screaming, 'Watch out! Dad's gonna have a hernia if you wreck the paint job!' So much for sneaking up to peek in the window. We might as well have brought our trumpets along and played a fanfare."

"Aw, Hardy had heard us long before then," Caleb said.

And it was true. He *had* heard them drive up and had immediately retreated to the bathroom and closed the door. It was the closed bathroom door, in fact, that made them all suspicious. The boys scrambled up onto the top of the van first, pressed their faces against the windowpanes, and reported to Blake what they saw. Hardy had left a half dozen empty pop cans scattered on a table, along with a few small yogurt cartons and a potato chip bag, but, as Caleb put it, "That didn't really mean much since everybody knows coaches are a bunch of slobs. They could've left all that stuff out."

"The bathroom door, though," Joshua said, "now *that's* what got our attention. Why would it be pulled all the way shut if nobody was in it?"

"I noticed it first," Caleb said.

"You *mentioned* it first. That's the first thing I saw when I looked in. I didn't say anything, though, 'cause I wanted to see how long it would take you to notice it."

Caleb hooked his fist and faked a swing at his brother. They went on to tell how Blake had finally pounded on the door of the building and called to Hardy, telling him they knew he was in there, that Philip was all right and kept asking to see him, that they were getting ready to call the principal on Blake's cell phone and get him to come out with a key unless Hardy wanted to go ahead and unlock the door from the inside.

They told Barb about the first two things Hardy said when he did open the door only seconds later. The first was to be expected, given Hardy's general bravura and refusal to concede defeat. He swung the door open and said irritably, "You're early. Dinner won't be ready for another hour. I was just frosting the cake." To which Blake replied without missing a beat, "Oh, we don't mind. We'll wait in your parlor."

Hardy dropped his mask for the second thing. "Is Flip really okay?"

It turned out that Hardy had let himself into the athletic house with a key. He had a dozen or more keys, in fact. Back during the summer when he had done his three days of custodial duty at the high school to pay for sandblasting the back steps, he had somehow managed to pocket the key, get it copied at a hardware store, and add it to his collection. Blake confiscated the whole bunch, of course. "He even had a key to both of our cars," he told Barb and Curt later, "and one for the concession booth at the pool where Olivia works." He shook his head in bewilderment, not so much, Barb thought, as if he wondered *why* his son would do such a thing as steal keys but rather *how* he could get away with it.

"I asked him where he was planning to go on Monday after school started up again," Blake said, "and he said he was in the process of weighing his options when we found him." Again he shook his head. "He mystifies me. He thinks of things that never crossed my mind when I was his age."

When the Chewnings went down to the hospital after church that night, Catherine grabbed Barb in a hug that almost took her breath away.

"He's back! He's back safe and sound!" she cried, pointing to Hardy, who was sitting on the foot of Philip's bed with his head down, playing with a loose thread from the blanket, wrapping it around his finger tighter and tighter until his fingertip turned blue.

"Yeah, it's me all right," said Hardy, not looking up. "Back from Cancun."

If someone had asked Barb a week ago to predict what kind of changes Catherine Biddle would undergo in the face of a crisis, she wasn't sure what she would have said, but she knew for a certainty that she never would have expected Catherine to turn so . . . she couldn't even think of the right word for it. *Mild* maybe. Catherine's sharp-edged tone of voice had faded—at least for the time being. It seemed that she had been suddenly tenderized within the space of a few short days.

When she caught sight of Joshua and Caleb in the doorway behind her, Catherine left Barb and walked over to them, almost shyly it seemed. "You boys are . . . well, you did something that . . ." She clasped her hands in front of her and tried again. "I just can't . . . well, you did it, and . . . it's just . . ."

She paused again, and Josh said, "Wow, Mrs. Biddle, you really have a way with words. Can you help me with a speech I'm writing?"

Barb winced but was glad to see that instead of taking offense, Catherine was smiling. She gave up trying to talk and embraced each of the boys somewhat timidly. Josh and Caleb as usual covered up their embarrassment by clowning around, crossing their eyes, and letting their tongues loll out as if she were choking them to death. And though she never actually said "thank you," Barb felt quite sure that the twins understood her intent.

Blake came over to shake the boys' hands and thank them again, and even Olivia stood up from her chair by the window, tossed her hair out of her eyes, and did a rare thing—she actually smiled. Everyone was laughing and talking at once, and Philip looked on with an openmouthed grin. His head was bandaged where he had struck it, and one leg was in a cast, but his face was bright with happiness.

Della Boyd entered the room just then with a bucket of ice and said, "Oh, look. We have guests!" She set the ice down. "Philip's ice bucket was just full of water," she said. "I've been trying to keep the nurses on their toes."

Blake laughed. "They all think she used to be a nurse the way she's taken over. We haven't told them she was just a volunteer."

Della Boyd busied herself around the room and pulled an empty chair around to the end of the bed. "Here, somebody can sit here, and, Sarah, you can sit over there by Olivia on the window seat if you want to."

Sammy, who hadn't said a word to this point, suddenly leaned out of Curt's arms, waved at Philip in the bed, and said cheerfully, "Hi, Phiwip!"

Everyone laughed, and Philip waved at Sammy. "Hi there, Sammy," he said.

Della Boyd approached Joshua and Caleb almost reverently, laid a hand on each of them, and said, "I knew you were good boys." She looked at Curt and Barb. "I've always known it. These are two good boys you have." Then she looked back at the twins. "You're such good boys."

Caleb elbowed Joshua. "She thinks we're good boys."

Della Boyd motioned to the chair again. "Here, Barb, go ahead and sit down."

"No, no. We're not staying," Barb said. "We just popped in to say hello. There's too many of us to fit in here. Anyway, I've got to take this hungry bunch home and feed them. We just wanted to let you know we've been praying for you. Our whole church has been. Curt gave a testimony in the service tonight and told them all the good news."

Blake cleared his throat. "Well, thank you. You folks sure have been good to us through all this. There's no way we could ever repay you."

"I wish you'd stay," Della Boyd said. "We could get more chairs." She stepped back toward the twins, again reaching forward to pat them on the arm. "Oh, you are two *dear* boys. Thank you for what you've done. And you, too," she added, addressing Curt and Barb again. "Telling all your friends about us—how thoughtful. Your preacher and his wife came by the hospital twice already, and that nice Eldeen Rafferty came by with her daughter, too."

"I'm sure she made things lively," Curt said. "Eldeen is quite a character. She's never met a stranger."

"And I've never met a stranger woman!" Catherine interjected, then laughed gaily at her joke and added quickly, "But it was nice of her to come. Dottie Puckett came, too, and I really appreciated that. After all she's been through . . . well, it was awfully kind of her."

"We could get some chairs from another room," Della Boyd said. "And you two boys could sit here on this end of the bed, only be careful not to—"

"No," Barb said again. "Really, we can't. We just wanted to see you for a minute, and our minute's up." She walked over to the foot of the bed and touched Hardy's shoulder. He was wearing what looked like a pair of old tuxedo pants, with a satin stripe down each leg, and a faded blue T-shirt with *DEAD IN THE WATER* printed across the back and a picture of a dead frog floating belly up beside a lily pad. "It sure is good

to see you, Hardy. The neighborhood hasn't been the same without you."
Barb liked Hardy. She always had. She had seen him in some of his most
obnoxious moments, but she still liked the kid. "And by the way," she
said, "you might want to shave one of these days."

Without cracking a smile, Hardy ran his fingers through his mop of
dark hair. "Yeah, good idea, Mrs. C. I was just sitting here thinking about
that. This stuff gets hot, you know."

Della Boyd hooted with laughter. "Oh, now, isn't Hardy just the biggest cutup? Imagine him with his whole head shaved!" She laughed so
hard that Hardy reached over and patted her on the back.

"Don't bust a gut, Auntie Deeb," he said. "It wasn't that funny."

"Oh yes, it was! It sure was! You're just a real cutup!" Then she looked
around at the others, her hands clasped as if in ecstasy. "Nobody's a bigger cutup than Hardy." She stepped forward again and touched the twins
on the hand, one at a time. "You two sure are good boys."

"Hey, Josh, I think this lady likes us," Caleb said.

Della Boyd laughed again. "And *you're* a couple of cutups, too!" she
said.

"What's a cutup anyway?" asked Philip, and everybody laughed
again.

Olivia rode to school with the Chewnings the next morning. Blake had
taken Hardy early. He had arranged a meeting with Morton Hollings
about the unauthorized use of the athletic building over the Thanksgiving holiday and the key he had discovered in Hardy's possession.

As she walked across the street to the Chewnings' van, Olivia was carrying her silk flower arrangement in one hand and swinging a purse the
size of a small envelope in the other. She was wearing jeans and a short
brown corduroy jacket. Her long blond hair caught the sunlight like pale
gold silk. Caleb slid open the van door for her and pretended to reach for
the flowers. "For me? Oh, you shouldn't have."

Without even blinking, she thrust the arrangement at him as she got
in and said, "Yeah, well, see, you're such a nice guy and all, you know,
and I just thought, 'Now what could I do for that sweet kid across the
street?' and at first I was thinking of, like food and cars and sports and
stuff like that, and then I thought, 'Nah, I know what *he'd* like—he'd like
a flower arrangement.' "

Josh guffawed. "Ooh, she fried you!" He licked the tip of a finger, put
it to Caleb's ear, and made a sizzling noise between his teeth.

Caleb took it good-naturedly, holding the arrangement up high and
studying it from all angles. "Well, I hate to sound ungrateful, but you
could've at least asked about the colors in my bedroom. These are all

wrong." And he gave the flowers back to Olivia.

Barb smiled at them through the rearview mirror. Only once or twice before could she recall Olivia even speaking to Josh and Caleb, but never had she teased with them. She made it clear that she wasn't carrying it too far, however, because a minute later when Josh asked her why girls bothered carrying purses that would hold less than a sandwich bag, she just shrugged her shoulders and turned to ask Sarah what grade she was in.

Smart girl, thought Barb. She must sense that you couldn't give the Chewning goofballs too much leeway. Pull out the stops all at once and you were asking for trouble. Barb wondered if Olivia were suddenly worried about the twins following her into the high school like two eager puppies, catching up to walk beside her and flanking her down the hallway, trying to outdo each other with their wisecracks and foolish jokes. She was probably regretting her earlier banter already. If things were still the way they were when Barb was that age, it wouldn't do for a popular senior cheerleader to be seen in the company of two silly sophomore boys.

She let them out in front of the school, then headed toward the elementary school to deliver Sarah. She had several things to get done this morning, and on her way home she recited them for Sammy: "Living room, Laundry, Library, LEGOs, and Grocery store. Four *L*'s and a *G*. Think I can remember all that?"

"Wemember all that," Sammy echoed.

A couple of years ago, Barb had gone through a phase of trying to write lists of things to do, but there was only one problem. She kept misplacing the lists. She'd find them lying all over the house days later in odd places, and upon reading them over would discover that the items had somehow gotten done already or else had ceased to be important.

The boys had ribbed her ceaselessly about her lists, reeling off silly puns like "Mom can't remember what to do next when she's listless," or "Uh-oh, she's listing again! Prop her up!" She had given it up after a few weeks, telling her family she was tired of wasting all that good paper. Now she tried various mnemonic devices. Four *L*'s and a *G* shouldn't be hard to remember, she thought now. If she could only remember what the letters stood for, that is. She also needed to get back to her poem since the Women Well Versed had their November meeting tonight. So now she was up to four *L*'s, a *G*, and a *P*.

The meeting was to be at her house again, though it had originally been scheduled for Catherine's. Two days after Philip's accident and Hardy's disappearance, Barb told Catherine she would call everybody and have them come to her house instead since she knew Catherine wouldn't feel up to playing hostess considering what all was going on. That had been on Saturday night, after Philip had regained consciousness but before Hardy had been found.

Catherine had accepted her offer, nodding as if in a daze, but Della Boyd had looked vaguely disappointed. "I'll still bring the refreshments," she had said. "I was planning to make these little cookies called toffee crescents, you know, and I've already bought the toffee candies the recipe calls for. You crush them up, you know, and mix them in with the . . ." She had trailed off, shaking her head. "Maybe Hardy will—"

"The doctor said Philip might get to come home on Thursday or Friday if everything still looks okay," Catherine interrupted. "And he can probably go back to school sometime the next week, he said, but he'll have to take it slow and use crutches, of course."

Naturally, Barb hadn't gotten around to telephoning everybody about coming to her house instead of Catherine's, but the way she figured it, she could just post one of the boys outside in the driveway to inform the ladies of the change after they parked their cars. That would sure take a lot less time than making all those phone calls. So the first thing to do was get the living room in order. She'd have to vacuum for sure and probably dust the furniture, then get extra chairs from the kitchen and dining room. But that shouldn't take long. Maybe she'd have time to hang another picture or two. There was that grouping of five small original watercolors she kept meaning to get up in the entryway. She thought she could find them easily since she had only a few boxes left that weren't yet unpacked.

Unfortunately, however, when she got home, she found that the living room was in worse shape than she had thought. She wondered how other people managed to keep their living rooms so meticulous all the time. She had never seen so much as a sofa cushion out of place in the Biddles' living room, for example. How did other women do it? Barb's family always seemed to spill over into every room of every house they lived in. She had thought this house would be different because it was larger, but not so. The very same thing was happening here.

Evidently the twins had played some board games in the living room at some point during the last week or so, for there were three different games laid out, one of them strewn all over the coffee table as if they had suddenly stopped in the middle of the game and never come back to it. Maybe they had played a game with Joe Leonard when he had come over on Thanksgiving Day. That whole day was practically a blur in Barb's mind now. Only four days ago, but it seemed more like four weeks. And Sarah was working on a 3-D puzzle of Big Ben, which for some reason she preferred to do in the living room, so there was all that clutter on the floor in front of the fireplace. A load of unfolded towels that had been dumped onto the striped Queen Anne chair was Barb's own contribution to the general disorder. She couldn't even remember what day she had done that.

"Okay, Sammy, Mama's got her work cut out, doesn't she?" Barb said as Sammy waddled forward to investigate the board game on the coffee table. "Here, you can help me put all this back where it belongs, okay?"

"Okay. I help," Sammy said agreeably, picking up two dice and clicking them against each other.

Of course, it took twice as long with Sammy's help, but he loved helping her sort out all the cards of the same color and putting them in the right slots in the box. Then when she turned around to attend to the Big Ben puzzle, he started taking everything back out again and laying out piles of cards all over the coffee table so that they had to do it all over again when she finally noticed him. But even with the delays, she was done by ten o'clock. She saved folding the towels for last so it would remind her of the next thing she had to do—laundry.

How six fairly normal human beings could generate so many dirty clothes was beyond her comprehension, but there was no denying the evidence as she opened the door to the laundry room off the kitchen. At least they were already sorted into four piles, but the *size* of the piles almost took her breath away, not to mention the smell of the pile containing all the children's play clothes, which of course included the twins' athletic shorts, socks, and T-shirts. She looked ruefully at her Maytag washer. Too bad I have only one of you, she thought.

"Come on in, Sammy, time to check pockets, okay?" she called, and Sammy pedaled in from the kitchen, straddling a large blue plastic dolphin on wheels.

"Okay!" he said eagerly. He dismounted the dolphin, turning it on its side in the process, and headed for the pile of play clothes. He knew his job perfectly by now. While Barb began loading the washing machine with pocketless garments, Sammy began picking out pairs of pants and shorts from the pile, sticking a hand into each pocket, and feeling around with a look of intense concentration in his blue eyes. It was a rule of the house that he got to keep anything he found, and already his little clown bank was getting heavier from laundry proceeds alone. The money didn't mean much to him, of course, but loose buttons, rubber bands, and gum wrappers excited him. "See, Mama!" he'd crow excitedly as he held up each treasure. Sometimes Josh and Caleb would leave a piece of candy in a pocket on purpose, and even Curt had been known to play the game.

Once Sammy had pulled a brand-new miniature fire truck out of a pair of Curt's khaki pants, never thinking it the least bit strange that his father would leave a toy truck in his pocket.

After getting one load started, Barb packed Sammy into the van again and headed for the library. Margaret Tuttle had quoted Robert Frost so often that Barb wanted to get a collection of his poems to study. Not just the common ones every Tom, Dick, and Harry knew—things like "Birches" and "Mending Wall" and "Stopping by Woods on a Snowy Evening" and all those other familiar poems—but other lesser-known ones, too. She wanted to spend some time examining what he did with rhyme and meter. She wanted to look at one poem in particular that Margaret had read at the last meeting. "Out, Out—" was the title. It was about the sudden death of a boy on a farm. For some reason the poem had kept coming back to her, especially during these last several days since Philip's accident, and she wanted to look at it more closely.

She had intended to go to the library right after the last meeting so she'd have time to study the poems before the November meeting, but here it was the day of the meeting, and she still hadn't done it. Wasn't this the story of her life? She smiled as she remembered a teacher she'd had in high school. A Miss Barton or Barkley or something like that who taught trigonometry and calculus. One of the woman's favorite things to say when somebody turned in a late assignment was "I am *not* a believer in 'Better late than never,' Mister So-and-So. *My* motto is 'Better never late!'" Well, Miss Barton or whatever her name was hadn't had a husband and four children to look after, Barb thought as she drove down Highway 11 toward the Derby Public Library.

Two hours later she was on her way home again, feeling proud of herself for having taken care of two *L*'s and the *G* on her mental list. At the library she had found a good collection of poems by Robert Frost as well as a whole stack of picture books to read to Sammy and several books for Sarah. Then she had stopped at Wal-Mart and bought a new set of Technic LEGOs for Philip as a combination coming home and birthday present. He would turn thirteen on the last day of November, and the doctor had said he would probably be home by then. The grocery store had been her last stop, and she had whizzed down each aisle, hoping her eyes would light on everything she needed since she had no list. The only hitch had come at the check-out lane, when she realized she had used up her last check at Wal-Mart. She rummaged through her billfold and came up with only eleven dollars, so she gave the cashier that and then charged the rest on her credit card.

"We'll eat lunch as soon as we get home, okay, Sammy boy?" she said after buckling him into his car seat. It was after twelve o'clock by now.

Sammy squealed and kicked his feet. "Okay!" he said. *Okay* was one of his favorite words these days.

What with lunch and reading to Sammy before his nap and looking through her Frost collection and trying to fix some troublesome lines of her own poem and picking up the children from school, it was after four o'clock that afternoon when it hit Barb that she never had gotten back to the laundry room after lunch. Where did the day go? And now she had supper to think about and then at seven the poetry meeting. At least she had gotten the living room tidied up.

As she transferred the wet clothes from the washer to the dryer and put another load of dirty clothes into the washer, she kept going over what she had read that afternoon. The introduction of the book of poetry said that Robert Frost had begun writing poetry when he was sixteen. She tried to imagine Josh and Caleb writing poetry—serious poetry, not the silly rhymes and limericks they tossed off at the drop of a hat. She tried to imagine Hardy Biddle writing poetry.

As she measured out a cup of detergent and sprinkled it over the clothes, she thought of all the ironies of Frost's life—his trying to be a farmer when he was allergic to hay, his having to travel all the way to London to get his American poetry published, his ability to write about life everywhere while describing cameo scenes in Vermont, his students' love for him even though he was known to throw away their compositions in fits of impatience. She thought of that haunting line from his poem "Out, Out—": "Little—less—nothing!—and that ended it." She measured out another cup of detergent but caught herself before she dumped it in. She'd done that more than once—put in a double dose by accident, ending up with piles of suds frothing out the lid of the washer.

"Uh, Mom, are you okay?" Caleb asked. He was standing at the door of the laundry room. "I mean, is this a special ritual or something—staring down into the washing machine? Is there a chant that goes with it?"

"Oh, sure," Barb said. "It's like a wishing well. I throw things into it and make wishes. You should try it sometime." She closed her eyes and muttered some gibberish, then shut the lid and twisted the knob to *Start*. "I wished for clean clothes," she said to Caleb. "And it always works! It's like magic."

Caleb narrowed his eyes and stared at her for a moment. "I bet you do this all day long, don't you? While we're plugging away at school, you're at home playing games with the washing machine." He shrugged. "Oh well, whatever it takes to make you happy, Mom." He looked at the remaining piles of laundry on the floor. "Say, have you seen my basketball shorts? That's what I came in here for. I need them."

And wasn't this another irony of life, Barb thought—that children, who were supposed to be creatures of fantasy, were so often the ones who brought you back to reality?

A Most Pressing Matter

19

Philip loved his LEGO set. He opened it right at the table at Pop's Pizza Palace, where they all gathered ten days later to celebrate his thirteenth birthday. He had come home from the hospital on his birthday, the last day of November, but at the doctor's suggestion they had postponed his party until the following week. Barb had been surprised that the Biddles had asked them to share the occasion, but Blake had insisted. He had walked across the street to issue the invitation on Wednesday night after prayer meeting as soon as he saw their van pull into the driveway.

"Philip wants you to come, and so do we—all of us," he had said. "You've been such a help coming to the hospital so much and taking care of things for us at home, and then all the food you've brought over this past week. Not to mention helping us find Hardy. We couldn't have asked for better neighbors." He paused for a few seconds, looking at each one of them in turn.

"So anyway," he continued, "we asked Philip what kind of birthday supper he wanted, and he didn't even have to stop and think about it. Pizza—what else would a kid say? Pop's over in Derby has this buffet on weeknights, so we thought we'd go there. And we want all of you to come—our treat. Oh, and Catherine said to tell you we're having cake here at home afterward if you can join us for that, too. I know the kids all have school the next day, so we won't make it an all-nighter or anything."

Barb had never before heard Blake say so many words in succession. There was a brief moment of silence, during which all of them had looked at each other.

"Well, if we're taking votes, make mine a yes," Joshua had finally said.

"I second that," Caleb said.

Curt had smiled. "I think it's going to be unanimous. Nobody in our family is going to turn down pizza."

Barb knew this was a sacrifice for Curt. Generally, the last thing in the world he wanted to do after a long day of seeing sick kids was to spend the evening socializing. The last time they had been out for an evening was probably three months ago, when they had taken the Biddles to the Purple Calliope and the parenting seminar.

Blake seemed genuinely pleased. "Well, good, then why don't you give us a call when you've checked out your last case of diaper rash tomorrow, and we'll go from there?"

Of course, as Barb could have guessed, Curt was late getting home the next day. He had his receptionist call Barb that afternoon to warn her that unless he had several no-shows, it was going to be a long day. And his prediction proved true, as Barb knew it would. He had been overbooked as it was, and then his last appointment of the day was a new mother with a legal-size page of questions front and back. The twins had to stay late at school for basketball practice, too, which Barb had forgotten about, so at five o'clock she called Catherine to tell her about all the delays. Everything worked out, however, because Olivia's cheerleading practice had gone longer than usual, and Blake had run into a snag at work and wasn't going to be home for at least another hour.

"At least he's in town, though," Catherine said over the phone. "I can't count the number of times he's missed the kids' birthdays." She sighed. "This is really a red-letter day, I guess. I honestly can't remember the last time the whole family did something together on one of our birthdays."

"And you're sure you want us horning in on it?" Barb asked.

"Of course we do!" Catherine said. "Don't be ridiculous. We wouldn't have asked you if we didn't. Why don't you call as soon as Curt gets home, and we'll compare notes? Maybe we can shoot for around seven. Hardy will probably be a grump by then, but he can always tide himself over with a snack."

Catherine had called ahead and reserved one of the two big tables in the party room at Pop's Pizza Palace. When they finally arrived at seven-thirty, they were ushered back to the party room by a perky teenaged server whose name tag identified her as Erika. It seemed that Erika knew Olivia and Hardy, for she spoke to them by name. Olivia just nodded in response and looked away moodily, but Hardy said, "Hey, Eureka, you found it yet?" after which he looked at Philip and said, "Don't even ask.

It's a private joke, and you wouldn't get it."

Erika must have recognized Josh and Caleb from school, too, but she seemed to be having trouble figuring out why they were in the company of Olivia and Hardy. She looked back and forth a couple of times before saying, "Y'all together?"

"Yeah," Joshua said, "but please don't tell anybody at school about it. I'd die of embarrassment if people found out. That's why we asked to sit in the back room away from everybody else."

Erika gave a puzzled smile. "Y'all related somehow?"

"Related to *them*?" Caleb said, pointing to Olivia and Hardy and smacking his forehead with his palm. "Please don't get a vicious rumor like that started. That's even worse than being seen with them."

Erika laughed and tossed her head. "Okay, I won't tell a soul."

Upon arriving at the door of the party room, they found that the other large table was occupied by a family of Asians. They looked Vietnamese to Barb, maybe Filipino. Upon seeing them, Catherine stopped dead in her tracks at the doorway, and her eyes narrowed. "Well, I was hoping we'd have it all to ourselves," she said. "It looks like they could go down to that House of Chan restaurant for their party." Barb couldn't help smiling. Now that Philip was on his way to a full recovery and Hardy was back home, Catherine seemed to be more like her old self again.

Fortunately, no one in the other group had heard her. They were too busy talking and eating. And laughing—there seemed to be an unusual amount of laughter as they talked. Barb wondered if what was being said was truly funny, or if it was just part of their speech pattern, a built-in inflection that sounded like laughter to anyone who didn't know the language.

This wasn't the first time Barb wished for a better memory so she could capture some of life's unexpected moments. She had a feeling that this whole evening would be great in a story, but she knew that by the time she got back home, she would have forgotten most of the details. When they were first married, Curt used to tell her she was a live-for-the-moment type, and he liked her just that way. "Otherwise you might remember all my mistakes," he said. Not that she forgot everything, of course. But where her memory was concerned, there didn't seem to be any pattern to the things that stuck and the things that fell out.

She looked around now at the bright green wallpaper flecked with red stars, the large white globes suspended from the ceiling on chains, the framed travel posters of Italy on the walls. The music playing over the speakers was jaunty and rhythmic, although it actually sounded more Spanish than Italian to Barb. She saw one of the Vietnamese men stand up and lift a baby in the air. The man had a streak of pizza sauce on the front of his white shirt. Several others pointed to the baby and spoke something almost in unison, lifting wedges of pizza as they spoke. Barb wondered if they were celebrating something. Was this part of a Vietnamese christening ceremony? How she wished she could film all of this and go back later to review it. Life was so colorful, but the frames sped by so fast.

They finally got themselves seated around the big table after a great deal of effort on Della Boyd's part to appoint everyone a chair. "Here, Philip, you're the birthday boy, you sit here at the end—or would you rather sit down there at the other end with all the other children and let the adults sit up here closest to this end? What do you think, Brother? Do you think he should sit down there between Olivia and Hardy and let the twins sit next to them, one on each side? Then little Sammy can sit— oh, won't we need one of those booster chairs for Sammy? There's one over there against the wall if you'll go get it, Blake. And, Sarah, honey, you can sit there next to Caleb if that's all right with everybody—or is it Joshua? I still can't tell you boys apart. And Barb, you and Curt, why don't you take those next two chairs so one of you can be by Sammy? Or would it be better if—let's see, Catherine, why don't you—?"

Barb was somewhat surprised that Catherine had let Della Boyd go on so long. "Oh, good grief, just find a chair, everybody, and sit down!" she finally cried. By then, though, almost everyone had taken the seats Della Boyd had assigned. Erika was standing by patiently, her smile still a bit perplexed, as if trying to sort out the relationships among them all.

When everyone was settled, Erika stepped forward and said, "I can get your drink orders now, and then you can help yourselves to the buffet."

Down at the far end of the table, Caleb said something, and all the kids laughed. Olivia's smile died quickly, though, and she replaced it with a bored look, crossing her arms and looking down at her lap. Hardy said something Barb couldn't hear, and Philip replied with, "Oh, sure you did! Like we're all gonna believe that."

"Aw, go ahead, let's all pretend to believe him," Josh told Philip. "It'll make him feel so important."

So Philip fixed Hardy with an innocent, adoring look and said, "Really, Hardy? You really did that? Wow, you're so cool! I'm gonna tell all my friends at school tomorrow how totally cool my big brother is."

Hardy leaned back in his chair and looked up at the ceiling with his hands clasped behind his head. "Oh, Pip, you could *try*, but you couldn't begin to tell it all. There just wouldn't be enough time."

Olivia yawned audibly and flipped her hair away from her eyes with the back of her hand.

"Besides, it would discourage your little junior high pals," Hardy added. "They'd all be wishing they could be like me, and that just ain't gonna happen."

"Yeah," Caleb said, "'cause he's already bought all the good threads from the Salvation Army store, and there's nothing left for the rest of us."

At the moment Hardy was wearing a pair of white knit pants, along with a Hawaiian print shirt. He not only loved making costumes of others' cast-offs, but if he could wear them out of season, that was even better.

"Yep, you got it," Hardy said. "People like me, we're called trendsetters."

"And when does the trend catch on?" Josh asked.

Hardy shook his head sadly. "Oh, it usually takes years and years for all the average people, the *followers*, to get with it."

"Hardy's gonna let me wear his Meadowlark Lemon sweat shirt to school tomorrow," Philip said.

"Yeah, I'm doing what I can for the next generation," Hardy said. "They're just so pathetic—all that matching Bugle Boy stuff and Tommy and Polo." He looked at Philip, who was wearing a new Tommy Hilfiger T-shirt, and shook his head. "Sad, very sad," he said.

Barb didn't know how things really were at home between Hardy and Philip since the accident, but one thing she had noticed over the last week was that although the two of them still smarted off to each other like typical brothers, a good deal of the rancor had subsided. She couldn't help wondering what had been said between them the first time they saw each other after the accident.

Erika brought over a chair so Philip could elevate his broken leg, and anybody could see that Philip enjoyed the extra attention she was giving him. When she asked him how he broke it, he said, "Oh, it's kind of a long story."

"Actually, the story's short," Hardy said. "The flight of stairs is what was kind of long."

Then out of nowhere Della Boyd piped up and said, "Tomorrow is Friday."

There was a short silence before Hardy said, "Freaky."

Everyone laughed, including Della Boyd, who added, "Friday has always been one of my favorite days!"

After Erika finished with the drink orders, Blake said, "Well, I guess we can head on out to the buffet." He cleared his throat and looked at

Curt. "Would you like to say a blessing for us first?" No doubt he was remembering the time at the Purple Calliope, when Curt had prayed before the meal. Catherine shot him a startled look but clamped her lips together and didn't say anything.

"I'd be happy to," Curt said. Somewhere in the middle of his prayer, which wasn't long at all, Barb thought of something. She remembered how shocked she had been the first time she ever heard Curt pray. It was well over five years ago now. She might have trouble keeping track of some dates, but she knew that one for sure. It had been on the fifth day of April, which was only two days after their anniversary.

They had both accepted Christ on the same night, during a revival campaign at the Church of the Open Door. It was the first time during their entire fourteen years of married life they had ever been to church, and they wouldn't have been there that night if it hadn't been for the persistence of one of Curt's patients—actually two of them, along with their mother and, later, their father.

Edna Hawthorne was the wife of the pastor of the Church of the Open Door, and her two daughters, Hannah and Esther, were quite the little evangelists. Only four and six at the time, they kept inviting Curt to come to their church whenever they came to the office, which was fairly often after their baby brother, Levi, developed an ear infection that hung on for months. The older one had looked at Curt once and asked, "Does Jesus live in your heart?" Curt had told Barb several times that he dreaded the day when the baby started learning to talk because then he'd have three little people pestering him about coming to church, and two was more than enough.

Edna Hawthorne herself always reiterated the girls' invitations but never in a pushy way, which was a relief. "We know you're a busy man, Dr. Chewning," she'd say, "but we'd be so pleased to have you and your family visit our church some Sunday."

He might have been able to put her off indefinitely, but the day came when her husband brought little Levi in for his checkup. They had been ready to talk about tubes, but finally a new antibiotic had seemed to do the trick, and Levi's ears were beginning to clear up. Theodore Hawthorne was smaller than the average man, but something about him made him seem much bigger than he was. When he looked up with a pair of the steadiest, most sincere eyes Curt had ever seen and urged him to consider the eternal destiny of his soul as a matter of gravest importance, Curt could think of nothing to say in response. And when the pastor had asked point-blank if he would attend one of the special services at their church that very week, Curt had looked him in the eye and said without hesitation that he would. For some reason, he explained to Barb later, he suddenly felt that this business of eternal life *was* a most pressing matter, one that he couldn't ignore.

They had gone to the church that very night, arriving a full fifteen minutes late because of another long afternoon of appointments, but had found seats near the back. They had sat down just in time to hear Edna Hawthorne sing "Some Golden Daybreak" and then had listened closely to every word the preacher said in a simple yet persuasive sermon titled "The Most Important Decision You'll Ever Make." They had brought the children with them, and at the end of the service when Curt stepped out from the pew, Barb was right behind him. She had no idea until she reached the front that Josh, Caleb, and Sarah had followed her down the aisle.

They had gone into a Sunday school classroom for counseling, and a man named Harvey Gill had talked to them all at the same time. Of course, Sarah was too young to understand it all, but the twins did, and by the time they left the Church of the Open Door that night, Curt, Barb, Joshua, and Caleb had settled once and for all the matter of their eternal destiny.

And that night was the first time Barb had ever heard Curt pray. She remembered how astonished she had been to hear him. He sounded like he had been praying all his life. Harvey Gill had prayed first, followed by Curt, who had always been a man of few words, although no one would ever have known it from his prayer that night. It was another one of those things Barb wished she could have recorded for future study. All she could remember now was that his prayer was powerful, eloquent, and unquestionably heartfelt, for at the end he had broken down and cried. All of them—Barb and the three children—had lifted their heads and stared at Curt in surprise, at which time Barb had seen tears flowing down Harvey Gill's face, too. Barb had felt that her own prayer, which followed Curt's, was a paltry thing compared to his.

When Harvey Gill had learned the twins' names, he had smiled at Curt and Barb. "Well, it's clear that you know something about the Bible already," he had said. He had found it hard to believe that they had named the boys after two uncles, not even aware of the Biblical story of the two faithful spies at the time. "Well, you boys have two big names to live up to," he had said, shaking their hands vigorously. "Joshua and Caleb were two great men of faith. You'll have to read about them in the book of Numbers." And they had—that very night when they got home, in fact. The whole family had sat around the kitchen table and read from the thirteenth chapter of the book of Numbers in the Bible that Harvey Gill had given them.

Salvation had touched Curt instantly and deeply. He hadn't had any major vices to give up or a hot temper to overcome, but he was a changed man in ways that Barb found hard to describe. He had always been what Barb would consider a focused and purposeful man, but after that night, his vision and drive intensified. He had set up a four-pronged program of Bible study at home—with the children, with Barb, with the entire family, and by himself. Whereas he had always been solicitous of his patients' physical and emotional well-being, now he had the eternal soul of each baby and child to consider. "They're not the same kids I saw last time," he told Barb when he returned home from his office the next day, but she knew what he really meant. They were the same kids, but he wasn't the same man.

"Earth to Pluto. Earth to Pluto," Josh said now, waving a hand in front of Barb. She saw that the others were leaving the table, heading toward the buffet line. She heard Della Boyd say, "I always *did* like Fridays, even when I was a little girl. And then when I taught school, why, it was everybody's favorite day. There's just a special feeling about Friday." Sammy was pounding on a package of crackers with a spoon, and Curt was leaning across the table, looking at Barb in a way that let her know he had just asked her a question and was waiting for an answer.

"Come again?" she said.

"I said you want to go ahead and get your pizza, and I'll stay here with Sammy?"

"No, no," she said, waving him off. "You go on. I'm not in any hurry. Just bring back a piece of cheese pizza for Sambo. I'll go get mine when you get back." She looked down the table at Philip, who was still sitting with his leg propped up, waiting for his mother to bring his pizza. "I'll keep the birthday kid company," she added.

Barb watched Curt rise and saunter off after the others. He was wearing his olive green slacks that she liked and a plaid flannel shirt the boys had given him last Christmas. As he went through the door toward the buffet line, he ducked his head, a protective habit resulting from going through too many low doorways.

It suddenly struck Barb as a surprising thing, as it often did when she observed Curt from a distance, that she was actually married to him. At times she would look at him and think, I hardly know you. I fix your meals, wash your clothes, sleep with you, mother your children, and make major purchases with you, yet I hardly know you. It never happened when they were close together—say, sitting side by side at the kitchen table—but only when she viewed him across a large space or in an unfamiliar room, as now. She wondered if other women ever had similar thoughts about their husbands.

How could you ever say you really *knew* someone anyway? A person was so complex that the most you could ever hope for was to peer briefly into a tiny corner of his soul. Maybe you could even step inside for a minute or two on rare occasions. She often wished she could have more of her husband, that his work didn't consume so much of his energy and attention. Maybe if he were home more, he could help her keep things more organized.

And they could talk more. He was often so tired at the end of a day that the last thing he wanted to do was talk. All his words had been used up with the mothers of those babies and children he saw day after day. Sometimes Barb joked about the "other women" in Curt's life—not only the ones who made appointments and came to his office, but all those who accosted him in public places to ask questions about their children's fevers and sores, sleep patterns and toilet training, and the ones at church who dragged him back to a Sunday school room to check out a strange rash or a swollen gland. Most parents thought he was a psychologist to boot, for they would bombard him with questions about their children's shyness, fears, aggression, stubbornness, demands for attention—you name it.

And then he came home emptied of words, with a look that said, "Give me something to eat and a soft chair." But Barb knew it was the same with most other women. One of her friends back in Asheville years ago had claimed that her husband never talked, he only grunted and used hand signals.

Yet, paradoxically, for all his human complexity, Curt was also amazingly uncomplicated. He was a good man—that simple phrase summed him up better than anything else Barb could think of. Given any situation, she could almost always predict what course of action he would choose. She might wish at times that he weren't so quiet, that she could feel closer to him, that he were a bit more adventurous and less serious, that his work didn't pull so strongly at him, but she knew for a fact that she couldn't wish for a better man.

Through the doorway she saw Curt pick up a plate and proceed through the buffet line. She saw him look down to the end of the line before making his first choice. Methodical and unhurried—that was Curt. It was a double-sided line, and Catherine was on the side opposite him. She said something to Curt, and he nodded politely.

Barb had no way of viewing him objectively after all these years of marriage, but she wondered for a moment how he looked to other people. Women who brought their children to his office often told her what a wonderful man he was—so patient, so gentle, so caring, and so forth. But what did he look like in their eyes? Barb had always considered him an attractive man, but maybe she was giving him too much credit for his character. Did Catherine Biddle, for instance, think Curt was a handsome man? She knew she only had to ask her, and Catherine would give her unvarnished opinion. She could hear her now. "Heavens no! He's *nice* enough, but he's not in the least bit nice *looking*!" Or "Why, what a silly question! Of course he's handsome. You must be blind as a bat if you can't see that!"

Forty minutes later Blake leaned back and said, "I'm not so sure they made any money off us tonight." They had just about finished, except for the twins, who were eating one last piece of chocolate chip pizza each.

The Vietnamese group had packed up and left ten minutes earlier, and Catherine had said, "Well, thank goodness!" as they made their way to the door in a great commotion of rapid talk and laughter. During the last couple of minutes the baby had set up a squall that sounded to Barb exactly like any other American baby. "They need to get that baby to bed!" Catherine had said several times. Hardy had cut his eyes sideways at his mother and watched her for several seconds, smiling slightly, but hadn't said anything.

Catherine and Hardy seemed to have reached a temporary truce, Barb had noticed. Whereas they had freely slung insults and sarcastic remarks back and forth before Philip's accident, she hadn't heard them talk much at all to each other since Hardy had returned home. That Catherine was happy to have him back was clearly evident, but they seemed to be stepping around each other cautiously as if they weren't sure of the rules of the game anymore. Barb couldn't help wondering what Catherine had said to Hardy that Sunday afternoon when Blake had found him in the athletic house and brought him to the hospital. What would be the first thing you'd say to your son after three days of convincing yourself that you would never see him again, remembering the whole time what you had last said to him?

"What about the present, Mommy?" Sarah whispered. "Didn't you bring it in?"

"Sure did," Barb said, reaching under her chair and pulling out a gift bag. She hadn't been able to find any tissue paper at home, so she had substituted last Sunday's comics as a filler. It actually looked quite planned and cheerfully appropriate for a kid, she thought, but she knew she wasn't fooling Catherine. She knew Catherine was probably thinking,

Well, of all the tacky things—if she had written tissue paper on her shopping list, she wouldn't have had to make do with part of the newspaper!

"Here, pass this on down to the thirteen-year-old," Barb said, handing it across the table to Curt. "Sorry it's late, Philip. I've had it for over a week, but I'd forgotten where I put it. I got it the same day I went to the grocery store, and somehow it got stuck on a shelf in the pantry. I found it last night right next to the saltine crackers." She laughed. "Anyway, we thought you'd like to open it here at your pizza party."

"He could open it at home," Catherine said. "We don't have to make a big production of it right here at the table." But the bag was already being passed down the table.

"Oh, a little more clutter won't matter," Blake said, eyeing all the dirty plates, glasses, and napkins on the table.

Then Sammy removed from his mouth a piece of pizza crust on which he was gnawing, pointed to the gift bag, and said plainly, "That's LEGO."

They all laughed. "Well, I guess little Sammy let the cat out of the bag, didn't he?" Della Boyd said.

"Cat?" Caleb said. "I thought it was LEGOs."

And Della Boyd actually let out a shriek of laughter. "You boys are so quick!" She turned to Blake. "Aren't they quick?"

Barb had chosen a LEGO set called Spy Runner, which, from all appearances, was a hit with Philip. He turned it over to the back and studied all the models that could be constructed from it, saying the whole time, "Thanks, hey, thanks a lot. This is cool! Hey, thanks, everybody, thanks!"

And on their way out of Pop's Pizza Palace a few minutes later, Barb heard the twins telling Philip about a new LEGO line they'd read about, called MINDSTORMS.

"We saw an ad for them in *Popular Mechanics*," Josh said. "They're these robot-looking things."

"Oh, goody," Hardy said, in a nasally little-boy voice. "Can I come to your house on Saturday and play with LEGOs?"

"Aah—I don't know," Josh said slowly, as if considering the matter carefully. "Do you think you could follow the directions?"

"Him?" Caleb said. "I mean, all you have to do is look at the way he puts his clothes together. We'd probably have to start him out on some DUPLO sets."

Philip laughed loudly.

Hardy stuck his face in front of Philip's. "Hey, Pip, if you care about your other leg, you better watch out what you're laughing about." But anyone could tell he really didn't mean anything by it.

Barb was right behind the boys, carrying Sammy. As they all stepped outside into the parking lot, she looked up at the black sky. The November rains had temporarily stopped, and the night was spangled with stars. There was only the faintest sliver of a moon. It reminded Barb of a tiny fingernail clipping. It was strange to think that although the moon must look like this every twenty-eight days or so, or actually fourteen if you counted both the waxing and waning stages, she so rarely noticed it.

She wondered what would have taken place in her life by the time it once again turned into the slimmest of crescents. Things could change so fast. This time two weeks ago Philip had been in a coma, and tonight he had eaten pizza. Barb watched Catherine and Blake walking across the parking lot toward Blake's black Lexus, and she breathed a prayer. She hadn't heard many cross words between Blake and Catherine recently. Could things be repaired between the two of them? she wondered.

She remembered one of the last things she had heard Blake say to Catherine before Philip's accident. He hadn't meant for Barb to hear it, of course, but she had come to the kitchen door at just the right moment. Or the wrong moment, as it turned out.

". . . and my father always took his clients out on the yacht in the summers," Catherine was saying to Della Boyd as Barb entered.

Blake was sitting at the table with what looked like a pile of bills spread out in front of him, but his back was to the kitchen door, so he didn't see that Della Boyd had waved Barb in before she had even knocked.

"I wish you'd quit calling that leaky houseboat a *yacht*," Blake had said. "You'd think you grew up next door to the Vanderbilts to hear you talk." Before anyone could signal to him that a neighbor was standing in their midst, he rushed on. "Has she told you about their house servants, too, Sister? Two toothless old crones who couldn't possibly have gotten a job anywhere else. And, yes, her father was a trial lawyer, but he did mostly court-appointed trials for lowlifes who couldn't afford to hire a lawyer."

When no one responded, Blake had turned around in his chair and seen Barb. She would never forget the look on his face as he swallowed and said, "Of course, the court paid him good money for all those trials."

A Special Case

20

The next night a bowling activity was scheduled for the church teen-agers, and Barb had volunteered weeks earlier to go along as a driver. She had learned a long time ago not to count on Curt for things like this, but she at least hoped he wouldn't get called out that night so he could stay home with Sammy and Sarah. She had a funny feeling about it, though. Curt's schedule had been surprisingly uneventful lately, with fewer emer-gency calls than usual. Any day now she expected things to turn upside down. It was strange how things like that usually went in cycles.

He got home at six and sat down to eat supper about six-thirty. He had eaten only a few spoonfuls of chicken noodle soup and a few bites of a grilled cheese sandwich, when the telephone rang. *I've got to find somebody else to stay with the children* was the first thought that went through Barb's mind when she heard the first ring, for she was certain that the call was some kind of hospital emergency. She had always told Curt she could tell just by the way the phone rang whether it was a normal call or a medical one. Sure enough, this one was medical—a newborn with a high fever. Within two minutes he was backing his Volkswagen out of the driveway.

"We need to leave in ten minutes, Mom," Joshua said. "Everybody's supposed to be at the church by seven." He was eating the other half of Curt's sandwich.

"I know, I know," Barb said. "Let me think a minute." The only baby-sitters she had ever used were church kids, but they would all be going bowling tonight. She reached for the telephone. Though she doubted that Olivia would be available on a Friday night, or, even if she were, that she'd be the least interested in baby-sitting, Barb couldn't think of anyone else at the moment. She hated to ask Catherine or Della Boyd to baby-sit, but if Olivia couldn't do it, she might have to.

She might have allowed herself to become peeved over the inconvenience Curt had left her with if she hadn't for just a moment thought of the mother whose baby had a high fever. She's at the hospital right now wondering if her baby is going to live, Barb thought, and my biggest problem is finding someone to watch two of my four healthy children so I can take my other two bowling. Finding a baby-sitter suddenly seemed like a very small worry indeed.

"Mom, you gonna use the phone or just hold it?" asked Josh. "You want me to look up a number or something?"

The Biddles' phone was busy, so Barb ran across the street. Finding the garage door open, she went through it to the kitchen door. Through the glass pane she saw Della Boyd in the kitchen, wearing a bibbed apron over a lavender housecoat. She was standing stock still in the middle of the floor staring at the telephone receiver in her hand, looking somewhat confused. Barb tapped on the glass, and Della Boyd turned her head slowly and squinted toward the door. When she saw Barb, she walked over and opened the door, still holding the receiver. The two of them started talking at the same time.

"Oh, hello, Barb, honey, how are you, I was just trying to . . ."

"Della Boyd, I'm sorry to bother you, but I have the biggest favor in the world . . ."

And then suddenly, all the voices began to register with Barb. Not just Della Boyd's voice, which was still droning on, as soft and pleasant and absentminded as always, but other voices in the background. She heard a woman's voice on the telephone Della Boyd held and recognized it at once as the prerecorded message requesting the caller to hang up and dial again. Della Boyd must have heard it, too, for she stared down at the phone and said, "Why, who can that be? I haven't even dialed the number yet."

The door to the basement was standing open, and the muted sound of voices and canned laughter from Hardy's television wafted upstairs. But the voice that rose above them all was coming from the direction of the den. Barb recognized it immediately as Blake's.

". . . and what did you think—that I'd forget about it? That I'd change my mind? How many times am I going to have to tell you that I mean business about this? The answer is still no."

Barb suddenly felt like an intruder. How many times was she going to walk in this way right in the middle of one of Blake's speeches? She was going to have to start going to the front door and ringing the bell as a warning from now on.

". . . and dialed a wrong number," Della Boyd was saying, "so I started to try again, and then I couldn't remember who I'd set out to call, and then you knocked on the door, and now . . ."

Then came another voice from the den. "Why are you doing this to me?" It was spoken shrilly, almost a scream really, and at first Barb couldn't tell whether it was Catherine, Olivia, or Philip who had said it.

"Because we've got to straighten things out around here!" came Blake's heated reply. "I'm tired of my kids running wild, that's why! I've been letting things go too long—that's another reason! I laid down the rules over a month ago, and you heard every one of them. You sat right in there at the kitchen table with your brothers and listened to every word. I meant what I said then, and I mean it now. You can hate me if you want to, but . . ."

"So what's she supposed to do—sit at home every night for the next two weeks?" It was Catherine's voice. "She's got a game to cheer for to-morrow night, for crying out loud! It's not like she can get a substitute! The cheerleading squad doesn't have understudies. The season's just started! She's spent hours practicing! What's she going to do—tell them she won't be there because she's *grounded*? I can't for the life of me figure out why you have to be so *extreme* about everything!" So much for not hearing cross words between Blake and Catherine recently, Barb thought.

"Anyway, Mom said if I . . ." Olivia was crying now.

Barb stepped back to the side door. "I'll come back another time," she told Della Boyd quietly.

Della Boyd looked back toward the voices coming from the den, then at Barb, then at the telephone in her hand. The recorded voice had finally stopped, and now a series of electronic beeps could be heard. "I think this telephone is broken," Della Boyd said. "Why would it be making a sound like that? I need to tell Brother it's broken." She looked back toward the den again with a worried look. "I think he's busy right now, though," she said, then dropped her voice to a whisper. "Olivia hasn't been acting very cooperative."

"Oh, I know how that goes," Barb said. She took another step back.

". . . not helping matters any!" Blake was saying. "We've got to do this, Catherine, and you can't always be undermining . . ."

"You see, Olivia came home late on Wednesday night, and Blake—"

"Oh, you don't have to explain anything to me," Barb said. "I need to go anyway." She had just taken hold of the doorknob when she heard feet pounding up the stairs and Hardy leaped into the kitchen from the open basement door. The fact that he was dressed totally in black gave his ensemble a more unified look than usual, although the individual garments themselves were as unconventional as always.

He had on black nylon warm-up pants that snapped down the sides, but none of the snaps were fastened, so the legs of the pants flapped freely, exposing his own legs beneath and the black knee-length mesh shorts he was wearing. He had on a black T-shirt with a large yellow *M&M* imprinted on the front and a rumpled black velvet dinner jacket over that. A pair of black work boots minus the laces completed the outfit.

"Hey, Mrs. C, this is lucky," he said amiably. He glanced toward the den and smiled. "Ahh . . . sweet sounds of family harmony." Looking back at Barb, he said, "I was just coming up to call you."

"Me?" Barb said. "What for?" She knew he must be kidding, but she didn't see his point.

"To see if you were home."

"Well, I'm not. I'm right here. I was just leaving, though. I've got to take the boys somewhere." She opened the door.

"I'm going to hang this phone up," Della Boyd said. "It must be broken." She walked across the floor and replaced the receiver firmly. "There. I don't know how they expect people to use the phone when it's making all that noise." She looked at Hardy. "Some woman I didn't even know was on there a minute ago," she said.

Hardy gasped. "You didn't hang up on her, did you, Auntie Deeb? She might've been calling to tell you you'd won a million dollars."

Della Boyd was convinced that she was going to win a sweepstakes someday, and she entered them all in hopes that she'd strike it rich. It had become a family joke by now, although Philip was her staunch ally, often declaring, "Somebody's gotta win, and Aunt Della's got as good a chance as anybody."

Della Boyd stared at Hardy and put a hand to her mouth. She spoke in a hushed tone. "Why, I wonder if that's who it was. I never thought of that!"

"Hardy's just teasing you, Della Boyd," Barb said. "That voice was just somebody from the telephone company asking you to try your call again. I've heard that message lots of times."

"Oh, is that a fact?" Della Boyd said, relaxing. "Well, they do notify people by telephone sometimes when they've won something. That man last year who won the *Reader's Digest* prize said he was fast asleep on his davenport when they called him. I read about it. He said he gave them a snippy answer at first because he didn't understand what they were talking about. Imagine—waking up from a nap and finding out you're a millionaire!"

"Well, I've got to go," Barb said. "Bye, everybody." She knew Josh and Caleb must be wondering what was taking her so long.

"Hey, wait, Mrs. C, you're not going without me, are you?" Hardy said.

Barb didn't know what to say. What was Hardy talking about? "We're going bowling," she said. "It's a church activity."

"Yeah, I know all about it," Hardy said.

"You do?"

"Yeah. Hey, what is this?" Hardy said. "You reneging or what?"

"Reneging?"

"Yeah, you know—going back on a promise. Sorry, I thought you'd know what that word meant, Mrs. C."

Barb laughed. "I guess I'm just not catching on. You don't mean you're going bowling with us, do you?"

Hardy looked at Della Boyd. "Listen to her, will you? She's practically begging me not to go." Pitching his voice to match Barb's, he exaggerated what she had said. " 'You *don't* mean *you're* going bowling with us, *do you?*' " He completed the effect with upraised hands and a look of horror. "Okay, Mrs. C, you win. You don't want me going, then I ain't going."

"Oh, Hardy, I'd love for you to go!" Barb said. "I just think you're pulling my leg, that's all. The boys didn't say anything to me about you going."

"That's 'cause I just now decided I was going," Hardy said.

"You mean they invited you?"

"Hey, is that so surprising?" Again he looked at Della Boyd. "She thinks nobody'd invite me. She doesn't know I'm the main man in demand. People line up for miles, Mrs. C, just to get a glimpse of me."

"I don't doubt that a minute," Barb said, smiling.

" 'Course, I told your duo I was already booked for tonight, being who I am and all, but hey—the main man can change his mind anytime he wants to, and that's what I did. Thought I'd give the duo a thrill, even though it's gonna mean major disappointment for lots of others."

"Well, so what are we waiting for?" Barb said. "You going to stand here bragging on yourself all night? We're ready to go."

Apparently the argument in the den was over, for Blake wandered into the kitchen just then. He looked tired. Barb wondered if he had won the battle against Catherine and Olivia. "Oh, hi, Barb," he said, "I didn't know you were here." Barb wondered if he was tempted to add *again.*"

"Not to stay," she said. "I just got here, and now I'm leaving."

"She came to get me," Hardy said. "I'm going with her."

Blake frowned. "Where?"

"To church," Della Boyd said. "Hardy's going to church with the Chewning twins. Isn't that nice?"

Barb could tell that Blake opened his mouth intending to laugh, but something made him stop.

"Where?" he repeated.

"Church," Hardy said, enunciating carefully. "You know the thing with the steeple on top?"

Blake turned to Barb. "What's this all about?" he said. "Hardy's not supposed to be going anywhere this weekend."

Now Barb understood Hardy's sudden interest in coming to a church activity. He must be grounded, too. She had to admire Blake for trying a tough approach, but she couldn't help wondering if grounding would even work for someone like Hardy. What would keep him from just walking out of the house, getting on his skateboard, and disappearing into the night? Wasn't Blake afraid he'd run away again? But Blake's word must carry some kind of weight, she decided, or Hardy wouldn't still be hanging around. He certainly wouldn't be scheming to exchange a night at home for a night with a church group.

Barb held up both hands. "Oh, please, I'm not trying to interfere with anything," she told Blake. "I guess the boys asked him to this young people's activity at the church, and I just came over to . . ." She trailed off, not knowing what else to say. She had already decided she'd just have to take Sarah and Sammy to the activity with her. Things seemed too tense around here to bring up the baby-sitting matter.

It wasn't hard to guess what had been going through Hardy's mind. *If I can't do anything fun tonight, I might as well go to this little Sunday school deal. Surely Dad'll be a sucker for that.* Pretty slick of him to try to pull this off. But it sure put Blake in a tight spot.

"Look, I don't want to complicate things here," she said. "I didn't know anything about any of this, really, and I don't want to get in the middle of a family matter." She looked back and forth between Blake and Hardy.

"What kind of activity is it?" Blake asked.

"Bowling," Barb said. "We're meeting at the church, then taking them all bowling. Then we're having banana splits back at the church later." She decided not to mention the devotional time before the banana splits. "We'll get back around ten or ten-thirty, I'm guessing."

"You keep saying *we*," Blake said. "Are you going, too?"

Barb nodded. "I'm one of the drivers." She paused, then added, "Even though some of the kids in the group have their driver's license, we always like to have adults drive for things like this." She didn't mention that she had been the one to push for such a policy when the twins had first joined the youth group. Teenaged drivers by themselves didn't really worry her too much, but teenaged drivers with a car full of teenaged passengers did.

"Oh, I think that's an excellent idea," Hardy said seriously. "It's much safer that way."

Barb smiled. "It just works better, you know," she told Blake. She glanced at the clock on the wall. "We're supposed to meet at the church at seven."

"And you'll be with them the whole night?" Blake asked.

Barb nodded again. "I sure will." The more she thought about it, the better she liked the idea of Hardy going along. This must be the fourth or fifth time the twins had invited him to an activity at church, and even if it did turn out to be a lesser-of-two-evils kind of acceptance, at least it would get him there.

Blake had his hands jammed into the pockets of his jeans, and he was chewing on his lip as he stared at Hardy. "Tell you what I'm going to do, Hardy. I'm going to let you go to this thing tonight." He shifted his eyes to address Barb. "But if he so much as steps one foot out of line, I want you to bring him straight home. No, better yet, call me and I'll come get him. Don't take any junk off him." Hardy accompanied his father's speech with a straight-faced pantomime, pretending to step over an imaginary line, drive a car, talk on the telephone, and so forth.

Della Boyd was watching him with a look that was part delight and part puzzlement. "Oh, Hardy, all the boys and girls at the church are going to get such a kick out of you!" she said, and Hardy, without smiling, sprang into the air and executed a series of swift kicks. Della Boyd laughed gaily. "I think bowling is such a nice thing for young people to do," she added. "I wonder if they still have hayrides anywhere. I went to a hayride one time years and years ago in Yazoo City with a girl in my class at school. They had a wiener roast, too, and sang songs around the fire. Things like that are so much more wholesome than going to the movies. The movies nowadays are just shameful."

"I agree one hundred percent," Hardy said solemnly. "The violence is shocking."

"Let me know the minute he gets out of hand," Blake said to Barb.

"Oh, I'm sure he'll be fine," Barb said, though she wasn't nearly as sure as she made herself sound. She knew Hardy was capable of pulling any number of shenanigans. "Well, then, if you're ready, we can go," she said to Hardy, glancing down at his unsnapped warm-up pants.

"I'm ready," he said, following her glance. "Ventilation, you know—

my legs get hot." Then he frowned suddenly. "Hey, you don't gotta wear suits and neckties to this little church dealie, do you?"

Barb smiled. "No, no. You're fine just the way you are. You can go on over and get in the van if you want to. We're ready to go." She knew the sponsors of the youth group talked to the church kids regularly about making visitors feel welcome and looking past their appearance. She just hoped the kids were up to a challenge like Hardy.

Blake shook his head and sighed as he watched Hardy walk out the door. "You know, it's funny," he said to Barb. "I used to blow a fuse everytime I looked at him in one of his getups, but I guess I've gotten used to it. I'd probably have a heart attack if he came out wearing something normal." He smiled wearily at Barb. "I sure hope taking him along isn't going to be a burden on you. Is Curt going with you?"

"No, he had to run to the hospital."

"Are there going to be any men at this thing?"

"Oh yes, at least two, maybe three," Barb said. "And believe me, they've all got plenty of experience working with teenagers. Everything's going to be okay."

"Well, keep a close eye on him."

"I won't let him out of my sight," Barb said, smiling. "We'll have a great time. Don't worry."

Catherine walked into the kitchen just as Barb was leaving. "Hey, what's all this?" she said. "I just looked out the front window and saw Hardy walking across the street. Where does he think he's going?"

"He's going to a church activity with Barb and the twins," Blake said.

"Church?" cried Catherine. "Well, I never!" She looked sharply at Blake. "I thought he was supposed to be—"

"He's got a three-hour reprieve," Blake said firmly.

"I think a church bowling party sounds like such a nice thing," Della Boyd said. "Maybe he can make some new friends."

"Well, Olivia's going to love this!" Catherine said. "Wait till she finds out you let Hardy go somewhere but not her. All we're going to hear is the big 'U' word over and over—'Unfair, unfair, unfair!' "

"Would Olivia want to go, too?" Barb asked. "There's plenty of room in our van."

Blake started to say something, but Catherine spoke first. "Olivia already *had* somewhere to go tonight"—she glared at Blake—"but somebody put the kibosh on that."

"Well, she'd be welcome . . ." Barb began.

"No, she's not in any condition to go *anywhere* right now," Catherine said. "I can just imagine what she'd say if you invited her to go to church!"

"Well, if she decides she wants to go, we'll be leaving in a couple of minutes," Barb said.

As Barb headed out through the garage, she heard Della Boyd say, "I've never been bowling in my whole life. I sure wish young people today did more things like that. That and hayrides and picnics and—"

"Well, it's not exactly picnic weather, Della Boyd!" Catherine snapped, and the door slammed shut.

Hardy was already slouched down in the backseat of the van when Barb raced up the driveway and flew into the house. "Hurry, Josh, get the diaper bag, will you? Caleb, find Sammy's jacket. Sarah, put on your coat, sweetheart. We're all going bowling!" She threw on her own jacket and grabbed her purse. "Oh, and you'll never guess who else is going with us," she said to the twins. She should have known better than to say such a thing to them. They could take an innocent comment like that and beat the life out of it.

"Dennis Rodman?" asked Josh.

"Al Gore?" asked Caleb.

"Arnold Schwarzenegger?"

"Pope John?"

To each guess, Barb said, "Nope," but she knew they could keep it up much longer than she could. And they did. She finally stopped responding, but they kept it going all the way out to the van, firing away with machine-gun rapidity.

"Pete Sampras?"

"Bill Gates?"

"Queen Elizabeth?"

"Oprah Winfrey?"

"Tom Clancy?"

"Mark McGwire?"

"Tiger Woods?"

And so forth. When they slid open the van door and looked inside, they both groaned in mock disappointment.

"You gotta be kidding!" Caleb said. "Look, it's only Hardy!"

"Big-time letdown!" Josh said. "Way to dash our hopes, Mom." The boys climbed into the van.

"Yeah," Caleb said to Hardy, "Mom says to us, 'Guess who's coming with us?' So naturally we're getting all excited expecting somebody really . . . well, you know, somebody like—"

"Wynton Marsalis," Josh said, "or Luciano Pavarotti or Itzhak Perlman or—"

"Whoever they are," Hardy said, still slumped down in the seat.

"Whoever they are?" said Josh. "Don't you know anything about music?"

Hardy adopted a condescending tone. "I know plenty about music."

"Of course he does," Caleb said. "Haven't you ever seen his CD collection featuring all those groups with highly intelligent names like the Flying Burrito Brothers and the Squirrel Nut Zippers and the Goo Goo Dolls?"

They were out of the driveway by now, heading down Brookside toward DeLaney. One of these days, Barb feared, the twins were going to carry their teasing too far. She had already cautioned them to go light with Hardy. "You're going to make him mad," she had said more than once, "and then you won't have a chance with him."

"We know how to handle Hardy, Mom," Josh had said once. "Trust us. Just wait, you'll see. Somebody like Hardy, you gotta keep 'em backed up against the wall, or they'll walk all over you. We've got a plan, see. Like I keep telling you, it's two against one. One of us always takes over when the other one lets up. You gotta keep him on his toes. He's a special case." Barb wasn't so sure about their plan, but she had to admit Hardy was a special case.

"Well, anyway," Josh was saying to Hardy now, "I guess it's okay you coming along tonight and all. We'll get over it. I mean, if it couldn't be Shaquille O'Neal, then we'll just have to settle for old Hardy the Har Har Biddle, huh, Caleb?"

"You little boys are a laugh a minute," Hardy said.

"Aw, is that all?" Josh said. "I think we can do better than that."

"Maybe we can work up to a laugh a second if we try harder," Caleb said. "I've got a good joke book we can use."

"My sides are aching already," Hardy said.

"Right or left?" Caleb asked. "It might be appendicitis."

For just a moment Barb felt a twinge of pity for Hardy. Two against one didn't seem very fair. As she turned onto Highway 11 and headed toward Derby, she prayed silently that the twins wouldn't interfere with the working of the Holy Spirit tonight. She could see just the top of Hardy's head through the rearview mirror. Please work a miracle in this boy's life, dear God, she prayed. But she knew even as she prayed that her hopes weren't very high. She glanced up at the black sky with a soft sigh. If the universe depended on her faith to remain suspended in space, she knew the planets would spin off into nowhere and all the stars would fall.

Just Another Adventure

21

Barb had heard her pastor, Theodore Hawthorne, preach on the difference between "head knowledge" and "heart knowledge" many times during the years they had attended the Church of the Open Door. That night as she drove her van along Highway 11 and then through the streets of Derby to the parking lot of the church, she knew in her head that God *could* answer her prayer, that He *could* work a miracle in the life of Hardy Biddle that night. If anyone had challenged her on the subject of God's power to do the impossible, she could have delivered a stirring speech, complete with Bible verses, to prove the point that God could take what seemed like a hopeless situation and turn it into a victory.

So as far as head knowledge went, she had an abundance. With heart knowledge, however, it was a different matter. Although she knew that God *could* transform Hardy Biddle—and He could do it that very night— she didn't really have the faith that He *would*. Hardy wasn't an ordinary boy. She couldn't help thinking it was going to take a thunderbolt to get his attention. Hardy just wasn't the type to be gently persuaded, at least not in Barb's opinion. He wasn't a Peter, Andrew, James, or John, who simply heard the call of Jesus and followed. He was more like Paul, who had to be struck blind on the road to Damascus before he would turn to Christ. But even as these thoughts went through her mind, she was chastising herself for her lack of faith. Who was to say how the Holy Spirit would deal with a person?

As she pulled up next to Willard and Jewel Scoggins' station wagon in the church parking lot, Barb tried to shake off her doubts, but she kept seeing images of Hardy losing his temper and hurling a bowling ball at one of the other teens or slipping a can of beer out from under his jacket and taking a swig or shouting some obscenity when he didn't get a strike or making a pass at one of the church girls. She felt a sudden rush of panic. Why had she agreed to bring him along? What was she thinking of?

The twins had told her a few things they had seen and heard at school, things about Hardy's extracurricular interests. They had seen him smoking in Jordan Baxter's car after a football game earlier in the fall, and the rumor was that it wasn't just a cigarette. The boys saw the kinds of girls Hardy hung out with at school and heard the way he talked in the hallways. His bad temper was legendary, as were the stories about his classroom antics. He himself had told them that he had failed world history the year before because, among other things, he had cheated on the final exam, defaced his textbook beyond repair, and turned in a term paper lifted straight from a library book. Berea High probably had fewer incidents of drugs, violence, and sex than the national average, but no one pretended it was perfect. It might seem like it was out in the middle of nowhere, but the kids were by no means sheltered. Barb wondered how much Catherine and Blake knew about Hardy's conduct away from home.

Still, Barb argued with herself, God can do anything. A lot of what boys that age did was only for show anyway. Maybe this was all a big act Hardy put on to impress people. Maybe underneath he was a soft touch. There was no doubt that he was a kid of many moods, and she knew she hadn't begun to see them all. Frankly, it surprised her that Hardy had come tonight, even if it was just a ploy to get away from home. She couldn't help wondering what he had in mind. She wouldn't be surprised if he tried to sneak away at some point. She would have to stay alert.

The boys were getting out of the van now, but Hardy remained in the backseat, scrunched down next to the window with his arms folded and his eyes closed. Sarah hopped down onto the pavement, and Barb went around to the passenger side to lift Sammy out of his car seat. She could tell he was already getting sleepy. He had taken only a short nap early that afternoon. He put his head on her shoulder and stuck a finger in his mouth. Poor kid, a bowling alley sure wouldn't be the easiest place to fall asleep.

"Come on, Biddle, you getting out?" Josh said, leaning back into the van. "We're going to divide everybody up into groups out here."

Hardy didn't budge. "I'm stayin' right here," he said. "Groups get on my nerves."

"Okay," Josh said, unperturbed. "We'll tell them we brought a visitor, but he's too shy to get out of the van. We'll make sure you get put in our group, though, don't worry."

"That's a huge relief," Hardy said.

Josh slid the van door shut and went over to join the group of boys gathered under a tree. The parking lot was lit by two bright streetlights. It was a cool night but not really cold, especially considering it was already the first of December. Good jacket weather is what Barb called it. Willard Scoggins was telling the boys something, stopping to laugh frequently and making wide gestures as if describing something of enormous proportions. His wife, Jewel, was standing beside him, nodding her head and smiling.

Barb smiled and waved at Jewel but decided to stick close to the van since she had promised Blake not to let Hardy out of her sight. She hoped she got a chance to talk with Jewel tonight, though. The whole church was buzzing with Willard's announcement during a recent service that Jewel was going to have a baby. Barb wasn't certain about Jewel's age, but someone had told her that she was almost forty-eight. She knew for sure that her only other child, Joe Leonard, was seventeen, and she had heard that Jewel had thought for years before he was born that she couldn't have children.

Barb never knew Jewel's first husband, who had died six years ago, but she knew it had been a drowning accident. When Willard Scoggins, the choir director, had started courting her over two years ago, everyone at church had been delighted, including Barb. When they were married less than a year later, Barb had helped serve punch at the reception.

Watching Jewel now as she stood beside Willard, Barb thought of how her friend's life was going to change with the coming of a new baby. Jewel's mother, Eldeen, could talk of nothing else. The way she talked about it, you'd think she was the one having the baby instead of Jewel. She had even written a poem titled "My New Baby"—not "My New Grandbaby," mind you, but "My New Baby"—and read it at the last meeting of the Women Well Versed.

Barb could feel Sammy breathing heavily against her neck now. Sarah busied herself with the dry oak leaves scattered across the parking lot, first gathering a small heap. Barb knew what would come next.

Sarah would make a shape out of them, some kind of animal most likely, maybe even using acorns for the eyes and nose. It was one of her favorite things to do. One Saturday several weeks earlier she had painstakingly formed a big giraffe in the driveway at home, complete with an amazing patterned coat, all made out of colorful fall leaves. It had taken her most of the day, and afterward Barb had meant to take a picture of it but discovered that the camera needed film. During the night a strong wind had come up, and the giraffe was scattered to the four winds by the time they got up the next morning. Sarah had taken it in stride, but Barb had felt a sharp stab of sorrow when she realized that all that was left of the giraffe was a memory, and knowing her own memory, that wouldn't last long.

Barb was happy to see the Finches here also. Rob and Glenda Finch had moved to Derby from Alabama a couple of years earlier so that Rob could coach and teach biology at Derby High. Their daughter, Tricia, was away at college now, but they had a thirteen-year-old boy, Clayton, who had just joined the youth group this year. The Finches were great youth sponsors. Rob's experience teaching high school and Glenda's skills as a practical nurse had served them well in a number of emergencies.

Last year alone, Rob had broken up a fistfight between two boys sitting behind the youth group at a Greenville Braves baseball game, found three lost eighth graders on an overnight hike, and persuaded a fifteen-year-old girl who had come to a Film Night activity as a visitor to give him her switchblade. Glenda had bandaged wounds, removed ticks, and administered medications. She had also known exactly what to do when another visitor had suffered an epileptic seizure in the middle of a scavenger hunt last year.

The other two adults for tonight's outing were Howard and Roberta Harrelson, whose son, Howie, was a senior in the youth group. It was, in fact, the sight of Howie Harrelson, standing with the other boys by the tree, that reminded Barb again that God could transform anyone. Howie had been saved two years ago, largely through the testimony of Jewel's son, Joe Leonard. Howie and Joe Leonard had both been in the band at Derby High and had played on the basketball team together. From a hostile, profane, cocky fifteen-year-old, Howie had changed into a cheerful, well-balanced seventeen-year-old who was now as outspoken for Christ as he had once been for himself.

Willard Scoggins had finished telling the boys his story and was now scanning the group gathered in the parking lot. "Okay, listen up, everybody," he called out. "Come on over here, and let's divide up."

"Yeah, let's divide," Caleb said. "We can have two teams—the Amoebas and the Protozoa."

Rob Finch laughed. "Glad to see you remember your biology from last year, Josh."

"I'm Caleb."

"Yeah, right," Rob said, "that's what you said the day you two switched places and went to each other's classes."

"Hey, you still remember that, Coach?" said Caleb.

"Yes, Derby High hasn't been the same since you two left," Rob said. "How's Berea holding up? Poor old Morton Hollings is a friend of mine. I considered warning him about you guys but decided to let it be a surprise."

By now everybody had moved together in front of Willard Scoggins, who was counting heads aloud. ". . . twenty-six, twenty-seven, twenty-eight. Okay, twenty-eight teens, that's great!"

"And we have one more," Josh said. "We brought a visitor. He's waiting in the van. He's shy and gets nervous in a crowd."

Willard looked at Barb quizzically, as if to verify the report. She nodded. "I've got Sammy and Sarah with me, too," she called. "A last-minute change of plans. But I can still take two or three more if they sit close."

"Okay, so we have twenty-nine teens," Willard said. "Too bad we don't have one more to make it an even thirty."

Caleb spoke up. "Joe Leonard has a split personality! Does that count?"

Joe Leonard grinned as he reached over and pretended to throttle Caleb. Barb had always liked Joe Leonard. Like the twins, he was tall and thin, but he was totally different from them in personality. She was glad they were friends. Even though he was two years older, he put up with them good-naturedly and actually seemed to enjoy them as much as they did him. He didn't talk much, but what he did say revealed both good sense and a good sense of humor.

Since the Finches had brought both their station wagon and van, there were five vehicles. Willard quickly assigned each teen to a driver. These would also be their bowling groups, he explained, since he had rented five of the twelve lanes at the Derby Tenpins Bowl-a-rama.

Barb ended up with six boys in her van—Joshua, Caleb, Joe Leonard, Howie, a friend of Howie's named Zack, and Hardy. Caleb sat in one of the captain's chairs with Sarah in his lap, both of them strapped in with the same seat belt. Howie took the other captain's chair, which left only the rear seat for the other four boys.

"Where's the other end of my seat belt?" Howie's friend Zack said. He had a high, thin voice.

Caleb introduced everyone to Hardy after they had all fit themselves in and were pulling out of the church parking lot, but Hardy didn't even bother to lift his head or open his eyes. "Yeah, well, whoever's sittin' next to me is jammin' me," he said, "and I don't like to be jammed, see."

It was Josh who was doing the jamming. "Yeah, well, your elbows don't feel so great either," he said. "Maybe you'd rather get out and ride on the luggage rack."

"I read about a boy getting killed that way," Zack said. "They do it for fun. It's called car surfing." Zack was a fair-haired boy of slight build who wore glasses and a worried look. Barb wondered how he and Howie knew each other. She couldn't imagine that it was through sports, for she couldn't picture Zack holding a baseball bat or dribbling a basketball. He had the look of someone who wished he were at home taking a computer apart or working with complicated math formulas rather than on his way to a bowling alley.

"Yeah, I've done that," Hardy said.

"You've gone car surfing?" asked Zack. His voice sounded breathless.

"Sure, lots," Hardy said. He yawned loudly as if to suggest that car surfing was so mild it was almost boring. "You close your eyes, and if you get going fast enough, it feels like you're flying."

"And you were on top of the car?" Zack asked.

Hardy's laugh had a derisive edge to it. "Yeah, I was *on top of the car*," he said, making his voice tremble and crack.

"How did you hang on?" Zack asked.

"Any way I could."

No one spoke for a few seconds, then Josh breathed an elongated "Wow!" in an exaggerated tone of admiration. "That is so majorly awesome, Hardy. How come you get to have all the fun, huh? Hey, Ma, can me and Caleb go car surfing with Hardy sometime, huh, can we, please, huh, pretty please?"

Caleb picked it up. "Yeah, Hardy did it, Ma, can we? We wanna be just like Hardy. Can we go car surfing, please, Ma, please?"

"Sure," Barb said, "right after you go over Niagara Falls on a boogie board and bungee jump off the Empire State Building."

Zack laughed—one of those nervous, choking laughs that goes on too long. Finally, as if to cover for him, Howie broke in with a question. "Did you ever play Chicken in a car when you were growing up, Mrs. Chewning? My dad said he used to do that when he was in high school." Zack's laughter stopped abruptly as if he didn't want to miss Barb's answer to Howie's question.

Barb was taken back. What had made Howie ask such a thing? And how was she going to get out of answering it? She couldn't lie about it, but she surely didn't want to tell the truth either. A feeling of sickness swept over her. The last thing she wanted to talk about was her high school indiscretions.

"Uh-oh," Caleb said. "Mom's hesitating."

"And you know what that means," Joshua said.

Caleb lowered his voice as if he were the anchor on the six o'clock news. "Tonight another sordid detail from a local resident's checkered past comes to light," he said. "It was revealed tonight on the way to the bowling alley that Mrs. Barbara Chewning, mother of four and wife to the respected Dr. Curtis Chewning, local pediatrician, participated many years ago in a game of Chicken, the deadly pastime of—"

"Was it just once, Mom?" Josh interrupted.

Barb's mind raced in circles. She had never tried to give her children the impression that she was the ideal kid growing up, but neither did she want to give them the full story of her foolish, and often rebellious, behavior. There were simply some things your kids didn't need to know.

"Again she hesitates," Josh said.

Caleb continued in his newscaster's voice. "Correction. Mrs. Chewning participated in *many* games of Chicken, the deadly pastime of immature teens behind the wheels of motorized vehicles—"

"Otherwise known as cars," Josh put in.

Zack laughed again, a shrill explosion that ended with something sounding like a hiccup.

At some point in college, Barb had actually tried to count the number of times she could have easily been killed before her twentieth birthday. She had come up with the number eighteen, she recalled, but now she couldn't begin to separate them all into specific incidents. She did know, however, that playing Chicken in her father's 1970 Mercury Cougar during her junior year of high school accounted for at least six or seven of the eighteen times.

She had had the reputation of being a daredevil during her teens— had first earned it, in fact, during elementary school. She had always been willing to try anything, and she viewed Chicken as just another adventure, like diving off the side of a cliff into Lake Shiloh, which no other girl in their school had ever tried, or deciding she wanted to break the girls' state track record in the 880, which she did during her senior year. She could still remember her father standing by the finish line at every race she ran in high school. "The thrill of victory!" he would bellow as she crossed the line. "The agony of de feet," she would always reply as soon as she had turned and trotted back and could get her breath.

Afterward she could never explain why she had played such a stupid game as Chicken. She only knew that the next time she was challenged, she always accepted. All the guys thought it was funny, and she naturally liked the attention she got. Of course, she knew all along that the boys bailed out sooner and swerved to safety because she was a girl, but that was okay with her. It gave her a perfect record in the game and the nick-name of Fearless Frazier at school. And she probably would have kept playing Chicken, knowing that the guys would continue to humor and protect her, if she hadn't wrecked her father's Cougar one Friday night after a football game when seven of her friends were packed in tighter than sardines and whooping it up as they flew along a country road with the radio turned up as loud as it would go.

That wreck had slowed her down, temporarily at least. Even though no one was hurt very badly, she had begun to get the first inkling of an important truth—that she wasn't invincible, that another ten miles per hour and a collision with something more solid than the rickety, aban-doned barn in the middle of a flat, rain-soaked field might have snuffed out lives, her own included.

And though she and her friends had laughed about the wreck after-ward, teasing each other at school and making it into such a big jolly joke that a reference to the event was even printed in the school yearbook, Barb had never played Chicken after that. When Jimbo Porter had chal-lenged her the next weekend, she had declined, grateful for the excuse that she couldn't drive till her dad's car was fixed. When he challenged her again weeks later, she had waved him off. "I'm learning judo now," she had said. "Anytime you want to be humiliated, let me know and I'll take you on."

"Don't worry. She does this all the time," Caleb was saying now. "One minute she's there, and the next, she's gone—poof!" He made a noise like a jet engine and began singing. "Off she goes into the wild blue yon-der..."

"We know it's really just an escape mechanism, though," Josh said. "It's that old when-you-don't-want-to-face-it-just-ignore-it-and-it'll-go-away trick."

"You mean the one your dad and I always tell you not to use?" Barb asked.

"Hey, folks, surprise! She's back!" Josh said. "Fast trip, Mom. How were things in Ma-Ma Land?"

Zack laughed again, this time a cascade of hooty giggles. Barb decided that this kid must have a whole repertoire of laughs. She wondered if he had any that sounded normal for a boy his age.

"I have no idea what you're talking about," she said to Josh. "I've been right here the whole time, and I've heard every word you've said."

Caleb laughed. "Sure, Mom, sure." Then he whispered loudly to the other boys. "And she's taught us everything we know about denial."

"I bowled a two-sixty-eight one time, you know," she said.

"Yeah, we know," Josh and Caleb groaned in singsong unison.

"We only hear about it every time we go bowling," Josh said.

"Is two-sixty-eight good?" asked Zack.

Hardy groaned loudly. "Is two-sixty-eight good?" he mimicked in a falsetto.

"Hey, watch it," Howie said. "Zack's never been bowling before."

"Somehow that doesn't surprise me," Hardy said.

"Yeah, Zack, two-sixty-eight is good," Joe Leonard said. "Three hundred's the top score. Anything in the two hundreds is good. The first time I went bowling, I bowled a sixty-one."

Barb was thankful that she had succeeded in diverting the boys' attention from the subject of playing Chicken, at least for now. "If any one of you boys back there can beat a two-sixty-eight tonight," she said, "I'll give you a prize."

"Yeah, but didn't you bowl your two-sixty-eight when you were in a league, bowling two or three times every week?" Caleb said.

"Yeah, Mom, that's not really fair," Josh said. "I mean, we go bowling, what—maybe three or four times a year?"

"Right, but I'm a woman," Barb said. "You're all big, strapping teen-aged males." As soon as she said it, she wondered if the other boys had turned to look doubtfully at Zack.

"You gotta figure she'd try that one on us," Caleb said.

"And why wouldn't I?" she said, pulling into the parking lot of the Derby Tenpins Bowl-a-rama. "Men can outdo women at anything athletic, can't they? I'm sure I've heard those very words come out of the mouths of my own two sons."

"Well, I'm not so sure bowling can be called *athletic*," Caleb said.

"Even though," Barb continued, disregarding Caleb's comment and raising her voice, "neither one of the two sons whose mouths I just mentioned can beat me at tennis yet."

"Hey, we haven't even tried since summer," Josh said.

"And you weren't really *trying* then, right?" Barb said, laughing. "Isn't that what you told me at the time?"

"Ooh . . . your mom plays dirty," Howie said.

"Believe me, this is mild," Caleb said. "You wouldn't believe the abuse we have to endure at home on a daily basis."

Barb shut off the ignition and turned around in her seat. "So is anybody going to take the challenge?" she asked. "Bowl a two-sixty-eight, and you get a prize."

"What's the prize?" Howie asked.

"Probably a fifty-cent package of Skittles," Josh said.

Zack laughed breathily, as if gasping for air.

Barb shrugged. "Wait and see." She noticed that Sammy was fast asleep now. The digital clock on the dashboard said 7:29.

Hardy spoke up. "I got a better idea, Mrs. C."

"What's that?"

"You bowl with us right now, and if we beat you, we get the prize. Forget the two-sixty-eight thing."

The eyes of all six boys were on her. Hardy unfolded himself from the corner, sat up, and opened his eyes, although only partway. He was studying her solemnly from beneath his eyelids. She looked at them one by one, then smiled slowly. Without question she could beat Zack, and she felt pretty sure about Josh and Caleb. Joe Leonard and Howie might give her trouble, though, and she had no idea what kind of bowler Hardy would be. Of course, she hadn't bowled for years. She might have lost her touch. But hey, this was an adventure—just like diving off the cliff or setting the 880 record. She had always been fueled by competition. Surely she could rise to the occasion again.

"Okay, guys, you're on," she said. "You've got to help me keep an eye on Sammy, though. He's asleep right now, so it shouldn't be too hard."

"You sure you have enough money for six packs of Skittles, Mom?" asked Josh.

"I'm not one bit worried," Barb replied.

After they all got out, Zack stooped beside the van to tie his sneaker. Barb went around to the passenger side and was unfastening Sammy's safety belt when she heard Zack clear his throat behind her.

"Uh, Mrs. Chewning, I was wondering . . ."

Barb's heart sank, for she knew what was coming. "Up we go, Sambo," she said softly. Sammy lifted his head briefly, then immediately laid it against her shoulder and closed his eyes again. Sarah stood nearby, holding the diaper bag in one hand and Barb's purse in the other. "You can go on and catch up with the other boys," Barb said, smiling at Zack. "I don't think I need any help here." She closed the van door and started walking.

"About what Howie asked you, you know, back there in the van," Zack said, trailing behind her. "I was sort of curious, you know . . . Did you really ever play that game Chicken when you were our age?"

Barb stopped and turned around to face Zack. There were two little creases between his eyebrows. With a quick sweep of the eye, she took him in, from his extremely white sneakers up to his flattop haircut. She took in his neat khaki jacket, zipped up to his neck, and his stiff, brand-new jeans with the cuffs rolled up. She wondered for a moment what he would do if she told him the truth point-blank. "Yes, Zack, I played Chicken on dark, narrow rural roads, not just one time but quite a few times. One time I took the speedometer up way past a hundred before the other kid chickened out."

Would he say anything, Barb wondered, or would he simply go straight inside and call his parents to come get him? "Mother, Father," he might say, "I found out that Mrs. Chewning used to play dangerous games when she was driving, and I didn't think you would want me to ride home with someone like that." And though Barb knew looks could be deceiving, Zack had the appearance of a kid whose parents would come right away to pick him up and whisk him home to safety.

"Zack, what do you hope my answer to your question will be—yes or no?" she asked. "Do you want me to say no, that I was a very safety-conscious teenager, or do you want me to say yes, I had a wild, naughty streak a mile wide?"

The creases between his eyebrows deepened. "Well, I don't really know," he said, looking confused. "I was just wondering if . . ."

"Well, I'll tell you what," Barb said, tilting her head and smiling at him. "You think about it, and when you can tell me the answer to my question, I'll tell you the answer to yours. Okay? Now, come on, let's get inside. We don't want to hold everybody up, do we? There are games to be played! There are prizes to be won!" She felt sure the matter wasn't closed, but at least she had bought a little time.

Together they walked toward the entrance of the Bowl-a-rama, neither of them saying another word. Zack appeared to be thinking very hard. And Barb was thinking, too. Though she certainly hadn't wanted to ponder her many mistakes as a teenager, she decided that the subject of playing Chicken had probably served a good purpose tonight, for it had reminded her on a very personal level of the fact that God could work around—and often *through*—youthful weaknesses. And playing Chicken was certainly not the worst of her youthful errors. God had salvaged *her*, hadn't He? Who was she to question whether He could do the same with Hardy?

A Great Sum

22

Barb had to admit that the twins had good instincts about how to handle Hardy. The bowling activity taught her that. As she watched Hardy that night and saw him bravely trying to maintain his air of cool, bored superiority in the face of so many opponents, she knew he was facing a losing battle. One on one with any of the church boys—Josh, Caleb, Joe Leonard, or Howie—it might have been a different story. He might have had a better chance. But any two of them in combination put him at an extreme disadvantage, and all four together made a formidable team. They were too quick for him, never letting him get the upper hand. If one of them flagged for a moment, there were three more to move in and take up the contest of wits.

Zack stood by with his mouth hanging open a good part of the night, laughing nervously at anything and everything, blushing wildly every time his ball veered off the lane into the gutter. He had taken his jacket off by now to reveal a long-sleeved yellow knit shirt snugly tucked into his jeans and a leather tooled belt with his name monogrammed on it: *ZACHARY*. Hardy, seeing a scapegoat in Zack, was merciless.

"Hey, Zack, how d'ya do that, huh? I mean, on my last turn I *tried* to throw a gutter ball, but I couldn't do it. How do you do it every time, huh?"

Howie came to his friend's defense, clapping him on the shoulder in a brotherly way and saying, "Hey, don't worry about it, Zack. I used to stink at bowling when I first tried it."

Josh joined in. "Yeah, too bad we don't have a video of old Hardy the Har Har Biddle here the first time he ever bowled. Bet he gave some excellent demonstrations himself on the art of gutter-balling."

"What do you mean, the first time I ever bowled?" Hardy asked, as he stood to take his turn. "This *is* the first time."

"Yeah, right," Caleb said. "And you play with Barbie dolls, too."

"And Mr. Potato Head," Josh said.

"I bet he's on a T-Ball team, too," Howie said.

Joe Leonard even contributed a line, addressing Hardy with feigned earnestness. "Maybe you can move up to coach-pitch next year."

Hardy emitted a girlish squeal of laughter, no doubt in imitation of Zack. "Oh, you fellows are just so, *so* funny! I'm just rolling on the floor!"

Bolstered by the support of the others, Zack ventured a comment. "That's what a bowling ball does." He smiled proudly at his cleverness.

Hardy lifted a ball off the return ramp and then turned to Zack with a look of open disgust. "I'm trying to decide," he said, "whether you're better at bowling or telling jokes, and I gotta tell you it's a real hard choice."

"Well, don't think about it too hard," said Howie, who was ahead of Hardy in the sixth frame by just a few pins, "or you might lose your concentration. We'd sure hate to see you step up there and blow it, wouldn't we, guys?"

"Yeah, don't choke, Biddle," Caleb said.

"Nice and steady," said Josh. "Don't even *think* about the big wide gutters. Just keep your mind on that little narrow strip down the middle."

"Yeah, keep your mind out of the gutter," Howie said.

Hardy shook his head. "Oh, you boys just try so hard, don't you?"

"Actually, we hardly try," said Josh. "It just comes natural." And everyone laughed except Hardy, who turned around and launched the ball down the lane with such force that the pins flew apart as if blasted with dynamite. He ended up with an impossible split, however, and then rolled the ball right down the middle on his second throw, advancing his score by only eight that frame. He curled his lip, shuffled back to the bench, and said, "Who cares?"

"Is that a rhetorical question, or are you expecting an answer?" Josh asked, but Hardy ignored him and flung himself onto the bench with an air of supreme nonchalance. Having taken off his black warm-up pants and velvet jacket earlier, he looked a bit underdressed for December in his black shorts and T-shirt, but Barb knew it was all part of his goal in life—to be different.

The other boys did such a good job of keeping Hardy in check that Barb stepped in to rescue him from time to time. "Okay, guys, come on. You're slowing down the game with all this chitchat. Look at the girls on lane two. They've already finished one game and are partway through another one."

It had been settled that the contest would include their total scores for two games. "That way we can get loosened up in the first game and then really get down to business in the second," Barb had said.

"Which probably means she'll just toy with us in the first game," Joe Leonard had replied, "and then annihilate us in the second."

Barb won the first game with a 178, but Howie was close behind with 169, and Hardy with 161. Joe Leonard bowled 148, Josh 135, and Caleb 129. Zack's final score was 39.

Once again Howie encouraged Zack. "Hey, it's just a game," he said. "If it was something important, like a chemistry test, we'd probably end up in reverse order—no offense, Mrs. Chewning." Howie grinned at her. "But what do I know? Maybe you're an ace in chemistry, too. I know I'm not. I never would've made it through if Zack hadn't been my lab partner." So that's how they knew each other. Barb figured it had to be some connection like that.

Behind all their tomfoolery, the boys were serious about the contest. Hardy was the only one who pretended to be indifferent about his performance, shrugging and muttering when he couldn't finish out a frame, but anyone could see that it was only a cover-up in case he didn't win. The other boys had determination written all over their faces when they stepped up to take their turns, and when they barely missed a strike or spare, they groaned openly and immediately looked at the electronic scorecard to see how the miss had affected their standings.

Barb bore down in the second game and pulled ahead early with a strike and two spares in the first three frames. When Zack knocked down six pins at one time in the third frame, they all cheered. He beamed with pleasure and looked at Hardy to make sure he had noticed.

Hardy laughed disdainfully. "I don't think I ever saw a ball roll so slow. It's a wonder it didn't stop before it got there. I thought there for a minute I was watching a slow-mo flick." He held up his forearm and slowly lowered it sideways to represent a sluggish bowling pin.

Sammy had awakened by now but sat mutely on the end of the bench beside Barb, chewing the edge of his favorite blanket, his wide blue eyes full of awe at the sights and sounds around him. Occasionally, when it was Josh or Caleb's turn, he would laugh. "Ball knock 'em down!" he would cry.

Sarah was with a group of girls two lanes over and had even let them put her name on the scorecard for the second game. One of the girls, Marilee Tucker, found a lighter ball for her and showed her how to throw it.

Sarah clasped her hands together after her first throw and watched the ball roll lazily down the lane, veering sharply to the left at the very end but clipping two pins. She turned around with a smile and gave a celebratory handclap when she saw the 2 recorded by her name on the scorecard. She looked over to where Barb was seated and waved. Zack, who was watching Sarah, too, looked deflated when she knocked down six more on her second ball.

Barb's margin of victory was wider on the second game, but among the boys the scores were closer. She bowled a 223, making her the overall winner. Hardy came in second in that game with a 159, then Joe Leonard with a 155, then Howie with a 149, Caleb with a 144, and Josh with a 139. Zack more than doubled his score, bowling an 87.

Zack added everyone's total scores in his head, announced the rankings, and then figured the average score per game. "Let's see," he said, tilting his head and studying the scorecard, "that's a grand total of two thousand fifteen, divided by fourteen since seven of us played two games each, which makes . . ." He paused no more than five seconds. ". . . an average of one hundred forty-three point nine per game or two hundred eighty-seven point eight per person." He looked around at the others and tittered. "Which means that those of us who scored less than a total of two hundred eighty-seven for both games pulled the average down."

"Oh, great," Caleb said. "Way to twist the knife in a little deeper. Like it's not enough to tell me I came in sixth, huh? Now you've got to go and batter my ego by telling me I pulled down the average."

Josh, who had ranked fifth by scoring one point higher than his brother, puffed out his chest. "Yeah, I'd be mortified if I came in sixth. Maybe I can give you some pointers next time."

Howie held out his hand to Hardy. "Good job, Biddle. I thought I had you there for a while, but you pulled away from me with those last three throws."

Hardy looked at Howie's hand as if it were infectious. Howie didn't retract it, however, but extended it even closer so that Hardy at last lifted his own hand reluctantly and allowed it to be shaken.

"Yeah, okay" was all he said.

"Don't get too confident, though," Howie said. "I want a rematch."

Hardy shrugged and looked away.

"Way to go, Mrs. Chewning," Howie said. "No prizes tonight, guys. She creamed us."

"Yeah, Mom strikes again," Josh said.

"Oh, spare us," Caleb said.

"Very, very punny," Joe Leonard said.

Zack let out a snorting laugh. "I get it—strike and spare, like in bowling, huh?" He laughed again, then stopped suddenly and asked Howie, "Is it time to go back to the church for banana splits yet?"

Hardy stared at Zack without expression, then sighed and shook his head. "Little things please little minds. What do you do for fun, kid?" he asked. "Watch the weather channel?"

Zack glanced at him quickly. "Sometimes. Do you?"

Hardy opened his eyes wide. "Yeah. Oh yeah, I love the weather channel. I especially love it when the Doppler radar shows lots of storm activity, don't you?"

Zack's eyes brightened, and he sat up straighter. "I have a video called *Monster Storms*. It shows tornadoes forming out of supercells."

"Really?" Hardy said. "Can I borrow it sometime?"

"Sure," said Zack. "It tells about this special meteorological program out in Oklahoma called Vortex that tries to forecast tornadoes early by using weather balloons and airplanes."

"Come on, let's start another game," said Howie. "We've got time. You go first, Caleb."

As Caleb took his turn, Zack continued talking. "And it shows this thing called a downburst, or microburst, that makes planes crash at takeoff or landing. It's this violent column of air that strikes the earth and then rebounds upward in a swirling wind." He formed an imaginary column with both hands, moving it downward suddenly and then letting it spring upwards, his fingers flying apart to signify a whirling mass of air.

"Wow, I bet you're good at charades," Hardy said. "Anybody seeing you do that would immediately guess 'Downburst.'"

"Or microburst," Zack said. "It's sometimes called that, too. They first started finding out about them after a plane mysteriously crashed on the runway back in the seventies and killed over a hundred people."

Hardy yawned. "Frightening," he said, folding his arms and sliding down so that his head rested against the back of the seat.

When Hardy closed his eyes, Zack turned his attention to Barb. "Did you know that the United States has over a thousand tornadoes every year?" He went on to describe a tornado in Alabama that had lifted the roof off a church sanctuary during a Palm Sunday service, killing twenty people, and then he progressed to hurricanes, listing for her the statistics of the damage caused by Hurricane Andrew in 1992. Barb nodded and did her best to look interested. The whole time, though, she was wondering what kind of man this boy was going to grow up to be.

Barb let them play the third game without her. Sammy crawled into her lap and drank his juice, crowing with glee anytime one of the boys made a strike. "*All* fall down!" he'd say. Willard Scoggins came around when the boys were almost finished. "We've got about ten minutes before our time's up," he said. "Think you can get done?"

"No problem," Howie said cheerfully. He was presently ahead of Hardy in this game.

"Hey, Mr. Scoggins, want to see something amazing?" asked Josh, who was getting ready to take his last turn. He held the ball in front of him, then called over his shoulder. "Watch this smooth release."

"He said offhandedly," Caleb quipped.

There was a great deal of laughter as Josh let go of the ball, which whizzed down the lane and knocked down nine pins.

"Hey, no fair. You messed me up, duck-brain," he said to his brother.

"What are you talking about?" Caleb said. "That's the best throw you've had all night."

Willard grinned and shook his head. "These boys of yours," he said to Barb. "They don't ever stop, do they? Are they still making up those awful Tom Swifties?"

"Oh, heavens," Barb said, rolling her eyes. "I sure hope they don't get started on that again." Months earlier Willard had told the twins at a youth activity about the Tom Swiftie puns he used to make up when he was their age, and he had given them several examples: " 'Lay your weapons down,' Tom said disarmingly"; " 'Come to the back of the boat,' Tom said sternly"; " 'I can never hit the target,' Tom said aimlessly," and so forth. The twins had almost driven her crazy over the following weeks making up new ones until one day she had put her head in her hands and said, "Stop! No more! Never again! None! Not a single one! Nix! Nein! No, no, no!"

"She said negatively," Caleb had replied quicker than a wink. She had wanted to bean him but had laughed instead. How could she have expected him to resist that one when she had set him up so perfectly?

"What are Tom Swifties?" Zack asked now.

Howie and Joe Leonard groaned in unison. "Believe me, you really don't want to know," Howie said.

"Sure he does!" Josh said. "You heard him ask."

"Please don't do this to us," Joe Leonard said to Zack, holding his hands in a begging pose. "Tell them you changed your mind."

"But I didn't," said Zack earnestly. "I want to know."

"And we certainly wouldn't want to deprive the boy of something he wants," Caleb said.

"We're warning you—you don't know what you're doing," Howie said. He raised his voice in mock despair. "Can we please ride back to the church with someone else?" he wailed, and he and Joe Leonard hurried on to the service desk to turn in their bowling shoes.

All the way out to the van, Barb heard the twins ahead of her firing lines at Zack while he looked back and forth between them as fast as his neck could swivel, an expression of dazed delight in his eyes.

" 'I just had a blowout on the highway,' Tom said tirelessly."

" 'I don't like being on welfare,' Tom said dolefully."

" 'Hello down there on the barn floor,' Tom said loftily."

" 'We're all Boy Scouts,' Tom said uniformly."

Waving his hand, Zack interrupted. "Wait a minute, who's Tom?" he asked.

"Who knows?" Josh said. "That's just what the jokes are called—Tom Swifties. So they all end with 'Tom said.' "

"Oh, okay," Zack said. "Go ahead. You know any more?"

And the twins resumed.

" 'Flip on the switch,' Tom said lightly."

" 'You spilled the hot fudge,' Tom said saucily."

" 'I hate taking exams,' Tom said testily."

" 'I'm all out of Tide detergent, so I guess I'll have to use this other box,' Tom said cheerily."

They were still going strong when she quit listening. It was no wonder, when she stopped to think about it, that she had learned to tune things out so easily. It had to be a survival technique that every mother of hyperactive twins developed. It was necessary for sanity.

Hardy was in front of Barb, following Zack and the twins, his head down, his shoulders slumped. Barb wondered if he was thinking about his loss to Howie in the third game. He hadn't said a word after his last throw, which had knocked down only seven pins, but had wheeled around with his jaw clenched, and sat down and yanked off his bowling shoes, all but throwing them onto the floor. He had jammed his feet into his black boots, put on his black velvet dinner jacket over his T-shirt, and clomped off to turn in his bowling shoes, his warm-up pants wadded up under his arm.

After Barb fastened Sammy into his car seat and started the engine, she turned around and addressed the twins. "Okay, now that's the last one of those Tom Swifties I want to hear." Then before they could beat her to it, she supplied the ending. "She said with finality."

The boys laughed. "See what you started," Howie said to Zack. "We tried to warn you."

"Are we going to get to make our own banana splits?" Zack asked. "I like them best when the bananas aren't very ripe."

"Frankly, I wish we were having hot dogs," Josh said, then quickly added, "Don't yell at me, Mom, please don't. It wasn't a Tom Swiftie, really."

As they drove back to the church, Barb looked out at the dark December sky. She wondered how Curt was doing at the hospital, if the newborn was still in danger, if right this minute Curt was fighting for the baby's life. She made herself imagine the baby sleeping peacefully and Curt talking comfortingly to the parents, telling them he was sure things were going to be fine now.

She didn't like to think about the few times in his practice when a baby or child had died. Sometimes when she heard other women talk about their husbands' job frustrations, she was tempted to ask, "When was the last time your husband ever tossed in bed at night over what he could have done to save a child's life?" People often told her how wonderful it must be to be a doctor's wife, to see him doing so much to help others, to share with him in the joy of healing. And it was, of course. But there were those other times that were blacker than a year of midnights. And it was those dark times that she often feared had seeped into Curt and left a permanent sediment. "You've lost your sense of humor," she had told him on more than one occasion.

Often when Curt was at home, she knew his mind was at the hospital or at some sick child's bedside. Once when he had been sitting in his recliner with what she called "that faraway look" on his face, she had said matter-of-factly, "I'm thinking I might sell the house and move to Tahiti if that's okay with you." And hearing only the last few words, he had nodded absently and said, "Oh, sure." Of course, she had more than her share of lapses, too, she knew that, so she sure couldn't be too hard on him.

She recalled several times when one of their own children had been sick but Curt had been so busy caring for other people's kids that he had never even known it. And it wasn't that he didn't care—heavens, no. It was just a time thing. There were only so many hours in the day. So when other women told her how fortunate she was to be a pediatrician's wife, part of her agreed wholeheartedly and the other part wanted to take another vote. Not that she would ever in a million years want any husband besides Curt. But a different occupation—now she might at times be tempted to give that some serious consideration if the choice were hers.

It was strange that the very thing people often envied her for—being a doctor's wife—was the thing that she sometimes grew tired of, which she knew was just the way life worked. She had once read an interview with the wife of a world-famous pianist. When asked if she loved to sit and listen to her husband play the piano at home, the woman had replied, "Oh, my goodness, no. I've had enough of that. That's the last thing in the world I'd want to do!"

Barb knew enough by this point in her life to realize that things were rarely as rosy as they appeared on the surface. Take Blake and Catherine Biddle, for instance. The first time she had seen them from across the street the day she and Curt had moved onto Brookside, her first thought had been, *What an attractive couple*. And all three of their children were as good-looking as their parents. So from the outside, they seemed to have every reason to be a happy family—nice house, nice cars, good looks. But starting with the first conversation she had ever had with any of them, back in August when she had gone over to borrow a cup of sugar, one thing had become abundantly clear. These were not happy people. She had to hand it to them, though. Their recent efforts, especially Blake's, to straighten out some things at home were admirable. If only they could understand that real changes didn't come from things imposed on the outside but from a change of heart.

They were only a few blocks from the church by now. In the back the boys were discussing professional basketball. "Nobody could've ever beat Chicago if Jordan hadn't retired," Howie said.

"A great bronze bubble floating in a perfect arc"—These were the words that came immediately to Barb's mind at the mention of basketball. And it was from a sports write-up she had read just the evening before in *Time* magazine, of all places. It was amazing how you started noticing poetic devices such as the use of metaphor everywhere you looked once you became aware of them.

Margaret Tuttle, the leader of the Women Well Versed, had been urging them all to read not simply for content but also for style. "Even when you read the newspaper, be alert for the precise word, the apt metaphor, the well-turned phrase," she had said, "for these are the materials of poetry." Margaret Tuttle was another example of how different a person could look on the outside and really *be* on the inside. Barb would never have guessed from looking at her, so steady and unruffled and beautiful, that Margaret had suffered so deeply.

At their last meeting of the Women Well Versed, which had been held at Barb's house only a week and a half ago, Margaret had listened attentively to the poems the women themselves had written and had offered encouraging remarks concerning both form and content, along with tactful suggestions for improvement if they were still interested in further polishing. Barb hadn't shared her poem because she hadn't had time to get the ending right.

Before she went on to the lesson for that night about free verse, Margaret had read aloud a sonnet she had written and was "still refining," as she put it, titled "Tree of a Thousand Stars." She had brought with her a pretty little bonsai tree in full bloom with the scientific name of *Serissa Foetida* but commonly called by the poem's title—Tree of a Thousand Stars.

The sonnet was so lovely it had made Barb's heart ache. Into its fourteen lines Margaret had compressed a great many descriptive details. The number of images was stunning for so short a poem. There were literal stars in the black sky, the tiny snow-white blossoms of the bonsai, green leaves, loose soil, sunshine, roots, water, hands, laughter, and music, but Margaret had somehow woven them together into a moving tribute of her friend Birdie Freeman, whom she had lost less than a year ago.

After reading her poem, she had gone on to tell them how Birdie Freeman had come into her life and shown her the path to hope and salvation. She had given a brief summary of her unhappy past but had quickly turned from herself to a more general application and had ended with these words: "We must never forget that our small, daily acts can total a great sum of love. They can be the stars by which others find their way through the dark voyage of life. They can teach others to live by faith." She then told them that the bonsai was the first gift Birdie had given to her when they had known each other only a few days.

Dottie Puckett, who was attending the meeting that night, had spoken up. "Birdie gave me one, too," she said. "Only mine hasn't ever had quite that many blooms on it at one time."

"But you should have seen the puny little thing when she first got it," Catherine had told the others. "I was there that day. I didn't believe for a minute it would even *live*, much less *bloom*!" She had folded her hands in her lap and looked contrite. "I was wrong, though. I saw it in her kitchen a month or two ago, and I couldn't believe it was the same one. You could have knocked me over with a feather. It's the prettiest little thing now!"

Margaret had smiled, nodding her head slowly. "Forgive me, for I know what I am about to say is simple and obvious, to the point of triteness, but I cannot resist the opportunity. In honor of Birdie, I must not leave the truth suspended in midair, implied." She had taken a moment as if to select the best few words from among many. "We must not despise small things," she said at last, "for what at first glance may seem insignificant may well be the source of great beauty and truth." She paused and added, "Birdie was a small woman, but her impact on my life cannot be measured."

Everyone was silent, as if expecting Margaret to elaborate, but evidently she had said all she intended to say on the subject. When Della Boyd asked her, however, if she would read her poem once more, slowly, Margaret complied, and as she read "Tree of a Thousand Stars" a second time, everyone's gaze was fixed on the little bonsai.

Barb still remembered the closing line of the sonnet: "By the light of a thousand stars, I reached the shore." She had known Birdie Freeman, of course, for she had been the organist at their church before the car accident that had taken her life. As Barb imagined the many tiny white flowers on Margaret's bonsai, a peculiar picture began to form in her mind. Each little star-shaped blossom began to rise from its slender branch and drift skyward in a great multitude. One by one they filled in the outline of a new constellation in the shape of a large heart.

Having arrived at the church, Barb parked next to the Scoggins' station wagon in front of the fellowship hall. Make me like Birdie Freeman, she prayed. Make my faith in God and my love for others shine like a thousand stars. She sat for a moment thinking of how Birdie Freeman had touched Margaret Tuttle in such a life-changing way and of how Margaret Tuttle was now sharing her gift of poetry with other women and of how each of those other women . . .

The van door slid open, interrupting her thoughts, and she heard Zack's high, eager voice. "I sure hope we're going to eat the banana splits right away!"

The Real Thing

23

As they were getting out of the van, Zack once again lingered behind while Barb helped Sammy out. "Uh, Mrs. Chewning, I was wondering . . ." he began.

Barb dreaded what was coming. No doubt he was ready to resume their earlier discussion about the game of Chicken. He must have decided on an answer to her question, she thought, and was now going to demand an answer to his.

"Upsy-daisy," she said, lifting Sammy out and setting him down on the pavement. "Go on in with Sarah, and I'll be right there." She closed the van door and turned to face Zack. She'd just have to tell him the truth and get it over with. She couldn't even remember now how the subject of playing Chicken had come up in the first place. She surely wished it hadn't.

Zack looked at her expectantly, his eyes wide behind his dark-framed glasses. "I was wondering," he said, "if they're going to have maraschino cherries for the banana splits."

Barb smiled, relieved. "Oh, I'm sure they are. What would a banana split be without a maraschino cherry? That's like apple pie without ice cream. Come on. Let's go in. The sooner the devotional time gets started, the sooner it'll be time to eat."

"Devotional time?" Zack said, lagging two steps behind her. "What's the devotional time? Will it last long?"

"No, not too long."

"It's already past nine o'clock." Zack sounded a little breathless as he tried to catch up with her. "My grandmother is expecting me home by ten. She gets worried if I'm late."

So he lived with his grandmother. That put a new light on things. Barb wondered if both of his parents were dead. Or maybe there was a divorce. Or an abandonment. Whatever the case, one thing was fairly sure. A great deal of Zack's nervousness and social awkwardness had to be related to living with a grandmother who worried about him.

She slowed down, put a hand around his shoulder, and fell into step with him. "There's a phone inside. We'll be sure your grandmother gets a phone call if we see it's going to be later than ten, okay?"

As the ladies went to the church kitchen to get the things laid out for refreshments, the young people were directed to several rows of metal folding chairs by the piano. First they welcomed all the visitors by name and then sang a few choruses, during which Zack kept craning his neck to see what the women in the kitchen were doing.

Hardy was sitting on the end of a row beside Joe Leonard, who sang out enthusiastically. Hardy was slouched down in his chair, his arms folded, an undisguised look of revulsion on his face. Peering through the kitchen pass-through window into the fellowship room, Barb saw Joe Leonard sharing his songbook with him, though Hardy wasn't singing, of course.

When they finished setting up for refreshments, Barb and the other women went out to join the young people. Sarah and Sammy had gone back to one of the nearby Sunday school rooms to play with some puzzles and toys. Poor Sammy, Barb thought, he should have been in bed long before now. It was a good thing he was a low-key kid. All this late-night excitement would have turned the twins into crazed animals at his age.

After the singing, Rob Finch told the teens that for the devotional time he had asked Howie Harrelson to share his testimony. As Howie got up and walked to the front, Barb was once again reminded of God's power to change lives. She remembered the first time she had ever seen him, before she had even known who he was. It was at the public swimming pool in Derby. She had gone to pick up Josh and Caleb one summer afternoon and had run into Howie—literally. Or rather, he had run into her.

It must have been a little over four years ago now. The twins would have been twelve at the time, and they had practically lived in the water that whole summer. Barb had walked past the check-in window that day and had just rounded the corner to the pool area when she was almost flattened by a kid, who turned out to be Howie, running from the opposite direction as the lifeguard bellowed, "No running on the pool deck! I said, *no running!*"

Of course he was dripping wet, and Barb remembered that it wasn't only the actual impact that surprised her but also the sudden flying of water all over her face and clothes. He was around fourteen at the time, much too old to be running around the pool, and as solid as a cannonball. The lifeguard had come over at once and asked Barb if she was okay, then reprimanded Howie, who appeared to be deaf for all the response he gave. He had glared at Barb, in fact, as if the whole thing were her fault. And when the lifeguard asked if he didn't have something to say, he had first spit on the concrete deck and then opened his mouth and let loose with one of the most obscene strings of words Barb had ever heard.

The lifeguard had ordered him to leave and not come back for the rest of the summer, and as he swaggered off to get his towel, he had proceeded to yell at the top of his lungs exactly what he thought about the lifeguard, the swimming pool, the stupid woman who had gotten in his way, all the other people in the pool, and everybody else in the whole stupid world.

Josh and Caleb had told her his name that day, and she had never forgotten it, which was unusual since she often had trouble remembering names. When she met him again a year or two later, the first time he visited their church, she recognized him at once, even before she heard his name. In fact, she had walked up to him, extended her hand, and said, "Hello, Howie Harrelson." He had looked at her quizzically as she shook his hand but had never asked her how she knew his name, and she had never told him.

As Howie stood at the podium now, ready to speak to the other teens, Barb leaned over to his mother, Roberta, who was sitting next to her. "That's a good-looking boy you have," she said, and Roberta flashed her a smile.

Barb knew the general facts of Howie's testimony but had never heard it from his own lips. His introduction was simple. "By the time I was fifteen, I had tried just about everything there was to try," he said. "I don't want to go into a lot of detail about my old life, but I was a bad kid."

He looked at his father sitting in the front row and then at his mother sitting in the back next to Barb. "Unfortunately," he said, "my parents can support every word I'm saying. They know all the details. They tried everything they could think of to straighten me out, but I was just determined to be bad. I know I hurt them a lot, and I'm not proud of that." Barb saw Roberta Harrelson make a quick dab at her eyes.

"I was a punk drummer in a metal band," Howie said, "and every other night we'd all get wasted out in this old garage where we practiced. I'd sneak away from home and . . . well, like I said, I tried everything there was to try. I was just a fifteen-year-old hotshot trying to be cool, and I was totally messed up. I was a loudmouth, a show-off, a liar, a thief, a cheat—you name it. I had a dirty mind and a dirty mouth. I gave my teachers fits and made a game out of getting kicked out of school." He paused a moment. "Okay then, that's enough about all that," he said. "So why am I standing up here tonight? It's not to brag about all those past sins. I wish like everything I could erase them out of my memory."

He took a deep breath and glanced at Joe Leonard in the second row. "If it hadn't been for a friend of mine," he continued, "I might not even be alive tonight. This is where the good part of the story starts. I was in the band at Derby High my freshman year. At least on the days I decided to go to school I was in the band. I'm sure my band director looked forward to the days I wasn't there. But anyway, this friend was in the band, too, and sat kinda close to me since he played the tuba and I was in the percussion section."

By now several people were smiling at Joe Leonard, who was looking embarrassed. "This guy kept asking me to come to these *things* called youth activities at his church," Howie said. "All kinds of different things, like skating and cookouts and stuff, and I kept laughing in his face. Then finally one day I said, 'Okay, kid, listen, get this straight—I'm coming with you this one time, and then I want you to shut your mouth about it or I'll knock your teeth down your throat'—except what I really said wasn't nearly that polite."

Everyone laughed, and Joe Leonard blushed. "So I went with him and his little church buddies to play miniature golf one time. Whoop-de-doo. Putt the little golf ball around for an hour and get this guy off my back— that's all I was thinking of. So I put on a good show, acting like a real nice guy that night, and then afterward I told him he better lay off and leave me alone or I'd stuff his head down his tuba bell." Everybody laughed again.

Howie paused, exhaling slowly and lifting his eyes to the ceiling. "It was only a week or so later that this guy I'd treated like mud risked his life for me." The laughter stopped, and the room became dead still. "I'd been in lots of fights before, so that wasn't anything new," he continued. "But this day I got it from three guys at once. I had smarted off one too many times, and they ganged up on me after school to teach me a lesson. They had some very effective teaching tools with them called knives, and they were pretty skilled with them. Said they hadn't decided whether to cut my tongue out or just get rid of me altogether. That's when my friend showed up."

Howie looked straight at Joe Leonard. "Joe Leonard saw what was going on, saw it was me down on the floor and knew I probably deserved everything I was getting, but he jumped to my defense anyway. He saw the knives and knew exactly what he was getting into, and he did it any-way." Howie shook his head and smiled. "I don't know about you, but in my book that's a real friend who'll do that. And the funny thing is, I didn't even think of him as a friend then." He stuffed his hands into his jean pockets and looked down at the floor. "I used to make fun of him right to his face and call him Holy Joe Leo," he said softly. There was a sudden burst of high, tense laughter from Zack that broke off abruptly.

"So anyway," Howie continued, looking up and speaking louder, "we both got hurt, went to the hospital and all that, but as you can see, we both pulled through." More people laughed. "Now here's the point of all this," Howie said, taking his hands out of his pockets and grabbing on to the sides of the podium. He leaned forward earnestly and spoke even louder. "It wasn't just a lucky accident that Joe Leonard showed up that day to help me out. God had the whole thing planned. And it wasn't luck that we both came through okay. It was God. Now here's a question for you to think about. If you had been in my place, how would you have treated Joe Leonard after all that? Would you have treated him any dif-ferent from before? Just try to imagine it. One day you're making fun of him to his face, then the next day he saves your life. How are you going to treat him now? What's going to be the first thing you say when you see him after you get out of the hospital?"

Howie paused and looked around, his eyebrows raised as if waiting for a response. "Come on. Somebody tell me," he finally said. "Would you treat him the same or not?" Still nobody said anything. It appeared that all the teenagers were trying to imagine themselves in Howie's place. Barb half expected one of the twins to offer something humorous, but she was glad neither of them did. They were both studying Howie as if deep in thought. She knew they had both heard this story before, but this was the kind you could hear over and over. It was the kind that made you think. Hardy was still slumped down in his chair, his head down and his arms folded, and Barb couldn't tell from where she was sitting whether he even had his eyes open. She prayed that his ears were, though.

"I mean, when somebody's got a *scar* because of you, doesn't that change the way you think about that person?" Howie asked. Almost everyone nodded. "You're going to do a whole lot of thinking about what that person did for you, right? It's going to keep coming back to you."

Howie was on the debate team at Derby High and had won several state awards for public speaking, but Barb was sure that there had never been so much at stake in any of his school competitions as in the speech he was giving now. She knew where the story was leading, of course, and prayed for him as he neared the end.

"Well, since nobody wanted to make a guess a minute ago about what I said to Joe Leonard the first time I saw him afterward, I'll tell you," Howie said. He smiled slowly, then looked back at Joe Leonard. "Do you remember what I said?" Joe Leonard shook his head, and Howie laughed. "Well, I didn't say much of anything, remember? I just stood there . . . crying like a baby. Do you remember that part?" Joe Leonard grinned and shrugged his shoulders, and there was a murmur of laughter.

"Now, here's what I'm getting at," Howie said, addressing everyone again. "I came back to Joe Leonard's church after that, see, and I talked to him and spent time with him. I wanted to find out more about this guy who had saved my life. I didn't call him 'Holy Joe Leo' anymore. And I listened to what he had to say when I asked him what all this salvation stuff was about. And you know what? I found out that Joe Leonard wasn't the only one who had a scar because of me. I found out that the person's name I had been taking in vain all those years had scars because of me—and not just one. He was nailed to a cross through His hands and feet. He didn't just get hurt for me, He died for me. He did that to pay for my sins, and He did it because he loved me."

Howie stopped and took a deep breath. "After I found out about that, guess what? I didn't make fun of Jesus Christ by using His name in vain anymore. I listened to what He had to say in the Bible, and I wanted to find out more about Him. The day came real soon when I accepted Christ as my Savior, and nothing was the same anymore. Nobody had to make me stop hanging out with my old friends or stop listening to heavy metal or stop doing drugs and all the other stuff I used to do. It was like an old dead skin just dropped off. Everything was different—I just didn't want to do any of it anymore. Of course, I had a lot of damage to fix up from the stupid stuff I'd done, and I don't mean it was all easy and smooth after that, but God changed me inside, and I've never been the same since."

Barb handed Roberta Harrelson a paper napkin she had brought from the kitchen, and Roberta blew her nose.

Barb had always wished there were a word or phrase set above ordinary language that could adequately describe the experience of salvation. Nothing in common use could do it justice. At times when she heard herself or someone else say something like "He got saved," she almost winced at the unholy sound of it. Even the phrase "born again" almost seemed too trite for the wonder of salvation. She was glad, then, that Howie spoke of having "accepted Christ," of being changed on the inside.

After Howie finished, Rob Finch stood up and motioned Marilee Tucker to the piano. He read John 3:16, then asked everyone to sing the chorus "For God So Loved the World." Rob was partial to some of the old choruses he had sung growing up, and he never apologized for them. Barb was glad, for she couldn't think of a more perfect song for right now.

"I don't think you'll ever hear a clearer testimony than you heard to-night of how God uses people to lead other people to Christ," Rob said. He looked at Howie, who had sat down in the front row. "Thank you, Howie. That was excellent. It gets better every time I hear it." He looked back across the rows of teens. "We're getting ready to have a closing prayer and then move on to refreshments and games, but let me say one thing first. If anyone wants to find out more about what Howie used to call 'this salvation stuff,' be sure to talk to one of us before the evening is over. We'd love to tell you anything you want to know. We all have a good time at these youth activities, but our highest hope is to see young people come to Christ as a result of them."

Rob prayed and dismissed everyone to line up by the long refreshment table where all the bowls, spoons, napkins, scoops, bananas, and toppings were arranged. The ladies quickly brought out the gallon tubs of ice cream from the freezer, and the teens set about making their own banana splits with a great babble of talk and laughter. Josh held up a banana and cried, "Hey, let's split!" and Caleb responded with "Yeah, let's peel out!"

One of the girls said, "Oh, you two nuts!"

"Correction, the nuts are over there," Josh said, pointing to the table. "There are pecans in that bowl and peanuts in this one."

Zack was second in line, Barb noticed. She wondered if his grand-mother limited his intake of sweets. Maybe that's why he was so excited about the banana splits.

She looked around for Hardy and saw him still sitting in his metal folding chair, still looking half asleep. She supposed he would consider it beneath him to appear too eager about refreshments. She wouldn't be surprised if he refused to eat anything.

Howard Harrelson and Willard Scoggins were rolling out a Ping-Pong table and getting it set up. Rob Finch rolled out another one and called to Hardy to help him unfold it. That was the last thing Barb noticed for a while because just then someone knocked over a two-liter bottle of Pepsi on the refreshment table, and she ran to the kitchen to get a sponge and paper towels.

Several minutes later all the teens were through the line and eating their banana splits in the metal chairs they had taken out of row forma-tion and pulled into loose circles. Barb made small sundaes for Sarah and Sammy and took them back to the Sunday school room where they were playing. As she walked down the hallway, she was surprised—shocked would be closer to it—to see Rob Finch sitting in another room with none other than Hardy Biddle. The two of them were sitting in chairs facing each other, and Rob was talking. Hardy sat hunched forward, elbows on his knees, staring down at his black boots. Barb felt her heart suddenly pound with hope. She delievered the sundaes to Sarah and Sammy, then ducked into a rest room to pray.

None of the other teens had even been aware of what was going on, so when Hardy appeared back in Fellowship Hall again, looking slightly dazed, Josh called out, "Oh, there he is! Hey, Biddle, come on over! I was telling them about that thing called a Nehru jacket you found last week at that really exclusive store where you buy your clothes." Josh turned back to the others. "He wore it to school with a pair of red plaid pants."

Barb came up to Hardy and motioned him to the refreshment table. "Here, you don't have anything to eat yet. There's plenty left right now, but don't be too polite or it'll disappear." Hardy didn't reply but ambled toward the table and picked up a bowl. Barb looked around for Rob Finch but didn't see him. She knew she wouldn't be able to go to sleep tonight until she found out how his talk with Hardy had gone. Maybe she should just come out and ask Hardy, but Howie and Joe Leonard came over just then to replenish their bowls.

"Hey, save some for us, Biddle," Howie said.

There wasn't a lot of fanfare that night. Rob Finch wasn't the type to turn cartwheels and jump up on top of tables to stir everybody up with emotional speeches, so at first the evening proceeded as if nothing had happened. Rob jumped into action when he reappeared, organizing a short Ping-Pong tournament of seven-point games and offering to take on the winner. The competition was lively, coming down to a playoff between Joe Leonard and Hardy. When Hardy won with a sharply angled spinner that dropped only an inch over the net, everyone clapped. And then when he beat Rob Finch in a close battle, the twins starting chanting, "Speech! Speech! Speech!"

To everyone's surprise, Hardy held up his hands like a politician silencing the crowd. "Yeah, okay, okay," he said. He looked at Rob and shrugged. "Sorry it couldn't be you, but, hey, it's me the crowd wants." He held up his hands again to quiet the laughter.

"Okay, fans, here's what I got to say," he began. By the looks some of the other teens had given each other all night, Barb could tell that a lot of them didn't know what to make of Hardy and, with the exception of the twins and a couple of others, most of them seemed slightly wary of him. The few who went to Berea High knew him from school, of course, and seemed to regard his presence at a church activity with awe, as if they'd found a tiger sitting in their living room.

All eyes were on Hardy now, but he didn't seem in the least uncomfortable. He pursed his lips and looked around slowly, nodding his head the whole time. "Yeah, okay," he repeated. "Well, like I said, here's what I got to say. I came tonight 'cause my dad was makin' me stay home, and I figured this was better than that, but not by much." A ripple of laughter went around the group, and he continued. "So, okay, I get in the little family van and come along with the duo over there, and I'm thinkin', 'Going bowling—ooh, surreal!' And I'm also thinkin' the whole night how radically weird everybody here is." Nobody seemed to know whether to laugh at that or not, though after Josh whispered loudly, "Look who's talking!" there was no question. When the laughter died down, Hardy concluded his speech simply. "So now I still think you're all weird, but that's okay. 'Cause now I know why you're weird, and it's okay to be that kind of weird."

He appeared to be finished, so Rob Finch spoke up. "So are you saying *you're* a little weird that way now, too, Hardy?"

"Yeah, I guess. I mean, I *know*. Yeah, I'm weird like that, too." And his dark eyes crinkled at the corners as he smiled.

In years to come, Barb would never think of the night of the bowling activity without the word *miracle* coming to mind. She would recall the event, in fact, anytime she found her faith wavering, to remind herself that if God could work His saving grace on Hardy Biddle, He could do anything. She would think of it every time she was tempted to use the word *miracle* lightly. No, *that* was a miracle, she would tell herself as she remembered the night of Hardy's conversion.

As Rob Finch told it to the adults in the church kitchen later, Hardy hadn't responded when asked to help with the Ping-Pong table, so Rob had gone over and sat down beside him. "Hey, you want to talk about anything?" was all he had said to Hardy, who had looked up at him briefly with narrowed eyes, then curled his lip and looked away. "We could go back to another room," Rob had said, and Hardy had said, "Oh, wow, could we really?" To which Rob had replied, "Sure, unless you'd rather talk right here in the middle of all this noise."

Hardy had only shaken his head and slid down lower in his chair.

"I could tell something was eating at him, though," Rob said, "so I decided to push it."

He again invited Hardy back to another room to talk, and Hardy had snapped at him. "And what would I want to talk to *you* about?"

If his voice hadn't cracked just the least little bit, Rob said he probably would have backed off and dropped it right then and there with something open-ended like "Well, think about it and let me know if you change your mind." But that one little crack on the word *about* showed him there was something going on inside Hardy.

So he pressed one more time. "Oh, anything you want to talk about. Anything at all." He paused. "Want to?"

The upshot of it all, of course, was the miracle. Hardy had gotten up and shuffled back to a Sunday school room behind Rob Finch, and by the time they came back into Fellowship Hall to eat their banana splits, Hardy Biddle's name had been entered in God's book as a new believer.

It was funny to Barb when she reviewed the evening later how everyone seemed to understand exactly what Hardy meant at the end of his speech. She was sure no one had ever before given a testimony of salvation in such terms, but she also felt sure that what Hardy meant by the word *weird* was the real thing.

When the night was over—after all the tubs of ice cream were empty and the Ping-Pong tables were folded back up and put away and Zack had telephoned his grandmother to tell her he'd be home by ten-thirty—Willard Scoggins gathered everybody for one last farewell. "It's been a good night," he said, smiling. "A very, very good night. Thanks for coming and bringing your friends. Next month we're renting the gym at the Filbert Community Center for a volleyball tournament, so be making your plans for that." He looked around and lifted his hands. "Anybody have anything else to say?"

"I have a good joke," Caleb said.

"No, I've heard enough of those tonight," Willard said, laughing. "Anybody have anything serious to say before we close in prayer?"

"The national debt continues to rise," Josh said.

"Millions of fish have died because of oil spills," Caleb added.

"Inner-city crime is higher than it's ever been," Howie said.

"Okay, okay, it's time to go home," Willard said, pulling out his handkerchief and waving it in defeat. "Let's have a word of prayer."

Barb was struck again with the simplicity of it all. Hardy had come to the bowling activity. He had heard Howie's testimony. Rob Finch had talked with him. Hardy had accepted Christ. But one part wasn't simple. At least Barb couldn't comprehend it. The convicting power of the Holy Spirit and the saving grace of God were far beyond her understanding.

How thankful she was that her boys had invited Hardy, that Blake had grounded him, that Hardy had remembered the invitation and wrangled a reprieve out of his dad, that Howie had given such a clear testimony, that Hardy had listened, that Rob had urged Hardy to talk with him, that Hardy had finally agreed.

She thought again of Rob Finch's words: "God uses people to lead other people to Christ." Her mind went further back, to how the two little Hawthorne girls had planted the seed of the Gospel in Curt's heart during office visits with their mother and how that had eventually led to the salvation of the whole Chewning family. The ripple effect—that's what it was. One life touched another, then another and another. Then those others all touched new people, and the ripples just kept widening and widening into a great sea of believers.

Extra Space

24

"If this isn't the stubbornest old wallpaper I've ever seen!" declared Della Boyd. "I thought it was supposed to just peel right off. Here, Barb, honey, can you hand me that scraper again?" Della Boyd laid the back of her hand against her brow, then gazed up to the kitchen ceiling. "I once knew a man in Yazoo City who hung wallpaper for a living," she said in a dreamy sort of way. "Mr. Kilgore was his name—'I take off the old and put up the new' was his advertising slogan." She looked at Barb and shook her head slowly. "The funny thing was, Mr. Kilgore's wife told me he hated wallpaper himself and never would let her put up any in their house." She smiled, then sprayed the wall again and started scraping. "But I sure didn't know wallpaper was this hard to get off. Mr. Kilgore earned every penny he made." She scraped in silence for a few seconds and then added, "Mr. Kilgore's wife had the prettiest hedge of lilac bushes you ever saw. And such a wonderul fragrance—my, you could smell them from the other end of the street!"

When Shirley Grimes had set up what she called a "Lend-a-Hand Night" for Jewel Scoggins and her family, who were moving into a new house, Barb had been reminded of the barn raisings during the frontier times and had accepted the invitation at once. "I thought since we weren't having a poetry meeting this month because of Christmas and all," Shirley had said when she called three nights earlier, "maybe we could all congregate for a couple of hours at Jewel's new house and get a lot of those little things done for her that take so much time." Shirley's voice had a musical lilt and was full of pep. She loved to organize things. "With Christmas looming," she continued, "I know Jewel's wondering how in the world she's going to get everything done. And with her pregnancy and morning sickness and all the rest, I think she's about at the end of her rope, bless her heart." If there was anything Shirley loved to do, it was salvage a desperate situation. "I think this will tickle Jewel and Eldeen to pieces," she concluded.

Indeed, Jewel had seemed overwhelmed when they all showed up at her door at seven that night and had even broken down and cried as she tried to stammer out her thanks to them for coming. Her mother, Eldeen, likewise waxed grateful but with words rather than tears.

"I was settin' in there just a minute ago," Eldeen said, "tellin' Jewel she just better quit tryin' to get everything done yesterday 'cause people that get theirself all worked up over little details never make much head-way in the long run." She looked at Jewel sympathetically and wagged her head. "She's just about wore herself out burning the midnight candle at both ends. I told her she's got to guard her health. And the *baby*! Why she can't be frettin' about house chores when she's carrying our baby! I read in one of my health magazines that little babies'll be born all skit-terish and nervous if they have mamas that are the same way. It gets in their bloodstream somehow. 'Just settle yourself down, missy,' I says to Jewel. 'Nothin' has to be done so bad that you give yourself ulcers and migraines and indigestion and heartburn all rolled into one! You'll spoil the spirit of Christmas!' I told her. But did she heed my warning? No, sir, she didn't! She just kept right on scrubbin' them bathroom shelves to beat the band, and then the doorbell up and rang, and here you all are— must be a dozen of you—crowded in here in your britches and work clothes just a'smilin' and ready to put your hands to the plow—or the mop and broom in this case!" She broke off to take a breath and emit a snort of laughter at her little witticism.

Jewel's husband, Willard, had put an arm around Jewel and beamed with joy as he welcomed the ladies and expressed his appreciation. "This is what I call true friendship when folks like you will show up like this to donate your time and energy." He laughed robustly. "I was glad from the beginning that Jewel joined your poetry club, but I'm even gladder now!" Their son, Joe Leonard, had smiled shyly and nodded the whole time. He had a swipe of white paint across one cheek.

"This is a night of jubilation for sure and certain!" shouted Eldeen, raising her arms and waving them. "The Lord gave us this nice new house, and now He's done opened up the floodgates of His mercy and sent us a whole work crew. Praise the Lord, from whom all our earthly blessings flow—and our heavenly ones, too!"

Of course it wasn't a new house in the strict sense of the word. Barb guessed it to be thirty or forty years old from the looks of it, but it was certainly a giant step up from Jewel's other house, a tiny brick box in what used to be the textile subdivision of Derby. This new house had an extra bedroom, bathroom, dining room, and den that the other one didn't, not to mention the fact that all the other rooms were larger. It was a house with great potential, but one that unfortunately was going to require a lot of hard work before the potential was realized.

Shirley had been in her element assigning tasks to everyone. Barb and Della Boyd had been given the kitchen wallpaper to strip, which was thankfully the only room that had wallpaper—and only a wide border on three of the walls at that. It was a splashy design of bright green leaves with orange and yellow birds interspersed. Barb tried briefly to imagine what kind of person would choose such a pattern to look at every day. Maybe someone like her next-door neighbor, Loretta Whittington, who loved wild colors and was the regional chairman of the Protect Our Southern Wildlife Foundation.

The kitchen was quite crowded since Fern Tucker and Joan Dunlop were also in there peeling old contact paper off the shelves of the cupboards and wiping them down, and Michelle Ringwald was cleaning and polishing all the knotty pine paneling along one long wall. The odor of ammonia and lemon oil filled the air. Joan was telling Fern about a dish called Chicken Fandango that her husband, Virgil, had cooked for company the night before.

"He loves to cook," Joan said, "but he's usually so busy grading papers or getting ready for the next day that he doesn't have much time for it." Joan was a newlywed, even though she had to be at least forty. "So we usually just get in the kitchen together and rustle up something fast after we both get home," she said, then added, "Virgil says the kids at school are sure getting antsy for Christmas break."

Barb thought about all the nights Curt didn't even get home to eat supper with the rest of the family, much less help her fix it, and as for a Christmas break, forget it—that was usually one of his busiest times during the winter. Ear infections and colds were getting revved up among the babies and toddlers by then, and all the moms waited until school was out to schedule checkups for their older children.

Belinda Price and Margaret Tuttle were doing windows in the living room, vacuuming out the sills and sponging them clean, then shining the panes with Windex. Barb heard Belinda ask Margaret what her favorite poem of all time was, but just then Della Boyd exclaimed, "There! Look, I finally got that part above the door all loosened up and scraped clean!" so Barb didn't hear Margaret's answer.

Shirley Grimes herself was in the hall bathroom on her hands and knees, scrubbing the ceramic tile floor with a toothbrush and Clorox, and Lois Butler was in the other bathroom doing the same thing. Carrie Sue Gray was painting the baseboards in the entryway, and Marcia Grover and Dottie Puckett were putting masking tape along the baseboards in the living room and dining room in preparation for painting. Harriet Murphy was using a long-handled mop to wipe down the walls in the front part of the house. Meanwhile, Willard and Joe Leonard were in the back bedrooms painting ceilings.

"If you finish a job," Shirley had said to the women after assigning the tasks, "there are shelves to clean in all the closets and shelf paper to be cut and laid." She had rubbed her hands together excitedly. "Let's see if we can get everything on my list done!"

This was the way it should be, Barb thought. People should pitch in and help each other more. Jewel was walking from room to room, holding a dust rag and repeating the same thing over and over as if in a daze. "I just can't get over this! You are all so dear to do this for us. We didn't know how we were going to get all this done by moving day." Eldeen, who was hemming curtains, had stationed herself on a lawn chair in the empty dining room, in close proximity to the living room, kitchen, and entryway so that she could participate in several conversations at once.

Barb couldn't help thinking about the contrast between Jewel's new home and the few homes she had seen less than an hour ago when she and Sarah had gone to the annual Tour of Homes for the Berea-Derby-Filbert area, sponsored by the county library for the purpose of raising funds for new computers to be placed in the branch libraries. Catherine Biddle had helped to organize it, in fact had been *the* organizer up until Philip's accident, when she had turned over most of her responsibilities to her friend Elaine Berryhill. But she was still heavily involved and was acting as hostess tonight at the reception being held at what was called the finale home—the last one on the tour and supposedly the grandest. Actually, the three towns of Berea, Derby, and Filbert didn't boast a whole lot in the way of elegant living, so much of the tour was through homes on the outskirts of Greenville, several of them near a golf course.

Catherine had given Barb two free tickets for the tour, or else she never would have gone. Tromping through other people's homes for the sole purpose of admiring the posh decor and furnishings wasn't her idea of fun. She and Sarah had gone through only four of the homes before she had lost her patience. "Wood, hay, and stubble," she said to Sarah as they headed home in the van. "That's all those houses are, you know, honey—just wood, hay, and stubble. Someday they'll all burn up." Sarah had nodded seriously and studied the streetlights, which were beginning to blink on one by one.

Barb had often told Curt that she made a lousy doctor's wife. All the doctors' wives she had ever known were society women—fashion plates, interior decorators, partygoers, the whole works. But Curt had always said she was the perfect doctor's wife in his book. "Give her a tennis racket, a popsicle, and an old sweat shirt," he once said to a friend at church, "and she's as happy as a clam." And she had punched him in the arm and said, "Hey, don't forget to toss in some sneakers, a hamburger, and a few good books."

The tour brochure had amused Barb, with its overblown descriptions of the various homes. "A gracious haven with that magical blend of fun and formality, pizzazz and practicality." "A picturesque Charlestonian-style retreat, splendidly appointed with unique family heirlooms." "A charming hideaway with an eclectic decor of unparalleled creativity." And her favorite, "A spacious dwelling, a-dazzle with myriad lights, be-witching extras, and luxurious panache, providing the ideal environment for teenagers." As if teenagers required myriad lights, bewitching extras, and luxurious panache to thrive. She wondered if Catherine had written all these descriptions herself and if she had used her thesaurus to do so or if the phrases had just sprung into her mind ready-made. Maybe she copied them from real estate guides and then just recycled them every year.

Barb smiled as she thought of how a tour brochure would summarize her own home on Brookside. "An adequate ten-room house furnished with several nice pieces but lacking a sense of overall decorative unity; ample floor space in laundry room for large piles of dirty clothes; casual 'just-moved-in' ambiance created by unpacked boxes, unadorned windows, general clutter, and pictures leaning against walls waiting to be hung."

What would be missing, of course, was the same thing missing in all the other descriptions—any mention of the specific people living there who made the home what it was. To round out the summary of her own home, the brochure would need to include something like "inhabited by a kind pediatrician, a distracted wife and mother, two lively teenaged boys, one gentle little girl, and an adorable toddler." Even then the story would be far from complete. How could you sum up a family in one sentence?

Barb stopped scraping for a moment and looked down the hallway where she saw Joe Leonard moving a ladder from one bedroom to another. "Hold her tight, Clancy, she's tipping!" she heard Willard say jovially.

From the dining room came Eldeen's voice. "And then Marvella, she took that bumblebee out of her freezer and perched it on a leaf in amongst the flowers in her centerpiece for a special effect, only she must not've froze it long enough, because lo and behold right after they'd passed the fruit compote around the table, that bumblebee's wings started a-quiverin', and the next thing we knew he'd revived hisself right in front of our eyes and was a-buzzin' around her chandelier!"

Jewel came back through the kitchen holding a spray bottle. She smiled up at Barb, who was standing on a chair, and said, "It sure is nice of you to come help us out, Barb, when you haven't been settled into your new house all that long. This means so much to us. It's such a busy time of year for everybody."

"No busier than any other time," Barb said. "And I think most of our busyness is totally unnecessary anyway. I can't think of any better way I'd rather spend tonight than helping you out."

"That's awfully nice," Jewel said. She looked around and sighed happily. "I don't know what we're going to do with all this extra space," she said. "We're not going to know how to act!"

"Oh, you'll adjust without any trouble," Barb said.

"My house in Yazoo City was about the size of the one you're moving out of," Della Boyd said, "except it only had two bedrooms instead of three." She held her scraper poised in midair as she studied the wall. She sighed softly. "It sure was a cozy place, but it's all gone now. It burned right down to the ground." Again the phrase *wood, hay, and stubble* ran through Barb's mind.

Jewel gave a sympathetic murmur. All the ladies in the poetry club knew about Della Boyd's house fire by now, since she had read her villanelle at the last meeting and explained that the idea had come from a personal experience. In a low voice, almost like mournful singing, she had told about losing her house. She smiled sadly at Jewel now. "You can just lose things so fast, you know." She blew a puff of air as if blowing out a candle. "One little breath and they're gone. All gone, just like . . . well, it's like a song I know about pretty bubbles in the air." Her eyes traveled upward as if watching imaginary bubbles floating away. She looked back at Jewel and cocked her head. "But I sure am happy for you and your family. This is going to be such a nice house for you, Jewel. So nice and pretty."

Jewel left the kitchen a few moments later, and Joan Dunlop said, "She's got to be the most patient soul on the face of the earth."

And Fern Tucker agreed. "Jewel and Eldeen both deserve every good thing that comes their way."

It occurred to Barb that some people might not think the Scoggins' new house qualified as a good thing, considering all the work it needed, but it was solid and roomy nevertheless, the kind of house a Realtor would list as "an overlooked gem," one with "terrific promise" for the "buyer with vision." She was happy for Jewel, and for Willard and Eldeen and Joe Leonard, too. She had never known a family of such good-hearted people, all four of them. They were living proof that it didn't take a lot of space and luxury to make a happy home. Her twins liked nothing better than to go over to Joe Leonard's house, as cramped as it was.

"Did you ever notice," Della Boyd said, waving her scraper through the air, "how bubbles shimmer in the sunlight? You can see all the colors of the rainbow swimming around on them." She began humming.

Barb nodded. She suddenly remembered the time several years earlier when Sarah had run to her, trembling with excitement, and she told Della Boyd about it now. "Come see, Mommy! Come out here and *see!*" Sarah had said, pulling Barb out to the driveway, where she had been blowing bubbles. She lifted her little plastic wand and blew through the rounded end, then pointed. "See them? See all the *colors?*" She was taking quick, shallow breaths. "And you can see things in them, too, Mommy." She had looked up at Barb and held her breath for a moment as if too awestruck to find words. Then, in a voice filled with wonder, "It's like a mirror."

At the end of the story, Della Boyd gasped. "Imagine a child saying all that! Your Sarah is a very observant little girl."

Two hours later they were all seated on the floor in the living room eating the chocolate chip cookies and ice cream sandwiches Shirley had brought along for refreshments. Willard and Joe Leonard were out in the carport now, sanding doors. "You ladies go ahead," Willard had said when Shirley announced that it was time for a break. "Just save us some. Joe Leonard and I will eat the leftovers, which we don't usually like, but when it's cookies and ice cream, that's a different story!"

All the women were talking at once. Barb studied each face, thinking about the wide diversity in their poetry group. "Everything from soup to nuts" was how Curt would put it. Eldeen, the oldest in the club at eighty-two, hadn't gone past eighth grade, yet Joan Dunlop had a master's degree. There were several church members in the group, but a few others—Marcia, Lois, and Carrie Sue—made no bones about the fact that they used their Sundays to do yard work, play golf, go grocery shopping, or catch up on their sleep. Michelle Ringwald had six children, whereas Belinda Price wasn't married and said she didn't want kids if she ever found a husband. Margaret Tuttle talked like an English professor, but Fern Tucker couldn't make a subject and verb agree to save her life. Jewel was beautiful and pushing fifty, while Harriet Murphy, though not yet thirty, was as homely as a barn and almost as big. Shirley Grimes could organize things in her sleep, but Barb herself had trouble keeping track of anything—time, keys, people's names, appointments, sometimes even money.

Barb thought of the club members who weren't here tonight. Tracy Littleton looked like a china doll with an eggshell complexion, whereas Geneva Fowler, who carried herself like a linebacker, had deeply pitted skin. Catherine Biddle spoke her mind freely and dressed like a million dollars, but Nina Tillman hardly ever said a word and wore shamelessly mismatched clothes. Barb didn't have much room to talk there, though, since she had about as much patience with clothes as she did with fancy houses. It made her tired just thinking about the effort somebody like Catherine must put into her wardrobe.

But for all their differences, the Women Well Versed had a lot in common, too. They were all interested in poetry, for starters. And it was becoming increasingly clear with every meeting that most of them had suffered loss of some kind. Dottie Puckett had lost her only daughter in a freak accident on Highway 11 back during the summer, probably not long after all of Della Boyd's worldly possessions had gone up in flames in Yazoo City, Mississippi. Margaret had lost her mother and her little boy many years ago and her dearest friend more recently. Joan had lost her father, Jewel had lost her first husband, and Carrie Sue had lost both of her parents to cancer within two months of each other. Lois and her husband had lost their business and gone bankrupt. Nina had lost a job she had held for over twenty years, and Tracy had lost a two-carat diamond ring that had been in her family for four generations.

They had spent a good deal of time talking about loss at the October meeting. "Tell us briefly about your loss of someone or something of great value" was Margaret's request that night before they read Elizabeth Bishop's poem "One Art," with its repeating line "The art of losing isn't hard to master." For fifteen or twenty minutes they had gone around the circle listing things they had lost to death, natural disaster, poor judgment, carelessness, or what have you.

Barb had been last, and her contribution to the inventory had shocked everyone. It was the first thing she had thought of when Margaret introduced the topic and asked everyone to participate, and as each woman added to the pool of losses, it became evident to Barb what she must say when her turn came. It didn't matter that she had never told any of her friends about this. It was what she must share. And it wasn't because she wanted to be original or sensational. There was a bigger point to it all, and she hoped she could make it. She knew for a fact that it was what God wanted her to do.

The shock of what she was saying registered in a variety of ways—the looks on faces, the uncomfortable shifting in chairs, and several sharp intakes of breath. She could still see Eldeen's thick eyebrows suddenly lower, Marcia's jaw drop, and Catherine's eyes widen and freeze as she began speaking. Margaret had observed her evenly the whole time, Nina had clicked her tongue and then reddened, and Shirley had pressed her lips together hard. Belinda had leaned forward ever so slightly as if to hear better, and Carrie Sue had turned and smiled coolly at a painting on the wall. Others had cleared their throats, fiddled with their pens, shuffled their feet, or studied their fingernails.

"The summer I was eighteen, I lost my virginity," Barb had begun. She spoke boldly and matter-of-factly, which was probably a big part of the reason everyone was so surprised at what she said. "Part of me wishes I could lay the blame on someone else," she continued, "but it was no-body's fault but my own. So instead of *losing* my virginity, I guess I should say I gave it away. I was going off to college that fall, and I thought I was old enough to make my own decisions about everything. Hardly a day has passed that I haven't regretted that particular decision because it led to an act of sin and lasting consequences. What I thought was going to be so much fun ended up bringing me nothing but misery. I didn't go to college that fall after all because I thought I was pregnant. It happened at the end of summer, and by the time we learned it was a false alarm, school had already started. My parents were shattered, and our relation-ship was never the same. The boy joined the Marines, and we never saw each other again."

She had paused a moment and looked around the circle. Some of the women looked relieved that she had stopped talking, but others seemed to want her to keep going. "I was stubborn about the whole thing," she said, "and I accused my parents of making a big deal out of nothing. I had to sit out a semester before I went to college, and things were pretty tense at home that whole time because of my willfulness."

Barb looked around the room at her circle of friends. "Let's skip to now. God gave me a wonderful husband, which I didn't deserve, and four great children. Some of the best friends I have are sitting right here in this room. I go to a church that means more to me than I could ever say. I live in a comfortable house, drive a nice van, and am in good health. Best of all, I have the joyful assurance of eternal life. God has blessed me richly."

She took a deep breath. "But I've paid dearly for that stupid, sinful mistake I made when I was eighteen," she continued. "I lost something I could never regain. It was something of priceless value, and I didn't have it to give to the man I fell in love with and married four years later. He forgave me and loves me with his whole heart, and of course God has forgiven me and covered my past sin with the blood of Jesus. But the point is, sin leaves a residue. You don't ever get off scot-free. I'll always have a deep scar in a dark corner of my memory. My mother died while I was in college—before I ever told her how sorry I was about disappointing her so much. That's something I can't go back and fix, and I think about it nearly every day. This is something we need to impress on our kids. By God's grace we can be forgiven for our sins, but we'll still carry the knowledge of that sin around with us for the rest of our lives."

She had smiled and closed with "So that's what I've lost, and I don't think I agree with the opening line of this poem Margaret just passed out. I think the art of losing *is* awfully hard to master. At least it has been for me in this one area. I don't even know if losing is an art you'd *want* to master. But then, maybe this is one of those poems that doesn't really mean what it says."

And that was exactly the conclusion they reached after studying the poem together. It progressed from a bit of whimsy about losing trivial things like keys to more important things like a family keepsake and finally to a loved one. What Elizabeth Bishop really meant, of course, was that the loss of minor things in no way prepared her for losing the person she loved. Even though she said it wasn't "too hard to master" such a loss and suggested that it only *looked* "like disaster," she meant the opposite. She was really saying that the loss had nearly done her in, that she would never get over it, that it was indeed the worst kind of disaster. There was a time when Barb probably would have been annoyed over such a poem, would have said something like "Well, if that's what she meant, why didn't she say it?" But she was beginning to see that it was often far more powerful to say something by "coming in the back door," as Margaret once described it.

After discussing Bishop's poem, Margaret had used Barb's remarks about her past as a transition into another poem, this one by Adrienne Rich, titled "Living in Sin."

She had smiled at Barb after reading the poem aloud. "I could not have coached Barb to give a better introduction for this poem than the comments she made earlier. What she thought would be a fountain of great joy at the age of eighteen became a deep well of regret."

Margaret had stopped and asked Barb to reread the first seven lines of the poem aloud. She had presented the term *blank verse* to them, pointing out the lines of unrhymed iambic pentameter, then had turned again to the content of the poem. "Though I deplore much about Bishop's and Rich's personal life-styles," Margaret said, "I find a great deal to commend in their poetry. I like what Rich does in this poem by way of contrast. The phrase 'living in sin' is generally one of titillation, suggesting pleasurable naughtiness and forbidden delights. Adrienne Rich very vividly shows the reader through the conflicting feelings of the persona the dark side of what she had supposed would be unending gratification. The lines that Barb read for us reveal what the narrator had *expected* from the experience of living in sin, while the ones that follow reveal the reality."

They had examined the milkman in the poem as a symbol of guilt, and at the mention of guilt the room had almost exploded. Everyone seemed to have something to say about the subject. It was amazing how many things women felt guilty about, Barb thought as the women talked.

Margaret listened to the comments, nodding reflectively, and just as she was opening her mouth to speak again, Eldeen rose to her feet. "But my Bible tells me that Jesus washed it all away! Pffft!" She placed her large palms together, then whisked them apart to signify a speedy departure. "It's all carried away in the crimson tide of His precious blood. 'Scuse me for saying so, but I think it's the biggest waste of time in the world for us to sit around moanin' and groanin' about our load of guilt when Jesus has promised to lift it off of our backs forever and ever!"

She craned her neck forward and let her eyes travel around the circle, looking deep into the eyes of every woman. "And if you don't know the joy of sayin' good riddance to your guilt, it's high time you did! Margaret's done told me this isn't a religious meeting, and I understand that, but there's a time to speak up, and this is one of 'em. You can't take off your religion along with your coat and gloves when you walk in that door yonder." She pointed to the front door of Harriet Murphy's house. "You can't stuff Jesus down inside your pocketbook like a wadded-up tissue and pull Him back out later when you need Him. When He lives in your heart, He makes a difference in everything you do—even the way you read poems! So there, I've done spoke my piece, and I'll sit down now." She sat down heavily, and several women, Barb included, nodded in assent. And of course, everyone turned to Margaret to see how she would respond.

Margaret looked at Eldeen for a long moment, then smiled slowly. "I know I am repeating myself, but I could not have coached Eldeen to draw a better conclusion to this discussion than the remarks she just made. I would not have expressed it in exactly the same way. Indeed, my style would have been pale and flaccid in comparison. But I agree with every word Eldeen said. If anyone is offended, I apologize, but the truth, as stated so aptly by Eldeen, stands in need of no man's defense."

Catherine Biddle suddenly recrossed her legs and begun swinging one foot vigorously. Her contribution to the discussion of guilt had been short. "I still feel guilty sometimes about not going to my father's funeral even though he wasn't much of a father to me when he was living."

"Isn't that right, Barb?" Barb snapped back from the poetry meeting to Jewel's bare living room. She scanned the faces around her. Jewel, Belinda, Della Boyd, and Fern were all looking at her intently, but she had no idea which one of them had just spoken to her.

She was tempted to bluff her way through the moment with something generic like "Sure thing!" or "Yep, you bet!" but she didn't. Instead, she lifted one hand as if on the witness stand and said, "Okay, I confess. I was off in another world again. Sorry, but would whoever asked the question please repeat it?"

Della Boyd threw her head back and gave a tinkling laugh that would have sounded fake coming from anybody else. "Oh, Barb, that's what I just love about you. You're so . . . well, so *honest* about everything. Isn't she honest, Jewel?" Jewel nodded and reached over to give Barb an affectionate pat on the back.

"I was just telling everybody," Della Boyd said to Barb, "that Hardy sure had himself a nice time last week with your boys at that bowling party. And he's just not been at all like himself since then. Not that it's been a *bad* change—oh no, no. Not at all. Not a bad change at all. But he's just been so . . . *different,* and I was sure you must have noticed the same thing since he's been going over to your house a lot lately. He's been talking a lot about things he never cared about before—have you noticed? He's just been so . . . well, so . . . ."

"Weird?" Barb asked.

Della Boyd laughed again. "Isn't she cute?" she asked Jewel.

And Jewel patted Barb on the back again. "Yes, that's my friend Barb," she said. "Cute and honest both."

"Phooey," Barb said. "Cute and honest sounds so boring. I'd rather be gorgeous and deceptive."

There was laughter, and then the voices in the room washed over her like a strong tide. She heard Fern Tucker asking Belinda about her job at the bank. "Who pays for it if the cash don't add up at the end of the day?" She heard Della Boyd next to her. "No, no, it sure hasn't been a bad change at all." She heard Jewel answering somebody's question. "Yes, it's due in June, we think, but the doctor says we might be a few weeks off." And she heard Eldeen's voice from the other side of the room. "And so Mr. Grissom, he built hisself a fire in the fireplace and *roasted* them pesky squirrels out of his chimney!"

Happy Thoughts

25

Christmas Eve was unseasonably warm, even for South Carolina. Though Barb had pressed Curt into building a fire in the den fireplace after supper, it was more for atmosphere than necessity. As she carried a big bowl of popcorn into the den from the kitchen, Barb stopped and surveyed the scene before her. Curt and the children were decorating the tree. Even Sammy was taking part, carrying ornaments one by one in his cupped hands from the box to the tree, then gently placing the hook over a branch and announcing, "See, I do another one!" each time. Caleb had put on some CDs of Christmas carols, and Barb herself had lit the bay-berry-scented candles on the coffee table, where she had also set a big plate of sugar cookies shaped like bells, sleighs, stockings, and candy canes that she and the kids had made that morning.

The thought came to her that she ought to take a picture of this and label it "The Perfect Christmas Eve." Then suddenly she realized she could do exactly that because Curt had bought a roll of film for the camera last night on his way home. He had even loaded it later and taken a picture of Sammy and Sarah in their pajamas sitting on either side of Barb, who was reading *The Fir Tree* to them before bedtime.

Barb set the bowl of popcorn on the coffee table and went to find the camera. The Biddles would be arriving in about ten minutes, but for once she wasn't running around at the last minute trying to finish something. All the refreshments were ready—or pretty much. The hot chocolate wouldn't take long to make, and they had plenty of pop in the refriger-ator. Of course, she had hoped the tree decorating would be finished by the time they got here, but that could be part of the evening's activities if it wasn't.

She knew people thought they were crazy for waiting until Christmas Eve to decorate their tree, but that's the way they had always done it. It wouldn't seem like Christmas Eve otherwise. It had all started when Curt was in medical school and the two of them hadn't had two pennies to rub together. The trees were always marked down on Christmas Eve, although they were also pretty well picked over by then. But it had somehow developed into a tradition, and even after Curt finished med school and the children came along, they hadn't seen any good reason to change it.

Catherine Biddle had had her tree up for two weeks, prominently displayed in front of the double window of their living room. She liked to have it up by the first of December, but Philip's accident had thrown her behind this year. She was using mauve and cranberry for all her decorations. "I alternate color schemes every year," she had told Barb. "Last year it was colonial blue and terra cotta." She had looked incredulous when Barb told her they wouldn't be getting their tree until the twenty-fourth. And when she learned they were going to put it up in the den, where it couldn't even be seen from the street, she said, "Well, good grief, that's sure a lot of trouble to go to for nobody to see it!"

If someone had asked Barb what her color scheme for Christmas decorations was, she would have said, "Oh, I don't discriminate. I use them all." Their tree ornaments were a hodgepodge of this and that collected over the years. One of her favorites was a miniature sled made out of tongue depressors. Another was a tiny wreath made out of puzzle pieces glued together in a circle, spray-painted green, and studded with sequins. One of the children had made it in art class at school.

Barb found the camera back on Curt's bureau, where he had put it last night. She didn't want "The Perfect Christmas Eve" to be a posed picture, so she stood quietly in the doorway of the den, adjusting the focus and waiting till all five of them were in the frame. When she called out, "Hey, look at this!" everyone turned toward the camera, and she snapped the picture. It didn't occur to her until later that someone looking at the photo years from now might wonder where the mother of the family was. Maybe she should add a little personal note to the caption to explain that she had taken the picture. She could describe the feeling of total joy that had come over her at the sight of her husband and children decorating the tree, the fire glowing in the hearth, the smell of bayberry and cinnamon filling the air, "Away in a Manger" playing in the background. She could tell how she had tiptoed in with the camera and caught them all unawares.

It had been a long, long time since they had had a perfect Christmas Eve, if they had ever had one. It seemed that something unwelcome was always happening on Christmas Eve. She couldn't begin to keep all the setbacks straight, but she did remember that both Sarah and Sammy had broken out with chicken pox last year on Christmas Eve, and two years ago—or maybe it was three now—Curt had been at the hospital with the Chapman boy, who had fractured a leg, an arm, and three ribs on an icy slope and a pair of homemade skis. One year Curt's mother had had emergency heart surgery on Christmas Eve, and they had piled into the van to drive to Alabama, and another year Curt himself had come down with a bad case of food poisoning from chicken salad he had eaten in the hospital cafeteria. And they had wrecked their car one Christmas Eve when they used to live up near Asheville.

It had gotten to the place where Barb almost hated to see the calendar roll around to December twenty-fourth. But amazingly, it was already seven o'clock in the evening, and so far nothing bad had happened today, even though Barb had caught herself several times tensing up whenever the phone rang.

That was the problem with growing older, Barb thought as she returned to the kitchen to get out paper plates and napkins. You learned that nothing was certain, that the happiest of occasions could turn sour, that good times could evaporate in an instant. She knew there had been a time when she had never given a passing thought to what tomorrow could bring. She had always been firmly planted in the present—when her mind wasn't wandering, that is. Her memory was so unreliable that she often forgot things in the past, and when she was younger it never used to occur to her to wonder or worry about things in the future. She had risen blithely each morning, meeting whatever *did* happen in the course of a day but rarely thinking about what *could* happen.

Even after her moral fall at the age of eighteen, her belief in favorable outcomes had reasserted itself, and the next semester she had gone off to college believing good things were bound to happen. It had rankled her parents, her mother especially, that she hadn't seemed to be much affected by the scare she had put them all through, that she had skipped off to a college several states away just like any other freshman girl. Her mother had made it plain that she didn't think Barb had shown enough remorse for the whole business. She had wanted some kind of visible evidence of Barb's resolve never to make them go through such trauma again. Barb hated to think now about how she and her mother had hardly spoken to each other those four or five months before she had gone to college. She had known her mother was waiting for an apology. It would have been such a simple thing to do, and such a *right* thing, but she had held out.

She *had* been sorry, of course, deep down, but she had never been one to wear her regrets on her sleeve. What was done was done. In refusing to apologize to her mother, there had been a lot of pride involved, though generally it wasn't so much out of pride or shame that she hid her troubles, but mainly she just didn't want to think about them. Why talk about things in the past? Maybe this attitude was part of the reason she had always disliked history in school.

And she knew for a fact that it was part of what had made salvation and Christianity so appealing to her. Though the Gospel itself focused on Christ's death, burial, and resurrection in the past, the whole salvation experience led to the great shining pathway of eternal life in the future. Christianity looked forward, and she liked that.

At college everybody on campus thought she didn't have a care in the world. She had joined the tennis team, made scores of friends, studied enough to make B's, and kept everyone cheered up. She always found a way to see the bright side of even the bleakest situation. When her roommate had made a zero percent on her first statistics test, Barb had said, "Hey, don't sweat it, that's actually a very good way to start out because it gives you so much room to improve. It'll look great on a graph! Think of the upward curve!" Her college yearbook, in fact, had dubbed her "Queen of the Optimists."

Somewhere along the line, though, her optimism had faded to caution and sometimes nowadays to downright pessimism. It hadn't affected her salvation, she knew that, but it had caused her to step back and take a long hard look at life. Not that most people knew it, of course. No, people still applied all those cheerful words to her—happy-go-lucky, sunny, carefree, good-natured, laid-back, and so forth. But they didn't really know her.

These days Barb sometimes wondered if she'd ever be able to fully enjoy things again. These nagging little thoughts kept arising to cast a shadow over the nicest days. Here she was even today, wondering if every phone call was going to disrupt their Christmas Eve. There were still five hours to go before Christmas Eve would officially end. So much could happen in five hours. So much could happen in five minutes, or five seconds.

She remembered when they had moved into their new home on Brookside only four months ago. She had walked through the house with Curt the day before they moved, surveying the recent improvements— the brand-new carpet, the newly painted walls, the new kitchen cupboards, the newly polished hardwood floors, all of which they had paid good money to have done. It was all finished and ready for them to move in. None of this business of trying to remodel while you lived in the house.

But instead of appreciating the new carpet, she had thought, In no time at all it'll get dirty. It'll show up first at the doorways into the bedrooms, getting just a little darker and more beaten down every week. Then before long, traffic patterns will start to form all over the house, those narrow paths of ground-in dirt from the bottom of shoes. And there will be spills and stains, and the carpet will need to be steam cleaned, and before we know it we'll have to rip it out and spend thousands of dollars to replace it all.

Ironically, it was Curt, always considered the more serious, practical, and realistic of the two, who had had nothing but good things to say about the house. He had gone on and on about the texture of the carpet, the color of the paint, the style of the cabinets, the sheen of the floors. Barb had smiled pleasantly and agreed, but the whole time she was thinking about how the paint would nick and peel, how the cabinets would get gummy with fingerprints, how the hardwood floors would grow dull.

She thought of Jewel and Willard's new house now as she came back to the den with the napkins and paper plates. She thought of all the hours of backbreaking work they had put into it—the sanding, the painting, the scrubbing, the rewiring, the replumbing, and all the rest. They had done most of the work themselves to save on costs, and most of the repairs and updating had been completed by the time they moved in three days ago. The twins had been over to help them on moving day, and Barb had taken a big pan of lasagna to them for supper that night. Jewel's face had been bright with joy as she showed Barb through the house and pointed out all the renovations. And Barb was happy for her, too—truly happy. Still, she couldn't help thinking, Time and all its cohorts—gravity, friction, dirt—are eventually going to undo every bit of this.

She went back to the kitchen now and got out her largest pan. She filled it with milk and set it on the stove to begin heating. She had plenty of envelopes of mix, but hot cocoa was better when you made it the "real" way, as Josh and Caleb called it. She got out the cocoa and sugar and set them beside the stove on the counter, along with a measuring cup.

She looked out her kitchen window to the street. She wished it were colder outside. Snow flurries would be the finishing touch to today. At forty-five degrees, however, there was no chance for that. She looked across the street to the Biddles' house. Their Christmas tree, with its hundreds of twinkling lights and its cranberry and mauve decorations, cast a glow out into the yard. Any minute now they should be coming out their front door and ringing the Chewnings' doorbell. As Barb turned her attention back to the stove, she prayed that tonight would make a difference.

She wanted the evening to be as perfect as the rest of the day had been, and she was determined to enjoy it to the hilt. Forget the gloomy thoughts about time and catastrophes and dirty carpets, she told herself. You can do it. You're good at forgetting, so put your talents to good use. Every time her next-door neighbor, Loretta Whittington, saw her in the driveway, she waved extravagantly, her colorful scarves flapping in the breeze, her bangled jewelry clinking as she called out, "Yoo-hoo, Barbara, think happy thoughts!" Okay, that's what she'd do—think happy thoughts. That was easy enough to do if you put your mind to it.

She turned the heat up a little more under the milk and got out a wooden stirring spoon. She listened to Curt and the children in the den. One of the boys was in the middle of a story. "And then he comes jumping up like this and makes her slip and spill the whole thing!" he said. Actually, it must have been the end of a story because the others laughed, and Curt asked, "Did she get hurt?" Leave it to Curt to wonder if anybody got hurt.

Curt—now there was a happy thought. She thought about the new study Bible and the leather moccasins she was going to give him tomorrow morning. That was another happy thought. He would love them both. She thought of the Christmas program at church last Sunday—yet another happy thought. Josh had played a solo on his trumpet, and Caleb had sung a duet with Joe Leonard. The Biddle family had attended—all six of them—and sat with Curt and Barb in the third row. Hardy had worn a bolo tie he had found at the Salvation Army store, a long-sleeved orange shirt with *ALLIED TRUCKING & STORAGE* emblazoned across the back, and a pair of blue suspenders. He had opened the hymnal during the congregational singing and held it so that Catherine could see it. Catherine had even sung along, or at least she had mouthed the words.

Now the good thoughts started crowding in on one another. Barb heard Sammy squeal, "I do another one!" and Curt said, "You surely did. I like that little rabbit, don't you, Sambo?" To which one of the twins replied, "Hey, no fair, what's the Easter bunny doing on our Christmas tree?" Sarah giggled. "Look at this one, Daddy," she said. "O Little Town of Bethlehem" was now playing—a flute and guitar arrangement. Barb thought of the snapshot of "The Perfect Christmas Eve" she had taken a few minutes ago. She'd have to put it in a frame and set it out somewhere instead of sticking it in a photo album. She wanted to look at it often. Life might be a vapor, but it was filled with good times. And God wanted the hearts of His children to be filled with joy—she knew that was so.

For the first time since Barb could remember, Curt had been home all day on Christmas Eve. That was the primary reason it had been a perfect Christmas Eve, of course. Dr. Lawrence Shepard, a good friend of Curt's, had volunteered to take all his calls and make his hospital rounds today and tomorrow. Curt had been taken·back by the offer and had initially declined, but Lawrence had insisted. He was a widower with two grown children, both of whom lived out on the West Coast.

"Nobody's coming home this year," he had told Curt, "and I'm sure not going anywhere. I've decided I'm too old to be traipsing off during the holidays. It wears me out. So since I'm going to stay home, I'd rather be good and busy than sit on my duff looking at my four walls. You'd be doing me a favor to let me see your patients." So Curt had finally accepted with the provision that Lawrence join them for dinner on Christmas Day, which he had pretended to think about long and hard before giving in. "Oh, all right. If you're going to twist my arm, I guess I'll have to," he had said with a grin.

Barb stirred the milk, although it wasn't even hot yet. She heard Sarah say, "I think this is the best tree we've ever had." It *was* a beautiful tree— a huge twelve-foot Douglas fir Curt and the boys had brought home that morning. The man at the lot where they bought it let them have it for five dollars just to get rid of it. But first Josh and Caleb had put on quite a show for him. While Curt was on the far side of the lot, the twins proceeded to poor-mouth within earshot of the tree man. They'd told Barb all about it when they got home.

"Wisht Ma could cook us somethin' besides chicken necks fer Christmas dinner this year," Josh had said.

"Yeah, them possums she boiled up last year was sure good," Caleb had said.

"Mebbe Pa and us can shoot a coon down in the holler and Ma can fry it up with some grits and cornmeal mush," Josh had said.

"Yeah, 'cept a coon won't go far with ten young'uns," Caleb said.

Curt, who was looking at the larger trees, was too far away to hear any of this, but he came back in time to hear Josh say, "One of these times, we's gonna *git* us a tree I'll betcha, 'stead of jest comin' down to the lot to *look* at 'em on Christmas Eve."

They had told the man they were only teasing, of course, and had told him it was a family tradition to wait till Christmas Eve to get their tree. The man had laughed heartily and claimed he knew all along it was a hoax because poor people didn't dress like them or drive vans like theirs.

Curt had introduced himself to the man, apologized for his sons' prank, and assured him they had money to pay for a tree. The man had enjoyed the joke so much he charged them only five dollars for the biggest tree on the lot. "What I don't get rid of I'll just have to throw away," he told them.

Because of a wet December, the tree wasn't as dry as would be expected from having sat in a vacant lot so long, and Barb was delighted when she saw the size of it. The vaulted ceiling in the den accommodated it with a couple of inches to spare.

"Silent Night" had just begun playing when Barb saw the Biddles coming out of their house across the street. She smiled as she watched them emerge one at a time. Catherine was swinging a gift bag, and Olivia was carrying what looked like a large stuffed animal. Philip took the steps carefully one at a time, then hobbled along beside Della Boyd down the sidewalk. He had abandoned his crutches for a walking cast now.

Barb waved to them through her kitchen window, but no one seemed to see her. Blake was saying something and pointing up to the sky, and the others were looking up. Hardy suddenly sprinted ahead and took the Chewnings' front steps in a single leap. Without waiting for anyone to answer the doorbell, he opened the front door and came on in.

"Hey, hey, hey, everybody," he said.

"Hey, hey, hey? What kind of Santa Claus are you?" called Josh. "Didn't anybody ever tell you it's supposed to be ho, ho, ho?"

"Nah, only if it's a Yankee Santa," Hardy said, walking through the living room into the hallway. "Southern Santas say hey, hey, hey."

Curt went to the front door to greet the others and ushered them in.

"Hi, everybody. Make yourselves at home," Barb called through the pass-through window. "I'm out here in the kitchen stirring milk." She wasn't sure, but it looked like Hardy was wearing an old band uniform—probably another one of his Salvation Army treasures. It was red with gold braiding.

"Whoa, if it's not John Philip Sousa in person," Caleb said.

"Yeah, glitzy rags," Josh said.

"What instrument do you play—piccolo?" Caleb asked. "Bassoon? Oboe?"

"Nope, triangle," Hardy said, pretending to strike one daintily.

"How square," Josh said.

Hardy nodded. "Yep, I knew you were going to say that. I set you up for it, see. It was a predictability test."

A few days ago Josh had told Hardy he'd turned in a written proposal to Morton Hollings, the principal, that they adopt another category for the school yearbook—one for "Best Dressed."

"And I told him I wanted to cast my vote ahead of time for you," he had told Hardy. "I told him you needed to be honored in a special way for your refusal to be a slave to fashion."

"Nobody'd vote for me," Hardy had said. "The small minds at Berea High just don't get it."

Over the boys' chatter, Barb heard Della Boyd's voice lift rapturously. "Oh, *look* at the tree! Look at all the colors! It reminds me of the Finksteins' tree back in Yazoo City! Mr. Finkstein was the hospital administrator where I worked, and every Christmas he and his wife would have all the volunteers over for eggnog and apple cake. They always had a big tree like that just *groaning* with decorations of every shape and size. And every color of the rainbow!"

"Finkstein?" Catherine said. "Isn't that a Jewish name? What were they doing celebrating Christmas?"

"Well, now, I don't know," Della Boyd said, laughing. "But they did. They sure did. They celebrated Christmas in a big way. Mrs. Finkstein always gave each of us a gift. Last year it was little spice sets."

The milk was beginning to heat now. Barb could see the steam rising. Soon she would add the cocoa and sugar. You had to stir it a long time, she recalled, because the cocoa was slow to mix with the milk.

Barb looked into the den again. Olivia was kneeling in front of Sammy with the stuffed bear. "Look what we brought you, Sambo," she said. "His name is Mocha. He has a little collar around his neck with his name on it. You want to hold him?"

Sammy threw both arms around the bear's neck and pulled it from Olivia. "My bear!" he cried.

"Wait a minute. Can you say 'thank you' for Mocha?" Curt said, and Sammy did.

". . . all kinds of spices you don't normally buy for yourself," Della Boyd was saying to everyone in general. "Coriander and fennel and mace and tarragon and . . ."

"Here, let me help you get that," Blake was saying to Curt. "I'll get up on the ladder, and you hand it to me."

"Mrs. Finkstein was such a refined lady," Della Boyd said. "She had the prettiest little feet. Size fours, if you can imagine! She had to drive all the way to Jackson to get shoes."

Barb turned back to the milk. If someone had told her back in August that they'd be spending Christmas Eve with the Biddles and *enjoying* it, she would have scoffed. Even as recently as a month ago, she would have seriously doubted it.

"Hey, cut that out!" she heard Philip say, and the older boys laughed.

Catherine walked into the kitchen behind her. "Did I hear you say you were stirring milk?" she said. "Whatever for?"

"Hot cocoa," Barb said. She saw Catherine take in her baggy red knit slacks, green sweat shirt, and black canvas slip-on shoes. Catherine herself was a vision of style, as usual, wearing a coordinated outfit of red plaid slacks, a red turtleneck, and a dark green vest trimmed in the same flannel plaid as the slacks. Every hair was in place, and her earrings were little clusters of jingle bells.

"Hot cocoa?" Catherine said. "Haven't you ever heard of those little packets you mix with hot water?" Then without waiting for an answer, she shook her head and waved her hand impatiently. "Honestly, you and Della Boyd remind me so much of each other sometimes—doing everything the hard way."

Someone must have turned down the CD of Christmas carols because Barb could barely hear the music now. Or maybe it was just all the other noise covering it up. But they weren't done with Christmas carols tonight. Barb wondered what Catherine would say right now if she told her Curt was planning a carol sing for the twelve of them later on. She wondered if Catherine would object to the reading of the Christmas story from the Bible or if she'd just press her lips together and endure it.

The Passage of Time

26

It was the Friday after Christmas when Barb seated herself in the black swivel chair at Dottie Puckett's Be-Beautiful Style Shoppe. Dottie still had a wreath up over the sink and a strap of sleigh bells on the door. A single string of multicolored lights formed a crooked frame around one of the mirrors. "Okay, Dottie, you're in for the challenge of the century," Barb said, sliding the band off her ponytail and shaking her hair loose. "I told Curt when he left this morning to be prepared for a totally new look the next time he saw me." She laughed. "I think he's a little worried, to tell the truth. He asked me if I could at least keep it the same color."

Dottie smiled. "A new look for the new year, huh?" She hummed a few bars of "Auld Lang Syne" as she ran her fingers through Barb's hair. "This is going to be fun, Barb, but everybody else might be mad at me before it's over. People are funny—they get used to you the way you are, you know." She gathered Barb's hair in both hands and bunched it up on top of her head, then stooped and looked at Barb through the mirror to see the effect. "Do you remember when Birdie Freeman got her hair cut off and permed? Lily Beasley said she almost quit coming to me after that because of what I'd done to Birdie's hair."

"It was a big change all right," Barb said. "I thought she was a visitor when I saw her at church the next week."

Dottie sighed. "I still miss Birdie, you know it? She and Mickey were such a part of everything at church." Barb nodded. "Hardly a day goes by that I don't think of something nice she did for somebody," Dottie continued. "I learned so much just by watching Birdie live out her faith. She was a saint of God if I ever knew one."

On the one hand, Barb wanted to steer the conversation away from

Birdie Freeman out of fear that it would bring back painful memories to Dottie. Last April Birdie had been killed in a car accident on Highway 11, and not three months later, Dottie and Sid's only daughter, Bonita, had been struck and killed along the very same stretch of road. Birdie and Bonita were inseparably linked by their deaths, and it seemed to Barb that talk of Birdie would have to lead to talk of Bonita.

On the other hand, Barb wondered if maybe something inside Dottie longed to talk about Bonita. Maybe that's why she had brought up Birdie's name, hoping it would lead to Bonita. Barb wondered if tiptoeing around somebody's grief only made it worse for the person. Maybe Dottie was tired of people avoiding any mention of Bonita, as if she had never lived. Maybe what she really wanted was for somebody to look her in the eye and say, "Tell me about Bonita. What do you miss most about her? What's your favorite memory of her? Is it getting any easier to accept her death? How are you holding up?" It would have been almost six months ago now, Barb figured.

She tried to imagine what it would be like losing one of her own children. Wouldn't it bring some small measure of relief to talk about it? Or would she push it down inside her as she had done most of her life whenever she had met up with trouble of some kind? The death of a child seemed to be in a category all by itself, though—way beyond the simple word *trouble*. How could you push aside something like that and pretend it had never happened? How could you ever be the same again?

Dottie picked up a brush and ran it through Barb's hair gently. "So tell me what you have in mind. You want to look at some pictures in my books, or do you already know what you want?"

"Oh, I don't know," Barb said. "Something easy to take care of for sure. Maybe something a little like Catherine Biddle's except not quite so short in the back. Something breezy and casual I can just blow dry."

Dottie laid down the brush and began sifting through Barb's hair with her fingers again. "You have nice hair, you know it, Barb? Nice and healthy. Perms and color and all those things can really take a toll." She clucked her tongue. "You know, I guess I'm sort of a double-crosser in a way. I know all those things are bad for people's hair, but I keep doing them anyway—and I even take money for doing it!" She took a large book of hairstyles from the bottom shelf of her cart and started flipping through the pages. "Here, let's see if anything strikes your fancy." She pulled up a rolling chair beside Barb and sat down.

"There, that one." Barb pointed to a picture of a perky blonde who was holding a lollipop in one hand and laughing at something off to one side of the camera. "I like that style. That wouldn't be hard to keep up, would it?"

Dottie held the book up next to Barb's face and looked back and forth from the picture to Barb, nodding. "Yes, that would work, I think. I can see it on you. It's right for the shape of your face, and there's enough fullness so it doesn't look as boyish as some of the others. I could even make you a blonde like her if you wanted." Dottie's eyes twinkled.

"No thanks, I'll just stick with mousy brown," Barb said. "So what's next? Do you just look at that picture and start whacking my hair till it looks like that?"

"Well, sort of," Dottie said, getting up from her chair. "Actually, we just got through one of the hardest parts. You wouldn't believe how long it takes some ladies just to decide on a style. They'll look through every picture in every book I have and still not find anything that suits them. I like the way you do it—you sure don't waste any time."

"Oh, I waste plenty of time," Barb said, "but not on my hair, I'm afraid. Catherine has been after me for weeks now, telling me I ought to come out here and let you use your scissors on me. I think she's on some kind of campaign to improve my looks. She gave me a whole pile of clothes last week to try on—things she's tired of, she said. Beautiful stuff, but not the kinds of things I'd ever go out and buy for myself. I'm not even sure if I'll keep any of it. Putting it all together seems like it would take so much effort."

"I know what you mean," Dottie said. "A person could spend a fortune on clothes." She looked down at her loose blue knit jumper and laughed. "As you can see, I'm not one of them." The drop-waist style, which was probably supposed to conceal her plumpness, instead accented it somehow, giving her the shape of a tree stump. Still, she had a pretty face—smooth skin, green eyes with long eyelashes, and a lot of natural curl in her thick brown hair. She turned and led Barb over to the sink. "Here we go, Barb honey," she said. "Just sit yourself down here, and we'll get you shampooed."

Now's the time, Barb thought. I'll say something to her right now about Bonita. She decided to use the direct approach instead of trying to work into it gradually, and she was about to open her mouth and say, "Was Bonita as sweet at home as she was at church?" when just at that instant, as Dottie was easing her head back so that Barb's neck fit into the curve of the sink, the door of the beauty shop flew open and in walked—*floated* would be more like it, Barb thought—a tall woman with very black hair and lips the color of cinnamon red hots. She was wearing a red beret and a long, flared black coat with a sheen. A filmy scarf in a leopard pattern was wrapped around her neck. She seemed to use her hands in a theatrical way as she made her entrance, as if she were conscious of people watching her. Barb knew it was unfair, but she couldn't help thinking of Cruella De Vil.

"Well, hello there," Dottie said pleasantly. "Look what the wind blew in." She turned on the water at the sink, and aimed the sprayer against her hand. "What can I do for you, Elaine honey? I don't have you down for an appointment today, do I?"

The sleigh bells jangled as the door closed forcefully, and the woman stood still in the middle of the room instead of moving over to the tan vinyl sofa to sit down. She struck a dramatic pose, with one hand on her hip and the other wafting gracefully at her side.

"Oh, dear, I was *sure* hoping you wouldn't have anybody here right now," the woman said. "I need a quick touch-up on my chignon in just the *worst* sort of way. I have a dinner party tonight." Her southern accent sounded fake—too much elongation and swoop, and dinner was "dinnah." Although Barb knew there were women all over this part of the state who really did talk like that, this one just didn't sound real. She reminded Barb of all those Hollywood actresses who tried to play southern belles and never quite pulled it off.

"Well, I just got started with Barb, here," Dottie said calmly, "so I'm afraid it'll be a little while. She's going in for a new look, so I don't want to rush it. You're welcome to wait, though, or you could come back around eleven. I think I could work you in before Marvella Gowdy's permanent."

Dottie had already wet Barb's hair and was now working up a lather with a shampoo that had a cherry scent. The woman must have walked over to the sofa because Barb heard mincing footsteps against the tile floor and a swishing of fabric, then the creaking of the sofa springs as she flung herself onto it.

"I just can't *believe* it!" the woman on the sofa said with an exaggerated sigh. "Why do these things *always* happen to me? It's like disaster just comes *courting* me, you know what I'm saying? I was over in Greenville at my lawyer's office this morning, you see, and as I was coming out of the elevator some big, clumsy ox of a fellow holding a stack of folders up under his chin stepped right on the back of my heel and then *bumped* into me. He knocked my beret completely off and crammed those old folders right into my chignon. I'm sure I must have lost a dozen hairpins. I heard them hitting the floor like *sleet*! All I need, Dottie dear, is for you to comb it out, then retwist it and fix it all back up in a jiff. You have such a knack for it—why, it would take me *forever*! And anyway, I've got to be somewhere in thirty minutes, so I couldn't come back at eleven even if I wanted to, you know what I'm saying?"

Barb spoke up. "You can do her before you cut my hair," she told Dottie. "I don't mind, really. I'd like to watch you do it, in fact." She wasn't in any hurry since the twins were home to watch Sammy and Sarah.

Dottie turned the water back on to rinse Barb's hair. "Isn't it nice of Barb to offer that, Elaine?" Dottie said over her shoulder.

"Why, it certainly is!" exclaimed Elaine, rising from the sofa. "It's the most *charitable* thing I've heard of in ages! But I sure do *hate* to put people out like that." She raised her voice a little. "Are you *sure* you don't mind . . . what was your name again?"

"Oh, I'm sorry," Dottie said. "I keep forgetting all my customers don't know each other." She kept shampooing Barb as she nodded first toward Elaine, then back to Barb. "Elaine Berryhill. Barb Chewning," she said.

Then she smiled down at Barb. "I don't know—this might give you time to get cold feet. You might just head right out that door and get in your car and go home without your new look."

"Oh, don't worry about that," Barb said. "I don't bail out halfway through things." Which wasn't anything close to the truth, she realized as soon as she had said it. There were plenty of things she didn't follow through with, but it usually wasn't because she lost her nerve. Usually it was just her concentration that got lost. "Not on purpose anyway," she added.

"My meeting *starts* at ten-thirty," Elaine said. She was standing by the sink now. She had taken her coat off, and Barb could see that she was wearing a red silk pantsuit. "It's not something I'm making up, I *promise*. It's a special meeting of the library board, and I dread it like the dickens. I guess you've been reading in the paper about this group of fanatics kicking up such a *ruckus* about some of the books in the library. To hear them talk, the only things they want on the shelves are the *Bobbsey Twins* and Shakespeare!" She clapped her hand over her mouth. "But I better shut my mouth! You might both agree with them."

Then without giving either of them a fraction of a second to express an opinion, she picked right up again. "Anyway, I don't see *how* I can show my face in public with my chignon in such a state. I'd be *mortified*! I'm sure it's a hopeless wreck by now. I just grabbed my beret and stuck it back on to try to keep everything from flying apart!"

Elaine glided to the other side of the sink, as if to make sure that Dottie knew she was standing there waiting. "And then like I told you, I have that dinner party tonight," she said, "so I really *do* need a quick little fix-

up, you know what I'm saying? It's at Nate and Danette McQueen's—
the dinner party, that is. They have this new indoor garden that you just
wouldn't *believe*! Danette's parties are always out of this world. She's the
entertainer *par excellence* around here, even though she did make the ti-
niest boo-boo one time with a salmon loaf she served."

Elaine threw back her head and laughed, one hand placed artfully at
her throat. "Poor Danette, she's still *humiliated* over that!" She stopped
laughing abruptly. "Oh, and she told me that the mayor of Greenville is
coming tonight, along with his wife, of course, and I've been positively
dying to see what that woman looks like. She's *supposed* to be a real beauty,
although I'll have to say her picture in all the publicity brochures last year
sure didn't look like much. Anyway, it's going to be a *big* affair tonight.
The invitations said"—Elaine lifted one hand and pretended to write
with a flourish in midair—" 'You are cordially invited to an Eve of New
Year's Eve dinner.' Isn't that *clever*?" She laughed again, a gay tittering
laugh. " 'Eve of New Year's Eve'—doesn't it have a *lilt* to it? Danette has
such *savoir-faire*!"

"It sounds like a real occasion all right," Dottie said. She was now
well into the second lathering of Barb's hair. Barb couldn't remember for
sure the last time someone else had shampooed her hair, but she thought
a nurse's aide had done it for her in the hospital after Sarah was born.
Anyway, it was sure nice and relaxing. She closed her eyes, and when she
opened them a few seconds later, she saw that Elaine had moved back to
the other side of the sink again. Closer up, she looked a good ten years
older than Barb had originally guessed, and her hair did look in need of
help. It was lopsided, as if she'd had a restless night of sleep on it. She
had her arms folded now, and although she was smiling, it was a tight
smile. Barb saw her look at the Pepsi clock on the wall.

Dottie gave no sign of hurrying. She kept kneading Barb's hair slowly
as if enjoying the feel of it, almost as if she couldn't stop until she'd
counted a certain number of strokes. She appeared not even to notice that
Elaine was standing right at her elbow, but she had to know it. The
woman was practically breathing down her neck.

"Oh, and you'll never guess what that *silly* fellow said to me," Elaine
said.

"Who's that, honey?" Dottie said.

"Why, the big bull in a china closet who almost knocked me down
coming out of the elevator," Elaine said. "You know the *only thing* he said
to me as he was down on the floor picking up all his file folders?"

"What did he say?"

Elaine spoke in a doltish, reedy voice, stretching out each syllable even more. " 'I'm sorry for the inconvenience, ma'am.' That's *all* he said. The *sum total*!" She paused as if expecting an outcry of disbelief, but Dottie's only response was to raise her eyebrows at Barb. "*And* he didn't even have the courtesy to *look* at me when he said it," Elaine added. "You could tell he didn't mean a word of it, you know what I'm saying? I was halfway tempted to kick those folders across the lobby, I'll tell you!"

Dottie gave Barb a wink. "There, that does it, Barb honey. Let me blot it a little with a towel, and then I'll tend to Elaine if you're sure you don't mind." Dottie squeezed the water out of Barb's hair, then began rubbing it with a towel.

Suddenly something dawned on Barb. "I know who you are!" she said to Elaine. "It just now came to me. You're Catherine Biddle's friend, aren't you? I've heard her talk about somebody named Elaine connected with the library. Didn't you say you were on the library board a minute ago? You must be the same Elaine."

Elaine nodded. "Why, yes, of course I know Catherine Biddle. In fact, it was Catherine who told me about Dottie's beauty shop." She fluttered a hand and rolled her eyes. "Yes, Catherine and I go back a *long* way. When I moved here with my second husband, who was an electrical engineer with one of the big firms over in Greenville, Catherine was the first—say, now wait a minute, wait *just* a minute!" She batted her eyelashes and pointed one long finger straight at Barb. Her fingernail reminded Barb of a tiny red arrow. "You aren't that new *neighbor* of hers, are you? The one who—didn't she tell me your husband was a *doctor*?" Suddenly Elaine's smile seemed a little warmer, and she adopted a teasing tone. "Say, what do you mean dragging Catherine off to *church* every time I turn around?"

Barb laughed. "Well, I don't recall any dragging going on, but her family has come to our church a few times lately."

"Yes, like two Sundays ago, when I gave a brunch for all the ladies in the Library Patrons Society who helped coordinate the Tour of Homes. *Never* in my life have I known Catherine Biddle to turn down one of my Sunday brunch invitations! But what does she tell me this time? She's going to *church* to see her son get *baptized*, of all things! 'Which son?' I ask her, and when she says 'Hardy,' I am *totally* flabbergasted, you know what I mean? 'Is this some kind of *joke*?' I say."

Elaine lowered her voice and continued confidingly. "I didn't tell her this, but the last time I saw *Hardy* he was carrying on like a *lunatic* right in the middle of the parking lot outside the Diamond Movie House with this whole gang of wild teenagers standing in a circle around him. He was giving a one-man show—dancing, singing, cavorting all over the place, *totally* out his mind, it looked like. I felt like saying, 'Honey, do you have ants in your pants or something?' I'd be willing to bet you any amount of money that he was *stone drunk*. And now Catherine tells me he's getting *baptized*! Why, you could have knocked me over with a feather!" She fanned her face as if to ward off a fainting spell, then glanced quickly at the clock again. "Well, anyway, can we get my chignon fixed now? I really am on a tight schedule today."

Elaine whirled and walked trippingly over to the swivel chair, and Barb moved from the sink to the couch to wait. She watched Dottie unpin Elaine's coarse, jet-black hair and begin brushing it. Women who colored their hair so black had always puzzled Barb. She thought the whole purpose of dyeing your hair was to make people think that was the natural color. Did Elaine really think she was fooling anybody?

"Well, I wish you could see Hardy now," Barb said. "I've never seen anything quite like it. Talk about a change." Barb still couldn't get over it. Every day she was struck anew at how quickly God had broken down Hardy's defenses and turned him around. She was still rebuking herself for her weak faith. She hadn't told anyone this, but she had harbored a liberal amount of doubt those first couple of days after Hardy's salvation. She had held back just a little on her rejoicing because she was afraid his profession might be only temporary, that his conversion might not stick. How could somebody like Hardy undergo a wholesale transformation? It had just seemed too fast.

But the next week when Josh and Caleb had kept coming home and telling her about Hardy's change at school, her hope had begun to grow. If somebody were to tell her now about Hardy holding forth in the center of a bunch of kids, she'd know exactly what he was up to. He'd be telling them about the change in his heart, but not in conventional terms, most likely.

Caleb had told her about overhearing Hardy in the lunchroom one day before Christmas break, though "overhearing" was probably the wrong word, since Hardy was practically shouting across four tables to Jordan Baxter.

"Hey, Bax, you still thinkin' about what I been sayin'?" he had called, standing up to get his attention. Jordan had just sat down with a whole table of what Josh and Caleb called "the hulking, surly dopehead contingent," and Hardy was sitting with Karl Simons and Lance Partlow, whom the twins described as "Student Council types."

"I tell you, it's cool, man, trust me!" Hardy had shouted to Jordan. "You'll live longer this way—like, try forever! Take the next exit outa Dumbsville, Bax. Get on the freeway. Crawl outta your hole and climb the hill, man! Turn on the light!" Kids all over the cafeteria were staring at Hardy, and some were laughing. But Hardy had always loved an audience. "Spread your wings!" he said. "Fly! Breathe! Live!" He was waving his arms, Caleb had said, so that the big, blousy sleeves of his gold silk shirt flapped like flags in the wind. Jordan's only response had been an obscene gesture as he told Hardy where he wished he would go.

"Not me, Bax," Hardy had called. "I ain't goin' there, believe me. I'm headed way north to the other place!"

"How would you answer that, Barb?" Dottie asked now.

"Answer what?"

"Elaine just asked me if I had seen a difference in Catherine lately," Dottie said. "Said she doesn't seem as talkative as she used to be, like maybe something's bothering her. She came in on Wednesday, and I'm trying to think if she seemed quieter than usual, but I don't remember. It was a zoo that morning, so I really wasn't noticing much of anything. Muriel Spears showed up for an appointment she had canceled the week before, and things got clogged up for a while."

"She's not *sick*, is she?" Elaine asked, frowning. "I called her the other day, and it was like her mind was a hundred miles away. We used to phone each other at least twice a week—I'm talking *long* conversations here—but lately it's like she's forgotten how to carry on a decent conversation. We used to talk for an hour and just getting warmed up, but—oh, Dottie darling, can you pull down some little tendrils at the sides there like you did last time and curl them a tad? I liked the way that looked—sort of a cross between accidental and on purpose, you know what I'm saying? Just the least little bit *messy*, you know."

And then without pause she rushed on. "Anyway, I thought maybe one of you would know something. I was thinking maybe she'd been to the doctor and gotten some bad news. I also thought it might be something about Blake or one of her kids. Honestly, women have so much to keep track of, it's a wonder we're not *all* a little loony, you know what I'm saying? She doesn't exactly have the *easiest* husband to get along with, you know, and Olivia can be awfully bullheaded. Not to mention all the trouble Hardy's been in almost constantly since the day he was born." She took on a sarcastic tone. "Of course, now that he's been *baptized*, I'm sure he's a perfect little *angel*." Her laugh had an edge to it. "But anyway, there's *got* to be something wrong," she concluded. There was a downward inflection as she ended, as if her whole speech were based on irrefutable evidence.

"Well, I don't think she's been to the doctor recently except to take Della Boyd for an appointment, and I'm pretty sure they didn't get any bad news that day," Barb said. Della Boyd had in fact called to her from the driveway that day and told Barb she had just gotten a "clean bill of health."

"And that's another thing," Elaine said. "I think that sister-in-law of hers is just *sapping* her energy. I'd kill any husband of mine who opened up my house like it was some kind of *motel*." She made a repeated flashing gesture with one hand, clenching and spreading her fingers. "Just hang out a Vacancy sign! Come on, folks—free beds and meals! Men are awfully quick to offer things like that—that's because they don't have to do any of the *work*. Let them change sheets and fix three meals a day for a few days, and they'd change their tune fast enough, you know what I'm saying?"

Barb was amazed at how nimble Dottie's pudgy fingers were with Elaine's mane of hair. She watched her gather and shape it, then twist it up behind her head and start pinning it.

"Well, I really don't think Catherine sees Della Boyd as a burden," Barb said. "At least not anymore. Maybe she did at first, but I've been impressed with how they've all just moved over and made room for her."

"That's right," Dottie said. "In fact, Catherine was telling me not long ago right here in this same chair you're sitting in that Della Boyd was a big help around the house. Told me about how she can just whip up anything in the kitchen without a recipe and how she's always tackling some new cleaning project."

Elaine threw her hands up. "Well, you two sure aren't any help! All I know is that I'd go crazy if *my* sister-in-law moved in with me, and I don't think Catherine's any different from me. Well, at least she didn't *used* to be, but something's sure come over her lately."

"I think Philip's accident really set her to thinking," Barb said. "I think she's still getting over the scare of almost losing both her boys at one time. She told me not long ago she still has dreams about Philip lying at the bottom of the stairs like he was dead."

She realized what she had said too late. Dottie stopped pinning Elaine's hair and looked over at Barb. The only sound was the quiet thump of the second hand marking time on the Pepsi clock. Barb wished she could play the tape back and delete her words. The last few seemed to echo, *"Like he was dead . . . like he was dead . . . like he was dead."* Then suddenly there was a rush of footsteps through the kitchen adjoining the beauty shop, and a door opened and slammed, followed by the sound of a basketball hitting pavement. Through the window Barb could see Dottie's boy, Max, dribble in a tight circle, then fake a pass and take a shot.

Dottie turned her head slowly and squinted at Max through the window. "Yes, Philip's accident—that's got to be it," she said at last, nodding. "Let something happen to one of your children, and it changes you forever."

Something hit Barb at that moment. What had been the *last thing* Dottie had said to Bonita, she wondered, that day before she walked out of the house to check the mailbox and was hit by the careless driver along Highway 11? What a difference it would make if you understood that every word you spoke to a person might be your last.

Suddenly Barb wished fervently that she were more alert, more aware of the passage of time. She didn't know why the thought came to her now, but she wondered as she sat on the vinyl sofa in Dottie Puckett's Be-Beautiful Style Shoppe when Josh and Caleb had last sat in her lap. There *had* been a last time for it, a specific day, but she'd had no idea at the time that it would never ever happen again. She felt a sadness in the thought. What other last thing had happened recently that had slipped by unnoticed?

"Everything is temporary"—she heard the words spoken almost audibly as she watched Dottie resume her repairs on Elaine's chignon. A host of sad images rose before her. She saw Jewel's new house with the paint peeling off the gutters. She saw Sarah's leaf giraffe swirling apart in the wind and mounds of dirty laundry beside her washing machine. She saw broken platters, worn carpets, and medicine bottles. She saw dry needles dropping off Christmas trees, jeans with holes in the knees, wrecked cars, and eroded beaches. She saw herself and Curt as old people. She saw Birdie Freeman's gravestone and Bonita Puckett's sweet, round face in her casket.

Time was so short. She thought of all the things in life that other people accomplished—people who were more self-disciplined and well organized than she was. But just at the same moment when the despairing thought came to her—*With all my imperfections, how can I hope to do anything truly worthwhile?*—she had an answer. It hit her so strongly, in fact, that she was tempted to bolt off the vinyl sofa and drive her van home at once.

And here was the answer that came to her: *If I can leave behind me four godly children, I will have not have spent my life in vain.* And right on the heels of that came another thought. *And out of everything God has given Curt and me here on this earth, our children are the only things we'll take with us to heaven.* As Dottie secured Elaine's chignon with the last pin, Barb rose from the couch. She felt a powerful urge to finish up here at the beauty shop so she could get home to Josh, Caleb, Sarah, and Sammy.

February 17 – March 18

DELLA BOYD

Close Range

27

One Saturday in February as Della Boyd snipped three pale lavender crocuses and two white ones from the side of the house, she observed that their petals were translucent, like tissue paper. She knew they wouldn't last long after they were cut, but at least they would be pretty for a day or two. She liked the way the petals stood up and cupped around the center. Clutching the five small stems in one hand as a bouquet, she recited aloud a line of a poem Margaret Tuttle had presented at the last meeting of the Women Well Versed. " 'And grass and white and red morning-glories, and white and red clover, and the song of the phoebe-bird.' " It was from Walt Whitman's "There Was a Child Went Forth."

Della Boyd wasn't sure why she liked the poem so much, but she had felt a tingle as soon as Margaret had begun reading it aloud. Something about it made her feel clean and spare and tightened down. It was actually nothing like the poems she used to like. This one didn't rhyme and didn't have a regular beat. Besides that, she wasn't even completely sure what it all meant because the shine and echo of the words had blocked out Margaret's comments about the poem afterward. She thought, however, that it might have something to do with the way all the things around a person somehow became absorbed into him.

She loved the line about the mild mother "placing dishes on the supper table." She remembered her own mother doing that. The father, who was nothing like her own father, spoiled the effect a little in the next lines with his angry words and quick blows, but he was soon replaced by other, nicer pictures of ferries and wharves and waves and sea birds. It was such an orderly poem in spite of the fact that it was a little on the rambling side. The whole poem was really quite mystifying to her, but she knew one thing—something warm and smooth tipped and spilled over inside her when she heard it.

Of course, Margaret had not heaped upon Whitman unqualified praise. She had pointed out that much of his verse was dangerously centered on the aspects of man that were immoderate and bestial. "But he did bring to American literature a new perspective," she had said, "a broad vision of the common experiences and intense emotions of life fused with an unorthodox, somewhat sprawling style that mirrored our national expansion. He was an important figure in American poetry, though his erratic rhythms and choice of subject matter make him difficult to read in large doses." Margaret had admitted that Whitman was not her favorite poet, but his pivotal position in American literature made him a significant one. Della Boyd was glad that Margaret was exposing them to a wide range of poets, not just the ones she liked best.

Della Boyd placed the crocuses gently in a shallow basket, then moved down toward the row of daffodils by the fence gate. She set her basket down and knelt. "You are the most cheerful flowers!" she whispered to the daffodils. She chose four of the smaller ones to clip and added them to the crocuses in her basket, along with several of the tall spiky leaves. She intended to make a spring arrangement for the kitchen table with Olivia's help. Olivia had learned about flower arranging in a class at school.

Della Boyd stood up and looked wistfully toward the fence where she had planted iris bulbs last August. She wished she could see them bloom before she left South Carolina. She tried to remember exactly when her irises back in Yazoo City had come to life, but time crowded itself together in her mind. Was it in June? No, she thought it was earlier. Perhaps April and May were the months for irises. She counted on her fingers. May was three months away, and she would be gone by then. May was when Olivia would be graduating from high school. Maybe Blake would take a picture of Olivia in her cap and gown standing beside the irises. Della Boyd hoped they were all going to be purple irises.

She looked around the yard now for something else to add to her flower arrangement. Two low bushes at the corner of the house boasted large oval berries the size of grapes and as glossy as red lacquer. She had no idea what kind of bushes they were, but she liked the way the berries were nestled down protectively within the little branches and the way they were so much bigger than one would expect from such a small bush. "Where were you when we were looking for red berries at Christmastime?" she chided as she walked toward them. A bed of English ivy grew untended among some of the shrubbery, and after she had plucked two clusters of berries, she stooped and clipped a few trailing ringlets of the ivy.

Myron Abernathy's camellia bush next door had dozens of new buds and several full blooms which were well within Della Boyd's reach over the fence. Since she had a standing invitation from Myron to help herself to anything growing in his yard, she picked two open flowers and three buds to add to her basket. She walked farther along the fence to the forsythia bush in his yard and reached across the fence to snap off three sprigs. She studied them for a moment, remembering the forsythia bush that had grown right outside her bedroom window in Yazoo City.

Five crocuses, four daffodils, five camellias, red berries, ivy, forsythia—oh yes, and pansies! She had bought a pot of pansies last fall and had never gotten around to planting them by the front steps as she had intended. Instead they had sat on the patio in their black plastic pot all winter, stubbornly blooming right through the wet fall and the coldest months. She walked into the backyard now and stepped up onto the patio. "There you are, brave and faithful as ever," she said, and with her thumbnail she pinched off the stems of three pansies, all the color of deep purple-black velvet. "Let's see. Now that makes lavender, white, yellow, deep pink, red, green, and purple," she said.

Just then the patio door slid open, and there stood Catherine in a seafoam green turtleneck and slacks. "Are you talking to yourself again, Della Boyd?" she said. "Here, I want you to come look at what Arlene Babcock did with the window treatment in our bedroom and tell me what you think."

As they passed through the den, Della Boyd saw that Olivia was sitting on the floor in front of the television, her feet tucked under her, watching a video. Della Boyd squinted at the screen and saw cheerleaders. The picture was a little shaky and fuzzy, but the sound was clear. "Let your spirit show! Yell, go, Wildcats, go!" She knew that Olivia's cheerleading squad was going to Myrtle Beach the first week of April for some kind of competition and that their coach had been making videotapes of their practices and asking the girls to watch them.

She also knew Olivia and her co-captain, Roxanne Gower, were feuding over one of the new routines they were trying to work up. Another thing she knew was that Blake wasn't happy about the trip and kept threatening to not let her go. "I don't trust that coach, if that's what you call her," she had heard him tell Catherine late one night in their bedroom. "That woman looks like she got stuck in the Woodstock time warp." Della Boyd didn't understand what he had meant by that, but she did know that the coach's name was Mona something and she wore beads in her hair and around her ankles, and she wanted the girls to call her by her first name.

Della Boyd, still holding her basket, paused at the doorway. "I found some flowers and things in the yard," she said to Olivia. "I'm hoping we can make an arrangement for the table." She spoke this as a question.

"See, look at that!" Olivia said, pointing to the screen. "She can't get it right! She keeps doing this spazzy thing with her foot! She never can get it right!" She stopped the VCR, backed it up a little, and then started it again. "Let your spirit show!" the voices said again—such perky young voices.

"Any day now, Della Boyd," Catherine called from the hallway. "The draperies are back here. Are you coming?"

"I'm going to put my basket right here by the door," Della Boyd said, partly to Olivia and partly to Catherine. "I'm afraid the crocuses won't last long if we don't get them in water soon."

"She's going to ruin everything!" Olivia cried, pointing to the screen again. "Look at her wrists right there! She can't even do the easy stuff!" Olivia had let it be known several times that Roxanne Gower had gotten on the squad only because her father was one of the football coaches at their high school, and she had complained often about the girl's height. "She throws everything off balance," she often said, going on to explain that if there were an odd number of cheerleaders, Roxanne could be in the middle and the formation would look even, but with six girls, "she just sticks out like a sore thumb." In fact, Olivia had started calling her Roxanne the Tower.

"I'll be back in a minute," Della Boyd said as she exited the den. "I've got to go see your mother's draperies." Catherine had been fretting over the new draperies in the master bedroom for several weeks now. She had taken them back to Arlene Babcock twice already because she wasn't satisfied. Actually, it was Blake who didn't like them the second time, and Catherine had decided after two days of looking at them that he was right.

His comment had been "They're too boxy and symmetrical," which seemed like a funny criticism for draperies. Della Boyd couldn't help wondering why it would be important for cheerleading formations to be symmetrical but not draperies. She had decided not to ask the question, though. She knew the world was full of little inconsistencies like that. She was forever seeing rules shift for no apparent reason. Other people always seemed to understand the reasons, but there was so much that just didn't make sense to her.

Catherine was standing at the doorway of her bedroom with her hands on her hips, studying the two windows on adjacent walls. She glanced back as Della Boyd came up behind her. "There, what do you think now?"

Della Boyd didn't speak for a moment. She tilted her head and looked back and forth between the two windows. She had liked the draperies before, but now she could see what Blake meant. They did look better this way. It was very surprising to her. She would never have thought of hanging them like this. She felt as if her imagination were being pried open and stirred with a big spoon.

The draperies were the green of fresh pine needles, and the fabric was soft and flowing, like fine shantung. They weren't really *draperies* in the strict sense, Catherine had told her several times, since each one consisted of a single length of fabric framing the window instead of covering it. But they did drape around the decorative rod, and to Della Boyd's way of thinking that made them draperies, though she wouldn't for the world have argued the point. Each drape looped around the rod three times, forming two pretty scallops across the top, and then hung in graceful folds down each side of the window. Arlene had tapered the ends this time around so that they gave the effect of fading away softly, and—this was the most interesting part—she had shortened one end of each drape so that each one by itself looked lopsided, but together the scale was perfectly balanced.

"Well?" Catherine said. "Now don't go trying to be tactful. You know I can't stand that. Just come right out with it and say what you think."

Della Boyd walked past Catherine into the bedroom. "That one," she said, pointing to the window on the left, "hangs down longer on the left side and shorter on the right, and *that* one," she continued, pointing to the window on the right, "is longer on the right and shorter on the left."

Catherine pressed her lips together and gave Della Boyd a look that said *Really? You figured that out all by yourself?* But before she could open her mouth and actually say anything, Della Boyd continued. "Now if that one," she said, pointing again to the window on the right, "were longer on the left and shorter on the right like that one," and here she indicated the window on the left, "there would be something wrong. It would be—" She broke off to search for a suitable word. "It would be . . . choppy." Yes, that was a good word for it, she decided. "It would be choppy and . . . *shaggy*." There was another good word. "But the way it *is* looks . . . classic and . . . well . . . *fresh*, like you'd expect of a Greek sculpture."

Catherine gave a little snort. "Della Boyd, you always go around Robin Hood's barn, don't you? Well, okay, so I've got fresh *Greek* window treatments instead of choppy, shaggy ones. I guess that's good, huh?"

Della Boyd nodded. "Oh yes, it is. It most certainly is good. It makes such a nice . . . *arch* this way, with the two longer ends on the outsides." She made a long, sweeping motion with one arm. "It's like the windows are looking at themselves in a mirror. If it were the other way, it would look . . . wobbly." She smiled happily at Catherine. "It was sure a good idea to do it this way. I don't think I ever would have thought of it, but now that I see it, I can tell it's right."

Catherine nodded. "I like it, too. " She sniffed and waved a hand. "But it sure took Arlene long enough to get it right! You'd think an interior decorator would be a little quicker. I'm just glad she charges a flat fee for hanging. If I'd had to pay her every time she came out to hang them, we'd be eating pork and beans all month!"

Della Boyd looked around the bedroom. "This is sure a pretty room. I like the new shade of green. Blake did a nice job painting it." She had liked the name on the paint can. "Kiss of Kiwi." She thought of the two attic bedrooms he had finally finished a couple of weeks ago. He had painted them a color called Almond Mousse. "I never knew Blake was such a handyman around the house," she said, noticing how neatly he had painted the molding around the bedroom ceiling.

"Yes, it's surprising what people can do when they set their minds to it," Catherine said. "Well, I've got a whole list of things to do today." She turned and headed back down the hallway. "I wasn't expecting Arlene to stay so long," she called back. "I've got to run over to the Furniture Gallery in Greenville and see about those brass sconces I ordered." And two seconds later Della Boyd heard Catherine's Buick Park Avenue start up out in the garage.

She was about to leave Blake and Catherine's bedroom when her eye caught a picture on the dresser that she didn't remember seeing there before. She walked over and bent down to it. Why, it was Blake and Catherine in their wedding clothes. She wondered where the picture had been all this time and why it had suddenly appeared out of nowhere. She had dusted in this room every week since she had been here, and she was certain this was the first time she had seen it. She picked it up. It was a small picture, and the frame was sterling silver. "What a nice-looking pair you two are," she said aloud.

Blake was thinner back then, and Catherine's hair was down almost to her shoulders and curled. They both looked very happy. Della Boyd remembered their wedding day clearly. It had been down in Biloxi on a Sunday afternoon in early summer, and she had worn a dress of floral voile in rose, plum, and moss green.

Catherine's mother had worn a blue dress with a collar of beige lace.

Mrs. Ashton could have been a pretty woman if she had smiled, Della Boyd recalled, but she had looked nervous and miserable that day. In fact, she had looked sick to Della Boyd. She had been a redhead like Catherine, but the color was a bit faded in comparison to Catherine's. Mrs. Ashton and her husband had been as different as night and day. He was brusque and intense and very much *present* when he walked into a room, but she was like a little teacup taken from a china cabinet and wishing she could be returned to her shelf. Yes, Mr. Ashton was like a bull, and Mrs. Ashton was like a piece of chipped china. The old saying "A bull in a china shop" popped into Della Boyd's mind, and she smiled. She was linking so many things together these days.

She frowned again and wondered how the Ashtons had ever gotten together. One thing Della Boyd had noticed was that a lot of married couples didn't seem to match up. In fact, she had thought Blake and Catherine were opposites when they were first married. Catherine had inherited her father's temperament, it seemed, and Blake had been more reserved, like Della Boyd remembered their mother being. But something had changed after they were married. Since coming here in August, Della Boyd had seen a fiery side to Blake that she never knew existed. Why, the way she had heard him talk at times! She shook her head a little as if to clear it. But that wasn't really Blake, was it? The real Blake was mild and easygoing. So much had happened that she couldn't sift through it all.

To be truthful, Della Boyd was a little confused about the relationship between her brother and his wife. She wasn't sure how it had happened or when—or even *if* it had happened, really—but it seemed to her that things weren't like they used to be between Blake and Catherine when she first came. She closed her eyes and tried to remember back to August, when the taxi had brought her here from the bus station in Filbert. She couldn't recall much about that day except that Catherine had come home first and then Blake had come home from work and held her in his arms.

She put her hands to her temples now and pressed. "What was it I heard that first time?" she asked herself. "It was *something* . . ."

Then it all came back to her. It was late one night shortly after she had come to Berea, after she had been asleep for a good while. She had heard voices. They weren't shouting, but they sounded angry nonetheless. She had lain in bed for a few minutes trying to sort out where she was and why she was here, and then she had started trying to hear what the voices were saying.

She had gotten out of bed, tiptoed over to the door, and opened it a crack. That was before she had learned about the hole in the closet. She had stepped out into the hall and stood by Blake and Catherine's bedroom door. And that's when she had heard Blake say it. "You can't see past the nose on your face, can you? Your little universe has just one planet, and that's you!" And Catherine had said, "Oh, don't act like such a saint. As if you'd welcome *my* sister with open arms if she showed up with a couple of paper bags and some cock-and-bull story!" And before Della Boyd could retreat to her bedroom and scurry back to bed to pull the covers up around her ears, she had heard Blake's reply: "As if *your* sister would darken the door of your house." She had never heard Blake speak in a tone like that.

Let's see, thought Della Boyd, that was back in August. She put the wedding picture down and counted on her fingers again. That was almost six months ago. She didn't understand much about marriages, but she knew husbands and wives weren't supposed to talk to each other that way. She had still been a teenager when her own parents died, so her observation of a marriage close at hand had been cut short. She did remember her father combing her mother's long hair at nighttime, however, and she remembered her mother calling his name out the back door at suppertime. They were gentle people. Della Boyd couldn't imagine them raising their voices to anyone, much less to each other.

But now that she thought about it, she hadn't heard Blake and Catherine talking like that since . . . well, it must have been since around Christmastime. She had heard it a lot those first few months, and then something must have happened because it had dwindled and then all but stopped. She stared hard at the wedding picture again. How things could change—sometimes for the bad and sometimes for the good. Yesterday she had very clearly seen Catherine take Blake's hand, hadn't she? Yes, she was quite sure she had seen that, though she couldn't remember where it had happened or why. And once not very long ago at all, she had seen Blake place his large fingers around the base of Catherine's ring finger and then run them up and down the length of it several times. "That is one tiny finger," he had said. "I could break it like a twig." But Della Boyd could tell from the way he said it that he had no intention of doing that.

She turned from the doorway of Blake and Catherine's bedroom and looked into her own bedroom across the hall. The blinds on the windows facing the street were open, and she saw Barb Chewning in the Chewnings' front yard whirling little Sammy around and around under the bare Japanese maple tree. She was holding both his hands, and his little legs were splayed out, almost parallel to the ground. Barb gradually slowed him down until they stopped, and together they collapsed onto the grass.

Barb rolled over onto her back and crossed her legs, and Sammy flopped around on the grass like a seal. Della Boyd hoped Barb wouldn't let him play on the ground too long. February was still too chilly for that.

The sight of Barb suddenly made a flash in Della Boyd's mind. It was Christmas Eve, that's when it was that things had changed. They had all gone over to Barb and Curt's house on Christmas Eve, and it was after that that she had stopped hearing Blake and Catherine arguing in their bedroom at night.

Christmas had been a confusing time for Della Boyd. Philip had still been stumping around in his walking cast after falling down the stairs, and Hardy had undergone a very puzzling transformation. He had gone to church with the Chewning twins a couple of weeks before Christmas, then two days later had gotten into trouble for starting a fire in an old metal garbage can in the backyard. Blake had looked out into the back-yard, seen the fire, and rushed out hollering at Hardy. To give him credit, Blake was only reacting from sixteen years of bleak expectations con-cerning Hardy's behavior.

As it turned out—and this was most surprising considering the sounds that had come up from Hardy's room in the basement almost around the clock—Hardy was trying to burn up all of his music! Not written sheets of music, but little disks in plastic cases, dozens and dozens of them! Al-most overnight Hardy had turned into a different Hardy altogether. It was difficult for Della Boyd to explain, but he . . . well, he settled down in a very dramatic way. Oh, he still wore most of the same outrageous clothes—and this Della Boyd found strangely comforting—and he still made her laugh with his play-acting antics, but she had been forced to look closely at him every time he entered the room to make sure he wasn't some impostor dressed in Hardy's clothes.

Once she had even asked him, "Where is the old Hardy?" and Hardy had pretended to look in all the corners and under tables, then had said gravely, "He appears to have dismissed himself."

And then on top of Hardy's metamorphosis came Christmas Eve at the Chewnings' house, when they had sat around their Christmas tree and heard Curt read from the Bible. Della Boyd had liked the sound of Curt's soothing doctor's voice reading phrases like "And it came to pass" and "the house and lineage of David" and "good tidings of great joy." She was running the words over and over through her mind—she had es-pecially liked "a multitude of the heavenly host" and "made known abroad the saying which was told them"—when she realized that Curt had stopped reading and was talking earnestly. He spoke the name of Jesus many times, and it was odd to Della Boyd as she had looked around the room that Blake, Hardy, and Philip seemed to be paying close attention, while Catherine and Olivia were both fidgety.

And after that they had sung some carols and had some nice things to eat, and then later after Blake and Curt had gone into the living room and come back after quite a long absence, Blake had said to everybody, "I mean to be different from now on." And he had looked straight at Catherine and said, "Give me a chance, okay?" Catherine had looked away, toward the angel on top of the Chewnings' Christmas tree, whose little glittery halo hovered a good three or four inches above its head, attached by a wire running down its backbone.

Blake had gone on to say something about "doing things backward," about "trying to fix things by patching up the outside." Della Boyd had caught a glimmer of what he meant as she thought of how she had tried to patch up a coconut cake the week before. She had accidentally set one of the layer pans to cool on an eye of the stove that was turned on low, and by the time she had discovered it, the pattern of the electric coil had burned itself right through the pan and into the cake. She had gently sliced off the bottom, stacked the good layer on top of it, and frosted the whole thing.

But when she had served it that night, Philip had been the first to state the truth. "It tastes burnt!" Only the outside had *looked* burnt, but the bad taste went all the way through. She should have known better. She wasn't really sure if this connected in any way with what Blake was saying, but she thought it probably did. You couldn't fix the inside of something by making the outside look nice.

After Blake's little speech on Christmas Eve, Barb had smiled at him and said, "I've been praying for this!" right out loud. Then Hardy had sprung up and stood on his hands right in the middle of the Chewnings' den, causing Catherine to find her tongue and cry, "Not indoors, Hardy Ashton Biddle! How many times do I have to—?" And she had broken off to apologize to Barb. "Honestly, it's like talking to a brick wall sometimes!"

Barb had shaken her head and waved it off with a laugh. "Hey, I've got two boys of my own, remember." And then one of the twins had said indignantly, "Hey, *we* don't do things like that in the *den*—we do them in the living room, next to the grandfather clock and the antique cabinet with all the crystal figurines!"

Della Boyd had felt like the room was swirling in circles. She couldn't keep up. Everybody always seemed to be several steps ahead of her. When Hardy flipped himself right side up again a few seconds later, the Christmas tree shook just a little and one of the little bell ornaments tinkled faintly. Sammy shrieked and clapped his hands. "Do it again!" he cried.

And it really had seemed that Blake meant what he said. He had been different at home after that. He hadn't been so testy with the children, and he had done a lot of obvious things to try to please Catherine. And even though Catherine didn't make it very easy for him, Blake had kept it up. More times than she could count, Della Boyd had seen him open his mouth to say something back to Catherine, then change his mind and close it. One night only a few weeks ago Della Boyd had overheard Catherine crying in their bedroom, and she kept repeating one thing. "I know it, I know it, I know it, I know it." She hadn't sounded angry, though. It sounded like whatever she knew was something sad.

Della Boyd walked slowly down the hallway back toward the den. The basket of flowers she had set by the den door was gone, and the television was turned off. She reached the kitchen and caught her breath when she saw that Olivia was already at work arranging the flowers in a fan-shaped white ceramic bowl. Now wasn't this a surprise? Olivia hadn't even appeared to hear her earlier, and now here she was, doing exactly what Della Boyd had wanted her to do.

They were always catching her unawares, all of them—Blake, Catherine, and all three children. You'd get used to one thing and start expecting it, then turn around and get something entirely different. You could never count on anything predictable when you were living in a family. Della Boyd clasped her hands under her chin and watched Olivia's deft fingers as they lifted a daffodil from the basket and snipped its stem shorter with the scissors.

A Different View

28

Sitting in bed that night, Della Boyd wrote in her diary.

Picked spring flowers today and helped Olivia make an arrangement. Wish I'd had pussy willows to put in it but haven't seen any around here. Wish I could see Juanita Spracklin's pussy willow bush in Yazoo City right now. Want to have one of my own when I go back home.

Though she had many more things she could have written about the day, Della Boyd suddenly felt very tired. She laid her diary on her bedside table and closed her eyes for a moment but opened them again almost immediately when she thought of something. Where was the poem she had wanted to read again? It was a poem she wanted to show Margaret at the next meeting of Women Well Versed. She had found it in a book she had gotten from the library, and she had copied it out and put it some-where . . . maybe in the notebook she always took with her to the poetry meetings. She opened the drawer of her bedside table where she kept her notebook. As she removed it, she saw that a loose paper was sticking out. Yes, there it was. She felt pleased that it had taken so little time to find it, for it seemed that she so often had to look for a long time to find things she had misplaced.

She held the poem up and read it to herself. It was a poem about going home, titled "The Long Voyage," by somebody named Malcomb Cowley, and she was somewhat surprised to find herself crying when she finished reading it. She reached over for a tissue and patted under her eyes. Then she read it again. No, she was wrong. It wasn't about *going* home. It was about *leaving* home. She wondered why the person in the poem had had to leave, and she dabbed at her eyes some more.

There were lines she needed to study more before she could wrap her mind around them, but one repeated phrase leapt out at her—"my own country." She understood that clearly. The person in the poem was longing for his own country. Even though the trees and birds and seasons were the same as in many other places, the fact that it was his own country made all the difference. She kept reading the line that compared the folding back of the waters at the bow of the ship to "earth against the plow" and found herself crying again. How well she remembered the way her father's plow had dug into the Mississippi earth and parted it like dark waves. When he wasn't crop dusting, her father had cultivated some cotton on the small tract of farmland where they lived outside Yazoo City. When she was just a little girl, maybe four or five, he had put her on his shoulders one day and plowed a furrow.

She closed her eyes and pictured her father. He had been a handsome man, not as tall as Blake but with the same dark hair and eyes. She remembered the day when the men had come to tell her about his accident in the airplane. She had kept repeating over and over, "But Daddy is taking me to Vicksburg tomorrow to see Aunt Permelia."

Instead, Aunt Permelia had come to Yazoo City the next day and stayed through the funeral, then had gone home to Vicksburg and promptly died three months later, leaving Della Boyd and Blake with only a few distant relatives in Oklahoma. Della Boyd thought of the little graveyard in Yazoo City where her father and mother were buried. It was enclosed by a black fence of wrought iron next to a pecan grove. She wanted to go back to the graves, to sit beside them, to clear away the weeds and debris, to place fresh wreaths on the headstones.

Though the house where she had grown up had been torn down for a drive-in theater, and the house where she had raised Blake had burned to the ground, a single insistent thought kept vibrating in her mind. *I want to go home*. She wasn't thinking of a particular house, just Yazoo City in general. She yearned for Mississippi. It was her own country.

The whole idea of going back home to Yazoo City had stolen upon Della Boyd quietly. She wasn't sure when it had first begun to whisper to her, but all of a sudden it had become something she deeply wanted. It was as if she had seen a pot on the stove, lifted the lid out of idle curiosity, and found it to be boiling wildly. She had been amazed to find her longing so intense almost at the same moment she had realized its existence.

The idea of going home could have started when she had begun going on walks with Barb through the neighborhood back in early January, which was probably a strange time to start outdoor exercise. They averaged three times a week, and their route was usually the same—all the way down one side of Brookside to the cul-de-sac and back up the other, then right on DeLaney and over a block to Sweetbriar, all the way down to the end of Sweetbriar to where it ran into Lamar, two blocks on Lamar over to Windsor, up Windsor toward DeLaney, and back down DeLaney to Brookside. It was probably well over two miles, but the pace at which they walked didn't push their heart rates much. "It does other nice things for our hearts, though," Barb had told Della Boyd one day.

Barb had actually invited Catherine to walk with her first. Della Boyd had been in the kitchen when Barb had rung the doorbell on New Year's Day. It must have been six or seven weeks ago now. Catherine, who had been rearranging the greenery on the mantel in the living room, removing the red bow and holly berries now that it was January, had gone to the door. Della Boyd had heard Barb say something, and Catherine had answered, "Are you out of your mind? In the middle of winter? I don't think so!" Then Barb had said something else, and Catherine had replied, "Who knows? I can't ever predict what she'll want to do. You're welcome to ask her. Be my guest."

So Barb had come into the kitchen, where Della Boyd was chopping up an onion. She already had a little pile of diced celery and green pepper sitting on the edge of the cutting board. Though some recipes for chili didn't call for celery, she always added it. She liked to add a dash of vinegar also.

For once Barb didn't have Sammy with her, since the twins were home to watch him and Sarah. "How about going on a walk with me?" she asked Della Boyd.

"A walk?" Della Boyd had said. "Go for a walk?"

Barb had laughed. "I know, I know. I'm crazy. Catherine already told me as much. But I thought it would be invigorating. I guess I'm getting cabin fever or something. It just suddenly hit me that I *had* to get outside or I'd start climbing the walls." She had paused and raised her eyebrows. "So what do you say? You want to go with me? I'm not planning a marathon or anything, just a little walk for some fresh air."

Della Boyd had begun taking off her apron slowly. "Well, now, yes, I think I'd like that," she said. "I really think I would." She looked back at the cutting board. "But I do need to . . . I mean, I was just getting things started for supper. I'm making chili. Philip and Hardy both love chili."

"Oh, go right ahead," Barb said. "I can wait. I've got our supper pretty much planned—well, to be honest, we're just having leftover chicken casserole—so I'm not in any big hurry. I'll just go out here and talk to Catherine while you finish up."

So Della Boyd had browned the meat and added the onion, celery, and green pepper, then mixed in the tomato sauce, tomatoes, thyme, vinegar, water, salt, and pepper. She had stirred it all up, then put the lid on the pot and turned the heat down low. She would add the beans during the last thirty minutes or so.

". . . just *looked* at me and then let it drop," Catherine was saying to Barb when Della Boyd walked into the living room. "Ordinarily he would have jumped down my throat. That man has got something up his sleeve."

"Well, give him a chance to change," Barb had said. "Meet him halfway. Tell me, do you like Blake better the old way or this new way?"

"Oh, goodness, let's see," Catherine said, laying a finger on her chin and appearing to think very hard. "Let's see, do I like tar or gravy better on my mashed potatoes?" Della Boyd didn't see what was so hard to decide about that.

Barb laughed. "Well, give him a chance," she repeated.

Della Boyd had thought that sounded like good advice. Although she really didn't know exactly what they were talking about, she knew it had something to do with Blake. She opened the coat closet next to the front door and took out her new parka. Her gloves were in the pockets, and she put those on, too, then pulled up the hood to her parka.

"He brought me some of those malted milk balls the other day," Catherine said to Barb. "Whoppers—you know, those things in the milk-carton thing?" She fiddled with a few pine cones near the center of the mantel and stood back to study the effect. Della Boyd thought the mantel looked pretty. Like Catherine said, there wasn't any rule that said you couldn't have greenery on your mantel after Christmas. Catherine had a knack for decorating even though she usually paid other people to do things for the house. Of course, she usually complained about paying them, too.

"Whoppers?" Barb asked, laughing.

"I used to practically live on them," Catherine said, stepping forward again to move the pine cones over a little farther away from the white candle. "At Ole Miss I'd have them for breakfast, along with a Diet Rite."

"So he must have remembered, huh?" Barb said.

Catherine shrugged. "Beats me. Maybe. Or maybe it was just a lucky guess."

Della Boyd remembered seeing the box of Whoppers on Catherine's dresser when she had passed by their bedroom two days ago. She had thought they must be Philip's.

"Well, go easy on him," Barb said again. "He's trying to make good on his promise. Give him a chance." Which was funny, because that was the very same thing Blake himself had said a week or so earlier, on Christmas Eve, when he had told them all he meant to be different and had talked about making things right on the inside. "Give me a chance," he had said.

And he *had* been different after that. Things surely had changed around here since Della Boyd had first come. Nobody could deny that. First Hardy had turned into somebody different overnight, then Blake. Even Philip had started going to church, some weeks with the Chewnings and sometimes to a church over in Filbert with his friend Andy Partridge.

Catherine and Olivia were still pretty much the same, although Catherine had shocked Della Boyd to pieces recently when she had come home from a shopping trip empty-handed and said wearily, "It just all seemed so . . . *pointless*. I mean, all those racks and racks of new stuff I felt like I'd seen a million times before. I just couldn't make myself get excited about any of them." This was Catherine talking—Catherine, who wore the prettiest clothes Della Boyd had ever seen in her life! A couple of times lately Catherine had even taken some of her very nicest things over to see if Barb Chewning could wear them since they were so close to the same size.

Yes, Della Boyd thought, a lot of things had changed around here. Even her own bedtime routine had changed. Della Boyd tucked "The Long Voyage" poem back into her notebook now and returned it to the drawer. She laid her head back against her pillow and gave a small sigh. She used to have such an orderly ritual at bedtime, but now everything seemed so hodgepodge. She never had gotten back on schedule during the whole six months she had been here. Her habits of many years had been wrenched out of their orbits.

She used to write in her diary and then . . . what? She had always read several entries from an old diary to refresh her memory about past years. Of course she couldn't do that anymore because all her old diaries had burned up with her house. Then what came next? Was it working a crossword puzzle? Or rather, working *at* one. She could rarely finish one without cheating and looking in the back of the book for the solution. She had kept several copies of *Ideals* magazines by her bed also, which she read over and over, and at some point she would open one to wherever she had placed the bookmark and reread two or three pages of poems. She didn't much like that kind of poem anymore, though. That was another change.

And her *Reader's Digests*. She had always read them methodically, starting with the first page of each issue and reading straight through, usually four or five pages each night. Since she had been at Blake's, however, she had found herself flipping open old issues of *Reader's Digest* she had found on the den bookshelves and reading whatever her eyes lighted on.

In Yazoo City she used to listen to a local news program on her radio at ten o'clock every night. It was called *Around Town*, and she had liked the announcer because she thought he sounded a little like Orson Welles. After she had come to Blake's, she bought an alarm clock to put on her bedside table, but she didn't have a radio. The television was in the den, but she never watched anything after *Wheel of Fortune* went off at seven-thirty. All the other programs were so unfamiliar now. She didn't recognize any of them anymore.

She raised her head again and looked around her bedroom. It was a tidy room, painted light blue with ivory trim. From her bed, when she was sitting up, she could see herself in the mirror over the dresser. She studied herself now, flattening her hair with the palm of one hand, trying to get it to not fly up so erratically from her head. She needed to go back to the beauty shop where Catherine went, to see what Dottie Puckett could do with her wild nest of hair now that her permanent had grown out so much. It was odd that her hair hadn't had the least bit of curl when she was younger, but when it had started turning gray it had suddenly developed a mind of its own.

Through the mirror she could also see the picture on the wall behind her above the headboard. It wasn't a picture of anything in particular, but Della Boyd had grown to like it over the past months. She knew it was called an abstract. At first it had made her nervous with its bold pockets and shards of color and brilliant little speckles of paint. She had wished it were a picture of something nice—like a lady in a park or children wading in a stream or flowers in a vase—at least a picture of *something*, even if it wasn't something nice.

But it was curious how she had gradually stopped wishing it were something else and had slowly grown fond of it. She wondered if it had anything to do with the fact that different kinds of poems had begun scratching at the door lately. And she had begun letting them in, too. She liked looking at the painting through the mirror. It gave her a different view than looking at it head on. She ran her eyes all around the edge of the black frame now, several times, and then held her breath and let them plunge into the coral triangle at the very center of the painting.

It was good that she had come here—she believed that to be so. She had needed to leave Yazoo City when she did. Things had been so up-ended after the fire. She hadn't been able to sleep for the awful images of charred rubble in her dreams at night, and she had kept imagining that she smelled smoke and ashes. She remembered someone asking her why she kept pulling at her clothes, and she had no answer to give. She hadn't even known she was doing it.

For some reason the phrase "Finders keepers, losers weepers" suddenly sprang to her mind, and as she stared at the painting in the mirror she thought hard. *Finders keepers, losers weepers.* She started at the end of the phrase and thought backwards. *Weepers.* She had wept, yes—rivers of tears—but now for the past couple of months she had felt herself rising, as if floating free of her loss. *Losers.* In the fire she had lost everything she possessed. *Keepers.* But she had kept her life. *Finders.* And what's more, she had a strong sense of having found new things here at Blake's house. And many of them were good. She nodded. Yes, that was true. She had been part of a family again, and that was a good thing. It had been hard, but it was good. *Weepers, losers, keepers, finders.*

She looked away from the painting in the mirror and let her eyes travel back to the dresser with its comb and brush neatly laid side by side and her toiletries arranged in a row—her Oil of Olay, her talcum powder, her hand lotion. She saw her pocketbook on the chair beside the dresser and remembered all of a sudden that the letter was in it. The letter from Helena Ludwig, who had taken her into her home after Della Boyd's house burned down. The letter was the reason she had announced, to everyone's amazement at the supper table three days ago, "I want to go home."

She got out of bed and went to get her pocketbook. It ought to be over by her nightstand anyway. She liked to have it nearby when she was sleeping. Sometimes at night after she wrote in her diary, or sometimes before, she would reach for her pocketbook, take out a photograph, and look at it a long time before she turned out the light. It was the only picture she had of her father. He was standing beside his airplane almost fifty years ago.

Before she got back in bed, she took the letter from her pocketbook. She slid back under the covers and unfolded the letter, smoothing it down. Helena's handwriting was messy and a little hard to read, which was why Helena had liked it so much when Della Boyd had helped her write thank-you notes during the weeks they had lived together after the fire. "I surely could have used your services before now," she had said to Della Boyd more than once. Della Boyd already knew the letter by heart, but she read it again anyway.

Dear Della Boyd,
 I find that I'm not happy in Louisiana. I wonder why I thought I ever would

be. *Nothing is right. I feel like somebody crumpled me up in a little ball. I'm all cramped up inside this shabby little shoe box of an apartment, and it dawned on me that nobody's making me do this. I came here thinking my home should be where the rest of my family is, but it's not home, no matter who's here. They're all too busy to even know I'm around most of the time anyway.*

I want to go home, and I'm talking now about Yazoo City. But I want somebody to share a house with me. How are things shaping up for you? Are you all settled in there or would you entertain the idea of going in halves on a house back in Y.C.? I think we'd be able to accommodate each other's eccentricities, don't you? I will await your answer before I go it alone. I do mean to move back home within the next five months. That's when my lease for the cubbyhole where I reside will be over, for which I'm abundantly thankful.

Yours sincerely,
Helena Ludwig

The letter had made the idea shake loose, but the springs were already scrunched tight, like a Jack-in-the-box. The music had been playing and the little handle had already been turning for a good while without Della Boyd's even realizing it, so the letter was just the pop that made the lid fly up. And that night at supper she had echoed Helena's words, though they were really her own now. "I want to go home."

She could still see the circle of faces looking at her curiously around the supper table that night. Catherine had been the first to speak. "Why, whatever in the world are you talking about, Della Boyd? I thought you felt at home here. You're always talking about that magnolia tree out back and how it makes you think you're back in Mississippi."

"I guess what I really mean," Della Boyd said, frowning toward the kitchen window, "is that it makes me *wish* I were back in Mississippi. I guess I haven't been entirely open with you."

"But, Sister, your house isn't there anymore," Blake said gently.

"I know that. But I can get another house."

"Hey, I thought you said you wanted to see me play soccer," Hardy had said. "We start in March."

Philip had stared hard at his pepper steak, as if considering how their meals might change if his aunt wasn't there to help with the cooking, and Olivia had made an exasperated sound and said, "You mean you'd actually think about missing my *graduation*?"

"Well, now, I don't have all the details worked out," Della Boyd said, "but . . . well, I want to go home."

Blake had cleared his throat. "Sister, I don't really think you ought to live by yourself right now. You need to be here with us."

"I'll be living with my friend Helena," Della Boyd had said.

Catherine had let her fork fall onto her plate with a clatter. "So when did all these plans get made?"

"They aren't really made yet," Della Boyd had said. "But I believe they will be." She had stopped and smiled at each of them in turn, although Philip couldn't have seen her smile since he was still glaring down at his plate. "I believe they will be made quite soon," she said again.

Della Boyd refolded Helena's letter now and laid it on the nightstand. The letter had been followed by several telephone calls, and then Helena had driven from Louisiana to Yazoo City to look at some houses. One of them sounded especially promising. "It has a garden gate," Helena had told her, as if she had known that single detail would turn Della Boyd in its favor. If things went well, Helena thought the house might be theirs by the end of March.

Della Boyd laid a hand to her forehead and counted out the weeks. Six of them. In six weeks she might be back in Yazoo City living in a house that had a garden gate. She wondered if it would be a gate like the one at the white house on Sweetbriar. She and Barb passed the house every time they walked, and every time they passed it, Della Boyd slowed down just a little. It was painted white with dark green shutters, and the gate was on the side, under a white archway. Except for trees, she could never see much of what was behind the gate, but Barb thought the people had a grape arbor in the backyard. Maybe she and Helena could have a grape arbor in their backyard, and she could make grape jam.

She rearranged her pillows and eased herself down under the covers. As she closed her eyes, she began tracing the houses along the route she and Barb walked. Yes, it must have been the view of all the houses from the street that had stirred in her the desire to go home. Not only the houses, of course, but also the people in them. Barb already knew some of the people and stopped for brief chats sometimes, but others she met for the first time on their walks. Della Boyd liked the way Barb would wave and call out cheerily, things like "Hi there. Was today the day you invited us for supper?" or "It's a good thing you got that big pine tree cut down before a storm could knock it over" or "Hey, did somebody put that For Sale sign in your front yard as a joke? Surely you're not moving away from us!" She admired the way Barb could strike up a conversation so easily.

In Barb's company she had gotten to know almost everybody up and down Brookside and quite a few people on the other streets, too. Wilma Partridge had invited them in for hot spiced tea one day, and Trixie Thorndike had asked if she could walk with them a few times. A couple of times Loretta Whittington had run out to the curb to give them samples of something she had just baked. Last time she was wearing a billowing dress of bright lime green and black and dangly earrings the size of Oreo cookies. On a paper napkin in her hand were sitting two lumpy dark brown balls that she called Coconut Cream Cheese Fudge Spheres, which Barb had said would make a good tongue twister.

They had met such interesting people all along the way—a man who operated a pet crematorium, a man who had lost both legs in Vietnam, a woman whose father had known Dwight Eisenhower personally, another woman whose collection of ceramic pigs was on display in her bay window, a couple who vacationed in Jamaica every year, and a man on Windsor Street who claimed to have won over five thousand dollars in various sweepstakes.

This last man had particularly fascinated Della Boyd, for she had sent in hundreds of sweepstakes entries over her lifetime and had never won so much as a plug nickel. She had finally quit trying a couple of months ago, having decided it just wasn't meant to be. In fact, that's what Hardy had said to her: "Why don't you give it up, Auntie Deeb? It's just probably not meant to be." She had thrown the last several letters away, even the most recent one that had said in bold letters on the envelope, *YOUR NAME DELLA BOYD BIDDLE HAS ALREADY BEEN SELECTED FOR OUR THREE MILLION DOLLAR SWEEPSTAKES*. Hardy told her that millions of other people had received the same letter with their names on the envelope.

One day Barb had pointed to a woman who lived on DeLaney Street. They caught a glimpse of her grabbing her newspaper off the front porch and then scuttling quickly back inside. "She's a strange duck," Barb had said, "but as generous as they come." She had gone on to tell Della Boyd how the woman, a widow, had given hundreds of thousands of dollars to different charities. Though she hadn't spoken a word to the woman and had seen only the briefest flash of her pink housecoat, Della Boyd immediately liked her better than the sweepstakes man on Windsor Street.

It must have been watching all those people turn to go into their houses that had set things in motion for Della Boyd. Some sense of wanting a front door of her own must have been aroused, of wanting to be the person checking the mailbox or sweeping the front walk instead of the one walking by. Of course, all these houses out in this subdivision were much finer than her house in Yazoo City had been. It wasn't that she wanted a house like these. It was just having a place to call her own that she had missed without even noticing it.

Right before she drifted off to sleep, she saw a sudden vivid picture in her mind of a garden gate flanked by purple irises, and she whispered, "I want to go home."

A Huge Risk

29

The next morning, Sunday, Della Boyd awoke early, thinking for some strange reason about hummingbirds. At first she thought she might have been dreaming about them, but then she remembered the feeder she had hung outside her bedroom window two days ago. She went quickly to the window and opened the blinds. Yes, there it was hanging from a branch of the small Bradford pear tree. But evidently no hummingbird visitors had come yet, for it was still full of the red nectar she had mixed up and poured in just days earlier with such high hopes.

Maybe it was too early—that must be it. She needed to call a bird specialist or find a book that would tell her when hummingbird season started. She wondered if hummingbirds migrated to warmer climates in the winter. Helena Ludwig would know. Helena had had two hummingbird feeders at her house in Yazoo City, and Della Boyd had spent hours observing them after the fire. She would sit on Helena's screened porch and watch the little birds come and go. That would have been—Della Boyd stopped to think—over seven months ago now. Yes, February was probably too early. But you never knew. Maybe some of the hardier varieties of hummingbirds ventured out before the others. All that wing motion should keep them plenty warm.

She smiled as she studied the bright orange feeder. She knew she was a patient person. That's one gift she knew she had. Maybe one day before she left to go home she'd see a hummingbird hovering out there with its tiny wings whirring and its long beak pushed into one of the four little trumpetlike sipping cups. That would be a happy day.

Suddenly she remembered something and laughed out loud. The nectar she had mixed up for the hummingbirds two days ago looked just like cherry Kool-Aid, and the directions on the package had said to store the leftover portion in the refrigerator, which she had done. Before she had thought to tell anybody, though, Philip had found it and poured himself a glassful. She had walked into the kitchen on Friday afternoon just in time to hear him say, "Hey, this Kool-Aid tastes funny."

"Oh, Philip, I'm so sorry," she whispered now, placing both hands over her smile. Thankfully it wasn't poisonous, and everybody but Della Boyd had laughed about it at the time. She had been too frightened to laugh but had dug the nectar envelope out of the trash and read it carefully. Although there was no *HARMFUL IF INGESTED* warning, no skull and crossbones picture, she wouldn't rest until she had called the hotline for the Poison Control Center, after which she had immediately found a marking pen and masking tape and labeled the jar with big letters: *H'BIRD NECTAR*.

Della Boyd turned away from the window now and went over to the closet to get out her bathrobe. It was then that she discovered Catherine was going to church with Blake and Hardy this morning. She learned it by stealth, the way she had learned other things over the past months, ever since she had opened her closet one night back in September to retrieve a receipt she had tucked into a skirt pocket. She had just thrust her hand into the pocket when she had heard Blake's voice quite plainly from the other side of the closet wall. "Why is it always everybody else's fault, Catherine? Are you really that blind? Some of the responsibility has to belong to you. After all, they're your kids as well as mine, you know."

And she had heard Catherine's answer, too. "Oh, how *generous* of you to share them. You've stayed home all of what—three weeks now? And suddenly you're this big expert on raising children? Don't make me laugh." Blake had evidently gone into the bathroom after that because whatever he replied sounded further away and too muffled to understand. There was no mistake about Catherine's response, though. "Oh, don't quote that drivel to me! That man doesn't live in the real world, and you know it! Anybody who names their kids Noah and Ezekiel and Hosea and who-knows-what-else is living on a different planet. I don't care how many books he's written!"

Della Boyd hadn't been sure, but she thought they might have been talking about the parenting seminar they had attended with the Chewnings. The speaker had been a doctor with a big family of boys. Blake had come home fired up after the meeting, she recalled, and over the following days had tried to implement some drastic new rules for the children, all of which had met with vocal opposition. She remembered an especially ugly face-off between Blake and Hardy one night shortly after that, during which Hardy had bellowed, "Hey, you gonna hang around here all the time now making up stupid new rules? How come you ain't leavin' on any business trips no more? Me and Liv and Pip, we can help you pack your bags."

And Blake had bellowed even louder, saying if anybody was going to be packing his bags, it was going to be Hardy. Then he had immediately changed his mind and said no, he didn't think Hardy even deserved the courtesy of being allowed a suitcase, that he should be thrown out on his ear and he *would* be, too, if he didn't fix some things real fast. Della Boyd had been in the den when the scene had erupted in the kitchen, and even though she had put her hands over her ears, she had heard it all clearly. Chairs had been knocked over, and something made of glass had been broken.

So anyway, she had known about the closet since September. After that first time, Della Boyd had gotten down on her hands and knees and looked around inside the closet. Since the guest room and master bedroom were both at the end of the hall, they shared a common wall. What she had discovered was an actual structural problem that explained the way the sound traveled. Somebody at some time had cut a hole right into the wall between her closet and Blake's! Hanging clothes covered it up now, but it was a hole nevertheless—about the size of a half dollar. Della Boyd couldn't imagine why it was there. It looked big enough to put a small pipe through, but why would anyone want to do that? She wondered if anybody else knew it was there. Surely someone would have noticed it when they first moved in, but after the closets were filled with clothes, maybe it had been forgotten.

She had soon discovered that if Blake left his closet door ajar, which he obviously did quite often, and she opened hers, she could hear entire conversations through the wall. This presented another problem called temptation. Della Boyd knew she shouldn't listen to a private conversation and felt guilty whenever she did, but sometimes even after she had held out for a long time and given herself a strict warning not ever to do it again, she found herself creeping over to open her closet door.

Thus it was that she found out this Sunday morning that Catherine intended to go to church. Catherine had gone with Blake and Hardy a few times before, and so had the rest of the family, at Blake's insistence. But today, as Della Boyd heard through the wall, it was all Catherine's idea.

"Oh yes, you did," Blake was saying, and Catherine's response came at once. "No, I didn't! I never ever said that. You're making things up again!"

At first Della Boyd felt herself go tense. She had heard enough arguing in this house to last her a lifetime. She took a small step back and was in the process of trying to talk herself into closing the closet door when she heard Catherine laugh. It puzzled her at first why she should be so surprised, but almost at once she figured it out. It was because Catherine wasn't given to laughter, at least not the happy kind. It wasn't something Della Boyd had heard from her very often, certainly not when she and Blake were talking in the bedroom.

Again Blake said, "Yes, you did," and Catherine protested. It was then that Della Boyd realized they weren't speaking in anger, and she let out her breath and took a step back toward the closet.

"You shouldn't be doing this," she whispered to herself, but she did it anyway.

"Well, I don't care if you do say that I said something I never said," Catherine continued. "I haven't been married to you all these years without learning to turn a deaf ear to your crazy exaggerations. I never said I wouldn't go back to that church, and you know good and well I didn't. But it doesn't matter because I *am* going today anyway. I'm sure not going to miss my own son singing in public even if it is at a hokey little church in front of a couple hundred religious zealots."

"Hey, you better watch it," Blake said. "Curt and Barb might not appreciate hearing you describe them that way."

"Well, nobody's here but us two," Catherine said, "so unless you decide to tell them, I guess they'll never know, will they?"

It was funny, Della Boyd thought, how she could tell now when Catherine didn't really mean anything serious by her little tirades. Wasn't it funny how the very same words could be said one way and sound hateful but said another way they sounded like teasing? One thing Della Boyd had begun to learn here at Blake's house was how to tell the difference between the two.

It gave her a feeling of accomplishment that she was discovering how to do what Barb Chewning called "read" people. Not that she had mastered the art, but at least she had learned not to take everything at face value but to wait a little while and pick up more clues. Hardy could still string her along at times, but she knew she wasn't as easy to trick as she used to be. In fact, not more than a week ago when Hardy had tried to feed her one of his farfetched stories, she had looked at him evenly, pointed out the kitchen window, and said, "Yes, of course, and apples are going to grow on that magnolia tree, aren't they?" Hardy had screwed up his mouth and said, "Aw, Auntie Deeb, you're no fun anymore." But she could tell by his tone of voice that he didn't really mean that either.

Della Boyd quickly began planning what she would wear to church this morning. She pulled out her navy blue skirt and a red blouse that tied in a nice bow at the neck and laid them over a chair. She hadn't known about Hardy singing, but now that she did, she was like Catherine—she didn't intend to miss it. For the past couple of months she had heard Hardy singing around the house. Every day now the sounds of his singing drifted down from his new bedroom up in the attic, and they weren't the kinds of songs she used to hear pounding up the stairs from the basement. To her knowledge, Hardy had never sung in front of a lot of people, but it didn't surprise her at all that he was going to. He was never scared to try anything. That was one thing she admired about Hardy.

From the other side of the wall Blake said, "I'm almost out of clean shirts," and she heard the sound of hangers scraping against the metal bar. Catherine said something she couldn't hear, and then Blake said, "Okay, thanks." This was something else new. Della Boyd couldn't remember his ever thanking Catherine for anything when she first came here to live.

And this past week Catherine had done it, too. When Blake had come home at suppertime on Wednesday, which was Valentine's Day, with a bouquet of pink roses, Catherine had pretended to faint right on the kitchen floor. Della Boyd had looked at her sprawled out on the green ceramic tile and said, "Oh, my lands, I'm glad I just mopped that floor today!"

Catherine had opened her eyes after her little staged swoon, looked up at Blake, extended a hand, and said, "Here, Don Juan, help me up since it was all your fault. You haven't brought me flowers in a coon's age, you stinker."

Blake had pulled her to her feet. "Well, okay, I'll take them back if you want me to," he had said, laughing.

"Try it and you're a dead man," Catherine had said.

And Olivia, who was doing homework at the kitchen table, had said, "And where's the candy, Dad? Everybody knows you give a woman flowers *and* candy on Valentine's Day, not just one or the other."

Blake had looked momentarily crestfallen before Catherine had jumped to his defense. "Yuck! None of those big, tacky, heart-shaped boxes for me! There's no telling how far ahead they make that stuff and store it in warehouses. I hate those assortments anyway. There's only about one piece in a hundred I even like, but you have to keep taking all these little bites trying to find a good one." She had taken the bouquet of roses from Blake and cradled them like a baby. "Now *these* . . . these I like! Give me roses any day over chocolates." Then she had looked up at Blake, straight up at him, and said without the least reservation, "Thank you. They're beautiful."

Della Boyd had gotten a vase out from under the sink and filled it with water. She had thought for a minute that she might start crying. Philip had entered the kitchen just then, looked at the roses, at his parents, and at Della Boyd filling the vase, and said, "So what's going on in here?"

"Not a blooming thing," Catherine had said, straight-faced.

That night at supper Catherine had touched one of the roses and said matter-of-factly, "I want you kids to notice what your father brought me today. You boys need to do things like that for your wives when you get married, and, Olivia, you need to look for a man like your dad."

"Wouldn't he be a little old for me?" Olivia had said.

"I'm not getting married," Philip said.

"But roses are so common," Hardy had said. "I'm gonna do wild and wacky things for my wife."

But Catherine had shaken her head. "Nope. Give me common old roses any day over wild and wacky." She had leaned forward and inhaled deeply. "There's nothing like a rose."

"Ah, I hear a poem coming," Hardy had said. "There's nothing like a rose / When you sniff it with your nose."

Yes, things surely had changed around here. Della Boyd felt like she had been jerked out of the middle of one book and transferred to a sequel. The same characters were there, but the plot was totally different.

She closed her closet quietly now and turned to make her bed. As she pulled up the sheet and smoothed it with both hands, she was thinking about Catherine and Blake and those beautiful pink roses. So that must have been why Blake had brought home another carton of malted milk balls for Catherine last week on the day after Valentine's Day. It must have been because of Olivia's remark. That must have been the candy portion of Catherine's Valentine gift.

Catherine had emptied part of the carton into a candy dish and set it on the kitchen table to share, but the candy hadn't lasted long. Della Boyd had eaten only two or three before they were gone. She had held each one between her thumb and forefinger like a delicacy, taking a small bite, and then examining the porous center. She had never before eaten a malted milk ball, and she found that she liked them very much.

A few minutes later Della Boyd had finished making her bed and was standing at the mirror over the bathroom sink. She hoped she could tame her hair into some sort of shape this morning. She heard Blake walk past the bathroom door and tap on Olivia's door across the hall. "Hey there,

sleepyhead," he called out, "see if you can drag yourself out of bed sometime in the next ten minutes." She heard him proceed to Philip's door
and say, "Up and at 'em, bud. The morning's half gone."

For just a moment she let herself think what it might be like to have
a husband of her own who brought her pink roses on Valentine's Day and
woke up the children each morning the way Blake did. She remembered
hearing the sounds of soft crying late one night a couple of weeks ago,
and when she had opened her closet door, she had heard Blake say, "You
never told me about any of that before. Come here. Let me hold you."
His voice was so low and gentle that she could barely make out the words.
She had closed the closet door ever so quietly and crawled back into bed
feeling ashamed of herself. She tried to imagine having a husband who
said to her, "Come here, let me hold you."

She raised her brush and ran it through the top of her hair. As she did
so, the thought of Arthur Porterfield sprang to her mind again, as it had
done countless times in recent months. She wondered where Arthur was
now. It had been many years since she had seen him, but she had heard
before she left Yazoo City that he was living in Guam with a Hawaiian
woman he had met in the Philippines. It all sounded like such a complicated chain of events to Della Boyd, when he could just as easily have
stayed in Yazoo City and married a local woman.

Arthur Porterfield was another thing Della Boyd had lost as surely and
irretrievably as she had lost her house. She hadn't lost him because of a
fire, though. She had lost him because of fear. "Fire, fear, fire, fear . . ."she
whispered aloud. She had met Arthur at the junior high school where she
had taught for five years in Yazoo City in the early eighties. Arthur had
come to Yazoo City from Natchez during her fifth year of teaching remedial reading to seventh and eighth graders. He had been a fortyish
mathematics teacher and a very private, remote sort of person, though
always gentlemanly. One day he had held the door of the teachers' lounge
for her but had looked up at the transom and blushed bright red as he
did so.

They always seemed to be bumping into each other without meaning
to, and when she had started hearing teasing comments from some of the
students and even a few from her fellow teachers, Della Boyd had begun
trying to avoid crossing his path. She had learned his schedule and stayed
out of his way. But one day after mimeographing an exercise about dictionary skills, Della Boyd had exited the audio-visual room only to run
headlong into Arthur Porterfield, whose arms were full of test papers covering the perimeter, area, and volume of geometric figures. The two of
them had collided so suddenly and forcefully that they had dropped their

papers, and Arthur's glasses had been tipped sideways.

Della Boyd could close her eyes and still see all those papers on the brown-tiled floor by the water cooler—all those pronunciations and syllable divisions mixed up among triangles and trapezoids. She could still hear Frieda Threlfall's hee-hawing laugh when she rounded the corner and saw Arthur on the floor of the hall trying to collect their papers and Della Boyd standing with her hand over her mouth trying to collect her wits. "Well, well, well. What do we have here?" Frieda had brayed. "Too bad I don't have a camera! I can see the caption now—'Mr. Porterfield on Bended Knee Before Miss Biddle Outside A-V Room.' "

There was a tap at the bathroom door and Philip's sleepy voice. "Is somebody in there?"

Della Boyd realized she had been brushing her hair so hard that it almost looked flat in places now.

"Yes, Philip honey, I'm almost done," she said. She put her brush down and began trying to fluff her hair to make it look fuller.

"Oh, never mind, I forgot," Philip said. "I'll go upstairs." Philip had been assigned to share the new bathroom with Hardy, and Olivia was now using the bathroom in the basement most of the time, so technically Della Boyd had the hall bath to herself.

And the next day after their hallway collision, Arthur Porterfield had come to her classroom after school to return a dictionary exercise that had gotten mixed in with his test papers. Della Boyd had taken it from him without saying a word, and when he had asked if she knew his sister, who was a volunteer at the hospital where Della Boyd helped out every Thursday afternoon and evening, she had nodded mutely and turned her back to write a list of words with diphthongs on the blackboard.

"Serena said you work on the pediatric floor," Arthur had said behind her, and Della Boyd had merely nodded.

Arthur had cleared his throat. "She said you have a magic touch with the babies."

She hadn't answered and hadn't turned around, but her chalk had stopped midway through a word. She held her breath for a long time, and then she finally heard the sound of Arthur Porterfield's wingtip shoes leaving her classroom.

It had been a monstrous coincidence—that's all it was, she had tried to tell herself the next night when she had gone to the hospital as she had done every Thursday night since Blake had left home to go to college. She had been holding a baby, a very sick little eight-week-old baby whose mother had signed away her parental rights and left him at the hospital to die. He had been born six weeks early without a stomach. They called him Baby Kenneth at the hospital. Della Boyd had held Baby Kenneth and rocked him for four Thursdays now, watching him grow weaker. She had sung to him.

"She said you have a magic touch with the babies." Those were the words Arthur had said to her, and those were the words that echoed in her mind that Thursday night when Baby Kenneth died in her arms. Those were the words she heard as the nurse listened for a heartbeat and found none, and as the doctor arrived and pronounced Baby Kenneth dead. The words shouted at her as she picked out a tiny yellow gown for him to wear and as she watched the nurses press his tiny still hands and feet onto an ink pad for prints. *"She said you have a magic touch with the babies."* She heard the words over and over as she helped give him his final bath and dress him in the yellow gown. She had felt great sadness, of course, but anger, too. Evidently her magic touch hadn't worked on Baby Kenneth. Of course, looking back on it, she didn't know what else she had expected. Everyone knew the baby would die sooner or later. But why had he chosen Thursday night? Why had he chosen her arms to die in?

She had asked to transfer to another ward after that. And when Arthur Porterfield had tried to talk with her at school again a few days later, she had turned and walked quickly—no, had *run*, actually—down the hall. She resigned from teaching at the end of the year, and eventually Arthur left Yazoo City and traveled out to the Pacific coast and then to the Philippines and Guam and who knew where else. His sister Serena never really spoke directly to Della Boyd about Arthur, but one day at the hospital when Della Boyd was getting off the elevator as Serena was getting on, Serena had glared at her and said very heatedly, "Some people don't know a good thing when they see it!" And as the elevator doors eased shut, Serena Porterfield had added, "It's your loss!"

There was another knock at the bathroom door. "Aunt Della, I'm out of shampoo. Is there any extra in there?" It was Olivia this time.

Della Boyd opened the door. "I'm sure there is, Olivia. I'm done now, so it's all yours, honey." She touched Olivia's arm as she passed. "Why don't you go ahead and shower in here instead of going downstairs? Just use my shampoo there on the side of the tub. You've been so nice all these months to share your bathroom with me, and I want you to know I appreciate it."

Olivia opened her sleepy eyes wider and fixed Della Boyd with a look. "It's too early to be going around thanking people, Aunt Della." Just before she closed the door and pushed in the lock, though, she peeked back through the crack and said with the least bit of a smile, "At least we got rid of Philip." Della Boyd had to admit that the bathroom situation had improved considerably since Philip had started using the one Blake had added upstairs. Little boys weren't the neatest people to share bathrooms with.

Back in her bedroom, Della Boyd rubbed on a little rouge and patted her face with powder. She put on her red blouse and tied the bow at the neck, then stepped into her navy skirt. She took out the pearl button earrings she had bought at Wal-Mart and clipped them onto her ears. She stood back from the long mirror on the back of the door and studied herself. "A spinster named Della Boyd Biddle," she said softly. Then she stepped closer and added one word. "Why?"

By this she meant two things. First, why was she a spinster of sixty-two when all kinds of other women found husbands and got married? She remembered a woman she had seen at the grocery store just last week with two little dimpled children in her buggy. The woman must have weighed close to three hundred pounds, and Della Boyd clearly heard her say to one of the children, "Naw, not that kind. Your daddy don't like no raisins." How was it that a woman like that could marry and have children while Della Boyd couldn't? But even more specifically, her "why?" referred to Arthur Porterfield. *Why* had she been so afraid of him?

For the first time she wondered if that baby dying in her arms might have had something to do with it. Could her mind have made some frightening linkups without her even realizing it? She tried to think of what could have been going through her mind back then. If she had been nice to Arthur Porterfield, he might have someday asked her to marry him. She had no doubt about that. But marriage was so risky. It opened up so many unsettling possibilities. She knew of lots of people who didn't stay married, for example, and some who did but weren't at all happy. She wasn't even sure she could be a good wife.

Yes, she was certain these had been the kinds of thoughts she had had all those years ago. And children—that was a huge risk that came with marriage. Children could so easily turn out bad. She had seen many bad ones in her five years of teaching. She had seen many good ones, too, but it seemed like such a big chance to take. And children could be born with horrible defects. They could be like Baby Kenneth, born without a stomach. She might have a baby only to watch it grow weaker and weaker and finally die.

"Fear," she whispered to herself in front of the mirror. That's what it had been. She could see it so clearly now. By an awful coincidence she had seen a baby die and had immediately made a horrible decision without even knowing it at the time. *I'll protect myself by running.* That had been her decision. And when she had run down the hallway away from Arthur, she was running not only from the risk of being hurt but also from any promise of love. She was running back to her comfort zone.

That was a term she had heard Barb Chewning use recently on one of their walks. She was telling Della Boyd about when the twins had gotten braces on their teeth a few years ago. They had both struggled to adjust to playing the trumpet with braces, but Caleb had had an especially hard time. He had wanted to give up his trumpet, pointing out how crummy his high notes sounded now. "I told Caleb he had to keep pushing the top of his range," Barb had said. "I told him he had to get out of his comfort zone." She had gone on to observe, "That's what life is all about, you know—stretching yourself out of your comfort zone." Della Boyd knew she had a point. Barb was such a sensible person.

Moments later she opened her bedroom door and went to the kitchen where she found Blake pouring a glass of orange juice. He looked at her in surprise. "Why, you're already up and dressed, Sister," he said. "Where are you going?"

"To church to hear Hardy sing," she said.

Blake looked puzzled. "How did you know about that? Hardy just came downstairs an hour ago and told me he was singing today."

Della Boyd opened her mouth to say something but realized she couldn't tell the truth. She couldn't very well say, "I heard you and Catherine talking through the closet." She smiled and tilted her head. "I just know these things," she said.

And Blake, still frowning, had been on the verge of asking something else when Hardy had landed at the bottom of the stairs in the hallway and shouted, "Hey, guys, any sweet rolls for the starving masses on a Sunday morning?"

A Sign of Life

30

In Della Boyd's opinion, the Church of the Open Door looked exactly like a church should look. It was white with a moderate-sized steeple and had an encased lighted sign out near the curb that posted the times for the church services and bore a new pithy saying each time she saw it, which now totaled four. Today's saying was *PEOPLE MUST KNOW THAT WE CARE BEFORE THEY CARE WHAT WE KNOW*. She thought about that a minute and decided she agreed with it. The windows of the church, though not stained glass, weren't ordinary rectangular windows but were curved on top and came to a point like a bishop's hat. The panes were made of beveled glass that sparkled fiercely. Someone must clean those panes regularly, Della Boyd thought, for them to be so shiny.

Inside it looked well kept. She liked the burgundy carpet and the fact that there were fresh flowers in a big vase on a table in front of the pulpit. Today's arrangement was the biggest bouquet of jonquils and narcissus she'd ever seen. There must be every variety on the face of the earth in that bouquet! She especially liked the big blowzy frilled ones and the milky white ones with the golden orange center. Paper-whites—that's what the white ones were called, she was quite sure.

Nothing about the Church of the Open Door was fancy or overdone, but it looked like a church where the people considered it important for things to be fixed up nice, and she liked that. Of course Della Boyd didn't have a lot to compare it to, seeing that she had visited very few churches in her lifetime. Her parents had been good, moral, kindhearted people, but they hadn't been churchgoers. And after they were gone, Della Boyd had had her hands full trying to work and raise Blake by herself. The last thing she had needed on a Sunday was a schedule to follow. That was about the only day of the week she allowed herself to indulge in a few minutes of pure relaxation. She remembered sleeping until eight o'clock on Sundays and fixing Blake a big breakfast of waffles and bacon.

As they were ushered to a pew halfway down the aisle, Della Boyd saw her friend Eldeen a few rows ahead turning around to smile and wave at them. Eldeen leaned over and whispered something loudly to a woman seated on her pew. Della Boyd caught the words "Hardy" and "prettiest red hair" and "the Lord Jesus," but she couldn't put them all together. Across the aisle she saw Dottie Puckett sitting with her husband and son. Dottie was such a sweet woman.

Margaret Tuttle was playing the organ as people got settled in the pews, and after they sat down Della Boyd whispered to Catherine, who was sitting next to her, "Did I tell you that Barb told me Margaret Tuttle only learned how to play the organ about a year ago? My, you'd never know it, would you? She sure plays beautifully, doesn't she?"

Catherine laid a hand over the pretty gold and pearl pin on the lapel of her eggshell-blue jacket and whispered back, "No, you didn't tell me." A few seconds later she added, "I don't know if I believe that. She sure doesn't sound like a beginner." Della Boyd watched Margaret Tuttle reach over to one side of the console and adjust something after she finished the song she was playing, and when she started in on a new song, the organ was softer, with a lower, richer tone.

Hardy hadn't come with the rest of the family but had ridden with the Chewning twins. He was sitting down on the front pew with Josh and Caleb and Jewel Scoggins' son, Joe Leonard. Della Boyd liked Joe Leonard. He came over to the Chewnings' house sometimes and played soccer and basketball with the twins and Hardy. He was a quiet boy but wasn't any pushover. He never backed down in their driveway basketball games, getting right in Hardy's face to block his shots, and Della Boyd had even heard him tease Hardy and call him things like Hardly There and Har Har. He had asked Hardy one time if he had a brother named Hale. But when Della Boyd had seen Joe Leonard at church the Sunday Hardy was baptized and told him how nice he looked in his corduroy sport coat and emerald green necktie, Joe Leonard had turned as red as a holly berry and gulped hard before he said, "Thank you." In some ways he reminded her of Arthur Porterfield—his shyness and politeness.

As Jewel Scoggins seated herself at the piano, Della Boyd felt her heart give a little lurch. At the last poetry meeting, near the end of January, it had still been hard to tell that Jewel was going to have a baby. But today, only four weeks later, it was different. She definitely looked like a mother-to-be. It must be the loose top she was wearing.

Della Boyd looked up at the ceiling, took a few shallow breaths, and blinked her eyes quickly. She knew Jewel was in her late forties—Barb had told her that—and she couldn't help remembering that one of her reasons for rejecting Arthur Porterfield's attentions all those years ago, when she was only in the early years of her forties, was that women shouldn't start families so late. She had reminded herself of all the unexpected sad things she had seen in the maternity ward at the hospital where she volunteered. Anything could happen in those earliest hours of life. After all, her own mother had died giving birth to Blake when she was thirty-eight. Fear—there it was again. She had given up her chance at marriage and children because of fear.

Harriet Murphy, one of the other women in the poetry club, had expressed privately to Della Boyd at their January meeting that she thought it was very imprudent—that had been the exact word she had used, *imprudent*—of Jewel and her husband to be having a baby at their age. But Della Boyd had turned on her quite vigorously and said, "Oh, I think it's a splendid thing! I think it's going to be a bright and shining star in their home, and I don't think there's ever been a baby born who will be received with more love and tender care! Yes, I think it's wonderful!" Harriet had looked embarrassed, as if she regretted having brought up the subject. She had turned away from Della Boyd immediately and struck up a safe conversation with Geneva Fowler about the virtues of gas heat over electric.

Jewel's husband, Willard, came to the pulpit now as Margaret finished her organ prelude. He smiled broadly at everyone in the congregation before he cheerfully announced the number for the first song. Della Boyd could easily picture Willard Scoggins holding a baby, and as they all rose to sing the three stanzas of the song "Bring Them In," Della Boyd imagined Willard bending over a crib and gently lifting a crying baby, drawing it up toward his broad chest and talking to it in the softest and most loving of tones, his round face aglow with fatherly pride.

"Bring them in from the fields of sin," those around her were singing. Della Boyd glanced at Catherine and saw that she was frowning down at the hymnal Blake held. Della Boyd had once heard Catherine tell Barb Chewning that she hated the word *sin* with a passion. It was one day when Barb had run over on another of her borrowing missions and had stayed to talk for a few minutes. Somehow the word *sin* had come up in something Barb had said, and Catherine had flown off the handle.

After Barb had left that day, Della Boyd had tried to pacify Catherine by saying, "I think it's a very disagreeable word, too, Catherine, especially for such a little word. You're right, it's a very negative word."

But Catherine had pounced on her, too. "Oh, don't try to smooth everything over and make it all better, Della Boyd. I don't want to talk about it!" Clearly, Catherine was determined not to like anything anybody said about the word *sin*.

The second stanza of the song talked about the "wandering ones" and the "lost ones." Della Boyd could relate to those words, for hadn't she felt wandering and lost for the past seven or eight months since her house had burned? She didn't feel as if she really belonged anywhere. But she knew this song was about sinners, not innocent people who had lost their homes to fire.

Every time they came to the word *sin* in the chorus, Della Boyd felt a little prick of anger. She remembered one afternoon recently when Barb had tried to talk to her again about what she called "the new life." Of course Della Boyd had more or less brought up the subject herself without meaning to. They had been taking one of their walks through the neighborhood, and Della Boyd had expressed her ardent longing for springtime. "I love it when everything starts getting reborn!" she had said. Those had been her exact words.

And at the word *reborn*, Barb had turned to her, her blue eyes alight, and slowed her pace. They had been on Sweetbriar Street at the time, right in front of a house with two redbud trees flanking the driveway. Della Boyd could see the buds swelling on the branches and was even trying to calculate how many more weeks it would be until they started popping open when she realized that Barb had stopped dead still and was looking right at her. She must have said something.

"Do you see what I mean?" Barb said.

Della Boyd didn't have the vaguest notion what she meant, so she merely shook her head. Her eyes traveled back to the redbud tree. Probably no more than four weeks, she thought. There was nothing she loved better than a redbud in bloom unless it was the early pale green leaves dripping from the slender curves of a willow tree.

"Nature is just full of beautiful parallels of the new life!" Barb had said. "Springtime is the perfect illustration of salvation. Don't you see? Earth sheds her dead garments of winter and puts on a new robe of green!" Barb could get excited about almost anything, bless her heart. Della Boyd had looked up at the sky as if thinking about Barb's point, but in reality she was thinking about spring. Layers of foamy-looking gray clouds were stacked like dirty contrails, hiding the sun from view. They had had a few days of false spring early in February, but now it was winter again. Spring was coming, but not nearly fast enough to suit Della Boyd.

And the next thing she knew the word *sin* had come out of Barb's mouth, though she hadn't been listening well enough to understand the context. She heard the word, though, and it grated against her. She felt her mild passivity flee for just a moment, and she looked at Barb and cried out, "I am *not* a sinner! I have been a good, decent person my whole life!"

Barb had patted her hand and said, "Oh, Della Boyd, I'm not saying you're a wicked person. I can't imagine you hurting a flea. But the Bible says we've all fallen short of the glory of God." She started walking again, slowly, and Della Boyd did, too, glancing back at the two redbud trees. That phrase puzzled her—"fallen short of the glory of God." What exactly did Barb mean? Della Boyd wasn't pretending to be as good and great as God, for heaven's sake! Anybody would fall short compared to God.

". . . so I know that makes it even harder for somebody like you," Barb was saying. "Now for me it was a different story. I knew the first time I heard the plan of salvation that I fit right smack dab in the middle of the verse that said, 'For all have sinned.' I didn't have to think twice about it. But I knew that God—"

Della Boyd couldn't listen to any more. "I believe in God! I never said I didn't believe in God." Barb opened her mouth to say something, but Della Boyd rushed on. "But I'm not a sinner! Why, I never even said a mean thing about anybody!" she said. "There were lots of times I could have, but I never did. I've tried my whole life to treat other people like I wanted them to treat me! I . . . well, I . . ." But she couldn't think of anything else to say.

Barb had smiled at her. "Wow, I wish I could say that." They walked a little while without speaking, passing by the two-story brick house where the man who wore a kilt lived. Barb had told Della Boyd that the man was a real Scotsman and even owned a set of bagpipes. They had seen him out in the yard one time refilling a bird feeder, and he was wearing his kilt and bedroom slippers. Della Boyd had thought his legs looked cold. But there wasn't a sign of life in the Scotsman's yard today, not even any birds at his bird feeder.

Before their walk was over that day, Barb had tried once more. "But it's not just the words we say, you know, Della Boyd. We can sin by our thoughts and actions just as easily."

For a few uneasy moments Della Boyd thought of her eavesdropping through the hole in her closet. Was that a *sin*? she wondered. She remembered being angry at Catherine several times for things she had heard her say through the closet, like the time back in September when Catherine had said something to Blake about his "dingbat of a sister." Della Boyd clearly recalled wishing she had the nerve to put her mouth against the hole in the wall and say to Catherine, "Well, you sure don't mind letting a dingbat cook your meals for you and wash your dishes and mop your floors, do you?" She remembered being glad the next morning when Catherine had complained of a sleepless night and a sore throat. Good, she had thought, that serves you right. Now she wondered if such a thought qualified as a sin.

Della Boyd suddenly realized that everyone in the church auditorium seemed to be turned around staring at them. She glanced over at Catherine, whose mouth was stretched into a taut smile, and Blake, who nodded pleasantly. She glanced to her left and saw Philip wearing the expression of a cornered rabbit and Olivia, slumped down in the pew with her arms folded, staring glumly at the floor.

"Let's all be sure to make the Biddles feel welcome, so they'll keep coming back to visit with us," Willard Scoggins said, beaming at them. "And now," he continued, "as the instruments play through one verse of our next hymn, let's all stand and greet each other with the right hand of fellowship." And as the organ and piano started playing, people from all directions descended upon the Biddles' pew, smiling and extending their hands and welcoming them to the service.

Della Boyd hardly had time to take in one person before another was pressing in upon her. She heard Philip saying, "Yes ma'am, thank you, yes sir, thank you" over and over next to her, but she couldn't get a single word out of her mouth. She hadn't expected this sudden rush of friendliness, this babble of voices and blur of faces. They hadn't done this the other times she had visited the church, so why now?

She saw that Eldeen was standing down at the end of their pew, and she heard her calling her name. "Della Boyd! Della Boyd!" Eldeen had both of her large hands cupped around her mouth. "I got somethin' to give you after the preachin's done today! Don't you scoot out too quick, all right?" Della Boyd nodded in confusion. At last, to Della Boyd's relief, people started returning to their seats and things calmed down again.

The next hymn they sang was slower and more sedate than the first song they had sung. This one was called "My Faith Looks Up to Thee." It wasn't the most cheerful song in the world, Della Boyd thought as she scanned the lines, picking out words like *guilt, griefs, darkness, sorrow,* and *death*. As they started the last stanza, however, Della Boyd decided she may have misjudged the song. It wasn't all gloom and doom.

"When ends life's transient dream," it started out. Yes, wasn't that exactly the thought she had had quite frequently of late? Life was as short as a dream. There was no denying that. Sometimes she wondered how it could be that she had lived for sixty-two years already. A sudden, ridiculous image leaped into her mind of all those bubbles floating through the air at the opening of the *Lawrence Welk Show* each Saturday night on television. How strange it was to think of such a thing now. Why, it had been years since she had last watched Lawrence Welk on television! She had loved that part of the program—all those pretty bubbles floating upward.

"When death's cold sullen stream shall o'er me roll," the hymn continued. She thought, as she often did these days, of the little graveyard where her parents were buried on a knob of a hill on the outskirts of Yazoo City, and remembered all of a sudden that there was a small stream that ran behind it and disappeared into the pecan grove. She had loved going there in the fall and spending a whole morning tidying up the graves, sweeping off the headstones, replacing the flowers. She had always walked along the stream afterward, sometimes even taking a picnic lunch to eat under the golds and reds of the autumn trees. She hadn't thought of it as a cold and sullen stream, though.

"Blest Savior, then, in love," the people around her sang, "fear and distrust remove." If only it were that easy, she thought. If only with a simple prayer one could erase his worries and doubts. If one could awake one morning and be free of fear—what a glorious thing that would be. Fear of failure, fear of disease, fear of embarrassment, fear of change, fear of pain, of loss, of death—she had felt them all.

She liked the last line of the song. "O bear me safe above, a ransomed soul!" It turned everything around. Life was over, but so was death. How happy the thought of being borne heavenward, a ransomed soul. But didn't "ransomed" imply a rescue from something, from . . . what? She knew the answer immediately, at least the answer Barb Chewning and all these other people here at this church would declare in perfect unison were she to pose the question. *Ransom from sin.* She could almost hear them shout it as the hymn ended and the pastor came forward to offer what was listed in the bulletin as a prayer of consecration.

As the preacher began to pray, Della Boyd looked around. Willard Scoggins' head was bowed, and so were Margaret Tuttle's and Jewel's. Della Boyd wouldn't have blamed them if they had been leafing through their hymnbooks getting ready for the next song, but they weren't. On the first row in front of the organ Della Boyd saw the top of Edna Hawthorne's head. Edna was the preacher's wife, and she had a pretty face and a mass of red hair almost the color of Catherine's, although Edna's red had a little more orangey fire and a lot more curl. She was a little on the plump side, but she could sing like an angel. She had sung a solo the first time Della Boyd had come to church with Blake back before Christmas.

Della Boyd saw Hardy standing up front beside Joe Leonard and the Chewning twins. The four boys were almost exactly the same height, Della Boyd noticed. There couldn't be more than a half-inch difference between any of them. They were all tall, nice-looking boys, although Hardy had the other three beat by a significant margin in Della Boyd's opinion. Hardy's head was bowed, but she couldn't tell if his eyes were closed. If somebody made her bet on it, though, she'd say they were. Three months ago she would have bet they weren't, but then, three months ago you never would have caught Hardy standing inside a church either.

A few rows ahead of Della Boyd, Eldeen Rafferty's head was bowed low, and she moved it from side to side and up and down as if feeling every word the preacher was praying. For just a moment Della Boyd allowed herself to wonder what it was that Eldeen was going to give her after church. To be truthful, Eldeen made Della Boyd a little nervous. She had a big smile and big bushy eyebrows and . . . well, she was big all over. Whenever she volunteered a comment at their poetry meetings, she talked in a big low voice and used big hand gestures. She had an awfully big heart, too, however.

As the preacher's prayer continued, Della Boyd looked around at her own family. She liked sitting right in the middle of them like she was. At the end she saw Blake, tall and handsome, standing next to Catherine. He was leaned forward slightly, his eyes closed tightly and his big hands gripping the back of the pew in front of them. Catherine's eyes weren't closed. She was studying her left hand, running her right index finger over her diamond ring and wedding band.

Della Boyd looked over at Philip on the other side of her. His head was bowed respectfully, his red hair sticking up a little over one ear. Next to him, Olivia was staring straight ahead with her eyes wide open. Every now and then her jaws would work up and down silently. Della Boyd was sure Blake didn't know Olivia was chewing gum or he would have made her spit it out before they got to church. If there was anything Blake despised, he often said, it was seeing a lady chew gum. More than once Olivia had shrugged her shoulders and said, "So I'm not a lady, okay? I'm a girl." To which Blake always replied, "They are not mutually exclusive terms, Olivia."

Quickly Della Boyd's eyes darted back to Philip, then Catherine and Blake. She looked to the front again and saw Hardy's head of dark thick hair. The thought hit her suddenly that the men in her family were venturing boldly into the field of religion well ahead of the women. She had heard Blake praying with Philip at bedtime several times, and Hardy . . . well, Hardy was just completely different now. He had quoted an entire chapter of the Bible at supper only last night.

Della Boyd still remembered some of the phrases from the passage. They were lovely, poetic-sounding phrases like "my downsitting and mine uprising" and "the wings of the morning" and "fearfully and wonderfully made." Olivia had stared at Hardy through the whole recitation with a look of disgust, her lip curled back as if he were a leper. Della Boyd tried to imagine Olivia reciting some verses from the Bible or Catherine praying with her at bedtime, but the picture wouldn't focus.

Finally the pastor's prayer was over, and by the time everyone had gotten seated again, Hardy was standing up on the platform behind the pulpit with Joshua, Caleb, and Joe Leonard. Della Boyd sat up tall so that her spine wasn't touching the back of the pew. Joe Leonard looked uncomfortable, as if his necktie was cinched too tight. Della Boyd hoped it wouldn't hamper his singing. The Chewning twins didn't look the least bit ill at ease. In fact, Della Boyd wouldn't have been surprised if one of them hadn't bent toward the microphone and cracked a joke. And Hardy . . . well, Hardy looked very spiffy, Della Boyd thought. He was wearing a white silk shirt with a red and white striped vest and a flashy red bow tie. He had on trim, straight white pants like something a train conductor would wear. Hardy really had a flair for standing out in a crowd.

Someone behind her whispered, "He looks like the ice cream man," and someone else snickered. Next to her Catherine stiffened. Della Boyd had only a moment to wonder what kind of song the boys were going to sing before Jewel played a brief introduction and they . . . well, they took off—that was the phrase that came to Della Boyd's mind first. It wasn't at all the kind of song she'd expect four teenaged boys to sing, but then, she knew these weren't your average teenaged boys. She wondered which one of them had suggested this particular song and if the others had agreed right away. It seemed like such an old-fashioned song for teenagers.

"I am thinking today of that beautiful land I shall reach when the sun goeth down." That was how the song started. The harmony was so tight and true that Della Boyd had to look up at the ceiling. She wasn't sure why, but she thought she might start crying if she kept looking at the boys. She glanced over at Catherine and saw that her eyebrows were raised and her eyes were open very wide. "When through wonderful grace by my Savior I stand," the song continued, and then came a question. "Will there be any stars in my crown?"

Now what would make four healthy young teenaged boys choose a song like that? Della Boyd wondered. Were they really thinking about stars in their crowns when they got to heaven? Or did they just like the tune of this song? How did one go about getting stars in his crown anyway? This was the thought that came to her as the boys sang the chorus. "When I wake with the blest in the mansions of rest, Will there be any stars in my crown?" The stars wouldn't be real stars, she decided. They'd be gems of all colors, but they'd shine like stars. But then the thought struck her that maybe it wasn't literal at all. They had talked a lot about metaphors in their poetry club. Maybe it wasn't a real crown after all. Maybe it was just a symbol of accomplishment or approval.

Joe Leonard was singing the melody. Della Boyd recognized his voice floating above the others. And Hardy was singing the bass line. He was the anchor. Della Boyd had never heard him harmonize before, but he had a good ear for it. She knew the boys had been practicing together in the garage over at Joe Leonard's house, but she never dreamed they would sound this good. The Chewning twins were singing the two middle parts, but she couldn't tell one from the other.

She looked back at the four boys and tried to picture them in Joe Leonard's garage. There weren't any electric guitars or drum sets in her picture, just the four boys singing. She had heard Hardy say they liked to sing without accompaniment because it made them get their parts right. She thought about how Hardy used to shut himself up alone in the basement with the pounding cacophony of his rock music. How could it be that he now went to Joe Leonard's unheated garage and sang songs about heaven?

She had to look away again. "Oh, what joy it will be when his face I behold," the boys sang. "Living gems at his feet to lay down. . . ." She liked the sound of "living gems" and would have stopped to think about it if more words hadn't kept coming. She didn't want to miss any of them, especially since she sensed that the song would soon be over. The boys came to the chorus again and slowed it down a little. "Will there be any stars, any stars in my crown, When at evening the sun goeth down? When I wake with the blest in the mansions of rest, Will there be any stars in my crown?"

There was a profound silence when the last note died away. No one moved for the briefest of moments. It was as if everyone else was as disappointed as Della Boyd that the song had ended. Then Eldeen slowly raised one hand high in the air and said right out loud, "Thank you, Lord Jesus, for such a blessing!" This seemed to loosen everybody up, for many others spoke up then. "Amen!" "Praise God!" "Thank the Lord!"

Pastor Hawthorne came to the pulpit after the boys sat down, and he paused so long before speaking that Della Boyd thought he had forgotten what he was supposed to say. But then he looked straight at the four boys, who had sat back down on the front row, and said, "I can hardly find the words to tell you young men how deeply my heart was stirred by your testimony in song." He looked out over the audience. "Their song poses a thought-provoking question, doesn't it? It brings to mind the verse from Daniel that says, 'And they that be wise shall shine as the brightness of the firmament; and they that turn many to righteousness as the stars for ever and ever.' "

The pastor smiled at the boys again, then said, "I almost feel like we could have a closing word of prayer and be dismissed right now." Della Boyd wondered if she was the only one who wished he would do exactly that. But as Pastor Hawthorne began talking about the offering and the ushers moved forward with the shiny silver collection plates, Della Boyd knew he had no intention of letting them go before he had preached his sermon. She remembered the order of things from her previous visits.

Jewel began playing something on the piano as the ushers turned to pass the collection plates. Della Boyd watched Willard closely as Jewel played. He was sitting on a small pew up on the platform, and his eyes were fastened on Jewel. Della Boyd wondered what was going through his mind. She looked quickly away, down at her hands resting in her lap, down at her long slender fingers. She had never had a ring of her own, and her mother's wedding band, which she had kept in a velvet box on her dresser, had disappeared in flames along with everything else.

Though Jewel was playing a different song than the boys had sung, the only words Della Boyd could hear were "Will there be any stars, any stars in my crown, when at evening the sun goeth down?" As she stared down at her lap, she saw the faces of the four boys all lined up in a row, all shining and earnest, like four living gems.

As a Shadow

31

A couple of nights later, on Tuesday night, Della Boyd sat at the kitchen table with a book spread open before her. It was *Anne Frank: The Diary of a Young Girl*, a book she had checked out when she had gone to the Derby library with Barb Chewning recently. Olivia was at the table also, writing a paper for a course she was taking called Life Issues. Della Boyd couldn't understand the modern high school curriculum. The most unusual course they had offered when she was in school in Mississippi had been Beginning Spanish. They surely hadn't had anything called Life Issues. She wasn't even sure what it was about. When she had asked, Olivia had said it was "just one big gigantic waste."

The Life Issues teacher had assigned the students to write what she called a personal essay, and at regular intervals Olivia would emit an exasperated sigh, throw down her pen, and say something like "This is like the most retarded thing I've ever had to do! I'm just making this stuff up!" She had asked Della Boyd how to spell several words already, and when Della Boyd had finally suggested that she use a dictionary, Olivia had said, "Nope. If you won't tell me, I'll just make a guess, and it'll probably be wrong." Which Della Boyd doubted. Olivia was actually a very smart girl when she wasn't being lazy and stubborn.

Barb had recommended *Anne Frank: The Diary of a Young Girl* to Della Boyd and had expressed surprise that she had never read it before. Now that she had started going to the library with Barb, it appalled Della Boyd that there were so many good books she had never even picked up and read the first page of. As a schoolgirl, she had never been fond of reading. Then when both of her parents were gone, she had no time for reading, for she was suddenly in charge of rearing a two-year-old. When Blake was old enough to go to school, she had worked in the domestics department at Sears, Roebuck and Co. in Yazoo City and had always had so much to do after she got home that reading a book was the last thing on her mind—at least reading a book for herself, that is.

She had read plenty to Blake when he was little. In fact, she still retained in her mind vague memories of scenes from his storybooks—children picking blackberries along railroad tracks, mothers hanging out laundry behind cottages on hillsides, men driving apple wagons along dirt roads, bats whirring through damp caves, school yard scuffles—and every so often when one would float across her mind, she would have to stop for a moment and try to remember if it was something she had witnessed firsthand or seen on television. Then it would come to her that it was from a story she had read to Blake long ago. At some point during his school years she had stopped reading to him, of course, which had ended her daily handling of books. She had kept working at Sears right on up through Blake's graduation from college, and shortly after that she was busy getting a teaching degree herself.

Actually, Blake had been the one to put the idea of going to college in her mind. She doubted that she would have ever had the inclination, not to mention the courage, to get a college degree if he hadn't insisted on it. "It's your turn now, Sister," he had kept saying. "You've put me through, so now I'm going to put you through." He had been so enthusiastic about it that she hadn't wanted to hurt his feelings. He had looked into different colleges that offered courses by correspondence since Della Boyd made it clear that she wasn't up to attending classes with eighteen-year-olds, and together they had chosen Delta State University. Though Blake had gotten a job down in Biloxi and married Catherine well before Della Boyd finished her degree, he had still paid for every penny of her education.

So in spite of the fact that she had received a baccalaureate diploma, the truth was that she had never been much of a reader. The irony of it probably should have struck her when she was hired by the Yazoo City school system to teach remedial reading to seventh and eighth graders, but it never had. Even after she had started teaching at the junior high school, she didn't read books, although she often assigned book reports for her students and marked the spelling and punctuation errors on their papers and even wrote comments at the end like *Excellent choice for your book report* or *One of the best books ever written!* or *Isn't reading fun?*

Besides the college textbooks for her education courses, practically the only things she had read as an adult were her old diaries, her scrapbooks of Blake's school papers and sports awards, a few favorite poems, the newspaper, and of course, her monthly issues of the *Reader's Digest*.

She often looked through her photo albums, too, studying each picture at length and reading each caption carefully, in spite of the fact that she already had them memorized. So although she usually read *something* at least thirty or forty minutes a day, she never ever read books. They were just too long. It was not a pastime she cared to get into.

No, give her a copy of *Reader's Digest* over a book any day. She liked the bite-sized articles in *Reader's Digest* and all the witty little anecdotes. She always marked her answers for "It Pays to Increase Your Word Power" and usually scored quite well, especially for someone who had never been much of a reader. She was also very fond of the "Picturesque Speech" and "Quotable Quotes" pages. And the regular articles were a whole education in themselves! Why, she had read about all kinds of things in the *Reader's Digest*—the danger signs of diabetes, Hong Kong's economy, herbal medicine, the Roy Rogers Museum, New Guinea cannibals, Claude Monet, social security fraud, KGB spies, Afghan nomads, how to make a tourniquet, and hundreds and hundreds of other things.

It was funny, she thought, how she had had to move all the way to South Carolina before she became a reader. And it had all started when she had gone on that first walk with Barb Chewning and heard her talk about a book she was reading, and then one day a week or so later Barb had asked if she'd like to go to the library with her. In many ways Della Boyd felt as if she had stepped into a whole new phase of life that day when she first accompanied Barb to the library. She was enjoying *Anne Frank: The Diary of a Young Girl* and knew she would finish it tonight. She was going to read *To Kill a Mockingbird* next and in fact already had the book sitting on the nightstand beside her bed. Barb had recommended that one also, had called it one of her all-time favorites.

And after *To Kill a Mockingbird*, she was planning to read *The Count of Monte Cristo* because Hardy had just finished reading it for his English class and had told Della Boyd there was "this really cool escape from a sewed-up bag" in it. She wasn't a terribly fast reader, though, so she might have to wait on that one until she had moved back home to Yazoo City and gotten settled in her new house with Helena Ludwig. Maybe she would take a book outdoors on pretty days and read by the garden gate. They could get one of those nice wooden swings to sit in, and she could take a glass of iced tea or lemonade with her.

She had just begun reading the first sentence of Anne Frank's entry for July 21, 1944, when she realized she would have been eight years old at the time Anne was writing these words. It gave her a funny feeling to think of herself living on a little cotton farm outside Yazoo City with her parents at the same moment Anne Frank was living with seven other Jews in a cramped hiding place above a warehouse in Amsterdam. They had been completely unaware of each other's existence at the time, yet here she was now, reading Anne's most personal thoughts.

She read several more sentences, then paused again from her reading and looked up at Olivia, who was chewing on the end of her ballpoint pen and scowling at something she had just written. In 1944 Anne's older sister, Margot, would have been about the same age as Olivia was now. Della Boyd tried to imagine Olivia in Margot's place, eating rotten potatoes, studying Latin and French and bookkeeping by day, wearing clothes she had outgrown, sleeping on a cot, bathing in shared water in a washtub, and having no social life apart from talking with the same seven people every day. She knew that hardships were often the making of people, and she wondered now if Olivia would have risen to the occasion had she been forced into hiding and deprivation.

Just then Olivia flung her pen down, pushed back her chair, and said, "There, the dumb thing's done!" She let her head flop straight back, her hair falling behind her like a shimmery gold curtain, and made a very unladylike gagging noise with her mouth wide open. Then she stood up and said, "I gotta have a Coke before I *die*," and she walked over to the refrigerator, barefoot as always. Catherine was always telling her to wear something on her feet, but Olivia never did. Della Boyd didn't see how she had made it through the winter so far without catching her death of cold. She knew her own feet would have frozen and fallen right off if she had gone around in cutoff denim shorts and bare feet the way Olivia did!

Della Boyd turned back to her reading. She felt a pang of sympathy for Anne Frank as she continued the entry for July 21, 1944, in which Anne rejoiced over "the prospect that I may be sitting on school benches next October." Bless her heart, thought Della Boyd, Anne was trying so hard to not let her hopes climb too high, yet she had already been in hiding for two whole years, and as the war turned in the Allies' favor, she could hardly contain herself.

Della Boyd had seen a program on television many years ago about Anne and her family, however, and she knew that Anne Frank had not survived the war. As she moved on to the entry for August 1, 1944, she couldn't help thinking sadly of all the things Anne could have accomplished had she lived through the war. She could have become a famous writer for one. She was such a plucky girl—and so smart and ambitious!

Della Boyd began reading slowly because she realized she was nearly at the end of the book, and it suddenly came to her that she wasn't at all ready for the last word, whatever it might be. The final entry started out on a meditative note, exploring the contradictions Anne felt within. On the one hand, Anne wrote, she was amusing and lighthearted and rather superficial, while on the other she was serious and deep and quite sensitive. She got herself all worked up by the end of the entry, scolding herself for hiding her true feelings and showing her weak, immature side so often.

And then it was over. Just like that. The last word, not counting her usual closing—"Yours, Anne,"—was *world*. She was right in the middle of wondering "what I could be, if . . . there weren't any other people living in the world" when her diary ended.

A brief epilogue on the next page told how the police had made a raid on Anne's hiding place a few days later, arresting all the occupants and sending them to concentration camps. Anne's diary was later found by friends in a heap of old books and papers on the attic floor. Anne's father was the only one of the eight who survived the concentration camps. Anne herself died in March of 1945 at Bergen-Belsen, only two months before Holland was liberated by the Allies.

Della Boyd felt tears welling up in her eyes. Poor little Anne Frank! She was just beginning to feel the pulse of young love, the power of independent thinking, and the joy of future hopes when the door to their hiding place was suddenly smashed down and all her bright dreams punctured. She was so close to being free . . . and then it had all fallen apart.

She saw Olivia stop in the middle of a swig from her Coke can and walk back toward the kitchen table. "Are you crying, Aunt Della? What's the matter?" Olivia looked back and forth from the book on the table to Della Boyd's face. "Did you, like, read something *sad* or what?" she asked. She pulled out a chair next to Della Boyd and sat down.

Before Della Boyd could compose an answer, Hardy blew into the kitchen, waving a sheet of paper. "Okay, everybody, listen to this . . ." he started, but he broke off when he saw Olivia bending toward Della Boyd, who was now wiping her eyes with a paper napkin. "Hey, what's up?" he said. "What's the Deeb crying for?" He rolled up his piece of paper like a scroll and stuck it in the front pocket of the overalls he was wearing.

Della Boyd shook her head and lifted her hands. "I'm fine. I'm fine. You children should know by now not to pay any attention to your foolish aunt. It's just . . . well, it's nothing really. I was just . . ." But she couldn't finish. She pressed the paper napkin hard against her eyes. Maybe reading books wasn't such a good idea after all, she thought, if it was going to upset her like this. She couldn't let herself get so involved in the life of somebody she had never met.

"It must've been something in that book," Olivia said to Hardy, gesturing toward the table. She took another drink of Coke.

Hardy walked over to the table and picked up the book. It was an old copy that didn't even have the title on the cover, so he opened it. *"Anne Frank: The Diary of a Young Girl?"* he said. He leaned down over Della Boyd's shoulder and spoke softly into her ear. "You been reading this, Auntie Deeb?"

Della Boyd nodded. Hardy pulled out a chair, turned it around backwards, and straddled it. Then he flipped to a page at random, and said, "Okay, let me check this out." He started reading.

Again the picture of Anne flashed into Della Boyd's mind, perhaps sitting at her little writing table at the exact moment the police broke down the door of their hiding place and stormed in. Maybe she had even picked up her pen to write another diary entry when she suddenly heard the cries of alarm from the next room. Maybe she had simply been dreaming at the time—dreaming about going back to school, marrying Peter someday, becoming a writer, having children of her own. She couldn't have been prepared for such a terrible and abrupt termination of her dreams! For surely she knew what awaited her at Bergen-Belsen.

All of a sudden Della Boyd recalled Brother Hawthorne's sermon at the Church of the Open Door only a few days ago. It wasn't a very cheerful sermon. Taken from the book of Ecclesiastes, it seemed to harp on a single theme and kept repeating a very irritating phrase. If he had said it once, the preacher had said it two dozen times. "Vanity and Vexation of Spirit." She had looked over at Catherine once and noticed that her lips were pressed tight and her jaw set like a rock. She wouldn't have been surprised to hear her sister-in-law call out, "Oh, get off it! This is depressing!"

But Brother Hawthorne didn't get off it. He seemed intent on reminding everybody that there wasn't a whole lot to be happy about here on earth—at least in the first part of the sermon, which was about the only part she really listened to. She remembered part of one especially troubling verse he had read from Ecclesiastes: ". . . all the days of his vain life which he spendeth as a shadow." Another verse was even more pointed. As fish were caught in nets and birds in traps, it said, so were men "snared in an evil time, when it falleth suddenly upon them." And the worst part of it all was that nobody knew when this evil time might come! According to other verses, any small wisp of happiness one might feel was only fleeting. Della Boyd wondered if Anne Frank had been familiar with the book of Ecclesiastes.

Without comment, Hardy flipped over several more pages of the book and began reading another entry. He was chewing on the inside of his mouth as he did so and bobbing his head a little.

What had Anne been thinking, Della Boyd wondered, as she was marched out of the attic to her doom? What had been her last words to her father and mother? Had she continued to hope for liberation through the long months that followed, or had she learned her lesson about hope? These thoughts hovered briefly in Della Boyd's mind, but the one that kept returning to haunt her was that final, blinding moment of shock, of having successfully eluded discovery for over two years and then having it all undone in a trice, of being burst in upon, of being manhandled by hostile policemen, of being totally *unprepared* for the suddenness of it all.

Della Boyd still had bad dreams from time to time of finding herself unprepared. Most often it was showing up in class unprepared. Sometimes she was a student facing an examination for which she had failed to study, and other times she was the teacher rushing into a rowdy class with no lesson plan to follow. Often she was late. The bell had already rung and the test had already started or the students were standing on the desks throwing things at one another. And always she was powerless to turn things around. She would try to speak, to offer an excuse or to gain control over the students, but she could never manage more than a whisper even though she would labor to make herself heard.

Other times she would dream that she was in public improperly clothed or not clothed at all. She would think in her dream that she was, say, stepping into the shower when she suddenly found that she had instead stepped into a crowded room where a party was going on. She would awake from all these dreams in a tangle of bedcovers and always had trouble getting back to sleep.

Yes, the fear of being unprepared had dogged her all her life. And now she had to go and read something like this, something that would feed her fears. Of course, the one thing she had never had a dream about was her house burning down, and that was exactly what had happened, whereas she had never in her life gone to school unprepared or appeared in public without her clothes on.

How mild her silly dreams were, she thought now, in comparison to the things that really happened, like your house going up in smoke. And really, losing your house wasn't nearly as bad as having your whole life suddenly turned upside down like Anne Frank's and finding yourself being herded off to a concentration camp! So maybe this book was a good one to read after all, Della Boyd decided, if it would remind her to put things in perspective.

Hardy paused from his reading and reached over to pat her hand. "Hey, it's okay, Auntie Deeb. All this happened a long time ago, see." By way of illustration he jumped up and dashed across the kitchen to Catherine's wall calendar of Ansel Adams photographs over by the telephone.

"See, this is now," he said, jabbing a finger at the days of February underneath the picture of a crescent moon suspended over a gorge. "And you're here in Berea, see, and . . ."

"But you can lose it all so fast!" Della Boyd cried out. "Things were going along so well for Anne, and then all of a sudden her world was shattered. One minute you have it, and the next minute you don't!" She made a choking sound that could have been either laughter or tears, and there was a moment of empty silence. Then to her utter surprise—and most certainly to Olivia's and Hardy's, for she saw them look at each other almost stupefied—she started laughing.

Hardy looked at Della Boyd, then at the book he had left on the table. Slowly he reached inside his overall pocket and pulled out the scroll of notebook paper and unrolled it. "A great confluence of ideas is taking place here in this room," he said in a serious voice. "It's cool and creepy at the same time."

Della Boyd had no idea what he was talking about. By now her laughter had subsided, and she fanned herself lightly with one hand. "Oh my, now aren't I a basket case, as your mother would say?" She shook her head a little as if to unmuddle it and smiled brightly at Hardy and Olivia. "Well! There now, I got that all out of my system." She pushed her chair back to get up. "I need to go take a bath, so if you children will excuse me, I'll just—"

Hardy rushed back to the table. "Hold on!" he said, jumping a good two feet straight up in the air and twirling around as he did so. He swirled his hands above his head comically and landed with his feet splayed, flapping the piece of paper and holding it out toward Della Boyd. It still curled up slightly. Della Boyd laughed and clapped one hand to her mouth. One of the many things she liked about Hardy was that he was so nimble and uninhibited and so *acrobatic*!

"Ah say, wait just one minute!" he continued, lowering his voice and shifting into a Texan cowboy drawl. "Ah came downstairs to show you something, ma'am, and Ah mean to show it to you. You're not gettin' outa Dodge City without seein' it, and soon as ya see it, you're gonna say"—he changed his voice to a high-pitched imitation of Della Boyd—" 'Why, Hardy, I think that's the best thing I've ever seen in the whole—' " He broke off and screwed up his face. Reverting to his regular voice, he said, "How old are you now anyway, Auntie Deeb, is it seventy-five or eighty?" And then it was back to his Della Boyd imitation. " 'Well, anyway, it's the sweetest picture I've seen in the whole however-many years I've lived!' " At the end he flapped his wrist like a girl. Della Boyd shook her head in amazement. That Hardy! Nobody else could talk in three different voices in such close succession.

"Oh, Hardy, I don't talk like that, and you know it," she said, laughing. "And you also know good and well I'm not anywhere close to seventy yet." She took the piece of notebook paper and looked at it. It was a pencil drawing of a broken statue toppled over in the middle of what appeared to be a desert. Della Boyd had seen Hardy's artwork before. He favored cartoon drawings and was really quite good at them—little people with oversized heads and grotesque features. He drew them in little strips and wrote words coming out of their mouths, just like in the newspaper comics. Though Della Boyd didn't always catch the humor, she always exclaimed over the drawings with comments like "What a droll little fellow that one is!" or "My, look at her hairdo and the cunning little hairbow!" or "How do you think up these funny little folks, Hardy?"

But this picture was different in that it didn't appear to be a cartoon. Della Boyd cocked her head and held it out at arm's length. "Well, this looks like a . . . well, like a . . . it's a statue or something, isn't it?"

"Right!" said Hardy. "It's Ozymandias."

Olivia, still seated, reached over and pulled the paper down so she could see it. She made a face and shrugged. "Oh well, whatever," she said and took another drink of Coke. Then she started shuffling her papers around on the kitchen table and closing her books noisily.

Hardy tapped her on the shoulder. "Uh, excuse me, Olivia, soon-to-graduate-from-high-school sister of mine, aren't you taking *senior* English now, and doesn't that mean you already had *sophomore* English? And you're saying the name *Ozymandias* doesn't ring a bell?" Hardy said.

Olivia didn't look up. She snapped her three-ring binder shut and shrugged again. "Nope, I didn't hear anybody ring the bell. Was he selling something?"

Hardy cavorted around, clapping his hands above his head. "Yes! Liv tries to be funny," he said to Della Boyd. "Emphasis on the *tries*. She wants so much to be like me, but—" He broke off to shake his head. "But, well, at least she *tries*."

Della Boyd remembered a time when Hardy would have yanked a hair out of Olivia's head or squeezed the back of her neck or thumped her head as if shooting a marble when she made a wisecrack, but she hadn't seen him do that in a while.

He seemed ready to drop the matter now and turned back to the picture Della Boyd still held. "How about you, Auntie Deeb? Ever heard of this dude Ozymandias?"

"Ozymandias? Is that who this is?" She looked back at the picture.

"But he's all broken into pieces in this picture."

"Yeah, right, that's the whole point, see. He was this Egyptian guy—hey, Liv, listen up, you might learn something you can share with your cheerleader friends tomorrow at lunch—and he was, like, majorly stuck on himself. Ozymandias—that's his name, see. It's all in a poem by this dead Brit named Percy Shelley. This Ozymandias egomaniac has somebody carve this titanic statue of him—no I'm not talking about the movie here, Olivia. *Titanic* is just another word for gargantuan or colossal, or—here, I'll make it easier for you—*very, very big*, okay?"

He winked at Della Boyd and continued. "Anyway, he had these words carved on the pedestal, but see, I haven't gotten that part done yet. This is just a sketch of what I'm gonna do. See, we gotta do this project for English. Miss Eaves-the-dropper, she's big on projects. She's the *queen* of projects. Anyway, the point of it all is—and see, this is where it comes back to your Anne Frank thing and what you were saying a minute ago—this Ozymandias dude thinks everybody in the next ten thousand years is gonna be totally awed-out by this statue of him, but—"

"But he dies and nobody even remembers him," Della Boyd whispered. "He had it all one day, and the next day he lost it. One day he had fame, and the next day he didn't. One day he had money, and the next day he didn't. One day he had *life*, and the next day he didn't! It all just floated away . . . floated away like a bubble." And she let her eyes travel upward. For a moment all was quiet.

Then Hardy snapped his fingers. "Yep, you got it," he said. "Hey, that's an idea! I gotta write a paper for part of this project thing—maybe I could tie in Ozymandias with Anne Frank. I bet that'd make Miss Eaves-the-dropper split her spleen."

Della Boyd knew that Miss Eaves-the-dropper was really Miss Eaves. According to Hardy, Miss Eaves had a habit of dropping things—chalk, papers, her textbook, and what have you. One time one of her earrings had even dropped off in the middle of class, which Della Boyd thought was very funny.

Hardy never referred to his teachers by their real names at home. Mr. Mackey, his biology teacher, was "Holy Mackerel," and he always held his nose when he spoke of his government teacher, whose unfortunate name was Mrs. Gross, which he pronounced "Mrs. G-r-r-r-oss!" Miss Foster was "the Foster child." She wondered if he ever called them these things to their faces.

Olivia was over by the sink now, peeling a banana. "It'll be enough of a shock for her that you even *do* a project," she said.

Hardy ignored the remark. "Can I borrow your book, Auntie Deeb?" he asked. "Are you done with it?"

"Well, of course you may." Della Boyd handed his drawing back to him. "I just have one more thing to say, Hardy," she said very seriously.

"Yeah? What's that?"

Della Boyd fluttered one hand and spoke in a breathy, prissy voice. "That's the sweetest picture I've seen in the whole however-many years I've lived!"

Raising a thumb, Hardy grinned at her. "Oh, excellent, Auntie Deeb. Very, very excellent."

As she left the kitchen, Della Boyd couldn't help feeling a little bit proud of herself.

Further Clues

32

A week and a half later, Della Boyd and Catherine ran by Winn Dixie on a Saturday to buy a package of pork chops on their way back from the mall in Derby. For some reason she couldn't explain, Della Boyd had gotten it into her head to fix pork chops for supper that night, and she wouldn't hear any of Catherine's suggestions for alternatives, which were many.

"And not to mention we've got all that leftover stew we could heat up!" Catherine said, still trying to dissuade her even as the automatic door whooshed open. "And anyway, I don't even think Olivia's going to be home for supper tonight," she added, as if she had just thought of it, "and Philip might be spending the night with Andy again."

"Oh no. I think it's the other way around," said Della Boyd pleasantly. "I think Andy is spending the night with Philip. I heard them talking about it this morning. And Olivia isn't leaving tonight until seven." Della Boyd led the way toward the back of the store to the meat counter. Behind her Catherine was saying something she didn't quite catch, although she did hear the phrase "go to so much trouble all the time." This was one of Catherine's favorite themes, one that Della Boyd had learned to tune out. She was remembering how much she liked pork chops, especially simmered with gravy, brown rice, and mushrooms the way she used to do it in Yazoo City. She couldn't figure out why she hadn't fixed them during the whole six months she had been at Blake's. It was funny how things just slipped out of your mind that way for long periods of time.

Besides the pork chops, another happy thought was on Della Boyd's mind. She was feeling especially optimistic today, for she had just talked to Helena Ludwig last night and had received encouraging news about the purchase of their new house in Yazoo City. Helena was in Yazoo City this weekend, and a date for the closing on the house had been arranged for the middle of March. The present owners would be moving out by the last day of March, and Helena and Della Boyd could move in on the first day of April.

Arriving at the meat section, Della Boyd stopped to look at the ground chuck that was on sale. She picked up a package that looked just the right size for six people. It would be good for Spanish rice or skillet macaroni hash or spaghetti some night.

"Now don't get sidetracked, Della Boyd," Catherine said. "All we came in for was pork chops, remember—and we don't even *need* those." She sighed deeply and spoke again, as if to herself, although Della Boyd knew it was largely for her benefit. "There's that whole two gallons of chili in the freezer we could have tonight, too, but will she use something we have on hand? Oh *no*, it's *got* to be pork chops, she says. And we've got to traipse into the grocery store for that one item on a Saturday, the worst day of the week to go to the grocery store. Personally, *I'd* rather have the chili, but who cares what *I* want? She's got her mind made up. No sir, anybody who wants chili tonight is just out of luck."

"It'll keep," Della Boyd said amiably. "We'll be glad enough to have that on hand one of these nights." She remembered the day she had made the chili—it must have been close to two months ago now. It had been so cozy puttering around in the kitchen that day. That was the day she had gone on her first walk with Barb, she recalled. She must have gotten a little carried away with the chili because she ended up with an enormous potful that could have fed a family four times the size of theirs. Catherine had lifted the lid after supper to see what was left, even after both Blake and Hardy had eaten three huge helpings, and had said, "Good grief, Della Boyd, did you think the entire Holy Roman Empire was coming to supper?" They had already had it again for a Saturday lunch, and there was still enough left for another meal.

Della Boyd picked up a large package of pork chops from the meat case. "These look about right, don't you think?" she said. "Let's see, that would probably be about enough for two each and a couple left over."

"Well, I'd rather not have *any* left over," Catherine said. "We've got enough leftover stuff in the freezer to feed us till next winter. If the country goes into a depression, we're all set!"

Della Boyd counted the pork chops in the package. "And if Andy eats supper with us," she said slowly, "it would probably come out even." A man wearing a white apron came out from the back whistling and carrying a tray of packaged chicken breasts. "I'd hate to run short," Della Boyd said. "Maybe I should get this one other small package just to make sure." She picked up another package and smiled over at the man, who had set his tray down and was now arranging the chicken in neat rows. "Pork chops always keep their flavor so well when they're reheated," Della Boyd said to him, raising her voice a little. "They're one of the *best* meats to keep their flavor, I think."

He nodded politely. "Yes, ma'am, they are."

Catherine looked at her watch. "Well, we don't need to conduct a survey about it. Let's just get whatever we need and go. I've got things to do!" She took the smaller package out of Della Boyd's hands and tossed it back into the meat case. "We won't need those. Trust me."

When they got to the express checkout line, Catherine started digging in her purse for her billfold. "No, no, no, you don't," said Della Boyd. "I'm buying these. It was my idea to have them, and I'm buying them. Put your money away." If there was anything Della Boyd was careful about, it was not taking advantage. She had insisted all along on paying for part of the groceries and in fact sometimes did a week's shopping all by herself and paid the whole bill. During her first couple of months here, she had heard more than one argument between Blake and Catherine through the closet wall about this very thing.

"I'm not going to have a guest in my home buying the groceries!" Blake would say, and Catherine would shoot back with something like "A *guest* doesn't stay for weeks on end! Let her contribute something if she wants to, for pete's sake!" To which Blake would reply, "As if she doesn't already contribute with all she does around here," and Catherine would answer with "And every bit of it is her idea! Nobody's putting a gun to her head, Blake. Nobody's forcing her to stay. Nobody even *asked* her to!" And so forth and so on. Thank goodness those arguments had subsided.

And the funny part was that now it was Catherine who was the most outspoken against Della Boyd's moving back to Yazoo City. "It's silly when you're all settled in here!" she kept saying. "Besides, you don't even really *know* this Helena Ludwig woman!" She had reminded Della Boyd many times that she had the hall bathroom all to herself now that Blake had finished replacing the tile in Hardy's old bathroom downstairs. One day recently she had even hinted that she was going to miss Della Boyd. "You're going to miss having five appreciative people to cook for" was what Catherine had actually said, but it was obvious that what she really meant was that *she* was going to miss Della Boyd's cooking. And, of course, by extension that meant she was going to miss Della Boyd herself.

Hardy was still complaining that if she moved back to Mississippi, she was going to miss most of his soccer season, which started in two weeks. And Olivia had been reminding her that she just *had* to stay and see her through the test for her driver's license. Now that Della Boyd had started taking her out in Blake's Lexus on weekends for driving lessons, Olivia was planning to have her license before she graduated in May. "You're the only one who's got any patience with me," Olivia kept saying. "I'm just starting to get the hang of parallel parking—you can't leave!" Philip's arguments usually concerned food. "You gotta stay and make your macaroni and cheese," he would say, or "Who's gonna make those oatmeal-raisin thingies for me if you go?"

Della Boyd had sympathized with Catherine from the outset. She knew it wouldn't be the easiest thing in the world to have somebody move in with you. Even though her sister-in-law had a sharp tongue at times, Blake hadn't exactly been a paragon of virtue himself. Della Boyd had heard him say some awfully hard things the first several months she had lived at his house—as if the children's problems were all Catherine's fault! Blake should have expected disagreeable consequences to his being away from home so much. Catherine couldn't be both mother and father, and Della Boyd had suggested as much to him. Of course Catherine had told him the same thing, but he seemed to take it better from Della Boyd. At least he hadn't snapped back and hurled accusations at her the way he used to do with Catherine.

Della Boyd had tried all along to put herself in Catherine's place and help out as much as she could. She loved to cook, so that was something she could do. She ironed and starched all of Blake's dress shirts, which saved on the laundry bill, and she pitched in with the housework right alongside Sparkle Flynn every Friday. In fact, some Fridays Sparkle didn't even need to come because Della Boyd had gotten everything caught up during the week. That's the way she used to do her own housecleaning in Yazoo City—one job a day instead of the whole thing at one time. That's the way she intended to keep her new house in Yazoo City, too. Since Helena planned to get her old job back at the city courthouse, Della Boyd would do most of the housework, which suited her fine.

Catherine was busy checking the bills in her billfold now, making sure all the twenties were together and the tens and so forth. She looked relieved that she didn't have to spend any of them on the pork chops. "Well, this whole pork chop thing is *totally* unnecessary," she said to Della Boyd, "but I'm just going to drop it. If you want to spend your money on something we don't need, I guess that's your business. I'm not going to say another word." She paused a moment, then continued. "It sure would be a whole lot easier, though, to just do the stew or the chili."

She looked at her watch again. "Or plain old soup and sandwiches— that's always a good, quick meal for a Saturday night." She craned her neck to see what the holdup was at the front of the line. "But I'm washing my hands of the whole business. If you want to waste your money, I'm not going to say a word."

Della Boyd smiled. "Oh no, it's never a waste to fix pork chops the way I'm going to fix them. You wait and see."

The woman directly in front of them had several items in her basket, and Catherine looked impatiently at the other check-out lines. "This express line always goes twice as slow as the other lines!" she said quite loudly. "On Saturdays they should have two express lines open." She gave a scornful laugh. "There must be another definition of the word *express* that I'm not familiar with. It sure doesn't mean *fast* around here!" The woman with the basket sneaked a quick glance at Catherine, then turned back around.

Apparently the man at the front of the express line had waited till the cashier had rung everything up, then had produced his checkbook. As the cashier pointed to the prominently displayed Cash Only sign, the man slapped at his pockets and shook his head fretfully. "I don't have a red cent on me," he said. He was a disheveled-looking middle-aged man in a wrinkled raincoat. He had a bushy mustache and wild tufts of frizzled dark hair springing from behind his ears. Poor man, Della Boyd thought, it wasn't hard to imagine somebody like that going through life failing to follow directions. Being unprepared probably wasn't a bad dream for him—it was probably an everyday occurrence!

"Wouldn't you know it?" Catherine said, pushing out her jaw and blowing a big breath upward. Her bangs flared away from her forehead. "Now they'll have to go find the manager, who's probably hidden away somewhere in the back talking long distance on the telephone, and they'll have to drag him out here to approve the check, and then Mr. Inept up there will discover he doesn't have any ID on him, so then he'll have to switch to his charge card, which probably expired two months ago, and then . . ."

But the manager had already shown up and was initialing the man's check while the man continued to offer profuse, rambling apologies to nobody in particular. "I didn't know . . . sorry, I didn't even notice. Well, that's the story of my life, so I guess . . ." He even turned at one point and waved his hand at the people in line behind him. "Sorry, folks," he said, shrugging, "it's my fault. I just wasn't . . . sure am sorry for the delay. . . ." Della Boyd waved back and smiled. Anybody could see the man could use a little friendly moral support.

Finally the woman in front of them inched forward and started removing her items from the basket and placing them on the moving belt. Della Boyd hoped for the woman's sake that she didn't have more than the maximum of ten items, or she might hear about it from Catherine. Sometimes Della Boyd found it hard not to be embarrassed in Catherine's company. She could be so *bold* in speaking her mind—almost rude! Of course, a lot of times she admired Catherine's boldness and even wished she could snitch a little of it for herself.

From the little bit Catherine had told Della Boyd about her childhood in Biloxi, it was easy to see how she'd acquired her boldness. Having been left to herself a good bit of the time and never feeling wanted or loved, Catherine had summed up her childhood bluntly. "So I had to learn to look after myself, since I knew nobody else was going to!" Della Boyd couldn't imagine having a mother who told you openly that you were more trouble than you were worth. If *she* had had a pretty little red-haired daughter like Catherine, she would have smothered her with love.

Della Boyd held her breath as the woman in front of them lifted out item number ten from her basket—a six-pack of Diet Sprite—and then reached back inside and pulled out a single bar of Dove soap and set it down with her other ten items. Della Boyd glanced at Catherine and knew the fact had not escaped her, that she was right now opening her mouth as if ready to say something about people who had trouble with simple mathematical functions like counting.

Della Boyd quickly tapped the woman on the shoulder. "I use Dove soap, too, and I just love it!" she said a little louder than she had intended. "It doesn't dry out your skin like a lot of soaps. Irish Spring and Coast, for instance—I feel *itchy* all over when I bathe with those, although I do like the way they both smell!" The woman was staring at her with her mouth slightly open.

"Dial is a good basic soap, and Zest is nice because it doesn't leave a bathtub ring," Della Boyd continued, "but it's not as creamy as Dove. Caress is fine, too, but I've always used Dove, so I guess that's why I like it best. I always find myself gravitating to things that are *familiar*. Do you do that, too?" She gave a chirping little laugh. She could tell from the look on the woman's face that she must be thinking, "This poor soul must be on drugs." But at least, Della Boyd congratulated herself, she had apparently succeeded in diverting Catherine's attention from the woman's violation of the ten-item limit.

"This person probably isn't terribly interested in your soap preferences, Della Boyd," Catherine said. "She's probably wanting to get out her *money* so she can be ready to pay when the girl finishes ringing her up, which she's doing right now."

"Well, by all means, you just go right ahead," Della Boyd said to the woman, who had now shifted her gaze to Catherine. "I didn't mean to hold you up. We wouldn't want this express line to come to a dead stop, would we?"

"You mean *another* dead stop," Catherine said. "The check writer already managed to do that, remember."

"I think I know who you are," the woman said slowly, addressing Catherine. "I thought I had heard your voice before, and I just now figured it out. You probably don't remember it, but I'm pretty sure we talked on the telephone once."

"Eleven sixty-eight," the cashier said, and the woman turned around and extended a crisp twenty-dollar bill, which she already had in her hand.

Della Boyd saw Catherine quickly size the woman up, from the fur collar on her leather jacket, which looked like real fur and real leather, to the suede flats just visible beneath the cuffs of her tweed slacks. Knowing Catherine as she did, Della Boyd could guess what she was probably thinking—that as long as this woman already seemed acquainted with her, she'd better put forth her best foot and be halfway cordial. After all, an attractive woman like this might be a good contact for some future social event or committee effort. Maybe she was somebody Catherine had phoned about one of her library projects. Maybe she had had something to do with the Tour of Homes back in December or the Used Book Sale in January.

As the cashier counted out her change, the woman looked back at Catherine again. "I teach at Berea High," she said by way of explanation. "I called you one time several months ago."

Catherine appeared to be dredging up a memory—not an altogether happy one either, for she was frowning.

"Math," the woman said. "Or more specifically in the case of your son, algebra. I have Hardy in my algebra class."

A mathematics teacher! Della Boyd thought. How mortifying that would have been if Catherine had said something insulting to her about not being able to count!

"Ruth Hadaway," the woman said as the cashier quickly bagged her items. She tucked her change in her jacket pocket and extended a hand to Catherine. "I did guess right, didn't I? You *are* Hardy Biddle's mother, aren't you?" She offered the faintest of smiles as Catherine took her hand.

"Yes," Catherine said, lifting her chin. "I'm Catherine Biddle." It was clear to Della Boyd that Catherine was waiting for further clues from Ruth Hadaway, who hadn't made it perfectly clear yet which way she was headed, whether friendly or hostile.

Della Boyd remembered the phone call now. It had been months ago and had concerned something about Hardy's class behavior, something not very complimentary. She remembered that Catherine had crashed about in the kitchen afterward, slamming cupboard doors and talking to herself about teachers in general and algebra teachers in particular.

Although Catherine had acted as if the whole thing were the teacher's fault at the time, she had done a complete turnaround at the supper table that night when she had brought up the matter to Hardy in front of everyone else. Della Boyd recalled her saying something about how humiliating it was to find out that her sixteen-year-old was "acting like a first grader" at school.

But Hardy had taken issue, acting offended by the comparison, slamming his fist on the table and saying no, first graders would never ever think up the stuff he did, that he was far, far more creative than a first grader, that they couldn't begin to compete with his level of skill in what he called "Classroom Diversionary Tactics."

Blake had jumped into the conversation at that point, and things had quickly gotten ugly. Della Boyd didn't like to think about all the times things had gotten ugly between Blake and Hardy during those days. It wasn't happening anymore, thank goodness—at least it hadn't for a couple of months now—but she still found herself holding her breath sometimes when the two of them were in the room together. They both had such definite opinions!

The fact that Blake and Hardy were now living peaceably under the same roof was, in Della Boyd's mind, almost the strongest proof of all that there was something to this "religious conversion" they claimed to have undergone. But to be a convert, one had to first be a *sinner*, she reminded herself. She felt a shiver go over her.

". . . at my wit's end with that boy," Ruth Hadaway was saying to Catherine. She took her two bags from the cashier and moved aside. Catherine stepped out of line, and the two of them stood beside a revolving rack of videos. "It was the most amazing thing I ever saw," Mrs. Hadaway said. "I kept meaning to call you back." It came to Della Boyd suddenly that this must be the teacher Hardy referred to as "That-away," always hooking his thumb sideways when he said her name.

"Uh, excuse me, ma'am, may I ring you up?" the cashier said, and Della Boyd realized she was still holding onto her package of pork chops.

She stepped forward quickly and set the package down. There were three other people behind her in line now, she noticed. She hoped they had more patience than Catherine.

"It couldn't have been more than two or three weeks after I talked to you," Mrs. Hadaway continued, "that Hardy came to school one day and was just . . . totally reformed. That's the only way to put it." She shook her head briskly to one side, just once, to move her dark brown hair away from her eyes. "Of course, what am I telling you for? You have to know this already. But . . ." Mrs. Hadaway seemed to be reaching for a way to say it. "But what exactly did you *do*? I mean, I know he says he's been 'born again' and all that, but . . . how did you get him to that point? I look at him now and can hardly believe he's the same kid I used to want to choke every single day he walked into class." She paused a moment and repeated, "How did you do it?"

They were standing beside Della Boyd now as she counted out the exact change into the cashier's palm, so she couldn't see Catherine's face when she answered rather breezily, "Oh, well, my husband and I just sort of . . . well, we knew *something* had to be done, of course, and so we laid down some new rules, and told Hardy that was just the way it was going to be, and well, one thing led to another, I guess!" Della Boyd smiled a little. She couldn't forget how Catherine had fought tooth and nail against some of those new rules Blake had laid down. "So many parents are afraid to be firm with their kids," Catherine added.

"Well," Mrs. Hadaway said, "he's as much of a joy to teach now as he used to be a . . . well, excuse my lack of tact, but a *pain*." She laughed apologetically. "And it's not just my class," she hastened on. "I hear it from all the other teachers. In fact, Karen Eaves was telling me about Hardy's English project just yesterday. She said it was pretty amazing—he wrote a paper and did some kind of elaborate art collage to go with it. Did you see it before he turned it in?"

Della Boyd wheeled around. "Oh yes! It was a splendid piece of work!"

"Yes, we *all* saw it," Catherine said. "That's about all we heard about for the past couple of weeks. I told him the silly thing was turning into a monster! I was sure glad it was due yesterday so he could take it to school and give us some peace and quiet at home."

Mrs. Hadaway looked at Catherine almost sternly. Della Boyd knew she must think Hardy didn't have a very cheerful and *encouraging* mother, but she just didn't know how Catherine was. So much of it was only talk. She didn't know that Catherine had been the one to suggest the idea of a collage instead of the single picture of the ruined statue and that she had recited a whole passage of *Macbeth* at the supper table one night when Hardy asked about famous plays that talked about the "transitory nature of life."

That was the topic of his project: "Art and the Transitory." He had come up with it on his own. All he had been required to do was write a short paper about a single poem, but he had decided to expand his paper. His thesis had been that the temporary nature of life on earth was a theme running through great works in all fields of art. Della Boyd couldn't imagine a boy Hardy's age thinking that up all by himself! And then the collage he had put together with pictorial references to all the works he had discussed in the paper—well, nobody could deny that Hardy was a very, very bright and creative boy.

Mrs. Hadaway had no way of knowing that after they had discussed Ozymandias another night at supper, Catherine had read another poem, this one by Gerard Manley Hopkins, a poem called "Spring and Fall" that Margaret Tuttle had discussed during the February meeting of the Women Well Versed. Mrs. Hadaway didn't know how beautifully Catherine had read the poem and how clearly she had explained to them all that it was more than just the falling of the leaves that was being mourned by the young child—it was mortality itself.

Mrs. Hadaway didn't know Catherine was the one who had told Hardy that it wasn't just writers and painters who dealt with the temporal aspect of life, but that she was pretty sure musicians did it also. She had urged him to ask one of the music teachers at Berea High about this, which Hardy had done. And so the project had grown to include music. After that they had heard works like *A German Requiem* by Brahms and *Death and Transfiguration* by Strauss playing on Hardy's CD player day and night.

No, Mrs. Hadaway didn't know that Catherine had actually *loved* the monster that Hardy's project had grown into. Why, she had petted and fed that monster! Of course, he had added a part to the end of his paper that Catherine had tried to discourage. "It's not scholarly to get off on a personal opinion like that," she had told Hardy.

"It's not opinion—it's fact," Hardy had said. "It's a very logical conclusion. Artists can mourn mortality all they want, but they've missed the boat if they stop there. The best artist in any field will use his thoughts on mortality to look for something more." He had jabbed a finger at the last page of his paper. "I wouldn't be telling the whole truth if I didn't add this part, see. All this other stuff leads intelligent people to a consideration of eternal life." Della Boyd marveled at the way Hardy could shift into such a *bookish* way of talking sometimes!

"Ma'am, your pork chops are right over here when you're ready for them," the cashier called to Della Boyd. "I put the receipt in the bag."

They walked with Ruth Hadaway out to the parking lot. "Keep up your good work with Hardy at home" was the last thing she said to them before she got into her maroon station wagon and drove away. Della Boyd wondered if she had children of her own or if she taught school to fill a void at home. She had seen right off that Mrs. Hadaway wore a wide gold wedding band. She wondered what kind of house she lived in and if she planted flowers in her yard. She wondered what kind of man Mr. Hadaway was.

"She sure is an attractive woman," Della Boyd said to Catherine as they got into Catherine's Park Avenue. "And very self-confident, too," she added. And as they pulled out onto the main road, she said, "And she seems to like Hardy a lot, so that makes her very intelligent also."

"Well, she's a cut above the average teacher, that's for sure," Catherine said. She was smiling, Della Boyd noticed, and she even started humming a little tune as they drove along, which was something that Catherine rarely did.

A Cold, Dark Feeling

33

Two weeks later on a Sunday night, Della Boyd crept into Olivia's bedroom. It was actually Monday morning, not Sunday night. Olivia's digital clock read 3:52 A.M. Tomorrow, or rather *today*, Della Boyd would be leaving for Yazoo City to sign the house papers with Helena Ludwig in the lawyer's office, but that wasn't the reason she couldn't sleep. Something else was on her mind right now. In fact, she was still so full of dismay she wondered if she would even be able to make the trip to Yazoo City. She already had her suitcase packed—really, it was a suitcase she was borrowing from Catherine because she didn't have luggage of her own—and her plane ticket was in her pocketbook, but she couldn't actually picture herself getting on the airplane and leaving. Not after what had happened to Olivia two nights ago.

There was a ladder-back chair against the wall near Olivia's bed, but it was piled with school books and articles of clothing. Quietly Della Boyd cleared it off, setting the books on the floor in a neat stack and tiptoeing to the closet to find hangers for the clothes. As she folded a pair of jeans, the thought suddenly seized her that these could have been the same jeans Olivia had been wearing two nights ago when *it* had happened.

For the hundredth time Della Boyd asked herself the same question. *Why didn't I ever think about the possibility of Olivia getting hurt?* She had reprimanded herself over and over for not warding it off somehow. Even if you couldn't make yourself dream something in your sleep, you could dwell on it enough during your waking hours that it accomplished the same purpose. She knew this to be true, for it had worked any number of times in her own life.

Take the tumors, for instance. Della Boyd had spent so much time worrying about tumors that she had never had one. She hadn't thought about them as much since she had been living at Blake's, but there had been a time back in Yazoo City when a large portion of every day was taken up with imagining she had tumors. Not just one, but several—and in different parts of her body. That they were growing slowly was obvious, but she was also certain that they were severely malignant. She had never told a soul, of course, and the idea of going to a doctor for a physical checkup to confirm her fears filled her with as much dread as the thought of the tumors themselves.

Blake had finally forced her to go to a doctor over in Derby back before Christmas, though, and Catherine had driven her to the appointment. Della Boyd had been terribly scared about the whole thing. She tried to talk Blake out of making the appointment in the first place and then tried various excuses for canceling it, but nothing had worked.

At the scheduled time, she found herself sitting in the waiting room beside Catherine, who was blithely flipping through a magazine showing pictures of contemporary homes and luxuriant gardens. When the nurse called her name, she felt as if someone had suddenly cinched a rope around her neck. She could hardly breathe. When the nurse called her a second time, Catherine looked up from her magazine and said, "I'm pretty sure she means *you*, Della Boyd. I doubt if there's another Della Boyd Biddle in this room."

She remembered sitting in the examining room wearing a disposable paper gown and waiting for the doctor to come and tell her that the tumors were even more widespread and pernicious than she had suspected. By the time he arrived to examine her, she was taking short shallow breaths. She felt a little light-headed and couldn't even respond properly when the doctor greeted her and asked her how she was doing.

She could still see the look of surprise that came over his face when he laid his stethoscope against her chest and saw her flinch and heard her give a tiny, nervous gasp. He had lifted the stethoscope quickly and offered an apology. "Sorry, I forget these things can be awfully cold." He held the end between his palms for a moment and then slowly tried it again. This time she hadn't made a peep, although she had trembled visibly during the entire examination. The attending nurse had patted her knee at one point and smiled at her. "Just try to relax, Ms. Biddle. It'll be over before you know it."

When the doctor finally came back in after she got dressed and told her she looked "fit as a fiddle" to him, she felt her eyes welling up with tears. "What's the matter?" the doctor had said. He set his clipboard on the examination table and laid his hands on his knees, bending down to look into her eyes. "Did I say something wrong?" His eyes were a nice steady gray, and even though he was going bald, he was a handsome man. In many ways he reminded her of their neighbor across the street, Curtis Chewning, who was also a doctor.

Della Boyd tried to take deep breaths and compose herself. The doctor pulled a chair over and sat in front of her. He was a friend of Blake's, someone he used to play racquetball with, and she surely didn't want him telling Blake that his sister had had a nervous breakdown in his office.

She shook her head briskly and spoke clearly. "Oh no, nothing's wrong. I just feel . . . so relieved, that's all." She closed her eyes and concentrated on breathing in and out.

"Were you worried about something?" he asked. "Is there something you need to tell me? I only covered the routine things, but if there's something bothering you, I can sure check it out." His voice was very kind.

But she smiled and shook her head again. "No, really, I'm fine. I don't go to doctors very often, and I guess I had just gotten myself . . . well, all worked up. You know how easy it is to do that." She paused and laughed. "Well, maybe you don't know. I don't think most men have that problem." She remembered, though, that her own father had avoided doctors, and she had even heard Catherine remark that it would "take hell and high water to get Blake to break down and go to a doctor."

She didn't tell the doctor about the tumors, of course—or, rather, the fear of them. She left his office a few moments later, still feeling lightheaded, but in a different way now. She had lived with her worry for so many years that it had taken many days after seeing the doctor before she convinced herself she was tumor-free. And even then, she kept reminding herself, tumors started out so small that it would be hard for any doctor to detect them in their earliest stages, but at least this doctor hadn't seen any *signs* of any. Since that day, the thought of tumors had slipped from her mind for whole weeks at a time. Every now and then it would creep into her mind during an idle moment, but she would close her eyes and visualize the doctor's trustworthy face as he said, "Well, Miss Biddle, you look fit as a fiddle to me," and she would feel better at once.

She was so cheerful that day on the way home from the doctor's office that Catherine finally said, "What in the world's the matter with you?" at which Della Boyd laughed out loud because it was basically the same thing the doctor had asked her when he saw her crying not fifteen minutes earlier, though, of course, not in the same tone.

"Oh, nothing's wrong," she answered Catherine happily, which was also the same thing she had said to the doctor.

"Well, then, I wish you'd stop all that humming and fidgeting," Catherine said. "I'm having enough trouble concentrating on the traffic without you bouncing all over the place. I'm trying to *think*." That had been only a few weeks after Philip's fall down the stairs, and Catherine had appeared to be doing a lot of thinking during those days. She had been quiet for long stretches of time, Della Boyd recalled, and had stared at Philip and Hardy as if she couldn't get enough of them.

Hardy's drastic change had occurred sometime around then, too, she remembered, and that had set Catherine back even more. It was as if she were bracing herself for him to change back to his old ways at any minute. She watched him closely and somewhat suspiciously, Della Boyd thought. "I've been around the block a few times" was something Catherine said a lot during those days, along with "People don't just suddenly turn around a hundred and eighty degrees at the drop of a hat."

So all the rest of the way home that day Della Boyd tried to sit very still in the front seat of the car and not make a sound. When they finally turned onto Brookside and then pulled into the driveway at home, though, she was ready to burst. Catching sight of Barb kicking a ball with Sammy in the Chewnings' front yard, she had opened the car door and called out, "Yoo-hoo! Hello there, Barb. I just got a clean bill of health!"

Catherine rolled her eyes. "We could make copies of the doctor's report and put them in everybody's mailbox up and down the street," she said.

But Della Boyd threw her head back and laughed. "Oh, goodness me, I'd *never* do that!" And she waved at Barb and Sammy again, then went inside to start supper. She made Swiss steak that night with some top sirloin she had bought on sale.

In Della Boyd's opinion, thinking about the tumors so much had evidently kept her from getting them. It had worked with the bad dreams of showing up late and going out in public unclothed, too. And it had worked for lots of other things—car wrecks, for instance. She had worried all her life about having a car wreck, but she had never ever *had* one. When she was a little girl, she had been deathly afraid of snakes after a neighbor had been bitten by a water moccasin. But never once had a snake bitten her.

No, it was always the things she never thought to worry about that leapt out to assault her. Her father's plane crash, the baby dying while she rocked him, her house burning down—things like that. She had sat down one day after Baby Kenneth had died in her arms and after she had been transferred at her request to another floor at the hospital and had written a list of some of the horrible things that *could* happen to her. By so doing, she thought, she could prevent them from actually happening. She couldn't remember all the things on the list now, but she knew for a fact that none of them had come to pass. A heart attack—that was on the list, as well as being mugged and robbed of all her money, starving to death, losing her eyesight, drowning, being caught up in a tornado, and running over someone, especially a child, accidentally. Of course, she hadn't thought to include a house fire.

Philip's fall back in November should have taught her something. She should have taken precautions to protect him from further injury and to keep Hardy and Olivia safe, too. Youngsters were so prone to accidents and mishaps—she knew that, yet she had done nothing about it. If she had only *worried regularly* about their safety, then the terrible thing wouldn't have happened to Olivia.

She carried the chair to the side of Olivia's bed now and sat in it very gently, lest it should creak. The house was still, and Olivia's breathing was the only sound she could hear. The streetlight gave off a yellow glow so that Della Boyd could make out everything in Olivia's room quite plainly. Olivia was sleeping on her side, and her face was smashed so hard into the pillow that her mouth looked misshapen. Her long blond hair was spread out over the pillow like a fan, and even in the dimness, Della Boyd could see the bruise on her forehead where Olivia had fallen against the television in the den. Thank goodness it had only been a glancing blow, or she probably would have needed stitches, and that might have left a scar on her pretty face.

Della Boyd leaned forward and stared hard at Olivia. "You are a beautiful young lady," she whispered ever so softly, "and your auntie Della wants only the best for you." She started to touch Olivia's hand, which was curled up under her chin, but she decided not to at the last minute. She didn't want to wake her up. Heaven knows she needs her sleep after what she's been through, Della Boyd thought.

It had happened on Friday night. The way things had lined up was really odd—though Hardy called the way it turned out "God-ordained." This was just another example of how Hardy's whole vocabulary had changed over the past few months. Even though he had often spoken the name of God before that, it had never been very nice. He had certainly never put it together with a word like *ordained* to describe an outcome.

Everybody had plans to be away from home that Friday night. First, Blake and Catherine had gone to a retirement dinner for one of the men Blake worked for at Forrest Bonner. The man, Riley T. Bonner, was one of the original founders of the company and had been a senior partner for almost forty years. It was a catered, no-expenses-spared affair over in

Greenville, followed by an open-house reception at someone's home at which they were going to present Riley T. Bonner with a solid gold Rolex wristwatch and a Caribbean cruise. Blake had said they wouldn't be home until eleven-thirty or twelve that night.

Philip was spending the night with Andy Partridge down the street, but they wouldn't be back at his house until very late. Wilma Partridge was driving Andy and Philip to Charlotte for a Hornets game.

Hardy was going to something called a Reach-out with the Chewning twins, some kind of church activity down at the YMCA in Filbert. All the young people of the church invited their friends from school, and they played all sorts of games and then had pizza and a devotional time. He had said he'd probably be home around eleven.

So that left only Della Boyd at home that night, since Olivia was supposed to be going to a cheerleaders' party over at Kathleen Kane's house. Blake had quizzed Olivia pretty thoroughly on what they were going to do, who else was going to be there, and so forth. He had even called Kathleen's mother and talked to her, much to Olivia's embarrassment. "My word, you're treating me like I was eight years old!" she had protested. "Why can't you trust me?"

"Better safe than sorry," Blake replied evenly. "Don't take it so personally, Liv, I'm just looking out for you."

"You're *suffocating* me is what you're doing!" Olivia said. "I wish you'd just . . ." But she hadn't finished. One thing Della Boyd had noticed about Olivia—she knew when she could push her dad and when she couldn't. Lately she had found him pretty hard to budge, and she had started saving her breath. Evidently she didn't relish the idea of being grounded again. Olivia wasn't any dummy. She had begun to learn that she usually got further with Blake by acting compliant than by throwing a fit.

Olivia wasn't supposed to be seeing that boy Scotty Brooks anymore. Della Boyd knew that Blake had forbidden her to go out with him. But she also suspected that Olivia was seeing quite a lot of him on the sly. She had seen the look on Olivia's face sometimes when she jumped to answer the telephone and then listened intently for a few seconds before hanging up. "Stupid wrong number again," she would say, trying hard to look irritated. It seemed to Della Boyd also that Olivia stayed after school an awful lot for no good reason. And once when Olivia was pretending to do her homework at the kitchen table, Della Boyd had clearly seen *Dear Scotty* written at the top of the paper she was writing on.

Della Boyd fixed toasted ham and cheese sandwiches for supper that Friday night, but only for Olivia and herself since the others were eating elsewhere. In fact, both Hardy and Philip had already left by the time Della Boyd pulled the sandwiches out of the oven. Blake and Catherine were in their bedroom getting dressed up for their dinner party. Catherine was going to wear a pretty emerald green sheath dress with a string of real pearls. Della Boyd had pressed the dress for her that afternoon and fixed a little place where the hem had come unstitched.

Olivia kept glancing at the clock on the kitchen wall as she ate her sandwich. She was wearing a pair of denim jeans with a short-cropped black sweater that Della Boyd thought looked a little too snug. When the telephone rang, Olivia catapulted out of her chair and answered it, then handed it to Della Boyd with a sigh. "It's for you," she said.

Della Boyd rarely got phone calls unless they were from Helena Ludwig. They had been talking every few days lately, getting things settled about the purchase of the house. But it wasn't Helena this time. It was Eldeen Rafferty, one of the women in the poetry club. Della Boyd didn't quite know what to make of Eldeen, but she couldn't help appreciating her attempts to be friendly. At the last poetry meeting, Eldeen had latched on to Della Boyd as soon as she walked into Fern Tucker's living room and hadn't let go all evening. "Heavens to Betsy, that batty old Eldeen talked your ear off, didn't she?" Catherine had said on their way home, but Della Boyd had only smiled and said, "Yes, she's quite the conversationalist."

"Conversationalist, my hind foot!" Catherine had said. "A conversation usually takes two people. I think that woman could listen to herself talk all day. Why, she never gives the other person a chance to get in a word edgewise. I don't think she ever stops long enough to take a breath! She must have lungs the size of oil drums!"

Which really hadn't been the case at all. Eldeen *had* talked up a blue streak, as Catherine liked to say, but she had also asked Della Boyd a lot of questions and had listened closely to the answers. Della Boyd could still picture her, leaning forward with her bushy eyebrows drawn close together and studying Della Boyd almost hungrily, as if Della Boyd's words were food and she was starving.

So anyway, here Eldeen was calling her on the telephone right at suppertime on a Friday night. "And how's my sweet little friend Della Boyd tonight?" she asked after identifying herself. Della Boyd thought it was humorous that Eldeen called her "little" when she was actually taller than average, but then, compared to Eldeen, most other women *were* little.

"Why, I'm doing very well, thank you," said Della Boyd. "And how are you, Eldeen?"

"Oh, honey, I'm as well as can be expected for somebody my age," Eldeen replied, "and probably a whole lot better than lots of folks my age. Seems like I'm hearing about more and more sickness and disease every day. Just last week, in fact, a good friend of mine I used to be in a sewing circle with took sick and was gone within three days! Just like that! Pffft! Hadn't been having problems no more'n the usual aches and pains that comes with being past eighty, but there she was on her deathbed before she had time to blink her eyes good."

"I'm sure sorry to hear that," Della Boyd said. "I hope she didn't have to . . . well, didn't suffer much before she passed on." It always gave Della Boyd a cold, dark feeling to hear about cases like this. She hoped Eldeen wouldn't linger on this subject.

"Oh, but she did," Eldeen stated flatly. "She was in *excruciating* pain, and the doctors couldn't put their finger on it for the longest—and then it was too late, of course."

"Well, that's too bad," Della Boyd said. She laid her hand over her heart, which suddenly seemed to be beating faster than normal.

"And I didn't even catch the whole name of what it was she had," Eldeen said. "Something not many folks catches, I know that. Big old long name. And then, of course, with her being on up in the years, it made her whole system too weak to fight if off." She paused and then repeated, "And then it was too late."

"Well, yes," Della Boyd said.

"Charity Pretlove," Eldeen said. "That was her name, my friend who just took sick and died—Charity Pretlove. Isn't that a nice name? Did you happen to see it in the obituaries today? I always got such a kick out of her name. Fact is, I used to kid her and tell her she sure had the *loveliest* name I'd ever heard of!" As if uncertain that Della Boyd had caught her joke, Eldeen explained it. "Having 'charity' *and* 'love' both packed in her name, you see—now that sure makes a *lovely* name if I ever heard one." She laughed her unique laugh, which always reminded Della Boyd of a semi truck—a series of low hooty blasts—then she stopped abruptly and exclaimed, "My, the *quilts* that woman made!"

"Quilts?" Della Boyd said. She didn't know what it was, but she always felt as if she was barely hanging onto a conversation with Eldeen. New topics were introduced with lightning speed.

"Yes, ma'am, that was her specialty—quilts," Eldeen said. "In the sewing circle we was in, she'd always be working up quilt squares. The prettiest patterns you ever saw! She had this one I'll never forget called Prairie Flowers, I believe it was, and it was just full of the gayest, liveliest colors. And the funny thing was, every one of them little flower designs—

there must of been upwards of twenty different ones—was made out of little snippets shaped like triangles and squares. Nothing else. Just triangles and squares, that's all!"

"Is that so?" Della Boyd said. She became aware of Olivia motioning to her, so she covered the mouthpiece while Eldeen continued to talk and whispered, "What is it?"

"Somebody's supposed to call me," Olivia said. "How long are you going to talk?"

"Well, I don't know," Della Boyd said before realizing she had taken her hand away from the mouthpiece.

"Sure you do!" cried Eldeen. "You know how you can fit little triangles and squares together in all sorts of different ways to make different designs—just lay 'em out this way and that. Joe Leonard used to have this little game like that called something like Pano-grams or Fun-grams . . . oh, I can't remember it now, but it had 'grams' on the end, and anyways you could make pictures of people and animals and what have you out of nothing but squares and triangles."

Eldeen must have lifted the receiver from her ear, for her voice grew suddenly fainter, and Della Boyd heard her say, "What was the name of that game Joe Leonard used to have, Jewel? Where you put all them pictures together with little pieces of cardboard?" And then she was addressing Della Boyd again. "That's it! That's it! It was called *Tan-grams!* Well, I wasn't too far off in left field, was I? Anyway, that's what Charity Pretlove did, only she made all her pictures *flowers*. And she used cloth and thread instead of cardboard, of course, and appliquéd 'em onto the quilt. And they was all different colors, so it looked real busy and just *full* of life! But it made a real *clean* design, too, what with all them straight lines and shapes and all them gay colors on a white background."

"Olivia needs to use the telephone," Della Boyd said. She tried to say it politely. "I'm afraid I need to hang up."

"Well, then, let me quit my jabbering and state my business," Eldeen said cheerfully. Her business was actually an invitation to come over to her house that very night, along with Barb Chewning and a few other ladies in the poetry club, to make "something real, real special" for Margaret Tuttle. "To show her how thankful we all are for what she's been trying to teach us ever' month," Eldeen said. "She's sure had her work cut out!" she added. "Some of us old dogs don't take much to new tricks." She let loose another gust of laughter. Eldeen went on to tell Della Boyd that she had just talked with Barb Chewning, and she was coming, too, "So there's your ride right there at your doorstep! It couldn't be any handier than that."

"Well, now, I suppose I can do that," Della Boyd said slowly. "I was going to be the only one home tonight anyway."

"Oh, nobody likes to be rattling around in a house all by theirself!" Eldeen cried. "Come on over and join the party!" And so it was settled that Della Boyd would catch a ride with Barb over to Eldeen's. A scrapbook was the idea, Eldeen told her. "I've been askin' for copies of everybody's poems," Eldeen said, "and we're going to put 'em all in a fancy scrapbook Jewel bought at the Hallmark store. It says Treasures on the front of it in fancy gold letters and has the prettiest picture of a apple orchard on the front. Won't that be nice? Jewel had the cutest idea that we could paste little apples on all the pages where we'll put the poems, and then inside the cover we can write 'Apples for Our Teacher' in big curly letters. Harriet Murphy has a real good hand for writing things nice. She's coming over tonight, too. So you be sure and bring any of your poems you want to put in the book, all right? I don't think I've got any of yours yet. And Jewel's going to fix us some hot chocolate and gingersnaps. Matter of fact, she's over here makin' the gingersnaps right now. Oh, and I been meaning to ask you if you're still enjoying the little angel suncatcher I gave you a couple weeks ago at church."

"Oh yes, I am," Della Boyd said. "I surely, surely am. I stuck it on one of the windows in my bedroom, and in the late afternoon it gives out the prettiest colors!"

"I know! I know!" Eldeen cried. "I got a window full of 'em, and when the sun shines just right, our whole living room is just *spangled* with little rainbows!"

Finally Della Boyd had gotten away from Eldeen. She felt as if she had been pulling a heavy load over a great distance. She set the telephone down slowly on the kitchen table and picked up her sandwich. It wasn't very warm anymore and had grown a little limp sitting on her plate.

"So you're, like, going somewhere tonight?" Olivia asked her. She had already finished her sandwich and was pouring herself a second glass of ginger ale.

"Why, yes, I believe I am," Della Boyd said. "I need to call Barb and make sure I can ride with her, though."

Olivia drank some ginger ale, then took several grapes from the bowl on the table and popped them into her mouth. She labored a few moments at chewing them, then said casually, "You want to call her now?"

"Well, I hate to tie up the line again," Della Boyd said. "Your friend might be trying to call you."

"Oh, go ahead," Olivia said, which Della Boyd thought was mighty generous of her. "It won't take long just to ask for a ride, will it?"

After it was all arranged, Della Boyd took a few more bites of her sandwich before she decided she wasn't hungry anymore. She began taking the plates over to the sink. Olivia was standing at the counter now eating pretzels, the stick kind, snapping them off neatly as she ate them. "So what's the deal?" she asked Della Boyd. "You gonna be out all night like everybody else around here?"

"Oh no, not all night," Della Boyd shook her head. "Barb needs to be back home by ten, she said." Just then the telephone rang. "That must be the call you've been waiting for," she said as Olivia grabbed the phone. Della Boyd rinsed the plates and put them in the dishwasher.

"Yeah, right," she heard Olivia say. "Uh . . . yeah, okay. Well, no, let's make it ten minutes later. Yeah, well . . . oh, nothing. Maybe, well, never mind. I'll tell you later. Okay." And she hung up and headed downstairs to the bathroom she was using now.

Blake and Catherine came out to the kitchen only moments later ready to leave for their dinner. Della Boyd thought they looked absolutely stunning, and she said as much. "My, my. People won't be able to take their eyes off you two," she told them. She made Catherine turn around so she could admire her dress from the back, and she straightened Blake's black bow tie, which really didn't need straightening at all. Blake called downstairs for a quick, last-minute reminder to Olivia about when to be home, and then they left. Blake held the door open for Catherine, and as they went out, Della Boyd said, "You look like two celebrities!" If there was a nicer-looking couple, Della Boyd knew she had never seen them.

About fifteen minutes later Della Boyd went to Olivia's bedroom door and knocked. "I'm going now, Olivia honey. Is your ride going to be here soon? Will you be okay here all by yourself for a little while, or do you want me to ask Barb if we can wait until your ride comes?"

"No, Aunt Della, I'll be fine," Olivia answered. "You go on. I'll make sure the front door is locked like always when I leave. Don't worry about me."

And that had been how the stage was set for the horrible thing that had happened right here in this very house that night. Sitting by Olivia's bed in the glow of the streetlight now, Della Boyd reached out and touched Olivia's hair. There was no question that Olivia had been dishonest and sneaky that night, not to mention very, very foolish. Still, Della Boyd couldn't help feeling sorry for her—and loving her.

She stroked Olivia's hair softly and whispered, "I wish I could erase it all, honey." From far away she heard the sound of a train whistle. It was a lonesome sound. It made her think of how fast things could move in the dark and how hard it was to stop them.

May 26

DOTTIE

The Motions of Faith

34

Dottie Puckett raised the shade at the side door and flipped the sign from Closed to Open. She stood at the door for a moment with her hands on her hips, staring out across the driveway at the irises that were blooming under the beauty shop sign. Her eyes traveled upward to the lettering on the sign: *Dottie's Be-Beautiful Style Shoppe.* Sid had taken the hose just a week ago and sprayed the sign, then had gotten up on a stepladder and scrubbed it with a long-handled brush. From this angle she couldn't see the lettering all that clearly, but she knew it looked a lot better now that Sid had cleaned it all off. He had been right, of course—they hadn't needed a new sign at all. "I can get it looking like new," he had told her. "All it takes is a little elbow grease."

A thought had come to her one day recently. *I wonder how many times I've gone through this routine? How many times have I flipped this sign from Closed to Open? How many times have I heard the bell jingle when somebody walked into the shop for a style or a perm or a haircut?* After that her mind had kept wheeling around and around. *How many different ladies have sat in my black vinyl swivel chair? How many stories have I listened to from those ladies? How many gallons of shampoo have I used by now? How many little squares of tissue paper for perm rollers? If I had made a big pile somewhere of all the hair I've cut off, how high would it be?*

She had kept thinking along this vein for a while before the real question presented itself for her consideration: *Is what I'm doing really important in the kingdom of God, or am I just catering to women's vanity?* All this was a new way of thinking for Dottie. This same time a year ago thoughts like this had never crossed her mind. But then, a year ago seemed like another lifetime.

It was May now. She thought back to how happy she had been last May, how ignorant of what was lurking just around the corner waiting to knock the props out from under her. This time last year she had never once questioned the goodness of God. She'd always been the one to remind others of His goodness when hard times hit. Another thought came to her now as she stood gazing at the irises. *How many times did I quote "All things work together for good" to other people before I had my own collision with tragedy?*

And the worst part of it all was that she felt like such a hypocrite. If she heard one more person say, "My, you've been so strong through it all" or "Your faith is such a testimony" or "I don't know how you bear up with such a sweet spirit," she thought she'd go absolutely crazy. She was ashamed of how *weak* she had been through it all, how numb her spirit still felt almost a year later. And yet she had made people think she was a tower of Christian strength, just full of trust in God's wisdom and goodness. She had said the words she had heard all her life, she had kept right on going to church, and somehow she had even testified publicly of God's sustaining grace. But all the while she had felt an oppressive density inside, like a heavy blanket smothering the life out of her.

Sometimes when she woke up in the morning, she entertained the thought of not getting up at all. She imagined she'd be perfectly content to just lie in bed and stare up at the white ceiling all day long, watching it grow brighter as the sun rose higher and then change again to pale gray when dusk began to settle. She could make a study of that ceiling, all the barely discernible bumps and pits and the cracks Sid had patched, and feel she'd done as worthwhile a day's work as cutting and styling people's hair.

Every time those words came to her mind—"All things work together for good to them that love God"—she pushed them away. She couldn't see anything good, not one single thing, that had come out of God's taking Bonita. But she knew things like this took time. That's what everybody said. She hadn't expected to be *happy* about Bonita's death, of course, but neither had she expected to still be feeling cold inside almost a whole year later. She kept praying for God to come back in and warm her up, but then she felt guilty for praying that because she knew God hadn't gone anywhere. She was the one who had moved.

Not even Sid knew the extent to which she had misled people. Once when she had tried to tell him of the great gulf between the way she acted and the way she really felt, he had taken her in his arms and said, "You just don't know your own strength, sugar. You've been the one who's pulled us all through this. Why, if it hadn't been for you . . ." But he hadn't been able to finish. Sid was such a tenderhearted man. He'd been so patient with her.

She turned away from the door now and walked to the counter beside the telephone where she kept her appointment book. Fridays were always busy, and today was going to be especially so. One of the high schools was having its graduation ceremony tonight, and she had several mothers coming in to get fixed up for the big night. Of course, that was going to make today even harder. If Bonita were still here, she would be graduating from high school this year. She had looked forward to her senior year so eagerly, and then she hadn't even gotten to start it.

Dottie wished she could skip her first appointment. She used to tell Sid that Wendy June Cato's mother must have been a prophetess for naming her Wendy, only she should have spelled it with an "i." And Sid had always agreed wholeheartedly. He'd been in the beauty shop enough times when Wendy June was there "talking the spots off a leopard," which was a popular saying in Sid's family. It wasn't just that Wendy June talked so much, though. Dottie had plenty of customers who talked a lot, but Wendy June was a gossip and a busybody.

Running her finger down the morning's schedule, Dottie stopped at the eleven o'clock line. Catherine Biddle. She had forgotten Catherine was coming in today. She was usually a Wednesday customer. Not too terribly long ago she would have dreaded this appointment also—not as much as Wendy June Cato's, of course. But she actually looked forward to seeing Catherine today. And later in the afternoon was somebody else who would make a bright spot in her day. Barb Chewning. Barb hadn't been in for a haircut since . . . well, Dottie thought it must have been sometime around Christmas, though she wouldn't be willing to stake anything on it.

Dottie used to have such a neat, unfailing sense of the year's progression. She had always envisioned the calendar year in her mind as a long, straight horizontal sidewalk divided into twelve sections, with trees on both sides. As the winter months of January and February gave way to spring, the trees along the sidewalk began to grow buds and then full crowns of leaves as May and June arrived. And all along the sidewalk in her mind, certain vignettes were staged among the trees. She could close her eyes and see as clear as day her son, Max, for instance, at the midway point of the sidewalk, playing Little League Baseball in early July in a field surrounded by green poplar trees, or Sid further along, fishing up at Lake Jocassee with the autumn golds and reds against the banks.

Her visual concept of time had exploded, however, last summer when Bonita had walked out to the mailbox and never come back. Dottie had lost track of enormous blocks of time after that, and she still found herself having to stop and think not only *What day is it?* but also *What season is it?* And the year, too—more than once she had forgotten that.

 She had been writing a check at the grocery store not too long ago and realized all of a sudden that she had no idea what date to write in. She had hesitated and looked out through the front windows, hoping for some clue from the trees or some kind of seasonal decoration. The cashier, a gray-haired grandmotherly type, had tactfully said, *"It's the twelfth, ma'am,"* and had laughed good-naturedly. *"The days sure do get away from us, don't they?"* She had picked up a paper towel and spray bottle and wiped down the black rubber belt as she waited for Dottie to finish up with her check.

 Dottie would never forget the look on the grocery clerk's face when she had asked her quietly, *"And could you please tell me what month it is?"*

 The woman's smile had vanished, and her eyes filled with sympathy. She stopped wiping, her paper towel poised midair. *"Oh, darling, it's March,"* she had said, as if realizing this wasn't just an ordinary slip of mind.

 Dottie looked down at the date on her appointment book now. May twenty-sixth. Bonita had died on July sixth. Dottie wondered how she could ever make it through the day when July sixth rolled around this year. Somehow she had made it through Mother's Day and her birthday earlier this month. Sid and Max had planted four new rosebushes for her and had taken her out to dinner and presented her with a pretty pair of jade earrings. Every time her mind tried to drift to last year's birthday, when Bonita had baked her a strawberry cake, she had forced herself to say something out loud, something completely off the subject of birthdays and cakes. She remembered how puzzled Max and Sid had looked in the restaurant when at one point she had suddenly said, *"Which uncle was it who owned the sawmill in West Virginia?"*

 But she knew July sixth would be even harder. She knew she would replay Bonita's accident over and over that day. Sid had already suggested taking a trip somewhere over July fourth, and Dottie was sure he must be trying to think of a way to take her mind off what happened last year. He had talked about the beach or the mountains or, more recently, both. "First off, we could go to the beach," he had said, "and then after a few days of sunnin' and swimmin', we could head on up to the mountains to cool off. What you say, sugar? Think you'd like that?" Max was all for it, of course.

 Dottie would smile and nod halfheartedly. She would do it for Sid and Max, but she didn't care one bit about it for herself. She couldn't imagine finding the least speck of pleasure in sitting on the beach. And wouldn't she be a pretty sight to behold in a bathing suit with her extra twenty pounds? This time last year, though, it was an extra fifty pounds. Somehow, without trying to, she had dropped thirty pounds since last July.

Just as she was forming a picture in her mind of the only time she and Sid had sunned themselves on the beach—on their honeymoon twenty-two years ago—and of the large beach umbrella scooting off across the sand in a sudden, powerful updraft, the bell on the doorknob jangled suddenly as Wendy June Cato swept into the beauty shop. She appeared to be right in the middle of a conversation, for the first thing she said was "And I'd like to know when she thinks I'm supposed to find time to do *that*!" This was the way it was with Wendy June. She just continued her conversations from the last person she was with, always assuming that the next person knew exactly where she had left off and where she was picking up.

Somehow Dottie managed to get Wendy June shampooed and over to the swivel chair before she had to utter a single intelligible word. Wendy June could keep up a steady flow of chatter, requiring only an occasional "uh-huh" or a nod or a murmur of disbelief to keep her going. If Dottie had been forced to tell the truth, she'd have to admit that she generally didn't hear half of what Wendy June said.

She heard her clearly today, however, as she was combing through her wet hair and Wendy June suddenly said pointedly, "I bet that girl's mother told you all about it, didn't she? Now, let's don't try to pretend she didn't. I know you fix her hair."

"Whose mother is that?" Dottie asked.

"Oh, let's don't act dumb now." Wendy June shook her finger at Dottie. "You know what girl—that Biddle girl, the one we were just talking about." Wendy June unfastened the Velcro strip at the neck of the plastic cape, then pressed it down again firmly. She then raised the plastic cape, flounced it a little, and spread it over her lap again. She had a habit of redoing everything Dottie did. Several times she had even stood right there in the beauty shop and recombed her hair after Dottie had finished styling it, saying something like "No, no. We don't have it quite right over here on this side, do we? There, that's much better."

"Oh, Catherine never said all that much about it," Dottie said now.

Wendy June grabbed the comb from Dottie and reparted her hair. "When are we going to learn that I part it farther over?" she said, handing the comb back. "Well, I can't say I blame her for not talking about it," she went on. "If my daughter went and got herself raped in her own house, I don't think I'd go around talking about it either!"

"Oh, it wasn't that," Dottie said. "It wasn't . . . rape." She could feel her face flush pink. There were some words it was hard to say out loud.

"Well, we all know it was the next thing to it!" Wendy June said. "Mimi heard all about it at school."

Dottie could just imagine Mimi Cato hearing all about it. Mimi was a chip off the old block, as the saying went. Dottie could see her trying to ferret out all the tidbits of the incident and making up the ones she didn't know for sure, then spreading it all around school as fact.

Actually, Catherine had shared part of the story with the ladies in the poetry club two months ago, right after it had happened, and Della Boyd had talked about it, also, when she had come in for a haircut and perm in April after she had returned from a quick trip to Yazoo City. That was shortly before she had moved back to Mississippi for good. So Dottie did know more than she was letting on, but she didn't feel she ought to talk about it with Wendy June.

"I heard that the girl's brother went crazy when he found out," Wendy June was saying now. "Mimi said"—Wendy June lowered her voice, although there was no one else in the shop to hear her—"that when Hardy Biddle found that Brooks boy in his house with his sister he threatened to get a knife and . . . well, you know, make sure that boy couldn't ever do that to another girl."

Dottie had heard that Scotty Brooks had sported two black eyes for a couple of weeks after the incident, but she hadn't heard about any threats like the one Wendy June was suggesting. She wouldn't put it past Hardy Biddle, though. She could imagine him having a very strong sense of justice when it came to things like that. And something inside her felt that he couldn't be much blamed for such a threat. After all, he was defending his sister. Even though she had "asked for it" in some people's opinion, she was nevertheless his sister.

"Did you want me to trim off about an inch?" Dottie asked.

"Must we ask that every time?" Wendy June said in a singsongy voice. "Yes, an inch is fine, just like always. Anyway, I guess Scotty Brooks learned a lesson or two—well, you'd *hope* he did. Mimi says he has a horrible reputation with the girls." Wendy June stuck one finger in the air and wagged it at Dottie. "You better watch that boy of yours. They can turn bad before you even notice it. I've always thanked my lucky stars I had only girls—although girls aren't any picnic either!"

According to what Della Boyd had told Dottie, *she* herself had been the one to discover Olivia and Scotty Brooks together in the den, not Hardy. The whole family had made plans to be away from home that night, including Olivia, but Olivia had apparently changed her plans when she found out the house would be empty. Instead of going to a party at somebody else's house, she had decided at the last minute to have her own party at home and invite Scotty as her only guest. What she hadn't counted on was Della Boyd coming home so early, although in the end she was mighty glad for it when things had gotten out of hand.

Della Boyd had gone with Barb Chewning over to Eldeen Rafferty's house for the evening. "But you see, Barb had to leave less than an hour after we got there," Della Boyd had told Dottie. "Curt got an emergency call he had to go tend to at the hospital, which meant nobody would be home to stay with little Sammy and Sarah, so he called Barb at Eldeen's and asked her to come home."

And since Della Boyd had ridden with Barb, she decided to leave also to save someone else the trouble of having to drive all the way to Berea to take her home. "That was the night we were putting together the collection of our poems for Margaret," Della Boyd had said. "But I really don't think our leaving made much difference. Eldeen had invited a few too many people over to work on it, bless her heart."

So the way Dottie understood it, Della Boyd had walked into the house through the front door about half past eight o'clock. The front door was unlocked, which she thought was strange since Olivia was supposed to have locked it when she left. Standing in the living room, Della Boyd had heard voices in the den. Tiptoeing into the hallway, she had heard Olivia saying, "Stop it, Scotty!" Then she started crying and trying to talk at the same time. "No, *don't*—I said no. I want you to stop!"

And a boy's voice had laughed and said, "Aw, be still. You know you want it. Why else did you ask me over? Now just quit—"

Olivia had screamed, *"No!"* and there was a sound like a slap.

"I was practically paralyzed with fear," Della Boyd had told Dottie, "but I knew I had to be strong to help Olivia."

And so from the hallway she had called out, "We're home, Olivia! And you better stop that right this minute, Scotty!" As she walked purposefully toward the den, she heard rustling and thumping, more sobbing and a low angry voice.

"If I hadn't come home when I did, there's no telling what would have taken place," Della Boyd had said. "The boy must have been drinking because he was acting . . . well, he wasn't acting *rational*." She had shaken her head and covered her eyes. "What I saw when I walked into the den was . . . was just awful! If I hadn't come home, I just shudder to think . . ."

"But you did come home," Dottie had told her, patting her hand. "The Lord worked it out so you came home in time to prevent anything from happening."

"Oh, but things did happen!" Della Boyd had said. "Olivia fell and hurt her head when he pushed her, and she was so scared she couldn't do anything but cry after he left. She wrapped herself up in a little ball and just trembled all over. She couldn't even sleep that first night from crying. Why, she was nothing but a jumble of nerves!"

Della Boyd had been a jumble of nerves herself in retelling it all to Dottie. "I called the YMCA to get Hardy," she said, "because I didn't even know where to call to get hold of Blake and Catherine. You see, they got all dressed up for a dinner party and . . . and, well, Scotty ran out of the house saying terrible things, and he fell down the front steps, but he got back up and left, and I don't even know where he went. There wasn't a car parked out front—unless somebody came and picked him up along the way. Or maybe his car was parked down the street where I didn't notice it."

Hardy had gotten a ride from the YMCA and come home right away when Della Boyd had called. He had talked with Olivia a few minutes and had left again, even though Della Boyd had begged him not to. "He looked so . . . well, he looked almost out of his mind, and he said he was going out to find him."

"Who? Scotty?" Dottie had asked.

Della Boyd had nodded. "I think he did find him, but I don't know exactly what happened. I just kept hoping he wouldn't do anything like . . . well, when Hardy loses his temper, he can get so, so . . . oh, he's an *awfully* strong boy, and he looked like he was ready to tear somebody from limb to limb. I just begged and begged him not to go, but his mind was set on it."

Dottie was almost completely finished trimming Wendy June's hair when she realized all of a sudden that Wendy June had paused for a split second as if waiting for her to say something. Dottie tried her old standby first, however. "Uh-huh," she said, nodding pleasantly.

"Well, *did* you?" Wendy June said.

"Did I what?"

Wendy June clicked her tongue in an exasperated way. "We must learn to listen better, mustn't we? I just went through this big, long thing about that Biddle girl and what happened on that trip the cheerleaders took to Myrtle Beach last month. She got all of them together in a huddle or something before the big final competition and actually *prayed* out loud before they did their final show—*prayed* right there in the gymnasium with all the judges and spectators and everybody watching! Mimi got it all from a girl in her French class whose best friend is a cheerleader— Roxanne Gower. Her father's a coach at the high school, and her mother's the one who does all that flower decorating for that shop over in Filbert, you know—the one next to the bakery. She did a wedding I went to—all in white, the whole thing, not a stitch of color except white. Well, there was some greenery, of course, but nothing else. Bland and boring, if you ask me. . . ."

Thankfully, Dottie got Wendy June under the hair dryer without having to answer her question, whatever it had been. She didn't know anything about Olivia Biddle and the cheerleaders' trip to Myrtle Beach anyway, so she doubted that she could have answered Wendy June even if she had wanted to. She did know one thing for sure—sometime in March, Olivia Biddle had started attending their church regularly, along with the rest of her family, and she had even sung with the youth choir on Easter Sunday morning. Dottie remembered the pain of listening to the youth choir that Sunday, knowing Bonita would have been singing in it if she hadn't gone out to the mailbox that day in July.

After Wendy June finally left the beauty shop, still talking even as she closed the door, Dottie breathed a sigh of relief. She knew, however, that she still had to make it through the next seven hours somehow. She knew she still had supper to cook and dishes to wash and then the long evening to fill up. She hadn't picked up her needlework in almost a year, and she hadn't read a single book since Bonita's death. She had read a few poems, but no books. She used to read constantly, but since the accident she couldn't seem to muster up the energy to turn the pages of a book.

Dottie never expected the day to turn out as it did. She never suspected after Wendy June pulled out of her driveway that a turning point of life was bearing down on her. She was prepared only to endure the day as she had endured every other day for the last ten and a half months.

It all started with Catherine Biddle's appointment at eleven. They made small talk during the shampooing and combing, but while Dottie was cutting her hair, Catherine said something that made Dottie stop and hold the scissors absolutely still while the words worked their way into her heart. What Catherine said wasn't really all that astounding in itself, but the ramifications almost took Dottie's breath away.

"You know it was you more than anybody else who made me want to become a Christian, don't you?" Catherine said, and when Dottie didn't answer for a few seconds—in fact didn't even *move* for a few seconds—Catherine looked up at her. "It's true," she said. "I couldn't get your words out of my mind. I'd hear your voice at the oddest times, even during all those years when I quit coming to you. I'd hear things you'd said, like 'God loves you' and 'God wants the best for His children' and 'God is so good' and on and on."

Still Dottie didn't say anything, although she did start cutting again, very slowly.

"And I'll never forget that first time I came back," Catherine went on. "I came partly because I wanted you to do my hair again and partly because I wanted to see if you were any different after losing your daughter. And you know what?"

"What?" Dottie said almost in a whisper. Her mind was spinning.

"I found out you were still the same. You still had a knack with hair, and you were still talking about God."

Dottie shut her eyes for a moment and shook her head. Oh, Catherine, if you only knew, she thought. If you only knew how far away from God I felt back then, how far away I felt from everything connected with life.

"All the way home that day I heard your voice," Catherine said. " 'Bonita's in heaven'—that's what you said that day, just as calm and peaceful as if you were saying she had run out to the grocery store or K Mart. To be honest, it made me mad. Yes, *mad*. I had wanted to see you different—blaming God or something, I guess. But there you were, just going about your business, accepting what God had brought your way. That's when I knew you had something I wanted, even though I wasn't about to admit it yet."

Dottie held a swatch of Catherine's hair straight out between two fingers and slowly, neatly snipped a half-inch off the end. "And God had to take me through some really close calls before I'd give in to Him," Catherine continued. "I thought Philip was going to die when he fell down the stairs back in November, and then I thought I'd lost Hardy for good when he disappeared. And during all that your voice wouldn't go away. 'God wants us to have joy in our hearts,' you'd say to me in the middle of the night, or 'God esteems us in our lowly estate.' I wanted like everything for you to be quiet, but you wouldn't! During that whole time with Philip and Hardy, I couldn't get my mind off you. I kept wondering how in the world you kept going when you lost Bonita. I knew your God had to be mighty big if He could see you through something like that."

Only the sounds of Dottie's scissors and the hair dryer were heard for a few moments. Then Catherine laughed suddenly. "Poor Blake. He was trying for all he was worth to make me see things God's way. He woke up to the truth a long time before I did! He told me later that Curt Chewning had advised him to *act* like he loved me even when he didn't feel it, and that's just what he did. Barb and Curt are big on that—do what you know is right even when you don't feel like it."

Dottie nodded. Yes, wasn't that what it came down to so often? She felt as if something inside was on the verge of slipping into place, something that had been loose for a long time.

Catherine laughed again. "I'd get so mad at Blake sometimes because he wouldn't blow up like he used to. I'd try to get him to argue, but he wouldn't! He'd just bite his tongue and turn the other way. And I'll tell you one thing you probably already know anyway. When somebody keeps on doing and saying nice things to you, it's pretty hard to keep acting ugly."

The bell on the door jangled again, and Sid Puckett poked his head in. "You got a break for lunch coming up sometime, sugar?" he said to Dottie.

"About thirty minutes," Dottie said, nodding toward the woman under the dryer. "I've got to comb out Pearl after I finish with Catherine."

Sid left, and it was quiet again for a minute. "There, I think that's just about got it," Dottie said, holding out strands of Catherine's hair on both sides of her head to check for evenness.

"The whole time I kept coming back to you to get my hair done, I'd watch you like a hawk," Catherine said. "I wanted like everything to see you falter or to hear you complain or do *something* to show that your religion wasn't real. But you never did. And every single time you'd say something that would stick with me. 'God has a plan we can't see'—that was it one time I remember, and I heard you saying that over and over for I don't know how many days after that."

Dottie had no recollection of even saying such a thing, although she did believe it—she really did. Something was struggling to take shape in her mind, something that would settle a question—a big one.

"Finally everything came together for me," Catherine said. "I couldn't resist anymore. When I wasn't hearing your voice, Hardy was working on me. He had a different technique, though. When Hardy goes after something, he doesn't beat around the bush. It's funny, though—it was your voice that was the loudest in my mind. And there was always Blake, of course, just trying so hard every single day, and then of course Barb Chewning would put in her two cents' worth, and finally I broke. I just broke down and gave in and said, 'Okay, God, you win.' "

Dottie bent down to trim along Catherine's neck. "I keep thinking about how God used all the different people in our lives," Catherine said. "It was Curt Chewning who had such an impact on Blake, and it was those goofy twins of theirs that kept after Hardy. And then it was Hardy of all people who got through to Della Boyd, and Barb Chewning who came over and talked with Olivia for so long after that thing with Scotty

Brooks happened. And Philip heard it from all sides, even from his friend Andy Partridge down the street."

She paused, took a deep breath, then added, "But it was *you* more than anybody who finally got through to me, and I just realized this morning on the way over here that I had never told you that. So I wanted . . . well, to thank you. You probably never even knew I was watching you so closely."

Dottie smiled and shook her head. "No," she said. "I haven't really been aware of a whole lot, but I sure appreciate what you've said, Catherine." She set her scissors down and picked up the blow dryer.

Is what I'm doing really important in the kingdom of God? There it was—that was the question that kept wanting to be asked again. How could Catherine have known, Dottie wondered, that it was a question that kept begging for an answer? And who would have ever guessed that Catherine Biddle would be the one to provide an answer for the question that had been preying on Dottie's mind lately?

Yes, Dottie said to herself as she aimed the blow dryer at Catherine's hair. *Yes, what I'm doing is important. Someday I'll stand beside this woman in heaven and know I had a part in it all.*

Something else was coming to her also. It was something Catherine had said about acting and believing. What was it? Dottie was thinking hard as she ran her fingers through Catherine's hair. It was drying fast. "Do what you know is right even when you don't feel like it"—that was it. Could that apply to me? she thought. She had been saying all the right things for the past ten months even though she hadn't really felt them, and that was why she felt like such a hypocrite. But maybe God understood that. Maybe He didn't expect a mother to accept the death of her child right off. Sometimes you had to act in spite of your emotions, not because of them. Wasn't that what she had been doing?

Dottie picked up the round curling brush and began to style Catherine's hair as she finished blowing it dry. This part wouldn't take long. She felt as if she needed to sort her thoughts out quickly, before she lost them. *"Do what you know is right even when you don't feel like it."* She knew there was a connection she needed to make.

And then it came to her. Maybe, she thought, the test of grief for a Christian was whether you stuck by what you knew was right even though you couldn't feel it in your heart yet. Maybe talking publicly about "God's will" and His "perfect plan" and the "assurance of His love" was okay even though your heart was aching so badly you hardly knew what you were saying. Maybe going through the motions of faith in a time of sorrow wasn't as bad as she had imagined. Maybe it was all right sometimes to *act* as if you believed even if you weren't sure you did.

The habit of trusting God—could there be such a thing? Could such a habit be a lifeline when tribulations swept over you? Could you hang on to it during the worst of the storm without seeing any evidence that it was real? And then when the strongest waves and winds of sorrow had passed, could you realize that what you had held in your hands all along was genuine, that it was your means of rescue?

Light moves faster than sound—she remembered that from school. When a man is hammering on a roof far away, you could see each hammerblow before you could hear its sound. Maybe the same thing applied to faith in some way. Faith moves faster than feeling—could you say that? No, that wasn't right. She was straining for a parallel. She had caught herself doing that more than once since she had started attending the poetry meetings.

No, it wasn't a matter of the speed of faith so much as its power and permanence. That was it—faith outlasted sorrow. Grief might knock you off your high wire, but faith was your safety net. Or was that treating faith too frivolously? She surely didn't want to be guilty of that. She suddenly felt very certain about one thing, though. She knew it wasn't a sin to grieve in private yet proclaim God's goodness in public. That didn't make you a hypocrite. Sometimes saying something over and over was what it took for the truth to sink in.

"Dottie, are you okay?" With a start she realized that Catherine had turned all the way around and was looking straight up at her, with a hand lifted to shield herself from the hot air of the blow-dryer. "You've been curling that same spot for the longest time. And you've been so *quiet*. Do you feel all right?"

Dottie smiled and lowered the blow-dryer. "Sorry, I was thinking about something." She nodded slowly. "Yes, I'm okay. I'm feeling . . . all right. You've been a real encouragement to me, Catherine."

Before Catherine left, she told Dottie that they were driving to Mississippi to visit Della Boyd in Yazoo City after school was out. "We're going down to Biloxi, too, before we come home," she said. "That's where I grew up, and I still have a sister there."

"Oh, how nice," Dottie said. "I never knew you had a sister."

"I'm hoping she'll still claim me," Catherine said. "I haven't been a very good sister. I have a lot of things to make right."

"Well, tell Della Boyd hey for me," Dottie said. "Tell her I sure miss her at the poetry meetings—and at church, too."

"I'll do that," Catherine said. She shook her head. "You know, I miss her, too—we all do. Della Boyd's the kind of person who grows on you.

When she first came, she drove me up the wall." Catherine was standing by the door now, looking out into Dottie's driveway. "Your irises are pretty," she said. "Ours are just about gone now—the ones Della Boyd planted all along the side fence." She laughed suddenly. "Della Boyd called up the other night out of the blue and said, 'What color are they?' and I said, 'What color are *what*, Della Boyd?' and she said, 'The irises.' I told her they were all purple, every last one of them. A real pretty, deep purple. She was glad about that. And then she said, 'Have they come yet?' And I said, 'What, Della Boyd? Have *what* come yet?' And she said, 'The hummingbirds.' I told her Philip said he'd seen one or two, and she made me get Philip to the phone so she could ask him all about them." She stood still for a moment, staring out into the driveway. "That Della Boyd," she said softly.

Catherine suddenly snapped to life and yanked the door open. "Well, goodness, I can't stand here talking about hummingbirds and flowers all day!" She pointed to Dottie's bonsai in the windowsill. "I can't believe it's still living. Is it going to bloom again anytime soon?"

"Oh, sure," Dottie said. "It's like your son—you know, hardy."

Catherine smiled. "Very witty. Well, I'm off—I've got a whole list of things to do before tonight!"

After Catherine left and Dottie was combing out Pearl Fairfax, she thought of something Della Boyd had said at church the Wednesday night before she left Berea for the last time. It must have been in early April sometime. She had stood right up to give a testimony at prayer meeting and had spoken clearly, smiling in her usual distracted way and swaying back and forth the whole time as if she might take off and waltz across the sanctuary at any moment. Della Boyd was such a unique person. She seemed so flighty most of the time, but she was really a lot brighter than you thought.

"I'm going home to Yazoo City tomorrow," she had said at church that night. "I'm going in an airplane from Greenville to Jackson." She had tilted her head back and closed her eyes for a moment as if overcome with joy at the prospect, then had uttered an audible sigh of pleasure and continued. "My heart is just full tonight," she had said. "I'm thinking about how God had to take everything away from me and bring me all the way here to South Carolina and work on me so long in order to open my eyes. And"—she had looked over to where Hardy was sitting with Joe Leonard, Howie Harrelson, and the Chewning boys—"I'm sorry if this embarrasses you, Hardy, but I've got to tell everybody what it was you said."

Hardy waved a hand. "Since when did I mind being bragged on in public?" he called out, and everybody laughed.

When things quieted down, Della Boyd continued. "For all these months I've been here, I kept refusing to believe I was a sinner," she said, "but Hardy made it so clear to me one day a couple of weeks ago. It was as simple as could be. Like one plus one equals two." She leaned forward as if about to share a great truth, which indeed it was. "He told me he'd been thinking about the greatest commandment in the Bible, which was to love God with all your heart, and then he said—and this was just how he said it, for I remember distinctly—'Now, the way I see it, Auntie Deeb,' he said . . . that's what Hardy calls me, you see—Auntie Deeb. Anyway, 'Now, the way I see it,' he said, 'if that's the greatest commandment, then the greatest *sin* must be not keeping that commandment.' "

Della Boyd stretched out her hands and smiled radiantly at the small congregation. "And it was like a light just turned on in my head!" she said. "I didn't love God at all, much less with my whole heart—and that was a sin. So I *was* a sinner—a *great* sinner. And of course after I admitted that, well, the floodgate opened, and I was ready to admit all the other ways I had sinned during my life." She paused, then concluded with, "God is so good. He's giving me two new homes—one in Yazoo City and one in heaven. I'll enjoy the one here on earth for a few short years and the one in heaven forever."

When Barb Chewning came in for her appointment around three-thirty, Dottie thought the day had already reached its peak. Her heart felt lighter than it had for almost a year. She felt herself smiling every time she thought about Catherine's words. *"It was you more than anybody."* She never expected another happy revelation in a single day's time.

Barb's appointment was almost over when it happened. Dottie's four o'clock customer hadn't shown up yet, which wasn't a bit surprising, since Alma Wess had never been on time for a single appointment in the whole ten years she had been coming to the Be-Beautiful Style Shoppe. Dottie didn't mind this time, though, since it had given Barb and her more time to talk.

It had been a leisurely appointment. They had talked of many things, one of which was books. Barb had told Dottie of a particular novel she had just finished and had described it in such appealing terms that Dottie had finally said, "Do you think I could borrow it?" The thought of reading a good book was suddenly a very appealing one.

Then right before Barb left, as she was digging through her purse and extracting loose bills, she stopped all at once and looked at Dottie. "You could have another baby, you know." That was what she said—just came right out with it. That was so much like Barb. She was direct and honest—

never rude and nosy and bossy, but just refreshingly frank. For some reason Dottie didn't take offense at the suggestion as she might have on another day or from someone else. Neither of them spoke for several long moments.

This wasn't the first time such a suggestion had been made, of course. Dottie had thought about it herself but dismissed it each time. And once, months ago now, Sid had even dared to mention the possibility of their having another child. Dottie was filled with shame as she recalled how she had nearly bitten his head off. "Another baby won't bring Bonita back!" she had said. And Sid had meekly nodded and turned away.

For one thing, Dottie had been afraid she might resent another baby trying to take Bonita's place. She kept thinking back to the years of struggle she had gone through as a child when her stepfather had tried to fill the place of her real father. But all that seemed like a silly objection now. Children and stepfathers were totally different. The thought of holding a baby in her arms—her own baby—suddenly seemed like a very good thing. She could almost feel the warm weight of a baby against her breast. She remembered that feeling.

"I know what you're thinking," Barb said, still digging in her purse. She took out a rumpled envelope and frowned at it. "You're thinking you're too old."

"I'm almost forty-two," Dottie said.

"So? Jewel's older than that." Barb pulled out a wrinkled five-dollar bill, which she put with the other bills she had found. "Here, take this and keep the change for a tip. I thought I had some more ones in here somewhere, but I can't find them." She zipped her purse shut and looked back at Dottie. "God wants to give you something good—I just know He does," she said. "He's been ready to for a long time."

Dottie smiled. It sounded just like the things she used to say to other people.

"Have you thought about it—trying to have another baby?" Barb asked. "Oh, never mind—that's none of my business. But if you haven't, I think you should, for what my opinion is worth. I hope you're not mad at me for sticking my nose in, but I really felt like God wanted me to say that."

Dottie shook her head. "Oh no, no. I'm not mad at you." She stepped over to the little drawer where she kept her money. "I don't even know if I *could* have a baby," she said slowly, "but I don't guess it would be right to say I *won't*." Without even planning to, she turned and gave Barb a quick hug. "Thank you for being my friend, Barb."

Dottie walked with Barb out to her car. "What pretty irises!" Barb said, stooping to touch one. "I can't believe yours are still blooming out here."

"Sid sure is proud of them," Dottie said.

"I'll bring you that book on Sunday," Barb said. "You'll like it." She got into her van, started the motor, and rolled down the window. "You know, it's a funny thing about books," she said. "They're wonderful things, and I'd hate to try to do without them, but you know what? They can only go so far. I used to be such an obsessive reader I missed out on huge chunks of real life. I can still get so caught up in a book I forget about laundry and supper and everything else. I forget there's a world of real people all around me. I forget sometimes that the story in a book is only temporary." She waved and started backing away slowly. "After the last chapter is over, there's all this real life waiting for you."

Dottie waved back. Barb's words hung in the air even after her van had headed off down Highway 11 toward Berea. *"Real life waiting for you."* Dottie turned to go back into the house. She looked off to her left toward Sid's Texaco station. She heard a series of loud metallic clanks, then a whoop of laughter. From the driveway she could see Max's basketball goal in the backyard. She thought of how tall Max was getting. She thought of how she used to read to him before bedtime every night. That had stopped after Bonita's death, of course, along with so many other things. She wondered if Max would let her read to him again. He'd probably think he was too old. But there were other things she could do with him.

Behind her she heard a car pull into the gravel drive, and she turned to wait for Alma Wess to park. The grass in the front yard was already in need of a trimming, she noticed. Looking up, she saw that the sky above was a clear, strong blue for May, and she remembered something else from science class. Somewhere along the line some teacher had told them that the stars were always in the sky, even during the daytime. The stars didn't really come out at night—they were there all along. Just like the sun didn't really come up. So much of life was illusion. I know you're up there, stars, even though I can't see you, she thought.

As Alma Wess got out of her car, she called to Dottie. "You probably think I'm a hopeless case! Sorry I'm late again, but I got three phone calls right in a row just as I was stepping out the door!" Alma stopped in front of the beauty shop sign. "My goodness, just look at the color of those irises, will you?" she cried. "Scrumptious! I don't know if I ever told you about my aunt Evanna or not, but she used to take the prize every single year at the county fair in Missouri for her bearded irises, and . . . oh, fiddlesticks. I left something in the car I brought to show you. Let me go get it."

Here it is, thought Dottie, *real life waiting for me*.

Alma was laughing when she came back from the car. "I don't know how you put up with all of us, Dottie. I bet you could put all your customers in a book and nobody would believe it. They'd think that was too many crazy people in one book. You must go to bed totally worn out."

"Oh, I love it," Dottie said. "I can't think of anything I'd rather be doing. Come on in and let's get started." And she swung the door open wide.

Be the first to know

Want to be the first to know
what's new from
your favorite authors?

Want to know all about
exciting new writers?